THE ELEVENTH COMMANDMENT

Richard Van White, Jr.

ISBN-13: 978-0-9909648-0-3

Cover photograph ("NASA's Great Observatories Examine the Galactic Center Region" taken by the Hubble Space Telescope) is used with permission from The Space Telescope Science Institute (STScI)

Book design by Mark Chumley Singer

To Mom and Dad

Acknowledgments

This book would not have been possible without the continuous and unwavering help of my good friend and editor Jim Korman, who provided nonstop support and guidance on every facet of the project from its inception. My heartfelt thanks also go to Tony Shober for his critiques and ongoing inspiration and to Kent Eby for the hours he spent reading on the train. I am deeply grateful, as well, to my brother Craig for his support of my writing and for sharing my passion for science fiction through the years.

Many thanks also go to the art and production team that made publishing this book much less daunting. Liza Milli Baker provided tremendous help with formatting and logistics, and shared her critical opinions along the way. Big thanks as well to super-talented Mark Chumley Singer for designing the wonderful cover artwork and to Brian Miller for all of his fantastic viral wizardry.

Last but not least, to everyone else who patiently listened to me talk about "The Book" through the years—thank you!

PART ONE

CHAPTER 1

Prevail together or surely perish together.

—The Eleventh Commandment

The black of space is broken by a brilliant lightning-like wrinkle. A hyperspace window opens and the light coalesces into the sleek, shark frame of a Vespucci-class star yacht. Pfizer Ambros snaps off his jump harness and knows he won't be able to get any sleep. The bright monochrome blur of hyperspace is a poor comparison to the artistry of real space. There is a lurch that the yacht's a-grav fields and inertial dampeners cannot disguise. The reflected light of Sol from the outer system worlds fills the view port. Pfizer sees the distant interconnected modules, cylinders, spheres and geodesics of space habitats, drift cities, and deep space automated industrial platforms flashing their bright lights among the distant and constant stars. The yacht begins its slingshot maneuver over the ghostly ice blue surface of Pluto and seems an immense glowing comet streaking toward the distant yellow blaze that is Sol.

Pfizer gets up from the acceleration couch in a single fluid motion and walks across his workroom. From his worktable, he picks up an intricately carved brass telescope. The baroque piece is an anachronism amidst the CDCs (crystal data chips) and holographic clutter of the onyx black table.

Pfizer's attention remains on the twenty by twenty meter observation port behind the desk, a panorama of outer system habitats and complexes arrayed before him. He continues to stare, finding no emotional composure or solace in the vista before him.

Returning home. Earth my home? Place of birth perhaps, but not my home. Not my home, not ever. Pfizer left Earth when he was five, after his sister Oriana's involvement in the Anangan Insurrection. What Oriana had done even now causes a cascade of emotions and thoughts he'd rather not consider: Oriana became caught up in a scandal involving proscribed weapons, drugs, AI contraband and worst of all forbidden gene splicing and manipulation; in fact it had been a concerted effort to usurp his parents' government. Pfizer suppresses a shudder. As a result of Oriana's actions, neither their parents nor the Hane Blood Circle, with their impossibly high standards, would ever consider her ascension to the Imperial See.

It had seemed to Pfizer that it was only after Oriana's betrayal that his parents developed an interest in him. They had him tested, and analyzed for acceptance into the illustrious Academy on Tempel, the foremost and oldest center of learning in the Imperium. Of course this attention did not come with any great outpouring of emotion from his parents. The Empress-Executrix and the First Lord were busy, along with their CEOs and senior execs, ruling and administering an Imperium of more than a million planets.

To his parent's satisfaction the test scores were good enough and Pfizer Ambros was admitted to the Academy. Though two years older than the official entry age of three, they sent him a galaxy away. In case he failed, his parents had two other children, Pfizer's younger sisters Gabrielle and Zoe.

Pfizer did not fail. Despite the crushing gravity, desolate climate, and sterile academic isolation, he excelled. When he was nineteen and in his fourteenth year at the Academy, the Arch-Chancellor Lurenga told Pfizer's parents that he would pass. Now, six years later, Pfizer is returning to Earth. *Not home. Home has become the diamond blackness of deep space expeditions.* Retrospectively, however, Pfizer can see his parent's machinations in even this. As Crown Scion he will one day be the hereditary ruler of the Imperium—the political framework of governments and corporations, some merely global and subglobal, others encompassing entire star systems, and some vast multiple star systems.

A rueful chuckle escapes him at the thought that he has been learning something that his parents and the other members of the Blood Circle and Imperial Council hadn't engineered. He tosses the telescope onto a pile of pastel cushions to the right of the observation port. In so doing he looks at his reflection and once more his thoughts wander. He is not the overweight, white-haired, timid little boy who left this star system more than twenty years ago. Now he is tall, with a V-shaped build. His short hair is a darker blonde, kept short because of its tendency to knap like wool.

His eyes are an electric gray that easily appear blue or violet depending on the light. All gifts of his parents prenatal gentechs. His hair can appear lighter or darker depending on the light, just as his eyes seem to change color. He has always been told that he looks nothing like the holos of himself in the holo news or info nets and this affords him a much-needed degree of privacy.

Pfizer sits back into the floating omniform a-grav chair behind his worktable. The chair, following its omniform programming, conforms to his position, cradling him and synchronizing with his body temperature. Within seconds he feels suspended in comfort. Pfizer kicks off his athletic shoes and leans forward in the chair until his feet touch the floor again. He feels the rumble of the yacht's sub-light conventional, or C-drive, thrusters travel up his tired legs.

"ETA until Earth orbit. Am I back on schedule?" he asks the workroom comp, not quite managing to keep the impatience from his voice, even though he is speaking to a machine. *Earth, Homeworld, our Sacred Home. The people revere this world and I dread it.*

From speakers hidden around the workroom comes the computer's synthetic voice, a blend of male, female, and something clearly artificial: "ETA to Earth Orbit five, thirty-four, fourteen … mark, lord."

"Five and a half hours," Pfizer mumbles to himself. *I'd rather spend the time in warp than feel time crawl the way it does when traveling in C-drive. Damn sub-light speed engines. At light speed it took merely ten minutes to travel from Sol to Earth. I traveled from Alpha Centauri, light years away, in the blink of an eye, and now because of in-system navigational hazards and intra-system traffic, speed has been reduced to a crawl.*

"Affirmative, lord," the workroom comp answers, snapping him from his contemplation.

"I was talking to myself," Pfizer says absently as he sorts through the piles of CDCs on the worktable.

"Why are you addressing yourself, Lord?" the workroom asks.

Pfizer looks up, then makes the awkward realization that he was about to explain human psychology to a computer. "I really don't have time to explain human psychology to you."

"Perhaps another time then, lord?" the workroom responds almost instantly.

"Whatever," Pfizer says, distracted as he holds up one of the CDCs to read its label.

"What time will be appropriate, my Lord? I can—," the room begins saying. Pfizer slaps the chip down on the table.

"Enough! What I said was rhetorical. Switch to servo mode."

There is a loud *click* as the comp changes function, and even though the workroom comp is not an Artie or AI (Artificial Intelligence), Pfizer has the vague notion that he has offended it. He sits back and he hears the omniform vibrate as it conforms to his new position. The growing AI Rights Movement is another issue and perhaps another storm on the horizon. From the right armrest compartment of his chair Pfizer retrieves his MentAmp and laces it around the back of his head and over his ears. The mental amplifier with its liquid crystal computer heart begins forming an analog of his mind, delivering micro-electrical charges to his brain, stimulating select neural transmitters and receptors in accordance with the biosoftware he's chosen for it.

Soon he will be in the interface. The data on the chip will be deposited directly into his mind. Not just data but sensory impressions as well. If Pfizer so chose he could learn snowboarding on the snows of Mars' Olympus Mons or Erosi Tae Kwan Do and have the experiences printed directly onto his nervous system—a vast advancement on the virtual reality systems of old. For most of the return trip Pfizer has been researching historical personages and their philosophies, looking for something to say when he touches down at the Cosmodome.

Pfizer sighs looking at the collected crystal data chips on the table. Most hold his own personal studies from Tempel but a significant portion of the chips contain work to prepare him for his duties as Vice-Prex of Terrax Corporation, Crown Scion of the Imperium... Suddenly everything about his life is the 'The Imperium.'

The discovery of an Outlaw nation of humans existing outside Imperial law is causing frightening levels of dissent. Thousands of years ago, after Naraji Ilkani's liberation of Humanity from alien invaders and his Eleventh Commandment, the fragmented Human Race engaged in an extra-galactic civil war, the Wasting. Centuries of unending war begun by a cult of genetically engineered racial supremacists, the Tene Thantos. The Wasting had nearly eliminated the race as surely as any alien invader might have. As a consequence the survivors had determined that to prevent another war all Humanity must be united under one government, the Imperium. No planetary system, family, or individual would ever again be allowed to possess anti-matter, fusion, or fission weapons. Only the Imperium maintained such weapons, as a possible last resort defense should an alien intelligence or human terrorist ever threaten Humanity.

Now the government of Pfizer's mother, Empress-Executrix Anastacia, is challenging the policy of immediate annexation of Outlaw nations, as implied by the Eleventh Commandment and established by Imperium policy in the

Declaration of the Aristos 1617 IC:

"In order to prevent the horror and scourge of intergalactic warfare, all Humanity must be united under one government."

The Oath of Unification and the Unification Wars followed and now fears of another war are common talk. The news nets are filled with images of protests by the Ilkani, fierce adherents to the Eleventh Commandment. Prominent government officials are engaging in political debates, and in some regions armed clashes are occurring. Probes project the Outlaw population at a mere forty billion, nothing to the trillions of Imperials. Are the horrors of the Wasting so firmly implanted in the human psyche that there can be no peace as long as all are not one, like some human hive?

What about goodwill toward one another of one's own free choice, not because it is the law? Pfizer sighs and leans back. He closes his eyes and taps the activation stud on the MentAmp's right side.

The effects of using the MentAmp vary from individual to individual. Pfizer experiences the nausea of a rapid fall, despite the comfort provided by the a-grav chair. He feels as if he is in a nightmare, falling swiftly through a dark tunnel. The sense of the nausea passes though, and Pfizer opens his eyes to find himself not in a stateroom on a hyperlight vessel, but in a firelit room.

The room is constructed of stone, wood, and simple mud plastering. He's read about such primitive dwellings, but the place is more ancient than anything he's ever seen. Thirteen people sit around a table. The smells of fresh bread, bitter herbs, and wine fill the room. Pfizer's stomach growls; the focus zooms in on the man at the center of the table. He is dressed in robes of some coarse organic fiber, his hair is brownish black and his brown eyes have an unnatural depth and serenity for one from this primitive time period. Pfizer feels his curiosity rising. There seems to be an almost tangible force in the room, like the presence of another, as if someone is watching over Pfizer's shoulder there ... No, here and now, *now!* ... Eleven thousand years after these recordings.

The other men around the table do not have the emoto-control of the man at the center of the table; they display their feelings and thoughts for all to see. They are in awe, some kind of rapture; combinations of anguish, sorrow, and reverence. The man at the center of the table is speaking. Mentally Pfizer increases the volume. "With fervent desire I have desired to eat this Passover with you before I suffer," he says.

The iris entrance to Pfizer's workroom expands open and Otto Buchanan, head of Pfizer's Bloodguard security, strides through. The iris closes behind him. A basketball tucked under his left arm, Otto quietly approaches Pfizer, who is sitting reclined behind his worktable, his eyes closed, the activity lights on his black MentAmp silently blinking. *Always with his head in a MentAmp. I wonder what he's studying now,* Otto thinks. Standing over the worktable, Otto wipes perspiration off his forehead and places the basketball into one of the two chairs in front of the table, then moves smoothly into the other, never making a sound.

"Pfizer," he says. Otto leans over the table, closer to his friend, and says again, louder: "Pfizer." *Pfizer looks so much better since he's removed his Tempellian lifesuit and allowed his hair to grow a bit. I forgot he had eyebrows. I forgot how normal he is. I'd begun to think of him as a Tempeler.*

Otto reaches out and picks up the workroom comp's manual console from the table. He sits back and hits a key. A holographic screen appears at eye level above the far right corner of the table. Otto reaches out and touches the holo's icons. The image moves closer to him so he can see the string of words running along the bottom of the holo screen as a voice reads:

"En'Zefi Survey Recording, Subject: Peaceful Coexistence." *By the Only God, the En'Zefi Survey,* Otto whistles with appreciation at Pfizer's efforts. Millennia of historical data had been collected by an alien race known as the En'Zefi. The lives of Confucius, Caesar, Siddhartha, and so many others had been recorded with an advanced sensory holographic device now adapted to be compatible with current MA, MentAmp, Solido systems. *Where are you now, Pfizer?*

When Otto was younger he never imagined that he would use the MA systems for anything but combat simulations and martial arts training. Yet ever since meeting Pfizer, he has used them to go on safaris across time and space. Otto has been amongst the desperate refugees of Pompeii as Vesuvius spewed burning ash. He has marched with Gandhi to the ocean to gather salt. Memories of the excursions cloud Otto's thoughts, but only for a moment. Originally assigned to Pfizer as his Bloodguard liaison ten years ago, Otto is now the Captain Praetor of Pfizer's Bloodguards, the genetically enhanced elite force created by Pfizer's ancestor Joseph Ambros to protect the Ambros and the other families of the Imperium's aristocracy. In the beginning Otto had viewed his assignment to Tempel as punishment. It was terrible being an Erosi amidst the cold intellectual Tempelers and Tempellians. However Otto had fallen in love with Tempel, the great libraries and school planets of the Academy.

I even met Mari there. He considers getting a MentAmp and joining Pfizer, but instead decides on a simple holographic tie in. Pfizer fidgets and his eyelids flutter. Years of Bloodguard subconscious conditioning come into play and before Otto can give it another thought he reaches across the table and turns off the MentAmp, his Bloodguard training to protect Pfizer causing him to act instinctively.

"Pfizer," Otto says.

Despite having known Otto for so long, Pfizer has never gotten used to some of the eccentricities of his protector. Otto is high-grav'd, so although he appears to be roughly the same weight and height as Pfizer, things are not what they seem. Otto's weight, or more precisely his mass, is twice that of Pfizer's. Otto is a native of Eros, home world of Pfizer's father's family, a planet with gravity twice that of Earth. The major cause of death amongst the original settlers to Eros were simple falls, heart attacks, and of course attacks from the indigenous flora and fauna that were twice as fast than their slow-moving prey. Snare vines with poisonous thorns had lashed out at the original settlers like whips. Grass panthers shattered settlement perimeters in blurs, green flashes mauling and dragging off colonists. To solve their problem the Erosi used their immense kelp wealth to employ gentechs to alter the molecular density of the first generation of Erosi embryos. These children handled the gravity of Eros as their parents handled the gravity of Earth: naturally. Now as a result, the high-grav'd in some ways are superhuman compared to those from Earth's normal gravity. When the Erosi, or anyone from the few high-gravity worlds they settled, are placed in a one-gravity environment, they are twice as strong, twice as fast. The high-grav'd are in demand as athletes, stunt persons, and soldiers. There is also the matter of Otto's Bloodguard conditioning—addicting them to tursapoi from birth and adding a hypnotic compulsion to allow no harm to come to the reigning Ambros and their immediate family. The Bloodguard are also leased to other Aristos to provide the ultimate in protection so long as their primary duty to the Ambros is not compromised. Another of the stipulations made by Joseph Ambros to insure the ascendancy and survival of his family.

Otto waits and watches in concerned silence for Pfizer to come out of his MentAmp fugue.

Pfizer rubs his eyes and there is Otto, a recruitment holo for the Bloodguard, face all planes and angles, lantern jaw, broad forehead, pale lime crystal green eyes. "Otto, tell me something. Do you ever slouch?" a smiling Pfizer asks thickly. Massaging his eyelids with his fingertips he tries to push the images of Yeiuda's betrayal of Yeishua from his head. Angry Aramaic shouts still echo in his mind.

Otto harrumphs, and decides Pfizer's question doesn't merit a response. There is fear in Pfizer's eyes though, the fear of the hunted. Otto runs a hand through his short corn silk yellow hair, and works his mouth as if to say something but then stops.

Pfizer smiles again to lighten the mood. Otto has never been one for emoto-control. His concern is written all over his face. "What is wrong, Otto?"

"Noth—. You tell me." Otto says in that sandpaper voice

Pfizer has never heard raised. "You do occasionally spend too much time in the interface. You're not a logician." Otto, clearly annoyed, grabs the worktable's application pen and waves one of the holo-globes into full display. Images of military and staff, their schedules and duties, flash in the bubble. The iris in Otto's left eye glows florescent electric yellow as the micro-MentAmp implanted in his skull establishes a datalink.

"I tell you ... I am vexed." Pfizer volunteers, admitting to himself he needs advice. "Sacred Home? ... *Earth*? The politics involved! I'd rather be at lecture or a cultural survey of a Back Zone."

"Me, too, Pfizer," Otto says startling him out of his introspection. Otto's glowing eye seems to wander past him, taking his mind off a sudden suspicion, but it is another of the holo-globes Otto is enlarging with a wave of the wand.

"The security considerations for Earth are the most complex I ever remember dealing with.... So many Aristos, so many Praetors," Otto comments.

Pfizer turns to the new globe.

Images of Earth, the O'Meara Cosmodome, and millions of people. "That reminds me ... I've made some changes to your wardrobe," Otto says quietly.

"Excuse me?" Pfizer asks. *He wants to talk about clothes?* Pfizer wonders.

"Nothing difficult. You'll see. Anyway, what was the En'Zef record about? I was going to link with you when you started getting ... fidgety," Otto says, attempting to be tactful and wanting the truth.

What is going on, Pfizer? Otto wonders.

"Hmm," Pfizer mumbles. It would have been comforting to have Otto there while those savages tortured Yeishua. *How could this record possibly be relevant? The crude, savage, completely immoral violence nauseated him. He asked for forgiveness—for them! Because they did not know what they were doing.*

"It was disturbing, Otto. Sometimes I don't think we've really changed spiritually.... Oh, yes, there've been physical and mental advances, but there's a downside. Our superior abilities breed superior ambitions and emotions. In some ways we have become worse."

"Pfizer, that's an interesting commentary but I think you need to concentrate on the reality of our situation, which is Earth." Pfizer has come to dread when Otto speaks in this way, almost mechanically, as if he's forcing himself to say something he doesn't want to, something he knows Pfizer does not want to hear. "You 'wear many hats,' as the Hane say. Cardinal of the Political Ministry suits you. You are also Crown Scion, and very soon you will be a Vice-Prex of the CIMB and inevitably Emperor-Executor." Otto's voice gains a dogmatic cadence. "Regent of Eros … Maybe one day even Kirin of the HaneNation." *Kirin of the HaneNation.* Otto speaks the words with frightening reverence. "There is extremism," he continues. "There is planet-wide rioting on some worlds. And it's all because your mother, the Empress-Executrix, wants to keep us from going to war."

CHAPTER 2

The greatest among you will be your servant.

—Matthew 23:11 Judeo-Orange Codex

Otto's pale, jewel green eyes have a disturbing refractive glitter. Mentally, Pfizer goes through emoto-control exercises. Instead of the telltale sigh, he keeps his breathing at pace, maintains his smile and eye contact. He even subtlety inclines his head and body toward Otto, a subliminal gesture of appreciation and acceptance. *I don't think you'd care so much about that if you've seen what I've seen*, Pfizer thinks. He knows that the return to Earth has been difficult for Otto as well. He can hear Otto's Erosi accent and that usually only happens when Otto's edgy or preoccupied. "It was important to those people who lived it, Otto. And I'm sure you know 'those that cannot remember the past are condemned to repeat it,'" Pfizer adds in a tone he uses to remind Otto to always speak his mind between them.

Otto genuinely smiles, Pfizer can seem so ... normal. Sitting there wearing a white Bloodguard A-frame, the Corps' logo emblazoned on the front, red shorts. The seriousness that had clouded the room seems on its way out the iris when Pfizer says: "I hope you didn't come by for a ball game."

"Huh?" Otto looks at the basketball. "No. Already played a pickup game between some Bloodguards and yacht crewman," Otto says spinning the ball absently, one finger then two, his ability seemingly lost on him.

"We divided the Erosi evenly and played without handicap. Only casualty was this crewman ... Nokosone. Phipps passed the ball a bit too hard for him—I guess he forgot Hideo was a one geepee—and he sprained both the guy's wrists. The interesting thing was—Wiktor, that sorry schmoozer, turned out to be a decent player." *A little too decent for the lazy sycophant I took him for. I need to review his background check,* Otto thinks. "Anyway, I stopped in because I needed to confirm touchdown site. Will there be any additional guests, or changes to your itinerary? I can make additional security arrangements."

"O'Meara Cosmodome is still our destination," Pfizer says matter-of-factly.

The corners of Otto's mouth turn down and he wishes his emoto-control were better, that he could have spared Pfizer the frown. "That's where your parents requested you touchdown," Otto says wishing he could stop himself. "I mean—Great, that makes my job easier. I just have to coordinate with the Lion." *Oh good, Mr. Smooth, 'It makes my job easier.' I can't get it through my thick skull that beneath all that emoto-control and emp-psych is my friend, whom I'd rather see happier. He cannot help but glance at a Solido of Pfizer, Ashim, and himself.* There is much more to life than security protocols.

"Lion or not, I'll make sure that if you want to remain on my staff, you will," Pfizer declares. The Lion, his father's brother, is the acting Grand Kurseg of Bloodguard Command. *Would he actually replace Otto? And is the Lion now in direct charge of my family's security? This means that Naval and Takazhr personnel are involved as well. Since when did protecting my family become a military operation? I need time. I need data. Luxvico. Dr. Tsimpo, and Ashim … but Ashim is dead.*

"Computer, check my schedule. I want to review Earth's current events," Pfizer commands. He knows that rage and frustration are still there in his voice for any emp-psych to hear. *What can I do?*

"Lord your schedule is full. However, there are several appointments that can be changed or canceled," the computer's tritone voice informs him.

"List," Pfizer orders the computer.

"After touchdown you are to board a Hane mega-zeppelin

15

for a twenty-minute meeting with the Executive Council while you're en route to the Imperios. A meeting with Dr. Tsimpo and Counselor Luxvico to discuss e-mortal allergic reactions to anti-geriatric drugs en route to visit the Earth-based division of Geritech Products. Directly following is a TAV flight from O'Meara to Rome to visit the Princess Oriana's incoming starship from Pandarata. The rest is labeled 'personal,'" reports the computer.

Well, Pfizer thinks, *the Executive Council meeting is unavoidable and I must speak with Rachel and Luxvico, but about Geritech issues? The Earth situation is too relevant. I certainly can't cancel the trip to Geritech with Otto present.* Otto's father reacted badly to an anti-geriatric and he began to age; however, many believe his death was actually suicide.

"Lord, will you amend your schedule?" asks the computer.

"Uh … No … Not at this time. Otto, any word from Melyssa?" asks Pfizer, mentioning the young paleogeneticist he recently met in the Roon Back Zone. Pfizer keeps a series of images of her on his worktable.

"No," is Otto's only reply as he begins working with Pfizer's lap console. Several holographic bubbles appear before Otto, some displaying geographic tactical data and others scenes from Earth or local news programs. Pfizer recognizes scenes from North America, the New Gate Bridge to Atlantis packed with traffic, the Berlin-Paris Cosmodome, and mega-zeppelins descending from orbit carrying tourists from across the Imperium.

"Nothing, Otto?" asks Pfizer again. This time Otto merely shakes his head. "May I have a few blank CDCs?" he asks as he begins to call up written text within the holo-bubbles. Pfizer now surmises Otto's teasing; well indoctrinated emoto-control keeps him from shaking his head or laughing. He decides to play along.

"Otto, are you certain your people have heard nothing from her? I mean, does she know I'm coming to Earth? Is she on Earth? I … I don't know if I want her on Earth if things are as serious as I'm beginning to believe," says Pfizer pushing a handful of CDCs across the table toward Otto.

He's got me, Otto thinks as he shuts down the holo programs. "Pfizer, Melyssa arrived on Earth a few hours ago and should be meeting your entourage shortly before the flight to Rome. If what Mari says about Rome is true, it's the perfect place to spend some time."

Pfizer sighs and pushes himself back in his chair, obviously relieved. "You should listen to your wife, Oz. I want to go over some of the ideas I have … What time is it?"

Otto closes his left eye and sees the yellow bioluminescent display of his eyelid chronometer. "It's about five now. An hour and half till shuttle departure."

"I've been in the MentAmp program for hours. We'll have to do this at the shuttle. I need to talk to Luxvico right now," says Pfizer, watching as Otto bristles. "I guess you'd rather be somewhere else while I talk to Lux," he adds, pulling off his socks and heading toward the workroom's lavatory. Otto nods and grabs his basketball.

"You mentioned something about my wardrobe?" Pfizer recalls, stopping before the iris to the lavatory.

God, let me get out of here before that condescending iceman robot gets here and I hit him in front of Pfizer, Otto thinks as he heads toward the iris out of the workroom. He stops and turns. "Just some alterations to your clothes for security purposes. We can talk later about that and your speech," Otto says, bowing slightly.

Pfizer puts his hands over his face failing to keep the fact that his friend feels obligated to show him this deferential treatment. "Yeah, Oz. See you at the shuttle," he says. The workroom iris spirals closed after Otto. Pfizer turns to face the view port.

The ecologically terraformed Luna shimmers in the distance now, a blue-white jewel much like Earth. Luna has been transformed from a cold cratered wasteland into a living world of vast oceans and fields by the Ambros and their empire-winning Terrax Corporation. Much of Earth's food is now grown on the surface and in the oceans of Luna by small communities of farmers and robohelpers.

Pfizer orders the workroom to start the chemsonic shower and then does a holographic search of his wardrobe before ordering the servospheres to gather his clothes. At his command three metallic silver spheres the size of Otto's basketball and covered with a-grav field generators detach themselves from an until-now-hidden rack of several more. "I'd like to see Counselor Luxvico in twenty minutes. Transmit request," Pfizer orders as the servospheres float silently away on their a-grav fields to gather clothes and perform other tasks.

Pfizer emerges from his shower dried by blasts of warm air and uv-tan lights. He feels lighter and cleaner, but the anticipation of earthfall and his speech has coiled around his heart like a boa constrictor. The servospheres return with his clothes: a double-breasted dark green jacket, with the holographic glyphs of the Academy's Political Ministry above the right breast pocket, white half-collared shirt with green and gold ascot, and gray pants with sewn in shoes. *Ugh! Horrible Earth and its ridiculous ornamental clothing*, Pfizer thinks. He begins to dress and notices the weight and feel of his clothes are distinctly different, especially of his pants and jacket.

"Computer!" Pfizer snaps. *The morning has already caught up to me and past me.* "Explain the different material composition of my clothing," he orders.

"Specify, lord," answers the computer.

Is it patronizing me? Pfizer wonders. "The clothes are not wool or cotton. The ascot is not silk," Pfizer replies.

"The clothing is a manmade compound, produced by Duquesne Corp., called GuardWear for protection against kinetic violence up to nine hundred meters per second, or one thousand kilograms per square centimeter, lord."

"Huh?" asks Pfizer.

"The harder the material is hit, the harder it gets within defined parameters, lord," answers the computer, and this time Pfizer is listening for a sigh of exasperation, but there is none. *I wonder if I'm the only person who wonders whether his workroom computer has emotions.* Pfizer runs his suddenly alien clothes through his fingers, dreading now to put them on as if doing so will precipitate the violence they are to prevent. *These are the wardrobe changes Otto was talking about,* Pfizer realizes.

The iris chimes and the workroom computer requests identification. The deep monotone voice of Counselor Luxvico responds: "Luxvico."

"Enter," Pfizer says.

CHAPTER 3

Located in the Riffellon Star System, the Academy
of Tempel, founded in the year '07 of the Imperial
Calendar, is accepted as the finest institution of
higher learning in the Imperium.

—*DK Planetary Guide*

Luxvico is a Tempellian, a native of Tempel, as well as a
graduate of the Academy's Political Ministry and thus a
Tempeler. Though Lux's degree is unknown, it is certainly
higher than that of Pfizer's degree of Cardinal. Like all
Tempellians, Luxvico wears the black lifesuit, a form-fitting
garment made of fine mesh that covers the entire body except
the face. Along the outer arms and down the legs is thin silver
tubing that circulates the suit's nutri-bath. The black garment
itself absorbs oxygen and beneficial amounts of ultra-violet
radiation and removes bodily waste via an odorless mist similar
to perspiration.

The suit maintains the body's integrity to such a degree that
no hair whatsoever grows on Luxvico's exposed face. The suit
also virtually halts the aging process shortly after neuro-
muscular apex between the ages of twenty-five and thirty,
making the Tempellians the longest living people of the
Imperium. Just how long Tempellians have lived is a secret that
they jealously and wisely guard. Over the black lifesuit is
usually worn some form of tabard, toga, or surcoat. If a
Tempellian is also a Tempeler, then an elaborate gold weave is
added to indicate the disciplines mastered.

Luxvico, with his protruding brow and square jaw, always gave Pfizer the impression of the old style automatons. Perhaps Otto is right about Luxvico. Luxvico's bow-shaped lips, which should have appeared sensual, are unanimated, simply a tight cruel line. Violet eyes are expressionless. Some genetic designer's masterpiece is wasted Pfizer thinks, in that cold face. Even after ten years Pfizer has never adjusted to the lobotomized stare from those glittering eyes. Though Luxvico bows and addresses Pfizer correctly, there is always something pedantic, superior in Luxvico's behavior toward others: *as if he were dealing with small and exasperating children.* "You asked for me, lord," Luxvico states.

"Yes, Counselor," Pfizer answers and finds his voice taking on some of the emotionless quality of the Tempellian's. "The current situation on Earth, I am grossly ignorant of current events there. I admit to being distracted by my mother's plan to decentralize the government. I'd like a brief idea of the political climate there."

The 1.57 gravities of Tempel have given Luxvico the stature of a shockball blitzer: wide shoulders, deep chest. Luxvico has an imposing regal stature and in the black lifesuit and his green surcoat with gold weave he seems something out of Arthurian legend. Luxvico removes a small palm-sized MentAmp link, for the chip in his head, from beneath his surcoat. "You are aware that for some time the Ambros, your family, have been trying to democratize the Imperium. Usually the Citizo have rebuffed these efforts, preferring the security the Imperium provides to the freedoms it prohibits. This trend has continued for thousands of years. Over the last fifteen hundred years the Ambros Press and Public Relations Corps, or PPRC, have initiated education, self-actualization, and determination programs—all subtly introduced to the populace through holo commercials, data feeds, entertainment—to allow the Ambros to abandon their stewardship of the race. Your ancestors saw the danger to the individual caused by the relinquishing of self-determination to the Ambros cult of personality. History is replete with horrific examples. The Roman concept of bread and circus—poor, starving masses screaming in adoration for free bread and wine, while blood was spilled and they worshiped their Caesars. Later, in the late 20th and early 21st centuries, billions in resources were squandered on broadcast sports spectaculars and reality dramas so that people would watch and adore and spend more while the Earth warmed and began to burn. When these things no longer distracted the people of Earth, their leaders used other means—fear of the collapsing planetary environment and the abnormal and mutated births since the ozone failure, and the worst tool of all, religious extremism. Then in the 22nd and 23rd centuries aliens invaded the birthplace of all the human races.

"I project that the Empress-Executrix's plan to break this cycle would have been successful within as little as fifty Earth years had the Outlaw Nation not been discovered. Since Earth is the capital of the Imperium, the factions have concentrated there. I can prepare a synopsis on factional alignment and their respective leaderships." Luxvico finishes.

What?! "Yes, Luxvico. By all means do so. I'll expect it before earthfall," Pfizer says distractedly, waving the Tempeler away in dismissal. *He said the plan would have been successful. Would have been! What in the True God's name did he mean by that?!* But the iris is closed and Luxvico is gone. Pfizer thinks to call him back, but before he can do so, strangely the iris spirals open and Luxvico returns to the room.

"Councilor, I'm glad you came back. I want—," Pfizer begins, but the sight of Dr. Tsimpo behind Luxvico cuts him off.

Rachel Tsimpo, Doctor of Psychiatry, Psychology and Communication, registered graduate of the Empathic-Psychiatry School of Bellerophon. She is a high-level director in the Ambros Public and Press Relations Corp. For more than six thousand years the PPRC has packaged, presented and spoon-fed the will of Joseph Ambros and his descendants to hundreds of trillions of the Imperium's citizens. Despite her considerable accomplishments, she appears younger than Pfizer. Rachel is tall and thin-boned. There is an air of frailty about her, but Pfizer can never be sure what gives him the impression. Her clothes he considers rather severe. Today, for example, she's wearing a black, fur-lined jacket, black skirt, black stockings, and black make-up. She is too beautiful to dress this way. She should be dressed like an elegant Mandarin lady, Pfizer thinks. There is never anything frail in Rachel's eyes. Rachel's eyes are the smoldering purple of an ocean sunset, far more expressive than the cold amethyst of Luxvico's eyes. They shine under jet black lashes that fringe out from delicate epicanthic folds. Perhaps it is the elfin quality of her nose, mouth, and high cheekbones that give her this seeming frailty. There is an stillness about her, a tranquility of purpose.

"I ran into Councilor Luxvico on the way out. I asked him back in with me because I know this is a difficult time for you," says Dr. Tsimpo, her voice a soft whisper, soothing and harmonious.

You bet I'm uncomfortable, Pfizer thinks. *And you'd be too, Rachel; that Tempeler was just in here and told me my mother's peace initiative was doomed.*

As an empathic-psychiatrist Rachel Tsimpo is an expert at reading facial expressions, body language, and voice atonals. *Yes,* Rachel thinks, studying Pfizer's strange regard of Luxvico as if Luxvico had just given Pfizer some awesome revelation. *What has Lux said to him?* "Did I miss something?" Rachel asks, eyeing Pfizer inquisitively.

"I believe it is the coming Fragmentation Resolution. I indicated earlier that I do not believe the Imperium Congress will pass ...," Luxvico begins saying.

This is a surprise to Rachel. Since joining the Unionists, a growing coalition of established political parties opposed to the Fragmentation, she has felt a renewed sense of purpose. After so many years of analyzing the feelings of others, she thought she had lost her own, until the Unionists had approached her. She had to discover what the Tempeler had revealed. "A lost vote does not mean an unsuccessful plan, Pfizer. Perhaps Counselor Luxvico would care to elaborate."

Luxvico looks at Dr. Tsimpo as if he is seeing her for the first time and she's some sort of insect. He repositions himself between Pfizer and Dr. Tsimpo, facing Dr. Tsimpo, his eyes see right through her and Rachel reminds herself she's wearing a T-shield in her necklace. "I will explain. If you two will sit."

Pfizer, relieved that he's getting an explanation, is now aware of an unidentifiable tension between Luxvico and Dr. Tsimpo. *What is going on between the two of them*, Pfizer wonders. He nods toward one of the a-grav chairs for Dr. Tsimpo, who sits in one graceful movement.

Not taking his eyes from Dr. Tsimpo, Luxvico begins saying: "As you are both aware, several technological applications supplied through the Ambros Free Fusion Authority are radically changing our society, namely, servosphere technology, interface tech, and Solido matter recombination.

"People have been, or are becoming, self-sufficient, and as a result, many government services and programs have become unused and unnecessary. The bureaucracies that administered these services and programs have become superfluous. The dissolution of these areas has proved successful since most of the bureaucrats welcomed their own unemployment. They saw this as a chance to continue actualizing and exploring their potentials. With this in mind, her Imperial Majesty Anastacia III put a proposal before the Executive Council to dissolve some of the offices of the aristocracy—most significantly, the Coronal Regents and the Stadtholders. All military representatives of the Imperium will be retired. Aristos will retain title and holdings but no longer wield executive or legal authority on the local or planetary level; instead, that power will be conferred upon magistrates and DemoPol reps."

"The Imperium would in effect become a cooperative of millions of independent but interrelated communities," interrupts Dr. Tsimpo. "Isolated, vulnerable, without guidance." Rachel stops, realizing she's vocalizing her secret opinion. Luxvico's scrutiny of her has intensified and even Pfizer is now staring at her with a look of comprehension.

"I did not know you shared the Unionist point of view," Pfizer says now smiling, the smile of learning something new about a good friend. Rachel can imagine him thinking of the interesting debates they will have. *But we won't, Ambros Prince. You and your family have lost the right to rule*, Rachel thinks.

"This is great for the nets. Imagine a vice director of the PPRC who doesn't share the Executrix view," Pfizer says jovially. "We can exploit this, show the Unionists we are open to opposition and willing to put the issue to a popular vote."

Spoken like a true Ambros. 'Let the people decide.' The people have been given too many decisions already. And contact with the Outlaw Nation is only going to increase the madness ... Genetically manipulated children from gestation pods! Rachel shudders at the thought.

Were such beings even human? However, the Ambros had allowed the practice, saying it was and is a matter of personal choice. Artificial Intelligences were being deregulated. What was happening to the Eleventh Commandment and defending the purity of the Human Race? Rachel was by no means an Ilkani, but Ambros liberalism seemed to be leading humans toward inhumanity. "I fear that with the general applications of these new technologies the people will need a strong central moral authority, and we are considering dismantling that authority," she says.

"Rachel, a 'strong central authority' be it moral, legal or otherwise means that our people must lose some of their will. Is it that their morals are not good enough? Must some inflict their morals on an entire society? And by what right does such infliction take place?" questions Pfizer.

"For the common good," answers Rachel without hesitation. "What do gestation pods and unrestricted genetic engineering represent for the common good?"

"An answer to the prayers of those unable to have children, the prevention of birth defects, the maximizing of potentials," responds Pfizer with equal conviction.

"What about women who want to use the pods simply because pregnancy is an inconvenience? What about single parent parthenogenesis weakening the gene pool? What about the dangers of creating another Aeonistic super race with no physical attachment besides raw genetic material?" says Rachel, pointedly staring at Pfizer and Luxvico in turn, both of whom are Aeon, e-mortals, engineered mortals like she *but top of the line, almost physically perfect.* Luxvico continues to listen emotionlessly as if Rachel is a form of flora that speaks.

"Shouldn't conception and the means of gestation be a matter of personal choice? And are you suggesting that we don't explore our potentials? That we stop evolving?" asks Pfizer.

"Excuse me your Imperial Highness, Doctor," interrupts Luxvico. "You both clearly demonstrate the amount of passion being expressed in this issue. Both sides are spending vast amounts to gain voter support but clearly the Unionists are using a very emotional 'gut' level approach similar to the points just expressed by Dr. Tsimpo. Using these tactics the Imperium Congress will not pass the vote unless the Ambros respond."

Is that all? think both Rachel and Pfizer, but for different reasons.

"Voter opinion has always been manipulated by various factors. However, we are dealing with an informed and rational public that can only temporarily be swayed by emotionalism," says Pfizer with rapidly returning confidence. He chuckles, "You had me nervous Lux, but this isn't over and the Ambros will carry the day."

"I ... apologize for having made you nervous," says Luxvico coldly. He is so emotionless that Pfizer imagines little stones dropping from his mouth as he speaks. "My analysis was based on current voter opinions, intended not to alarm but inform. Though I am not an empathic psychiatrist as the Doctor, I do know that when issues are this sensitive to those involved, and the passions run as high as those I just witnessed, violence often occurs. That should suffice as an explanation as to the general reasons for the rioting," says Luxvico. *Is he trying to tell me something?* Pfizer wonders.

Does it, Lux? Pfizer wonders, fingering the sleeve of his

armored jacket. *You've given me an explanation for the violence. But is this just the beginning? Or the end?*

CHAPTER 4

There are three motives for violence: passion, gain,
and self-defense.

—*The Takazhr Conduct Manual*

"Personal Log, Classified Entry 102123, Captain Basileus
Ahren reporting. Early this morning, 0200 Imperial Time, the
Imperial Navy received a distress signal from a Space Guard
monitor, a warning: 'Smugglers.' The signal was lost when the
monitor was destroyed by what long-range scans identified as a
nuclear explosion. My brigade was stationed at the Luna Low-
Gravity Deep Space Combat Facility and shipped out on the
Stealth Cruiser Narsoom. We intercepted the smugglers in low
Jupiter orbit. The firefight between the two ships was brief
before we boarded. Takazhr units have just finished
eliminating final smuggler resistance. These smugglers were
carrying and using tursapoi—"

Basileus Ahren halted for a moment remembering the
carnage he'd just participated in. *Tursapoi, one of the most dangerous
addictive substances in the Imperium. And now Father is coming to
investigate the matter personally, due to the severity of the incursion. It's
fortunate that he was on Sacred Home for the Uprising Ceremonies. That
was quite possibly the worst experience of my life,* Basileus thinks with
a shudder. He looks up at the main monitor away from the log
entry of the ghastly violence onboard the freighter.

Twirling end-over-end before him and above the swirling,
rainbow-covered Jupiter atmosphere is the charred hulk of the
smuggler ship. Once a sleek, smooth freight racer, now an
abandoned husk, burnt and pockmarked by the Narsoom's

weaponry. Flotsam from the battle makes fiery splashes of yellow orange and then black pyrotechnics as pieces burn in Jupiter's atmosphere. *Jupe flare,* the stellar enthusiast called them. They remind Basileus of a mentallia Solido of Jupe flare that the First Lord had once given his father. It would have been a spectacular sight were the flares not in fact temporary grave markers for a dead ship.

Basileus drops his head wearily and sees his mesh and plated hands in dark green armor. His hands are black and purple with dried blood. He feels sick and overwhelmed. He'd cry if he could, if it would help. The young captain leans forward on the armor rail of the command deck, trying to catch his reflection in one the communications officer's screens. What he sees increases his nausea. Blood stains his hair, smearing his aquiline features. Basileus removes his soiled mesh armor gauntlets from his armored forearms and runs his clean but sweat-soaked hands briskly through bristly straw-colored hair. He wipes dried blood from his light brown eyes, which are blank and look on joy or sorrow without change of expression.

It's just as well his emoto-control is so good. He can still feel the tursapoi drug, the war drug, flashing down his nerves like white fire; he still feels nine feet tall and bristling with razors. He remembers back in basic, the drill sergeants warning him of the danger of being in the presence of normals while still in the tursapoi drug's frenzy. Basileus realizes, as his face reddens with embarrassment, that he could have easily holoed the Narsoom's commander from the ship's barrack hold. Instead he risked losing control on the bridge. *But what I found on that smuggler unnerved me. I haven't been thinking straight,* Basileus thinks. Sobering rapidly Basileus thinks of the small obsidian and iron symbol he found on a dead smuggler. He'd left the forward combat area immediately with this find, and he'd thruster-packed over to the Narsoom. At the time he'd been deep in the tursapoi madness, and judging by the distance of blue and white uniformed bridge personnel from him, he'd probably been very unpleasant when he came on board. *I can be sorry later,* thinks Basileus. *Best to keep my mind clear, keep from getting excited. Excitement could throw me into frenzy, just seeing how awful I look just now almost made me lose control. If these Navy bastards knew what I found, they'd be worried about a lot more than a frenzied Takazhr on the bridge.*

Basileus steals a glance at the ship's master, Rogesh Feravi. Captain Feravi is watching Basileus furtively from the confines of his command console. The Captain's swarthy mustached face is eerily illuminated in the dim bridge light, by multicolored monitors and holographics that process information for him. Even now Basileus knows the Captain is studying him for signs of frenzy, white and gold flecked eyes, muscle jerks.

"I would like to apologize for any ill-mannered behavior when I came on board, Captain Feravi, sir," Basileus says, turning to face the Captain.

Captain Rogesh Feravi has never in his one-hundred-fifty-year-career as a naval officer been in a situation so unique, although in such a long career, he has experienced countless smuggler boardings. He commanded this very ship during the battles of the Anangan Insurrection. But never has a tursapoid officer or enlisted come onto his bridge. True there are the armored marineguards, but really, a Peacekeeper on the war drug, on his bridge giving orders. At first, almost immediately Rogesh had thought to order the bridge marineguards to remove this dangerous intruder, but he didn't, considering the potential for devastating violence in so sensitive an area. No this was no ordinary Peacekeeper not some tursapoi-frenzied trooper who'd left the smuggler ship and rocketed to the Narsoom in a thruster-pack because he couldn't tell friend from foe.

This is a son of Cato Ahren, a Viceroy and commanding Grand Kurseg of the Takazhr. For this child to make such a gross breach of combat conduct there was a legitimizing reason, there had better be. Rogesh's father had just retired, a Vice Director from the PPRC Diplomatic Group, and as the son of such a high-ranking diplomat, Rogesh had been exposed to the intricacies of emoto-control. The knowledge had served him well throughout his career; Captain Ahren had come on board in near hysterics, demanding to speak to the Grand Kurseg of the Peacekeepers.

Rogesh had asked mildly, trying to calm the soldier, what could be so important? However, the youth had insisted that he speak personally and immediately to his father. Rogesh had put down stung pride. Fear was written all over the still youthful face with its empty eyes. Those eyes now carried a discernible emotion, fear, not just for himself but those around him, and something else. It is an ugly kind of fear, almost paranoia. "No, my lord Captain, it is of no matter," replies Captain Feravi graciously.

What was so important? Will he tell me? Rogesh thinks. The naval captain speaks with an almost musical drawl, Serdian, from Serd. The peculiar melodious accents and rich spiritual life made them superb diplomats and negotiators. "My lord Captain, if I may ask ..." Rogesh stops in mid-sentence as Basileus' face begins to harden. *No, asking will yield no further information. Whatever it is he will not reveal it until he sees the Grand Kurseg,* Rogesh decides.

Basileus appreciates the older Captain's patience and diplomacy; he is left feeling embarrassed that he could not reciprocate. To make it worse the Captain had said: "I understand. If you'd like, a secure channel can be put to my workroom," but before Basileus could reply the Watch Officer intruded from the communication station.

"Forgive the interruption Captain sir. Lord Captain Ahren, a communication: 'The Grand Kurseg sends his compliments to both of you and your crews on an excellent performance and lord, Captain Ahren is to shuttle immediately to INS *Bismarck*.'"

"Thank you. See to that commander," Captain Feravi orders. "Lord Ahren, it has been an honor meeting you, young man," says the Captain. Basileus salutes crisply and with all sincerity says, "Thank you, sir. It was my privilege to meet so exemplary an officer."

Yes, he has the manners of the Court. But still to be so afraid, and of what? Rogesh wonders. "Whatever is going on, young man, it will be all right," he says. But the eyes looking into Rogesh Feravi's say otherwise and a sudden sense of apprehension settles over him as Captain Ahren heads toward the a-grav shaft.

"I hope so," murmurs Basileus to himself as the a-grav iris spirals open. He steps in and orders his destination: hangar deck, flight pads. The vibrating hum of the ship is replaced by the whine of the a-grav capsule as it speeds him along the Stealth Cruiser's four hundred meter length. Basileus sags against a wall of the capsule. *Nothing will be all right if the Tene Thantos have returned. Nothing, will be all there is, if they are back,* Basileus thinks bitterly. The iris spirals open and Basileus emerges onto the Narsoom's flight pad. Space-suited and uniformed personnel scrambled around him, like bees intent on specific tasks, as boarding pods return through the magnetic field that retains the flight pad's atmosphere. Landing lights and strobes blink under the thick exhaust of Basileus' arrowhead-shaped shuttle. Lieutenant Bernard Al-Feza, Basileus' executive officer, stands by the shuttle's boarding ramp with a duffel bag and data case. Al-Feza's dark, usually smiling, face is haunted and hollow-cheeked. Al-Feza looks into Basileus' eyes momentarily and then drops his normally steady gaze.

"It was horrible, sir," mumbles Bernard Al-Feza, shaking his head.

"Lieutenant, report," snaps Basileus. *I must lead by example. If what I fear is true, we will need every brave heart we can muster.*

Al-Feza is startled by Basileus' manner and gives an awkward salute. "Captain, the data case has the brigade officers after action reports. And I had some workgreens packed. You can't report to the Grand Kurseg in cybernetic battle armor, sir," he says, handing Basileus the data case and Takazhr duffel bag.

Basileus acknowledges the salute. "Better, much better, Lieutenant," says Basileus, taking the data case and duffel. "I want this scenario programmed into the base combat simulators with the objectives of increasing combat efficiency and minimizing casualties. Use a large number of variants, Bernard." Basileus hesitates momentarily, "If we have to do this again I don't want it taking such a toll on us. And Nard, I want you and the rest of our people to quarantine yourselves. Anyone wanting confirmation can contact the Grand Kurseg. No contact until further notice."

It is clear by Al-Feza's expression that he would rather pass a-mat plasma, the fuel that powered instellar ships, than go through the boarding again. "My men are depending on you, Bernard. Keep things together until I get back." Basileus slaps Al-Feza on the shoulder, salutes, and strides purposefully up the ramp.

Behind him Lieutenant Al-Feza yells: "Clear Sky, Basileus!" the traditional spacers' farewell and good luck. As Basileus climbs on board the shuttle he taps the communicator by the boarding lock signaling the flight cabin, "This is Captain Ahren. You may lift when ready." The pilot acknowledges and Basileus closes the lock. There are no omniform chairs in the passenger cabin. *Only the military could be so utilitarian,* thinks Basileus. He drops his helmet and data case in one of the tiny chairs and goes to the shuttle head.

Five minutes later Basileus emerges, shaven and wearing his work uniform, a single piece of comfortable black-green armored mesh, with a multitude of pockets. He manages to squeeze his one-hundred-kilo form into the miniscule chair in an almost bearable position. At least there are unshuttered view ports. He drops his head into his hands and rocks back and forth. That freight racer carried two metric tons of tursapoi, enough for his brigade for a year at combat consumption rate. Tursapoi meant only one thing, violence. (*Once, five thousand years ago hordes of tursapoid Tene Thantos had attacked this star system, so long ago that even to the e-mortals it seemed like legend.*) The enemy today on that freight racer had supposedly been just fifty unarmored, untrained smugglers. Maybe half of them had time to get to the tursapoi, the war drug, but those that did had put up a fearsome resistance. No, they didn't just resist; they attacked. They attacked the nearly two hundred cybernetically armored troops of his brigade and inflicted such casualties that Basileus had no choice but to order his troops to use their own tursapoi. He hadn't looked at the reports, but he doubted any smugglers survived and his people were trained professionals. They'd have tried to take prisoners, even on the drug, but the smugglers had ingested or injected probably lethal quantities, judging by the suicidal ferocity of their attack.

It was a Tene Thantos crucifix he found on the freight racer. That and the smugglers suicidal use of tursapoi made him feel a terror he'd not felt since childhood, when he was afraid of nightmares. As a child he'd been to the museums and memorials all across the universe on the planets that survived the Wasting. In fact, one of the memorials he saw, on the fourth planet of this system, Mars, was the remains of Sidonia—an entire city, a blackened glass crater with the partially melted skeletons of a few buildings as a grave marker for millions.

It could not happen again; it just couldn't. Yet right now there is a Tene Thantos crucifix in his pocket in a security capsule, and the ship he'd found it on was carrying tursapoi. The flight trajectory clearly indicated a course for Sacred Home, where most of the Imperial family and government where gathering. Family and many friends were on Sacred Home, the very birthplace of Humanity.

CHAPTER 5

To prevent the horror and scourge of intergalactic
war from being inflicted on future generations, all
humanity must be united under one government.

—Aristo Declaration of 1617 I.C.

"Mother of Ambros," Basileus whispers. "What's going on?"

"Captain Ahren? We're making final approach," says the bewildered voice of the pilot. For the first time Basileus realizes it is a women's voice and that he must have left the communicator on when he boarded the shuttle. Basileus stands and walks forward to the flight cabin. "Thanks," he says as he slides into the navigator's chair perpendicular to the pilot. At least this chair is one of the omniform type. The round-faced pilot with the corona of black hair is intent on her controls as she guides the shuttle on its final approach to the INS *Bismarck*.

The Dreadnought ISN *Bismarck* is a four-thousand-meter-long triangular wedge of armor, bristling with energy weapons, studded with accelerator tubes and launchers, a starship so large it awed by its sheer immensity. Yet if a frenzied suicide group could get onboard, they could conceivably destroy such a ship. Despite the great size and power of the Imperium of over a million planets, it too could be destroyed, if the population of just one planet were to go on a frenzied crusade, as the people of Anonjida once had. *Magdalene should have blasted it to bits along with every Tene. After all, it only took one decent a-mat device to crack a planet.*

"Captain," says the pilot, "strap in. We're passing through the hangar bay's magnetic field."

Basileus fastens his safety harness as the hundred-meters-wide entrance of the hangar dominates the shuttle's view port. Voices of hangar officers whisper over the communicator ordering touchdown procedures. Basileus gets up, goes astern to retrieve his belongings and departs wordlessly as the shuttle comes to rest on the *Bismarck's* flight pad. He leaves the young naval pilot astonished at the rudeness of her aristocratic guest.

Marshal Tsano Amin, the Grand Kurseg's chief aide, watches as Basileus walks away from the delta shuttle. Basileus appears tired but in relatively good shape, considering he's just been through the exhaustion of a frenzy. Basileus' eyes focus on Tsano and there is the glimmer of recognition in them, followed by a brittle smile. *If I could have prevented him from seeing combat I would have,* Tsano thinks. *Basileus had seen that which should never be seen.* To most citizens and even most soldiers of the Imperium the peace of the Pax Ambros had been broken only once in four thousand years.

Tsano and Basileus know different. They know there are those who must take, steal, pirate, or rape rather than create. The Takazhr and to some extent the Bloodguard hunt these aberrations, mostly shattered humans who were used or abused themselves and are now inflicting abuse on others. Once apprehended, they could be healed. The Imperium was not yet paradise but at least the organized violent sub-cultures of the past had been eliminated in a society that possessed the technology to create almost any device or food from its basic elements and free fusion energy. The one exception had been the Tene Thantos, originally a secret society of puritanical racial supremacist e-mortals. They spread their poison of intolerance, bigotry, and hate for so called 'lesser beings' to the citizens of the Imperium. The Tene Thantos made many e-mortals fear Citizo genetic regulations and laws and the Citizo fear e-mortals' enhanced abilities and lifespans. The Tene Thantos almost destroyed the universe. Surely that was one lesson humanity could not forget. Tsano hopes this generation will not be the one to repeat this mistake, but it seems inevitable. Basileus comes to a stop and salutes Tsano. Tsano returns the salute and asks, "What happened out there?"

"I can't talk about it here, Tsano," answers Basileus. "Where's my father?" *It is good to see a reassuring face.* Basileus thinks.

"In the executive officers' workroom. Your father never stops working, you know."

"Yes," Basileus says. When he thinks of his father he usually pictures him seated at a work station. On lush green Titan though, not an Imperial Dreadnought, especially not the flagship. Since the engagement he has had a longing to be planetside, to feel real gravity and breathe unprocessed air. He allows Tsano to usher him toward a bank of a-grav capsules. Basileus realizes it's getting difficult to concentrate, that this entire ordeal has taken its toll on him, physically and mentally. "I need some sleep, Tsano."

Tsano grunts agreement. "Don't worry. Just let us debrief you and I guarantee you'll get the rest you've got coming."

Basileus closes his eyes as the capsule speeds them through the starship. Tsano nudges him when they reach their destination, and as he opens his eyes he smells the perfumes of the Xanadu blossoms. Florescent orange, delicate blood red stamens. "I think I was dreaming of home."

"The Xanadu began blooming when we left," Tsano says as they approach a Bloodguard sitting ramrod straight at a receptionist desk outside the workroom. Basileus recognizes him as one of the household guard. He's glad that his father is using their regular Bloodguards instead of those available from the Diplomatic Protection Group.

* * *

His Royal Highness, Prince Cato Ahren, Viceroy and Grand Kurseg of the Imperial Takazhr sits quietly, suspended in the middle of the workroom. The workroom itself is a large circle twenty meters in diameter, some floor sections raised others sunken. Everything is Erosi blackglass, except the four-meter semicircular expanse of view port that shows swirling Jupiter and an ocean of stars. Several columns of light, some larger than others, dot the room, holograms of the battle with the smuggler and the holo logs of the officers commanding the engagement. Some of the holos contain information in print; others spew forth information in a haunting myriad of voices. Cato reclines in the suspended command chair, his left eye glowing from the MentAmp implant in his head. A buzzer from the desk below signals him that Tsano and Basileus are on their way.

"Lights, chair down and to station," commands Cato.

Soft white light illuminates the room and the chair floats to a blackglass rectangular conference table with seven identical chairs. Cato thinks of Glythsphr, the Ahren families' ancestral seat on far Titan. Cato wishes that Basileus had stayed on verdant Titan, gone to emp-psych school, maybe even Tempel, become a diplomat, philosopher or scholar.

Cato remembers chasing a laughing seven-year-old Basileus between the trees in orchards of tall gold grass. Not enough time, not enough of those times. He remembers playing in those same stands of pear and apple trees with Orion, his first son. Just as Cato's father Alexander had played with him. Cato knew sadly, had known since the day Persis had caused him to adopt Basileus, that he would outlive this mortal son. Persis never watched Basileus grow up, she died in shuttle accident.

Cato never encouraged Basileus in his Takazhr career; he supported but never encouraged him. However, Basileus had adored his adoptive older brother. When Orion at eighteen had packed the family gym with weights and gravitons, the eleven-year-old Basileus would often intrude in the dangerous area to emulate his hero. When Orion had gone to Earth and New Point, Basileus had declared that he too would attend the prestigious Takazhr academy when he was old enough. Then there was the bright summer day when they'd buried Orion in the orchards outside Glythsphr, just as he'd requested when he joined the Takazhr. By then Basileus had been a lieutenant and he and Cato had walked quietly through those trees, back toward home, as the sun set behind the broad canopy of emerald, rust, copper, and yellow leaves above the house. Cato pleaded that Basileus abandon his law enforcement career. He wanted to see Basileus grow old and play with his children in these very same fields.

The iris spirals open and Marshal Amin and Captain Ahren enter. "It could use a few plants, don't you think Basil?" said Cato, being the Grand Kurseg could wait a moment.

Basileus eyes the workroom with obvious distaste. "I have an Anorn tree that is crazy from space travel. Can you take it home, Father?" Basileus asks, walking toward Cato and embracing him.

Cato, from ancient Homo Deus bloodlines an Aeon, stands two meters tall, with fiery red hair and predatory golden eyes in a face like an ancient bronze of Alexander the Great. He looks down at his son, a face now older than his, and returns the embrace. *Basileus is frightened?*

"I have been well, but since I received your message," says Cato, still slightly leaning and embracing his son, "I have been nervous. I haven't ... Well, that is not important." Cato disengages and looks hard at Basileus, the unwavering and unnerving stare of the emp-psych-trained. "I'm sure you are aware that this amount of tursapoi headed toward an unknown destination does constitute a grave danger, but it is not an Imperium-wide disaster. You signaled me with a Code D Priority which means we should go to a State of Emergency. Is that what you believe, Captain?" asks Cato. Without meaning he has resumed his role as Grand Kurseg.

Basileus reaches into the holo control fields of a station at the table and activates the room's security system.

"They weren't just smugglers. They were Tene Thantos Deathmen." Basileus is pulling the security capsule from his worksuit. He tosses it on to the table and it skids to a stop in front of Cato. The secret he has kept since leaving the freight racer rushes out. "I saw one take enough tursapoi to kill an Invid. He then killed at least ten of my men ... Others are still in critical care ... We followed procedure, cybernetic battle armor. At first I didn't want to believe it, but now that our people and the Navy had a chance to go over that ship, I know there's more evidence than that crucifix. The bodies alone, the fact that they could ingest instantaneously lethal quantities of tursapoi, suggest that they were engineered or bred for this. Only the Deathmen were made that way."

The logic is cold and undeniable. Lomin, his Tempeler counselor, could not be more precise. Even so, Cato is almost willing to dismiss the very possibility that his son might be correct. There have been very few times in Cato's life when he's nearly abandoned the truth—but the loss of Orion and Persis have driven him close. Cato takes a deep breath.

"I want forensic and autopsy analysis immediately, Basil. Contact the Narsoom. Maintain the information quarantine. Then summon Lomin," orders Cato.

Cato turns to Tsano. Both of them served during the Anangan Insurrection, when Princess Oriana, older sister of Pfizer and first child of Empress-Executrix Anastacia, had made a desperate bid to save the life of her unborn child. She challenged the prohibition against Aeon, attempting unlicensed prenatal genegineering. She claimed she wanted to endow her child with abilities to aid in his or her stewardship of the universe.

Cato was of the belief that to genegineer away defects or enhance latent genetic characteristics was justified. He also supported the genegineering of humans for adaptation to high-grav worlds like Eros, and more important, so did the government GenTech Board, which issued genegineering licenses. Oriana, with the help of scientists of questionable ethics, to say the least, had genegineered the unborn fetus' extra-sensory and psi-kinetic brain functions.

The Wasting had proved how dangerous this was. During the Wasting Armingkon Quiso and his racial supremacist Homo Deus, Neo Deus followers, bred telepaths and telekinetics who had done as much killing as a-mat and fusion weaponry. Fortunately the 'Power,' as most referred to psi-kinetic ability, was unnatural at these levels and had quickly dissipated from the gene pool after the Wasting. Cato can see Tsano agrees—the universe won't survive another Armingkon Quiso.

The room bleeps for attention and informs them that Counselor Lomin is arriving. The workroom iris spirals open and Lomin, Cato's Tempeler Counselor, glides in.

Lomin is old. None of them really know how old, but they know he is older than anyone the three of them know.

Lomin wears a-grav units on his wrists and ankles, keeping his body in an a-grav field and suspended from the debilitating effects of gravity. His face, exposed by the black lifesuit of the Tempellians, is brown, weathered, and lined, a deflated shock ball with two bird-bright slits for eyes.

Lomin wears the yellow robes of the Academy Psychological Ministry. He floats to the table and nods to each of them—Cato, Basileus, then Tsano, opening his eyes just a little more. The gesture appears reptilian and distant. "Lords, Marshal Amin."

This is no time for amenities, Cato decides. "Lomin this is an emergency. Basileus has discovered a Tene Thantos artifact, and encountered what we believe to be Deathmen smuggling tursapoi and illegal weapons to Sacred Home."

Lomin gasps and it is the most emotion Cato has seen from him in fifty years. Cato experiences the odd sensation that Lomin is a museum piece from a lost time, but when? Lomin absently wipes saliva from his opened mouth. *He's astonished. Just like the rest of us, even he doesn't want to believe this is real,* thinks Cato.

"I must review the data ... I want to see the symbol ... the bodies," Lomin begins muttering. Basileus opens the security capsule and hands it across the table to Lomin. Deftly the old fingers, like black talons in the lifesuit, pluck the symbol from the capsule. Lomin brings it close to his face. *He said something—or did he sing it? He couldn't be praying, could he?* Cato wonders.

"You ... We must inform the Empress and the First Lord," says Lomin, turning toward the iris. "Cato, I must see the

41

bodies," he begins floating from the table.

"Lomin? Contact the Empress-Executrix without confirmation?" asks Cato rising from his chair, close to anger at the Logician's behavior.

"Cato," Lomin says softly, and it's the voice he used with Cato two hundred years ago, when Cato was a child, slow to grasp something. Lomin partially turns toward them, his face in shadow. "You will contact them. Then you must take me to see the bodies. I'm going to assemble an investigative team from the *Bismarck's* crew. I will meet you in the main hangar in fifteen minutes ... Please, Cato, be on time."

Lomin turns and floats from the room, leaving Basileus amazed at Lomin's treatment of his father, Tsano indignant, and Cato ... It has always been hard to read Cato, and now every emotion registers plainly.

"Father, when I gave Lomin the Thantos crucifix, he mumbled something," says Basileus.

"A prayer, my son. He was praying," answers Cato, watching the closing iris. The others must not have seen Lomin as he turned or there'd be more questions, Cato decides. But Cato did see Lomin's face as he left the room, and his eyes had been full of tears.

CHAPTER 6

Four things support the world: the learning of
the wise, the justice of the great, the prayers of the
good, and the valor of the brave.

—The Prophet Muhammad, Old Earth, (words
inscribed above the Imperios entrance)

She is a tall, strikingly beautiful woman. Her lips are full and
sensuous. Her eyes are light electric gray like Pfizer's, magnetic
and penetrating. Stately is the single word that best describes
her. Her severe black suit with gold buttons accentuates the
lovely curves of her figure and the shine in her dark copper
hair, which is tightly pulled back by a matching black band.
Her stateliness envelopes her like a force shield, a bubble that
none of the surrounding execs intrude upon unless permitted
to do so.

The execs whisper into microphones and peer into the
monocular viewers of the audvids that are linked to their
omnipalms; they exchange data chips with one another. It
seems like a dance that surrounds her, a dance of power. She is
Anastacia Mariko Isabella Ambros, Empress-Executrix of the
Imperium, Majority Share Holder of the Terrax Corporation,
and Chief Operating Officer and Majority Share Holder of the
CIMB—or Combine of Internetworked Mercantile and
Banks—and for better or worse she rules the known universe.

Anastacia folds her black-gloved hands in front of her. The
panoramic window of the reception tower presents a
spectacular view of the ocean of humanity gathered at New

Eden's O'Meara Cosmodome. The hum and din of so many people makes the air and walls vibrate. The tempo has been building for days as her family began returning, drawing these record crowds to Earth, the Sacred Home of the Race. Anastacia maintains an acute dislike for such titles. She knows they are meant to awe, that they are simply another form of government manipulation designed to encourage submission of the self to religious mystique. In the same way empath-psychiatrists of the Ambros Press and Public Relations Corps make her into the heroine, galactic goddess, mother of her civilization. They employ archetypes. She knows she is a woman; true she is an e-mortal, but she was born of a mother and a father. She is subject to time and space, with cares, desires, fears as human as the hundreds of trillions she rules. Sometimes such thoughts trouble her. *How easy it would be to slip into the leader mystique, the cult of personality created around me.* She knows how utterly foolish and destructive that would be. She has sworn to herself that she will free the Ambros of their stewardship of humanity, but the burden of freeing humanity from its old ways is enormous.

The sad truth, Anastacia thinks, *is that for untold millennia men and women have given up their destiny, a portion of themselves; either they willingly submitted or they did so without even knowing. Our ancestors were sold on the idea that some government, religion, corporation, or constitution held the keys to their lives, and they gradually lost their freedoms or like the ancient democracies forgot to think for themselves. Kings, presidents, electors, prime ministers, legates, prelates, senators, bishops, and Empress-Executrix—words made sacred and conferring authority. One placebo after another: religion, science, government, law. Somewhere out there people believed someone else had the answer to their problems. No. The simple truth was that given the knowledge, resources, and time, individuals could unlock their own destinies, find their true genius, self-actualize, be their own leaders, and the universe would blossom with Einstein and Tsasinov, Mozart and Caitlin, Angelous and Tzuens.*

Anastacia knows that any leader, if the word could still be used, who arose in such a world could only lead with the informed consent of his or her fellows, or the moral superiority of his or her positions. She has not picked an easy task; the government she seeks to dismantle has resisted. Certain technologies and industries have removed the need for many government services. With the advent of the Free Fusion Authority, servo-sphere technology, and matter recombination Solidos, communities and individuals have become self-sufficient and thus independent. Government services and programs have become unused and unnecessary, and the managers and workers of the system unneeded. In earlier times this would have been a problem, a dangerous problem. Government bureaucrats without jobs? With today's technology, however, these unemployed welcomed the time for personal pursuits. She had once thought that the bureaucracy would be the most resistant to change, but much had been phased out already, and as she observed, those bureaucrats welcomed the opportunity to explore their own lives.

Opposition increased, however, when Anastacia turned her attention to the legislative apparatus, the law makers. Things changed then; Oriana had rebelled. But Anastacia stuck to her convictions and now twenty years later, the reinvention of society continues, although at a slower rate than when it first began.

Unfortunately, with the discovery of the Outlaws things are changing once again. The Imperium has polarized. On the one side is Anastacia's "party." Its stance is to allow the Outlaws to advance at their own pace and when the time is right to allow them to join the Imperium, which by then will be more of a Cooperative of millions of communities. Her opponents, on the other hand, think otherwise. "Do it the way it's been done for thousands of years," they say, citing the fact that Imperial policy on the repatriation of rediscovered human colonies was a provision of the Aristo Declaration of 1617: "To prevent the horror and scourge of intergalactic war being inflicted on future generations, all Humanity must be united under one government."

That single statement had become the rallying cry of the

proponents of the entrenched bureaucracy, those who did not want to give up their power. The riots had broken out then and the opposition had begun using emp-psych media tricks, scandals involving her political supporters, and publicity campaigns to undermine her efforts. Creating the Omnividome had been her answer to their smear campaign. The Omnividome would be a communications device that would instalink her to every citizen of the Imperium. She would bring the issues of dismantling the government and the annexation of the outlaw territories to a referendum.

Anastacia is certain that most voters will embrace her ideas of self-sufficiency, independence, and self-actualization and reject the opposition's ideas of guidelines, limits, regulations, and thus mediocrity—a dreadful mediocrity that would stagnate the entire human race bound under it.

Anastacia believes that, simply put, her way of "scattering the eggs from the basket" would save humanity from extinction.

Anarchy!—the opposition said—Little tiny communities to be destroyed in a second Wasting, or worse to be conquered while divided and enslaved again by some non-humanoid intelligence! An appeal to fear is what the opposition counted on; fear of the stranger, the unknown, the different. Fear of losing the little creature comforts, of having to think and to be responsible for oneself.

Anastacia has prayed—yes, for this even she has prayed—that her fellow humans will not listen to their fear this time and will instead follow the voice of reason to infinite futures and continue in their support of her.

"Domina?" A voice interrupts Anastacia's thoughts, using the title exclusively used by the Bloodguard for an Executrix.

Anastacia turns toward the rich bass voice and looks into the brown face of General Houka Jamal, General Praetor of Anastacia's Bloodguard. Anastacia nods and Jamal advances. Two steps and he covers the ten meters between them in graceful fluid motion rippling with energy, a panther on steroids. Houka's biosculpted face is a work of art, with its high cheekbones, chiseled jaw, and dark brown eyes that smolder like live coals. His hair is shoulder length, braided, and adorned with silver, obsidian, and lapis lazuli. Anastacia has always become a bit breathless at his appearance. Houka seems some gen-tech's dream of a more evolved, elegant species. She wonders momentarily if his awesome appearance is the result of some Bloodguard think tank.

"Good Morning, Houka," Anastacia says. Her voice is a soft lilting contralto. She has gotten to know General Praetor Jamal quite well in the past two decades. His presence now assures her all is well.

"Good Morning to you, Domina. Captain Praetor Buchanan informs me Ambros Two has entered orbit and a shuttle is en route to New Eden."

There is a commotion at the main iris to the observation salon. Holo pickups and lights start clicking on as the media gathered around her staff begin turning toward the iris.

"The First Lord," Houka announces in explanation as the iris spirals open.

Millian DeHaaven Hane-Ambros is Anastacia's husband and upon her ascension to the Executorship of the Imperium he became the First Lord. Millian arrives with a wake of imperial execs behind him. The majority of Anastacia's execs are government directorate or military dressed in various uniforms, while Millian's execs are dressed in the height of cosmopolitan business wear. The exchange of information between Millian's execs is much more frantic than that among Anastacia's staff. Millian's execs talk numbers, commodity rates, stock portfolios, strategic resource inventories. Millian cuts a dashing figure in the black and red uniform of a Bloodguard retiree, General Praetor rank.

Where Anastacia is poised and regal, Millian is animated and charming, a showman who conducts his staff and the media like a maestro. At this distance Millian could be mistaken for Pfizer, although nearly two centuries separated the two in age. Millian's wedding earring flashes in the holo camera lights as he begins issuing directives to both staffs but

Anastacia catches the brief glance he throws her—the smile and the extra light in his eyes that is there only for her. He dismisses everyone with a wave of his hand and all depart except his older brother, Creed, the Lion. Millian excuses himself from Creed. Anastacia suppresses a shudder. Creed exemplifies all she dislikes about both the Erosi and her husband's family.

"My Dear," Millian whispers in her ear, knowing this tickles her. She smells ocean and salt air from Millian's visit to the outside. She steals a kiss from his lips and immediately the holocams begin whining. They both pull away and Millian quips, "Really, haven't you people seen enough? We've been married ninety-eight years!"

"And each kiss has been sweeter," Anastacia murmurs to the delight of the press.

Millian nudges closer to her. He looks at her with a look she has seen before, when he wants to gather her in his arms and tell her that he loves her.

Millian steps away from his wife and confronts the gathering of media people. "That will be all ... for now," he says with a mischievous smile. The crowd hums with polite laughter. "We'll talk again when the Crown Scion arrives," Millian declares, nodding to Houka, who steps forward and gently ushers the press away. The First Lord turns back to his Empress-Executrix.

Anastacia's lips form the word "Yes." Yes, Millian has always been the very soul of care. When she'd first began seeing him, her parents had been worried, worried this high-grav'd soldier would be too physically strong with their lovely girl. He could literally break her back hugging her. What would happen in a moment of passion? But Millian was nothing but gentle with her, no embrace too tight, no caress too heavy. It was this loving restraint of such great natural strength that had won her. She had also seen her beautiful man's face rock hard, cold, and his glacial blue eyes gleaming with frigid anger. Millian was a Bloodguard, conditioned to serve and protect the Ambros. Was it because of conditioning that he loved her? But in the end it hadn't mattered what planet he came from or what his family did or what his job was; all that mattered was Millian. The way he talked to her, touched her, made her see the world and shared it with her. As always thoughts of faults and problems melted away.

When Anastacia gazed at him this way, Millian invariably warmed and drew near her. It was his secret shame that he sometimes thought himself undeserving of the love in her eyes. If he was deserving he wouldn't have allowed these damnable negotiations with Yoshida Colonizers to take him away from her for the past three days or the press to eavesdrop on their moments together now. The attention from the media had become stifling. God only knew if Anastacia could end this with her plan. Their daughter Oriana's actions had proven a severe disappointment. Oriana, whose name meant 'daughter of the golden one,' had always been considered by Millian to be the child most like himself: extroverted, politically conscious, interested in the state of Ambros family in both government and financial matters. It hurt that much more that she had lead the Anangan Insurrection. In his view it deprived the Imperium of a ruler with vast potential.

To Millian his sullen son was an unknown variable in his wife's plan to dismantle the government. *The Scholar,* Millian thinks of Pfizer. *Like his mother, a dreamer. No, that was unfair, idealistic yes, and a shrewd philosopher scientist. But with zero practical experience in imperial or corporate affairs.* Millian groans in frustration. Pfizer did have strength of character though, enough certainly to defy Millian, and that he considered Pfizer's greatest attribute. If only Anastacia's timetable had not acquired its own awful momentum. Pfizer may conceivably be the last Emperor-Executor. Would he be strong enough? Millian had debated waiting for a grandchild who might possess the qualities he sought. But the Fragmentation, once it had begun, had gained a life of its own. To halt the plan would cause more problems for centuries, and then maybe the race would never be free but extinct.

"We'll see soon enough," Anastacia says, responding to his unspoken thoughts, and Millian grips her a little tighter.

CHAPTER 7

Failure to communicate is the source of all
conflict.

—An Ambros History: Anastacia II and the Omnividome

The Bloodguard Officers have begun whispering vehemently
with Naval Officers. Millian turns and his frost blue eyes
search the officers, looking for his brother ... Creed Hane.
Millian's brother and the ranking Grand Kurseg, commanding
general, of the Bloodguard, berates an Imperial Naval Admiral.
"Five and a half hours?!" roars Creed. An embarrassed silence
fills the salon.

Creed Goethe Duran Hane, 'the Lion' behind his back but
never in his presence—although Creed certainly knew the
nickname, and both Millian and Anastacia suspected he
enjoyed it. With his great mane of gold hair, his fierce sharp-
angled face, and the hunter's gaze in his pale blue eyes, he is
every bit the lion. There is something feline and predatory in
the manner of all Bloodguards, even Anastacia's beloved
Millian. But Creed exemplifies it, radiates it. A Vice Admiral is
dumbfounded by the pressure Creed exerts with his very
personality. Anastacia has never cared for Creed's
superciliousness; she's always fought a sense of resentment
towards the influence Creed has over his brother, her husband.
It is cat and mouse now with the Admiral. The Lion
antagonizing his prey.

"What were you thinking?!" Creed growls. "You track a
hostile UFO from Pluto Station ..."

Anastacia is familiar with the Naval officer, a Vice Admiral Majeski, an aide to Admiral Albert Rhodes of Naval Intelligence. She cannot watch this bullying any longer.

"Something the matter, Kurseg Hane?" she inquiries, bringing all the cold formality she can muster to her voice.

Creed stops in mid-harangue. He is delighted to answer the Executrix. He has been waiting for such an opportunity. *She is responsible for all of this and more.* Creed does not attempt to conceal his thoughts from evincing themselves through his body language and the effect is like a slap to Anastacia or anyone else in the salon who is well versed in emoto-control.

The media are going to have a field day, Millian surmises as his wife and brother square off.

"A UFO, an unidentified, flying, object," Creed says pedantically. "The Empress-Executrix is familiar with the term." Creed has turned from the Vice Admiral and is striding toward Anastacia. "In view of the unrest ...," He begins, but his eyes say, *that you created—you.*

God, he's going public! Millian thinks and positions himself between wife and brother. Creed fortunately does not make his disagreement with Anastacia public. Instead he says: "In view of the unrest, all ships within Pluto orbit must respond to hails and be identified."

"And the UFO, Kurseg?" Anastacia asks through clenched teeth.

"A misnomer in this case Majesty; the object has been identified. It is a long-range freight racer. Audio and visual communication attempts have not been responded to." Creed's reply is militarily efficient and polite, but the smile on his face is one of ... *Of what?* She thinks.

Damn him! "You assume hostility based on their failure to communicate, Kurseg?" Anastacia asks and regrets it immediately.

"The Executrix, architect of the Omnividome, should have to ask ...," Creed says with just the right amount of familial familiarity to keep Millian from being publicly offended. "Surely you of all people know that failure to communicate is inherently hostile."

CHAPTER 8

The power to make decisions is the beginning of
freedom.

—Pfizer Ambros, as quoted in *The Hane Commentaries*
by Aaron Charlemagna Invid-Hane

"There're simply too many media," Otto complains to Pfizer
for the fifth time, tapping his monoviewer. They are seated
next to one another in the passenger compartment of a
modified delta shuttle.

"Tell them interviews after landing," Pfizer suggests. "Tell
them no one is getting preferential treatment."

Otto turns to look at Pfizer. Pfizer has never seen his face
so hard. Then his expression softens slightly, and he leans
toward Pfizer whispering: "I remember a study at the
Bloodguard Cadre on Tempel. In the Anangan Insurrection
Tolan had planned to use memprogrammed media
personalities as assassins because of their access to government
officials." Otto's green eyes harden again. "I'm sorry. I have to
prepare you. You've got to know the possibilities. It can save
your life."

"Otto, is it really so bad?" Pfizer asks, reading in Otto's
expression that it is and that Otto would much rather tell him
something comforting than the truth. Otto, however, is sworn
to only speak truth to this future Domino of the Corps
Bloodguard.

"I think so. I've been viewing the nets. There's a lot of
passionate demonstrating going on down there," Otto says,

easing into the truth as best he can. Initial reports estimated some three million people had gathered around O'Meara Cosmodome. The Ambros had unleashed something in the populace. They came in record numbers across the vast distances of the galaxy, to this remote planet on the edge of the galactic spiral because of one family's dream.

The pilot has set the cabin viewer for the approach angle. The growing globe of Earth seems to swell before them. Already they are in the uppermost regions of the atmosphere. Otto hand signals to an armored squad of Bloodguards:

"Watch the crowd. We've got plainclothes to deal with the net people. Set scans for constant weapons surveillance."

The first slight bumps and jolts on entering atmosphere shudder the cabin. Staffers begin buckling in, grabbing handholds. Pfizer fumbles with his safety harness. On the viewer they pass through clouds to a dawn-painted vista below spectacular golds and oranges reflected off permacrete and silicon towers.

"Otto ...," Pfizer whispers. Then his mouth forms a great "O" of awe. Otto deactivates his monocle and looks at the viewer. Even at this distance the gathered mass of humanity is obvious.

"Gods, it's monstrous ...," says someone from the PPRC. Pfizer pulls the three playing-card-sized crystal sheets from his jacket pocket. His speech.

"Landing in two minutes," informs the pilot over the intercom amidst the astonished murmurs running through Pfizer's entourage. Thinking of the hiss and gurgle of water or waves of ammonia against current skimmers, Pfizer turns to Otto, but the Bloodguard is preoccupied with his comm equipment, receiving and transmitting through sub-vocal mike, ear transceiver, and monoviewer. Pfizer pulls a hand comp from another pocket and inserts one of the crystal sheets into it, but can't bring himself to read it. Staffers and Bloodguard are beginning to crowd around the cabin hatch.

"The essentials of the situation are the same as any other. Either you will control the situation or be controlled by it," says Luxvico, appearing black, green, and gold in the dim cabin light, as if out of nowhere. "Or find a way between control and controlled, serving and doing what you will. This will require your awakening."

Pfizer nods thanks to the Tempeler and he and Otto get to their feet. Dr. Tsimpo is at the hatch smiling reassuringly. The magbolts of the hatch are withdrawn and thud into place and the doors open to the silent whirling of yellow strobes.

The cool crisp air of this October dawn rushes in and rose-colored sunlight fills the hatchway. A sound like the humming of bees vibrates the very air in the shuttle. Pfizer lunges himself forward.

The thunderous greeting that meets him is so loud that he backs into Otto's immoveable form. Otto gently thrusts him back to more thunderous cheering. Giant holo screens relay Pfizer's image throughout the throngs of people. Pfizer waves his arms high above his head and the cheering intensifies, and Pfizer feels it lifting him up, like a wave that seems to carry him down the landing ramp.

So many people, so many differences, except the shared curiosity on the expectant faces. To see this and to set foot on Earth for the first time in years fills him with an unexplainable tingle and he feels the ache of raw emotion in his throat. He turns towards the reception tower.

"Madame Empress, First Lord Ambros," Pfizer says bowing. His voice is loud and rings throughout the crowd echoed by the holo screens. "Aristo, Citizo, ..." Pfizer stops and raises a hand holding the three crystal sheets of his speech. "I had prepared something to say to all of you. But being here on the birthworld of our race and seeing you, I can only speak from my heart."

Now, except for the throb and hum of so many people there is silence. "All of you know I have returned because of the Outlaw Issue that divides the Imperium. I thought that we had rid ourselves of our fear of that which is different, rid ourselves of false pride, false dogmas and idols.

"I thought the barriers that fenced the human heart—

Greed, Ignorance, and Apathy—had been torn down. Why do we raise them?" Pfizer stops and takes a deep breath looking out across the waiting mass of people and in a quieter voice he continues.

"Have we become so uncertain of our powers that we must steal or force what we create upon others with weapons?" Louder he goes on, "Please, in the name of decency, let this false craving for power over the destiny of others perish. Instead, seek to love, help, and enlighten them, as we love, help and enlighten one another. In peace and in fellowship."

All eyes are on Pfizer. As he continues speaking the crowd is drawn in not only by his eloquence but by his authentic sincerity. He needs no script. He has stirred their emotions, gained their full attention. The passion Pfizer is arousing in the gathered populace has become palpable.

High in the reception tower Millian and Anastacia look on in amazement. These are not new sentiments that Pfizer is uttering. Other prophets had offered them. But Pfizer speaks now with such hypnotizing sincerity and fervor that he seems to be minting each sentimental cliché anew. *Is this our son?* Millian and Anastacia marvel. *This commanding, thrilling orator? This saint?* A tear rolls down Anastacia's face at the effect Pfizer's words have on the people in the salon, on those down on the ground, on those following this on galactic networks. *Who could calculate the impact of these words?* Millian wonders. He feels a weight growing in his chest.

"Pfizer...," Millian mumbles. "Our son occupies the universe's center stage, and they"—he waves a hand to indicate the swirling madhouse of flesh and color—"are his."

In contrast to her husband, Anastacia feels as if a crushing weight has been removed from her. She is free ... free. Pfizer has taken the mantle of the dream. Millian gathers her to him and she weeps quietly, almost invisibly, against his chest. The media are swinging their attention toward her. Pfizer's entourage is coming through the iris. She sees her son in a knot of Bloodguards working the crowd outside the iris. Pfizer's Captain Praetor, Otto Buchanan, is speaking with Houka, the

Lion, several senior naval officers, and a giant in black whom she recognizes as a friend, Cato Ahren, Grand Kurseg of the Takazhr, with the floating black spider, Lomin. Creed detaches himself from what is becoming a livid conversation. Suddenly, Anastacia sees the alien emotions of concern and worry that cloud the Lion's proud visage. The tan face has paled and Creed's eyes briefly scan his brother's face.

"Domina," Creed says to her, using the Bloodguard title for the ruler for the first time, instantly alerting her and Millian. "I must confer with you and the First Lord in private and immediately."

Millian has rarely seen his brother so agitated, not even after the death of their father, or in confrontation with their oldest brother, Balthasar. "Creed, wha ...?"

"No," Creed says with hard and utter finality. Then softly: "Not here. Not now. Enough is already on the nets," he says, turning toward the confused media behind a cordon of Bloodguard.

"Houka," Anastacia calls, "inform the PPRC to issue a statement for me. I have urgent personal business. Immediately after you do that report to the Imperios. Millian, shall we?"

Millian extends his arm to escort Anastacia. "What about our son, Creed?" he asks turning and indicating Pfizer with a glance. Pfizer is surrounded by enthusiastic media who've returned their attention to him.

Creed turns to his nephew, who is smiling confidently, orchestrating the press just like Millian. Creed summons Otto over to him. "Captain Praetor Buchanan, escort the Scion to the Imperios when he's done here." Creed examines his hand comp. "Tell him his session with the Executive Council has been cancelled."

"Kurseg Hane, I want to leave my Bloodguards with Pfizer," says Anastacia. Millian and Creed exchange glances. "Best we don't Domina; it would be suspicious. He'll be all right. Buchanan's an excellent Bloodguard," says Creed. "Millian, tell her we have to go. Domina ... Ana, you and I may not agree, but I am still Bloodguard and even if I weren't, you are my brother's wife and those are my nephew and nieces. We are family. Trust me." Then Creed does something that convinces Anastacia. He drops his emoto-control, allowing her to see anguish, concern, ... and terror?

Something in the Lion's manner has changed. Anastacia isn't sure whether it is the self-effacing attitude, or his sudden display of human emotion, but she knows it is desperate.

"Domina, the press have been informed," Houka says returning. "I will return with you?" he asks, and Anastacia hears the warrior fanatic in his voice. "Yes," is all she can manage as she and Millian leave the observation salon, their and Creed's staffs following in their wake.

The Lion, standing at the window of the salon, hears the crowd roar for their return with love-choked voices, and he imagines the roaring crowd that killed his father during the Anangan Insurrection. He thinks to himself how ephemeral the line between love and hate.

CHAPTER 9

To paraphrase from an ancient Hebrew saying:
We are all responsible for one another.

—Anastacia Ambros, as quoted in *The Hane
Commentaries* by Aaron Charlemagna Invid-Hane

The woman responsible for the Anangan Insurrection watches the news from the O'Meara Starport as she paces the length of a great picture window, nearly one hundred meters long and twenty high. The absurd dimensions are testament to the fact that the window had once been the entrance to the penthouse skidder park, and although it could have been downsized, the view is too awe-inspiring to contemplate reducing. Here atop the Imperios, a one-hundred-twenty-story ziggurat of Erosi blackglass, is an Olympian view of New Eden, all of Stratadeen Island, named for the Terrax Corporation engineer who led the Atlantis Raising Project. It is here in Stratadeen that the Imperios is situated. Across the Nike River is the gleaming needle of the Pinnacle, Imperial Military Command. Skidders, shuttles, and every manner of a-grav conveyance weave fiery blue trails over the great megapolis in the early dawn, and the rising sun shines in the cavernous room with a celestial light.

A servosphere trails behind Oriana and projects the events at O'Meara before her eyes. It has been breath-taking. She is tempted to replay Pfizer's speech. She heard it only once, but it seemed to her that there might be forgiveness and an end to her exile. But to replay the speech now would send the wrong signals to others—to the two Bloodguards watching her at a distant door through the cybernetic eyes of their armor, and more important, to those who watched by more discreet means. Qamar had sent a message:

"Pfizer is coming. Visitors rerouted."

Nasir Qamar, Chief Executive and Operating Officer of Allied Autotechnics Galactic (AAG), the leading manufacturer and distributor of servospheres and various forms of robota and artificial intelligences. It had been Qamar's idea to use the servospheres as spies and communicators for the Unionists. His allegiance to the Unionists was based on Balthasar Hane's government-backed Anti-Monopoly suit against AAG. Qamar ruled an economic empire as vast as that of her family, and he held a chair on the board of the CIMB, as did the Ambros and her father's family, the Hane. Qamar would do apparently anything to keep it. From the moment Qamar had suggested they use the spheres as spies, Oriana had known they could also be used against the members of their coalition, but now she realizes Qamar may have an agenda larger than the obvious one of keeping his fortune intact. PPRC reporters confirmed that Qamar was involved in the Restorers. The Restorers: An Aeon Faction that had formed during the Insurrection. Qamar hates mortals and anyone with their blood.

Politics had indeed made for strange bedfellows. Oriana wants freedom. She wants freedom from Pandarata, "the Rock." She wants the freedom to choose from unlimited abilities and potentials for her children, freedom for all e-mortals living in the shadow of mortal morals and ideologies. Qamar, on the other hand, wants his Corporation intact and every mortal dead. And Rachel Tsimpo can't accept a universe without the Imperium, without order and the stability of the Law.

Oriana stifles an urge to gasp with the sudden realization that she will not be free. When the coup is successful, she will be Empress-Executrix, indebted to those who brought her to power, and obligated to provide her trillions of subjects with peace, justice, a stable currency, and secure space ways. *An impossible task.*

The Ilkani Church, rather than alienate the mass of faithful Citizo, will still insist that continued genegineering, e-mortality, and tech enhancement are against the Eleventh Commandment and she will still be frustrated from having the children she desires. Ilkani was the second largest single religious denomination amongst the Imperium's e-mortal population. They influenced the GenTech Board, and it had been the damning indictment of the Board that had put her, childless and a widow, on Pandarata.

Then another thought causes her to smile wryly. Half of the Church's hierarchy was either all e-mortal or had e-mortal blood flowing in their veins. The lure of increased lifespans, superior intellectual and physical abilities had been too great. They would come to see her point of view or they would at least turn a blind eye to it; after all, the Church had accepted e-mortals who converted and or married into it.

She raises her eyes and looks at her reflection in the cool blackglass. Almost thirty years of loneliness on the Rock, but her heart-shaped face is as youthful as it was on the day of her twenty-fifth birthday. She delicately traces the outline of small lips, and her small nose with her right index finger. Hers is a Madonna face, beautiful and serene. Beneath long liquid gold eyelashes are the genetic marker of the Ambros, gray eyes. But Oriana's eyes are not the bright neon gray of Anastacia's or Pfizer's eyes. Instead their pale retinas hold all glacial coldness of the Hane,. Fitting she thinks. She is her father's daughter. Her name means, "Daughter of the golden one," and while it was meant as tribute to her mother, she is an Erosi at heart.

All the Hane had been so proud of Millian's precocious little girl, especially her grandfather, Aaron The Great, the Hane ClanLord. Oriana had been his first grandchild. She'd called him after the conception of her child, and he had died protecting her from the riots that resulted when news of her act had spread. Her father, Millian, had suffered the worst, though. For on the same day he lost a father, he lost a daughter. Oriana found many sympathizers on Ferros, a high-grav'd world and the fourth planet of the Anangan Star

System, a hotbed of e-mortal extremist factions. Her Bloodguards were killed and she found herself the puppet of Restorers, e-mortal extremists. *Is the same thing happening again? Am I actually ensnaring myself in a greater prison then the Rock? Yes, Pfizer's speech at O'Meara has raised many questions. Qamar's message indicates that Pfizer is still coming to their pre-arranged meeting. Will they be able to talk then? Would it matter? "Rerouted visitors," indeed! A smuggling group had been intercepted.*

Oriana sighs deeply and leans against the great window. The message contained none of the codes that would alert her to any personal danger. She knows none of the smugglers will be taken alive. Is this how history is going to remember her, with all this mayhem surrounding her name? She turns toward her Bloodguards. She can stop this insanity before it goes any further. She can warn her mother and father, save Pfizer. Her Bloodguards turn away from her and open the far doors. Oriana stops and the motion causes the guards to turn toward her again, one of them announces."

"Lord Jovion Quiso, Bar—," the Bloodguard electronically augmented voice is interrupted, as Quiso says loudly:

"That's quite enough, her Royal Highness recognizes me." Quiso's oily, precise voice seems to thunder in the room. He would help her ameliorate and calm the new factions that would develop after the coup. He is the Unionists' political leader.

There is something hypnotic about Jovion's gaze, but it isn't mesmerizing in a sensual way; it is reptilian. If his presence weren't so unnerving she'd laugh. Why is he here all of a sudden? Are Qamar and the others really watching her through the servos? Where is Reza-Fahd?

"The Vicar went to meet his father. We're all to meet in the office adjoining the old chapel. Reza asked me to come and get you, your Royal Highness." Oriana imagines the serpent-like Jovion hissing the words in response to her unspoken thoughts.

As an Ambros, they want my assessment of the smuggler interception, they want to know what will be the reaction of my father and his family,

Oriana thinks. Despite her (current) aversion to him, she enjoys looking at Jovion. He has a breathtaking figure. His hair is silver, either a gene designer's choice or a biosculptor's. Oriana doesn't know which. But it is angelic and powerful above his tan face. Jovion's eyes are sky blue, open, and inviting; they seem to pull at her. She shakes her head roughly. It is difficult to concentrate around him. Yes, let him escort her. The confusion she felt is vanishing, like the dawn fog of the lawns surrounding the Imperios.

Yes, it was a good idea to escort her, Jovion thought. *She's been wavering, caught up in that sickening, debilitating tide of mortal emotion.* There were times when he considered her the weakest of these puppets he'd assembled. She wasn't though. She was a product of two of the most ancient and powerful e-mortal families, with gene strains and traits coveted by the Tene. She was flawed by her exposure to the weakling philosophies of her mother's family, and misguided paternalism of her father's, but she was the key to the galaxy. She was an heir to the Phoenix Throne, and a majority interest in CIMB, given certain circumstances. With her lineage and her resources, marriage with her would bring so much to his own resources. He could at last begin his plan to cleanse the short-lived from the universe.

Jovion extends his arm and Oriana graciously accepts it. Oriana has been so lonely on the Rock that this simple courtesy is a profound moment. Oriana's sentence is life. She is brought to Earth to attend the Uprising Ceremonies, the decennial holiday observing the beginnings of Naraji Ilkani's rebellion against the Rehl Enslavers, and then she is packed up like an unwanted gift and sent back into exile.

"Her Royal Highness is disturbed perhaps?" Jovion inquires, quietly stopping halfway to the great doors. Icy gray eyes glance up beneath gold lashes into Jovion's eyes. *She is on the verge of confessing something,* he thinks, a confession because of the way her wine red lips pout. Jovion is more than an ordinary emoto-control specialist; he sees that she has decided to tell him a half-truth.

64

CHAPTER 10

We do not hear the enlightenment offered into our
lives ... Unless it comes from the right voice.

—Oriana Ambros, as quoted in *The Hane Commentaries*
by Aaron Charlemagna Invid-Hane

"Pfizer," she says guardedly. She cannot forget the tone of
reconciliation, the tolerance for new ideas and alternative
lifestyles that permeated Pfizer's speech.

Jovion waits patiently. The difference between the warrior
and the fighter was patience. He'd been impatient once before
and it had cost him the universe. *Pfizer,* he thinks. Yes, the
brother had turned out to be quite a variable. The speech at the
Cosmodome had been impressive. Pfizer's inside handling of
that audience was no subtle use of emoto-control and crowd
psychology; it had been sincere, spontaneous, natural. Jovion's
analyst had begun pouring over Pfizer's previous appearances.
Jovion had demanded to know if this had just been an isolated
incident, a fluke, but it had not.

The records showed it was apparently an innate ability that
was maturing along with Pfizer. Pfizer's charisma was not a
studied charisma, and he possessed few of the attributes that
made up Jovion's own formidable abilities to persuade. Yet
look how he has captivated the people! It seemed to Jovion as
if for millennia the universe had been working against him.
Hate and frustration mingled white hot in his chest—he would
not be stopped this time! "What about your royal brother, the
Crown Scion? I understand you're meeting with him later. I'd

very much like to be a part of that interview."

How did it come to this? Oriana muses. What began as an attempt at completion has led to an attempt to escape loneliness and exile; it has trapped her in a conspiracy with idolaters, weapons runners, drug smugglers and murderers. *Jovion's scrutiny is stifling, he needs to be diverted, but how can I divert him.*

"The Lion has probably called for an emergency session of the on-planet Executive Council members," Oriana says, broaching the subject that she knows originally brought Jovion. A subtle nod of Jovion's head confirms her speculation. "The reaction of the Council will depend on who is conducting the initial smuggler contact investigation, and how much they uncover."

"Cato Ahren and his pet Tempeler, Lomin," Jovion snaps, eager to personally hear her assessment. "The ship was captured with cargo intact. The crew understandably did not allow themselves to be captured," he adds, waiting for her reaction to his initial comment. Oriana's only perceptible reaction is a quick intake of breath, which she covers by calmly saying:

"Then they know they are in danger. They will either move off planet or summon immediate reinforcements. Then again, Father will want to take advantage of the public sentiment after Pfizer's speech and not postpone the Omnividome broadcast. They will stay and fight. We ... He is Hane."

The fact that Oriana was about to side with her family does not escape Jovion. It only illustrates how tenuous the Unionist's hold over her is. But she also demonstrates her value with an insider's view of the First Lord's reactions. Jovion is about to ask about the Lion when they arrive at the doors of the secretary, a small office adjoining the Imperios chapel. The chapel itself dates from a time when the Ilkani had been welcomed at the Imperial Court.

The room is a circle within a circle. A blue, back-lighted, stained glass diorama of Naraji Ilkani's martyrdom winds around the wall. A second circle is then formed by nine columns of gold filigreed blackglass, which also supports the domed vault of the ceiling in which an intricate holo projection of the galaxy slowly rotates. Beneath the projection is a contemporary circular table of Erosi blackglass with eight comp terminals and corresponding omniform a-grav chairs. The floor is covered in a soft red wine-colored carpet. The room is well air-conditioned and redolent with the scent of rosemary and laurel.

"Fitting for the Magus Patriarch," Jovion whispers matter-of-factly. *This setting will give them the appearance of having deep religious convictions,* he thinks. *But the circular table has no head; it will have to go.*

"I wonder who chose this room," Oriana says offhandedly, unaware of Jovion's thoughts. "We seem to be the first to arrive. I suspect Rachel Tsimpo is behind choosing this room. The diorama is a nice touch."

"This is as it should be, your Royal Highness, for it was here we set in motion the will of God. We must be reminded of his sacrifices so that we can make our own," announces Assur-Banipal Banishar Saud, His Holiness, the Magus Patriarch, Prince of the True Church, Defender of the True Faith, Master of the Sacred Cities, and Executor of the Church's CIMB Shares. The Magus Patriarch is a tall broad-shouldered man who gives the impression of possessing great physical and moral strength. His face is strong, inspiring, his eyes soul-searching, probing. He wears the traditional white silk cassock and skull cap, and blue, gold, and scarlet tabard and vestments. The ring finger of his right hand bears the dazzling luminescence of a fire jewel from Inferno, which he extends toward Oriana.

During her exile Oriana had known she'd need the support of the Church if she were ever to return to power. In her second year of imprisonment she'd joined and become a practicing Ilkani. *Oh, yes, they'll ignore my plans, this time. After all, I am one of them now,* she thinks as she kisses the Magus Patriarch's ring and breathes, "Your Holiness."

Jovion Quiso watches the verbose Assur visibly expand

with pride at Oriana's gesture. The Magus Patriarch glances at Jovion, black eyes filled with triumph at an Ambros kissing his hand. But as Jovion's brooding impenetrable blue eyes stare back, Assur-Banipal, Magus Patriarch, sees in his mind's eye a fiery holocaust, a storm of howling fire raging out of control. He cringes and snatches his hand from Oriana.

"Reza-Fahd," the Magus Patriarch says, trying to cover his off-character gesture, "has gone to get the others. Let us sit and enter our data," he says, inviting them to the table with a sweeping wave of his arm.

The Magus has the voice of a Serdian but the body language and gestures of a Terran. Oriana remains standing while Jovion and Assur-Banipal sit at opposite ends of the table and begin entering their data. Holographic fields dance before them. The doors open and Nasir Qamar enters. Oriana sees Nasir's civilian bodyguards joining the Daakan and Bloodguards in their vigil outside. Nasir's gaze sweeps the room, unmoved by its spectacular artistry. He is a tall dark-skinned man with short curly black hair, a giant like Cato Ahren, with the intricate tattoos of the Chosen circling his right eye. His is a familiar face, especially now, with the anti-monopoly suit against him. He is a rabid Pro-E-mortal and anti-government extremist. Oriana considers him the most volatile of the Unionist. His relation to her is especially complex, for he too is Aeon, Neo Deus, even more so than Oriana, who inherited it from her Hane lineage.

Nasir glances at Quiso and then to Oriana. He bows his head and says, "Your Royal Highness" in a voice as chilly as liquid nitrogen. At no point does he acknowledge the presence of the Magus Patriarch. Nasir sits equidistant from both Assur-Banipal and Baron Quiso, as far from either as he can be. Qamar does not insert a data chip. He probably has some liquid crystal implant with compatible biosoft or wetware for the occasion. *The table's spy shield should disrupt any unauthorized recording devices*, Oriana hopes.

Nasir Qamar wears a simple black single suit of form-fitting metallic mesh, but on the left side, along a band that extends from shoulder to waist, are his Family Runes worked in precious gems and rare metals, a fortune that could buy a world. Yes, Nasir Qamar is complex.

The doors open again and Rachel Tsimpo enters. This means that Pfizer is somewhere in the Imperios or nearby. With Rachel is Grand Admiral Sir Nicodemus Von Haagen Zhao, Chief of Naval Operations, Hero of the Anangan Insurrection. Qamar seems to bristle when Zhao enters the room. The Grand Admiral and Dr. Tsimpo both kiss the Magus Patriarch's ring and then turn to acknowledge Oriana. Rachel bows deeply and says with all the honesty and adoration of one who serves the Ambros, "Your Royal Highness, this is indeed an honor."

Grand Admiral Zhao's hazel eyes look into Oriana's pale gray ones. Years before it was Zhao who commanded the forces that broke the gathering power of Oriana's forces in the Anangan Star System on the planet Ferros. Loyally, he led Anastacia's forces to victory and now he is betraying the mother for the daughter. There is shame in his eyes as he says meekly, "Your Royal Highness. It is an honor to serve you." He then salutes smartly and stands behind her. *He is working hard for forgiveness,* she thinks. *He'll need to,* she observes, watching the venomous Nasir glare at the Grand Admiral.

Reza-Fahd Assur-Banipal Orani Saud enters quietly and activates the door's security seals. "The Mimic can't be here; its cover would be disrupted," he says softly. Reza-Fahd wears the impressive dress tans of the Order of the Daakan Crusaders, the Ilkani Church's security force. He bows to Oriana and goes to kiss his father's ring and then returns to her side.

"Let us begin then," Oriana says, stealing the initiative. "Grand Admiral, the smuggling intercept?"

The Grand Admiral moves to the table and inserts a CDC in one of the vacant compu-funcs closest to him. A holographic of the Jupiter sub system blinks into view above the table.

"I'm sure you are all aware that Cato Ahren and planetary defense command intercepted the weak smuggling attempt," the Grand Admiral grates as the galactic holograph is replaced by a tactical representation of the interception of the freight racer. Reza-Fahd is stung by Zhao's comment, but his emoto-control prevents it from showing. Warily he takes a place at the table opposite Qamar and inserts a data chip. Zhao, who is still standing, turns his head from the holo display and looks down at the now seated Reza-Fahd. "You could have transported it on a Navy ship. No one would have asked any questions."

"He didn't, Nico. We didn't," says the Magus Patriarch. "How badly does this compromise us?" This question is directed toward Dr. Tsimpo.

"I don't know yet. I am to be briefed later this morning in preparation for a public statement about the interception," Rachel answers.

"What does it matter? We all know that no one survived on that smuggler, and there is no evidence that can tie it to us," says the quiet Reza-Fahd.

"Let us hope so, your Excellency," says Jovion in his dulcet Serdian tones. "Surprise is everything to our plan."

"Will the fact that the *Bismarck* is now in orbit change your plans?" asks Admiral Zhao, pleased at this opportunity to demonstrate his worth to the others.

"An Imperial Dreadnought is in orbit?!" exclaims the Magus Patriarch, rising from his chair. "That means what? An additional legion of marineguards and orbital fire support, a complete fighter wing?"

"Yes, ... Yes, about that, your Holiness," says Jovion. "And may I add, that's a very accurate assessment for a priest."

Smarmy, oily, bastard, thinks Assur-Banipal. "It is my business to know, my son. Besides, being the spiritual father of Humanity, I also command the Daakan Crusaders and I want to know how our plan ... *your* plan is going to hold up with that orbital weapons platform above us."

Jovion's angelic face hardens. "The plan will remain unchanged. At the appointed time the ships Nasir and I have assembled will engage all planetary and orbital defenses."

CHAPTER 11

Deathman *n., pl.* -men. 1. Cybernetic reanimated
dead Homo Deus or Homo Deus Dominus; the
soldier class of the Tene Thantos. 2. *Colloq.* A
person or persons viewed as overly opportunistic
or exploitative.

—*Webster's Universal Dictionary*, 6323 I.C. Edition

"How is your hastily armed mothball fleet of corporate
brigands and Qamar's robots going to engage the Imperial
Navy, and the planetary defenses of Sacred Home?" demands
Assur-Banipal.

"We may need to reassess—," begins Reza-Fahd.

"Reassess *what*, mortals? The whereabouts of your spines?!"
barks Nasir Qamar. "We are not going to engage them ship to
ship, or attack ground defenses. We are only there to get the
survivors and any who try to flee!"

At the appointed time nuclear and a-mat devices placed by
our agents and the Mimic will devastate all planetary and
orbital defenses, killing most of the planet's Naval, Takazhr,
and a good portion of the Bloodguard personnel, including
those on Luna bases. The fleet will prevent the survivors from
leaving New Eden, where the Tene Thantos Deathmen will be
razing the city and killing every Loyalist. Eventually,
reinforcements from Mars, Venus, and the System Starbases
will force our fleet to retreat, and her Royal Highness, the only
surviving Ambros of the Imperial Family, will rally the
surviving Bloodguard and military, and drive off the Tene

Thantos. The desperate and the grateful will make her Empress-Executrix, and as sole survivor, invest her with more CIMB shares than any Ambros has ever possessed."

And I will have an Empress-Executrix I can exert pressure on, and will at last end the suit—and the lives—of Balthasar Hane and his mortal-loving family, Nasir tells himself.

"Thank you, Nasir," says Quiso amicably. "I could not have put it better."

Assur-Banipal's face bunches with concern as he looks at Nasir Qamar. "Is that how simple it is? You two soulless machines—Some of the ground bases are near population centers and Tycho City is Luna Base! Use nuclear and anti-matter weapons on population centers? Kill Citizos? What of the Oath to Humanity? The Aristo must protect the Citizo from the horrors of the Wasting!" shouts the Magus Patriarch. "The damage to the biosphere could take many years to repair—." He stops abruptly as his fellow conspirators all gaze at him in frustrated bewilderment.

"You must smash a few atoms to create a reaction, your Holiness," Oriana says softly. "The surviving Citizo will want Tene Thantos blood, and the DemoPol parties will be reminded that their true salvation belongs in a strong central government, not some weak grid-locked assembly of confederated states. Times of trouble produce signs of faith."

"Another queen said something similar millennia ago and she lost her head. So we should do anything for the Phoenix Throne daughter of Ambros?" asks Assur-Banipal, the Magus Patriarch, after Oriana's casual rationalizations for mass murder.

The Magus has doubts that could shatter our fragile coalition. He must be reassured, thinks Rachel Tsimpo. She walks over to the angry Magus and lays a delicate hand on his arm.

"Your Holiness, in the beginning, before Naraji, Ancient Man was in many nation states, factions. They fought each other in horrible wars over the simplest of ideas. Then the Rehl Enslavers came and for the first time in our bloody history we were united. Our unity made us the most powerful species in the universe, one race, under one God, with one government and one religion. Now the Aeon and their allies have driven the Tene beyond the Boundary. The hatred that we turned outward once again turns inward. Without enemies, our unity is threatened. Once again we are poised to kill each other. The Anangan Insurrection is all the evidence we need. Surely more internal violence will follow, caused by those of lesser morals than those of our future Empress-Executrix or others in this room."

The Magus Patriarch looks into her brilliant violet eyes. "You are right, of course," he pets the hand on his arm reassuringly. "Naraji has sent us these Outlaws as a sign that we must return to the old ways. These Outlaws must be united with the Imperium for the survival of all. And when our coup succeeds, there will be war. We will be united again, our vitality restored," he sighs, drained by his internal moral battle. Spiritually weary, he droops in his chair.

Well done, Rachel. The soulless way Nasir and Jovian discussed the potential deaths of millions would unnerve anyone, Oriana observes silently.

"Grand Admiral Zhao," she says aloud, "rendezvous with our fleet and prepare to isolate this star system. Reza-Fahd, if you will mobilize the Daakan, the Tene will send a liaison to coordinate their strikes with you. The bombs are set?"

"Yes, Princess," says the quiet Reza-Fahd, who stands looking ferocious with a Daakan battle helmet tucked under his arm. He takes a breath and addresses the table: "Remember, we will strike at the height of the Umboshad. You then have twenty minutes to clear the area before the Deathmen enter. They will be too deep in tursapoi frenzy to distinguish friend from foe. Until we meet again as the new Executive Council, I wish you all good luck." With that and a long gaze at Oriana and his father, Reza-Fahd departs to command the Church's Daakan.

"Stay out of the fighting, and avoid Imperial installations," Oriana adds. The Grand Admiral salutes her and departs as the others rise from the table.

"Well," says Quiso to one in particular. "At last it begins."

For the first time since his outburst earlier, Nasir Qamar betrays the faintest of emotions in a slight upward turning of the corners of his mouth, but it is no smile. Rachel Tsimpo's skin crawls as he turns his gaze directly upon her, looking at her in the way that Pfizer's Tempellian looked at her, as if she's microbiota. "Leave with the Admiral," he says. Rachel, trained in every nuance of emotional psychiatry, realizes he is dismissing her as he would an animal. She turns to Oriana, ignoring Qamar to receive dismissal from her.

Oriana acknowledges Rachel's courage with a nod of her head. "Well done, Rachel. We shall talk later," says Oriana, releasing her graciously. Oriana meets the gaze of the standing Nasir. He is studying her with such blatant intensity that had her Bloodguard been in the room they'd have removed him.

"Yes," Qamar says. "They would try indeed. Perhaps, your Royal Highness, there is some hope for you after all."

Oriana throws back her head and laughs at Qamar with utter derision. "Nasir Qamar, sometimes you are little more than a rabid animal. Aeon? Chosen? You dishonor all e-mortals when you behave ... with such base emotion."

"It disgusts me to be in their presence. Contact with them is an act of desecration," grates Nasir, turning his burning gaze toward the Magus Patriarch.

"Your bigotry does not frighten me," says Assur-Banipal politely. "The Princess is correct. You emote like the Citizo you malign. Such behavior will break our alliance before we begin."

Oriana is impressed by the Magus' courage as well. *To insult this creature so.* Nasir is regarding him with unbridled hatred. "When this is over, I will—" She does not let him finish.

"You'll do nothing, or the Bloodguards will leave your worlds burnt and gutted, your factories and machines broken and ash."

"You would side with them over your own kind?" demands Nasir, spit flying from his mouth. *He is a loose cannon*, Oriana thinks.

"I will defend my subjects against any and all aggressors …," she begins.

"Hypocrite! You plot to murder your family for a throne!" shouts Nasir.

"For my *freedom!*"

"Your freedom—I'd say you were free enough already. Free enough to plot the murder of your family, kill thousands, and seize the greatest empire, corporation, and fortune in the known universe!"

"Careful, Qamar, or when this is over it is you who will have to worry," hisses Oriana.

"Who is rabid now, my future Queen?" responds Qamar, suddenly subdued.

To the silence Assur-Banipal mutters: "Indeed," and Jovion Quiso smiles.

CHAPTER 12

Being aware of a trap is just the first step in
avoiding it. The trap is still there.

—Creed Duran Goethe Hane, as quoted in *The Hane
Commentaries* by Aaron Charlemagna Invid-Hane

Anastacia leans her head against the cool armored glass of her
skidder limousine and half listens. She is in the passenger
compartment with Cato, Millian, and Creed. Cato recites the
tale of terror that began when a freight racer was intercepted in
the early morning with two tons of tursapoi and an assortment
of forbidden weapons of mass destruction.

Cato Ahren is insisting that Deathmen have entered the star
system, to the shock and dismay of Creed and Millian. Creed
has insisted they leave for the *Bismarck* immediately, but Millian
has been equally insistent that they remain on planet.

She is going to have to make a decision and Creed's seems
the best. Millian's earcom buzzes and his attention goes from
them to the voice on the other end. Millian's face hardens and
he turns his eyes toward Anastacia.

Her only thoughts are: *The children? My parents?*

"They are devaluing our CIMB shares," Millian announces
coolly. "Various Internet brokerage firms are selling blocks of
Terrax Corporation stock. EWN is reporting rumors that
we've over-invested in the Omnividome Project and will not
be able to pay this year's dividend, and that we've lost a freight
racer in Jupiter orbit trying to repair flaws in the grav wave
network. We can't leave, Ana. It will substantiate these rumors.

...." Millian pauses as his earcom hums more. "Allied Autotechnics Galactic and Tupolev Shipping are attempting to initiate hostile takeover procedures against Ambros Antimatter..."

Creed watches his sister-in-law's face pale as Millian repeats the list of directly owned Ambros companies and their subsidiaries under economic siege. His oldest brother, Balthasar, had warned him that the Ambros Omnividome Project was folly; Balthasar had wanted Anastacia to wait until the anti-monopoly suit against AAG had gone through, so that their largest CIMB competitor would be neutralized. Now they would be forced to remain on planet to calm their shareholders, and lose the security and mobility offered by the *Bismarck*. "This line of assault suggests that they have an inside knowledge of our personalities and options. They are deliberately directing us to positions they want us in," says the Lion.

"Are you still suggesting we abandon planet, Creed?" asks Millian.

"Even at the risk of losing our controlling share interest in the CIMB—thereby losing economic control over our Imperium?" Anastacia adds. "And surely you know political control is secondary to economic control."

They're both mad. Creed is stunned. *Cato tells them that Deathmen are in the same star system, and all they can think about is saving money.* "You will be alive and still in command of the military," he answers.

"I will not use military force to respond to legitimate economic actions no matter how dire. I would be no different than some despot or robber baron," declares Anastacia.

"There are Deathmen in the system, Majesty. They only mean violence. You must be prepared," says Cato, flatly stating the obvious.

"Prepared, yes, but we will not provoke," announces Millian, siding with his wife against all Bloodguard training. *Nasir Qamar should be arrested; Tupolev are nothing but greedy pawns. This whole incident of tursapoi and smuggled weapons has the stamp of*

Qamar, but the Deathmen speak of an evil no sane person would associate with.

Creed stabs his earcom with his finger. "Increase security on planetary Imperial Family members to Red One. I want to know everyone Nasir Qamar has contacted within the last two weeks. Begin immediate overt and covert surveillance. Tell Judge Advocates Office to prepare request to seize all records and assets of Nasir Qamar and AAG." His earcom hums in acknowledgement.

"No seizures, Creed, no arrests," insists Anastacia.

Creed fixes her with his polar blue gaze, disgusted at what he views as weakness. "Of course not, Domina," he says the word bitterly. *This woman is too weak to defend the throne and has emasculated his brother. Millian's Aeon will be hobbled by this liberalizing e-mortal.* "I just want to be able to arrest the traitor the minute I have evidence."

"We should get as many additional Naval Units in orbit as soon as possible," says Cato Ahren. Anastacia is just as stubborn as her mother the Empress-Executrix Isabella. *If she won't go, we are going to have to work with what we have here.* "I reviewed our resources on the way down from orbit. The Dreadnought Group *Bismarck* in orbit, Dreadnought Group *Washington* at L5 station Columbus, ..."

Anastacia tries to pay attention as Cato Ahren recites the list of available units in orbit and the star system. The list is long and detailed, and military strategy falls more within the expertise of Millian and her brother-in-law. *Maybe Creed is right. What am I going to do?* she prays silently.

"Useless!" shouts the Lion, drawing sharp glances from everyone. "The Empress has forbidden the use of force against these traitors. Tell me, Domina Anastacia, are Millian and I to die as our father did for Oriana?"

Creed's words knock the breath from her, and she bows her head in anger. Anything to keep from looking at either one of them. Millian lays a hand on her knee in comfort, and feels the minute trembling.

"Creed, I signed the order from the GenTech Board,"

Millian confesses. "What Oriana, my daughter, wanted to do was wrong. Ana didn't want to sign that order, and she didn't. If you blame someone for Father's death then blame me."

Ordinarily, such weakness from his brother would have pushed Creed beyond anger, but this time it makes him sad. The sadness is an ache in his throat and heart. "Millian listen to me. The flight path of that freight racer would have brought it over New Eden. One a-mat device and you and I, Kiritzia and Aaron, Basileus and Lomin, Anastacia, Pfizer, Gabrielle, and Zoe will die along with millions of others, the planet may be rendered nonviable," the Lion says, his voice suddenly sounding old and weary. "I am a Bloodguard. Let me do my duty."

"Majesty, the Kurseg is correct," agrees Cato. "Show pity, any remorse or lack of conviction in this struggle and it will be fatal to billions. Nasir Qamar is ruthless, amoral, utterly pragmatic, as soulless as the Artificial Intelligences of AAG. He is an Aeon. Unfortunately that makes some of us think that we are Gods. Life, whether mortal or e-mortal, isn't real life to him, just a series of organic equations. He will show no mercy, not any. If we are going to stay on this planet I would like to continue detailing our resources. We are going to need a plan of action."

Cato restarts his list of orbital and naval assets. Then a list of troop assets and configurations sequestered on Venus, Earth, Luna, the Mercury and Mars Colonies, Orbital Habitats in Lagrange Space. Millian and Creed question him on some, suggest possible relocations of others. Anastacia tries to stay interested but watches the morning sun turn the Nike into a sparkling cool blue ribbon. Moments ago she had felt triumphant. Now things are so uncertain and dire.

Every instinct of hers and those around her is to flee. *But how? How can I abandon my people in the face of such ... evil? Just as she believes God will not leave her, so she will not desert her people. If only Creed and Cato could understand this.*

The skidder convoy races along the South Nike Drive toward the shining towers and skyscrapers of New Eden and the ziggurat of Erosi blackglass that is the Imperios. The trees along the Nike are alive with the first burning colors of autumn and early morning. Anastacia wants to stop and go out amidst her people. Joggers, cyclists, gliders, boaters, walkers on the pathways, swirls of color everywhere sport outside the windows—life, before winter. *It's winter in my heart and with every word that Cato says I feel my freedom, even my choices, slip away.*

"I will accept moving the children off planet. And I'll understand if you want to move your respective loved ones off planet. In fact you may go with them," Anastacia says quietly.

Courage? Selflessness? "Thank you, Domina," whispers the Lion with a sincerity Anastacia has never witnessed in him. For the first time she sees how he and Millian really aren't so different. Creed has only been married eight years and has but one child, a very special boy according to a sealed report from the Bloodguard Breeding Index.

"After meeting with the Joint Chiefs and the Security Committee of the Executive Council I will send Kiritzia and Aaron home to Eros, to HaneHome," the Lion says flatly. "Thank you."

"Do it now, Creed. The council is probably compromised with traitors," says Millian.

"I can't. I will … Just not yet," is all Creed says, but he knows they all understand.

Millian knows his brother must see his own family. See them with his own eyes and hold them at least one more time. It is how he and Anastacia feel. *For Zoe and Gabrielle on the outskirts of the city, for Pfizer performing his duties, for Oriana, his daughter, a true Hane. Oriana who for almost twenty years was a Senior Vice President of the Terrax Corporation's Financial Operations, Oriana who since the age of twenty four had attended every session of the Executive Council … By the Only God!* "It's *her!* It's our girl," says Millian in a hoarse whisper. He quickly wipes his eyes. Mercifully, neither Creed nor Cato turn away in shame.

"If it is her Highness, the Princess Oriana, then surely the Ilkani Church—," begins Cato, who stops when he realizes that the Empress-Executrix and First Lord are stunned and dejected by the realization of their daughter's latest betrayal. "I am sorry, Majesty. I know what it is like to lose a child," he offers. *But not this way.'*

"It's worse than her being dead. She's selling her soul," says the Empress-Executrix, as she wipes away one of her husband's tears. Strangely, her own eyes are dry and the course ahead seems clear now.

"They're using her, Millian, preying on her naiveté. But now you will announce to our shareholders that the grav wave network is intact and as a sign of solvency we will be paying this year's dividends early. Furthermore our banks are to lower interest rates by three-quarters—no, a full percent. Creed, rotate in the best Bloodguards and other special forces you can. You'll have to have the best protection for the royals on planet and Creed, only the best evac and SAR pilots on standby.

"After you take care of that, Millian, I'd like you and Creed to talk to Balthasar. Tell him we will liquidate a significant portion of our strategic cash reserves to initiate a joint venture takeover of Tupolev and EWN. I will consider selling a portion of CIMB shares to guarantee our alliance. Then could we mobilize the sector fleet for war games? Or would that tip our hand?" Anastacia asks. "You see, I was—I *am* listening," she says to the startled Creed.

"We can't mobilize the sector fleet," says Millian, impressed and already implementing Anastacia's ideas. This is a side of her he wished the Hane, his family, saw more of. For the first time since this began he feels there is a chance to avert a bloody coup, or worse, all-out civil war. They may survive. "That's a logical move, but would only alert our enemies. It might provoke them into striking early, which would be devastating to us. The more time we buy, the greater our chances for survival. *Even Ana can't move off planet with the children*, Millian realizes.

The skidder limousine stops and the four exchange looks. "Be assured that they are aware that we know at least two things," says Cato Ahren. "One, there was tursapoi on that freight racer, and two, the Tene are involved. The press may even be aware of the intercept, though not the nature of it. I ask you to watch what you say until a proper statement can be released to the PPRC. And I'm sure there will be plenty of questions about the First Lord's upcoming announcements," Cato adds, as he steps from the skidder limousine, flashing a brilliant smile for the press.

The Lion grins. "After Millian and I contact Balthasar, I'd like to meet all of you and some select staffers," he says through his smile as he extends a hand for his brother.

"Agreed. The Pinnacle, Secretary Goldshef's situation room. Yes?" says Millian as he steps out into the roar of the crowd and extends a hand for his wife.

The crowd cries with unrestrained joy when Anastacia steps out. Holostrobes flash as the scene is recorded and beamed all over the Imperium. Then there are the questions.

"What did you think of your son's speech?"

"Are you going to reconsider the Princess Oriana's petition?"

"Is there any truth to the rumors that the grav wave net is down?"

Anastacia simply and dutifully smiles, ignoring most of their questions although she stops and waves to some of her favorite reporters.

A group of Bloodguard in cybernetic battle armor pour from the Imperios and replace her guards from the limousine skidder. The effect of Creed's upgrading security to Red One. Some of the press are already asking about the increased security, but she passes through the entrance and as the doors close behind her she thinks: *My security and that of my family have already been upgraded, but if the Deathmen are really in the system how will I protect my people?*

CHAPTER 13

The very act of observation changes the nature of
the observed due to the perceptions of the
observer.

—*Encyclopedia Galactica,* Vol. 6350, "The History
of Quantum Physics: the Heisenberg Principle"

Luxvico could not get away from his duties soon enough. Ever
since speaking with Rachel Tsimpo and Pfizer Ambros on
board the star yacht he has been calculating a temporal
projection. Not prescient but the next best thing, he foresees
violence and destruction for the Ambros. Rachel Tsimpo has
clearly been soliciting information from both of them and was
prepared for violence if they did not respond correctly. She
was wearing a telepathy shield but she overestimated her
emoto-control. Luxvico easily read her. She is no casual
Unionist. And if he is aware of this, then so is the Political
Science Ministry. Surely they must be.

Luxvico glances out of the view port of his trans-
atmospheric vehicle, TAV. The Tempeler embassy on Earth,
where he prefers to reside when he visits the planet, is in Death
Valley, Nevada, a subdistrict of the North American Precinct.
At least the weather is similar to home, he thinks. But the thick air
and light gravity of this planet always makes him feel nauseated
for the first few hours. The Executive Council meeting that
was previously scheduled has been abruptly changed,
temporarily releasing him; however, a Bloodguard has been
assigned to him, along with a government TAV. So he could

be back in New Eden in thirty minutes. Within the last four hours something has occurred to change the political and security climate of the planet. He quickly browses the Impgov news and the only strange incidents to occur were the interception a freight racer in Jupiter's orbit and now this sudden assignment of a Bloodguard.

The Tempeler Embassy is similar in design to the buildings of his home world—twenty stories, roughly copper-colored conical towers with heat dissipation fins and solar panels. The building hums with its a-mat power core and environmental control units. The entire Tempellian population of Earth is dispersed between nine other such towers. The TAV hums across the desert on its a-grav generators toward the metallic shining tower, and as they approach the Embassy, Luxvico observes how light bounces off the many windows. The building has many landing platforms for various forms of conveyance. Servospheres and servobots weave in and around the complex. An automated warning informs those who trespass that they are on territory belonging to the Academy of Tempel and if proper identification is not transmitted the local authorities will be informed. Luxvico removes his omnipalm from his surcoat and sends his personal recognition signal. A computer voice gives landing instructions for one of the upper landing extensions and the Bloodguard deftly pilots the TAV to the designated destination.

Luxvico has always thought one of the best things about the Bloodguards is that generally they are silent, not speaking unless spoken to. He has found the silence during the trip from New Eden satisfying. Three servobots now float towards him like upright hovering ants with no pincers, only two appendages, and a single marquise-shaped eye that glows green. Both servobots bear his crest on their torsos, the lead one's crest is gold, the other's silver. The lead bot speaks in the tritone voice of most machines: "Master, welcome home."

"S-One, I have a guest. Provide him with a locator beacon so he does not get lost in the tower. S-Two, see to it that quarters are prepared for him adjoining mine," commands

Luxvico.

"Excuse me,"—the armor-augmented voice of Bloodguard Chavez begins, as S-One hands him a pen-sized cylinder with a flashing red top, and S-Two zooms away silently—"but Corps Command has entrusted me with your safety."

"I am quite safe in this tower," Luxvico says, turning to face the Bloodguard. "Unless, Bloodguard Chavez, you have been instructed to keep me under constant surveillance as well," he says, cold violet eyes boring into brown ones.

"No, Councilor, only to protect you. With your permission, after I see to the safety of your quarters, I'd like to inspect the tower's security measures."

Perhaps my objections of Otto Buchanan have projected onto all Bloodguards. Though in all these years it's strange I have never noticed. "Very well, Bloodguard Chavez. I have important communiqués I must send. Inspect my quarters, and then S-One will give you a tour of the tower's security measures." *As if you'll understand them.* "Although if you check with *Corps Command* you will surely find this complex's security specifications on file."

"I am aware of the specifications, sir. I reviewed them after being assigned to you. It's procedure that I still inspect them, however," the young Bloodguard says softly.

Luxvico sighs and leads the Bloodguard through the tower.

They encounter no other Tempellians or Tempelers, although Bloodguard Ensign Etienne Chavez is aware of the swishing of clothes turning corners just out of sight, of figures standing back in shadow waiting for them to pass before they go on about their personal business. "We are a very private people within and outside our own homes. Because of my rank, they are affording me this privacy," explains Luxvico, sensing the Bloodguard's unspoken questions.

When Luxvico crosses through the iris into his personal quarters he is surprised. And he is not a man who is easily surprised. Waiting for him there are Councilor Lomin, the Tempeler to Viceroy, and Takazhr Grand Kurseg Cato Ahren. Luxvico sees the Bloodguard's soft smile at the widening of

Luxvico's eyes. "Venerable teacher," Luxvico whispers, bowing and therefore not realizing that the Bloodguard snaps to attention.

"Luxvico, I am satisfied to see you again. I have read your submissions to the Chancellery with growing interest. It is why I am here," says Lomin, although the bird bright eyes have been focused on the Bloodguard. "I see, my young pupil, that your emoto-control still needs study," the ancient Tempeler adds, the faintest corners of a smile tugging at his weathered lips.

"Your arrival was not anticipated, Excellency. I am satisfied to see you and that you are well," answers Luxvico, aware that despite his best efforts even now his cheeks are shading. "Forgive me, Excellency."

"What? Ah, of course. You were always the proper Tempellian. I shall make a confession to you. Sometimes I think we have been wrong in turning away from the passion of our Terran heritage. I must admit to a certain pleasure in the knowledge that you are still human. It lightens my burden."

For the first time since seeing his teacher Luxvico is aware of the great stress around Lomin's eyes and face, the rigidity of his neck and shoulders. "What troubles you Excellency?"

Lomin looks intently at the young Bloodguard. "We must speak alone. "Officer, could you pardon a teacher and his favorite pupil for a moment?"

The kindness of the old Tempeler speaks to something in Etienne Chavez's heart. He produces a palm scanner from a utility pocket and does three scans of the room. He bows his head toward Lomin and smiles briefly at the still embarrassed younger Tempellian. "The room is clear, sir." With that he turns and departs.

Later Luxvico will remember this fateful day. "There is something I must tell you, Excellency. I believe there is a conspiracy against the Ambros," he blurts.

Now it is Lomin's turn for shock and surprise "How do you know?"

"The Crown Scion's Media Officer, an Empathic-

Psychiatrist named Rachel Tsimpo, but I have yet to ascertain the true threat."

"The threat is with the Tene Thantos," says Lomin, recalling the crematoriums burning day and night, the blackened decimated cities, the howling, wailing, and suffering of billions. "I simply cannot fathom how any sentient being can ally itself with such evil," he says to Lux in disbelief.

"It's inconceivable that they have returned. Gert Hane pursued them beyond the Boundary. There has been no known sign of their existence in almost four millennia. The species' memory cannot be so poor as to allow such a horror again," Luxvico states.

"It has been my experience that the repetition of horrors decreases their perceived terror. If the human race can do it once, why believe it can't happen again? No, it could be far worse," says Lomin, whose mind fills with images of worlds exploding, of refugee ships burning above the glow of Riffellon, of the corteges for a dead Emperor and Empresses, of the grief of the Imperial Family. He pulls the security capsule from his robes and hands it to Luxvico.

Warily Luxvico takes the capsule from his mentor. "Increase illumination," he commands as he opens the capsule. As the lights turn up Luxvico sees the symbol from his history lessons and an avatar of his childhood nightmares. "Have you tested it for authenticity?" he asks. *No! No! NO! How much he wants this to be a mistake. Never in his wildest dreams never—.*

"It is made of solid molecularly molded neutronium, a crucifix and the rank symbol of an Ubervar. DNA samples show that the owner was an engineered human, an e-mortal, with a definite genetic modification towards tursapoi assimilation along with other enhancements. Additional samples taken from the battle site—"

"There's been a battle?!" Luxvico interrupts.

"Yes, a very minor one. An interception near Jupiter orbit. The intercepting ship scored a direct hit in one of the cargo bays, killing a group that had been preparing to use SAA— Space Assault Armor. Blood samples reveal bio as well as cybernetic nano enhancements. The profile discrepancies are negligible. They are or were Tene Thantos Deathmen. The Executrix, First Lord, and The High Commands of the Bloodguard, Navy, and Takazhr have been informed. I wish to contact the Arch-Chancellor and ask him what we are to do. When I realized you were here on Terra, I knew my best student would be aware of something if not the whole truth."

"Computer," orders Luxvico, "open a coded subspace communication channel to the office of the Arch-Chancellor of the Academy, Lurenga." Then he adds, "Authorization: Lomin."

A great bubble of static forms in the center of the room, the bubble blinks and is replaced by the face of another Tempeler. He wears the white of the Arch-Chancellor. Although his face looks as young as Luxvico's, his pale green eyes are as old as Lomin's. "Eminence," say Luxvico and Lomin in unison, both bowing from the waist.

"Lomin, Luxvico," says the Arch-Chancellor, mechanically viewing both of them. "May I say that it is especially satisfactory to see you again, Lomin." Behind the image of Lurenga the two can see the red skies of Tempel and the golden spires of the towers. Knowing actions are louder than words, Lomin retrieves the security capsule from Lux and displays its contents to the closest holo pickup.

Lurenga squints, and it is obvious that his hands are making swift adjustments to what is probably his holo resolution. "You may return home if you wish," he states evenly. "We will be issuing an advisory for all Tempellians in the Sol, Spica, T'ang, and Aquila star systems."

"You knew?!" blurts Luxvico. Lurenga's right eyebrow arches at Luxvico's impertinence.

"Of course we knew. We've known for almost fifty Terran years. This observation by the Political Science Ministry is about to draw to a close. You are to transmit your updated observations directly to Laurza, the Chancellor of the Political Science Ministry."

"But the Ambros—"

"We observe the affairs of the humans. We do not interfere."

"The very act of observation changes the nature of the observed. We have already interfered. Now we have to help," says Luxvico rapidly.

"Luxvico, as brilliant as you are, you were too young to be sent out amongst the humans. You have developed a sympathy for them."

"Aren't we Human?"

"Perhaps we were once, but we have evolved beyond Humanity. The only thing we have in common with them now is our appearance."

"Surely his Eminence has not forgotten that our relationship with the Universe is symbiotic. What happens here will affect all of us. This could be the prelude to another Wasting."

"The Military Science Ministry assures me that our planetary security measures are more than sufficient. You are to prepare to return home. You will not divulge the extent of our knowledge to your employers. I expect interesting observations from both of you. You are witness to the end of an era. Lomin, I hold you responsible for Luxvico's return home. Understood?"

"I understand, Eminence. We will be on one of our courier ships tomorrow. Lomin out."

"End transmission," orders Lurenga as the holo-bubble vanishes.

Dropping all pretense of emoto-control Luxvico turns to Lomin. "We cannot let this happen. Do you intend to make me return?"

"Silence," orders the older Tempeler, pulling his omnipalm from his robes. After making several adjustments to the device, Lomin says: "Computer, create a subspace link with the Academy Master Computer and download all files from the Political Science Ministry using the following encrypted codes and authorizations." Lomin then pulls a MentAmp from his robes making adjustments to it before he places it on his head and activates it. He quietly approaches Luxvico and gently touches the younger man's cheek. "We are temporarily shielded. Let me say first that I, too, am ... surprised. I have denied myself any kind of feeling for so long that it is difficult to articulate my emotions now. But I remember ... I remember," muses Lomin.

"You were there?" Luxvico whispers in awe. *Impossible! That would make Lomin nearly six thousand years old.* Although Luxvico himself is impossibly old by even e-mortal standards, he cannot conceive that any being could live six thousand years—or want to. *What have those eyes seen?* Luxvico thinks as he looks into the bright eyes of Lomin.

"More than you can imagine in your young life," says the older man, reading his thoughts. "The flashes of light from planets during orbital bombardment, the pyrotechnic blooms of mushroom clouds over a-mat strikes. I saw the city of Sidonia vanish in the heart of an a-mat detonation. But more than destruction, I remember centuries of beauty, the search for knowledge, and the discovery of things new. Most of all, I remember the love I have seen."

Still in awe at his teacher's display of emotion, Luxvico touches a tear on the old face.

Lomin smiles faintly. "Choosing you as my protégé was perhaps the wisest decision of my life. This is no exaggeration: you are the only one I know wise enough and human enough to do what must be done. You must take this data to the Bloodguard."

"There is a Bloodguard just outside this iris," says Luxvico as he heads toward the iris.

"No. Not him. We know nothing about him or who he reports to. Realize that we are placing our lives in danger by defying the Chancellery. Is there a Bloodguard that you know or trust here on planet? Cato's Praetor is on Titan."

Otto Buchanan's face comes to Luxvico's mind along with the customary distaste. "I know of one I am absolutely sure of. However, our relationship is less than cordial," says Luxvico, thinking of the Praetor assigned to the young Ambros idealist he'd help educate. Realizing that the tower's communications systems may be comprised, Luxvico activates his omnipalm and signals the Captain Praetor. Much to his surprise Otto's face appears on the second ring. *He must be keeping his omnipalm near him, and I thought he'd be vacationing with his family.*

"Lux? Excuse me, Councilor Luxvico. What can I do for you?" The Praetor seems unsurprised by the call. It's almost as if he'd expected it and his usual superciliousness appears to have vanished. Luxvico experiences a moment of doubt. But one look at Otto confirms that this is the Scion's childhood friend and not a Mimic. He hears a child splashing in water behind the Bloodguard. "I apologize for the interruption, Captain Praetor Buchanan. But it is urgent we speak in person … and in public," says Luxvico. Much to Luxvico's genuine surprise the Bloodguard simply says, "Where and when?"

"I have a meeting with his Imperial Highness this afternoon in the Capital. I understand you live in a suburb outside the city—Forstar County, the borough of Ellendale. I can meet you there."

Otto appears uncomfortable momentarily. "No, I live a good hour from that part of the city. Why don't I meet you at the Cosmodome, by the reflecting pool in front of the Pax Monument?" counters Otto.

"I have access to a government TAV. I can meet you anywhere, Captain Praetor—" begins Luxvico.

"Good," says Otto quickly. "We'll stick with the reflecting pool. One hour.," Otto adds, just as his image fades from the omnipalm screen.

Luxvico deactivates his omnipalm and returns it to his surcoat. He sighs and turns his attention to Lomin, who is still deep in interface with his MentAmp.

"I will follow Arch-Chancellor Lurenga's directive. I shall report to the Titan Embassy to contact my employer; however, once there I will request sanctuary," says the old Tempeler. He extracts a CDC from his MentAmp and hands it to Luxvico. There is a slight tremor in the old hand as the crystal data chip drops into the younger hand. "The Academy's observations on the resurgence of the Tene Thantos and their involvement in this Union conspiracy," Lomin says, and then he embraces Luxvico. "If I do not see you again in this life, I will surely on the other side. Peace and wisdom be your companions. Live well," says Lomin as he turns and drifts from the room on his a-grav devices.

Standing alone in the center of his quarters Luxvico is aware of an aqueous saline solution falling from his eyes. "Goodbye," he whispers.

CHAPTER 14

"...That was Marisol Fitzgerald Buchanan with a rerelease of 'Look What You've Done.' I'm Simon Rishay. Stay tuned and we'll continue bringing you the best music and the finest coverage of events here in New Eden."

—*The Simon Rishay Musical Hour*,
Hanenet, 12:35 Imperial Time

Otto shifts his Davini into fifth climb and pulls into the two hundred meter altitude traffic. The afternoon sunlight off the many colors of airborne traffic is spectacular. At this time of day there is little traffic in the fifth climb zone. But with the Uprising Ceremonies and the Omnividome Project, even this high the skidder zones are jammed.

Pfizer has graciously (not that Pfizer was ever ungracious) given him time off to go and see his family in Forstar County outside the Capital. Otto is looking forward to bringing them into the city for the celebrations. It will be his son Agust's first time seeing New Eden, and maybe if they can find a sitter he and Marisol can see Nova Roma as Pfizer suggested.

Even at this altitude he can smell the ocean air and the chlorophyll of the grasslands beneath him, and he is reminded of his home planet, Eros. If only Earth's gravity weren't so light and the air so thin. Oh well, at least their house here is state of the art, environ-controlled. The gravity is set to a comfortable 2.3 gees and the air pressure appropriately dense.

Pfizer's reception at the Cosmodome was memorable. Never in his thirty-two years has Otto ever seen a crowd of that size or seen such a unanimous outpouring of acceptance. Maybe Pfizer has the answer to this crisis.

The skidder's auto-navigator informs him that he's approaching the Singing Rock exit. *'Exit.' The term would be 'point' if we were headed to his home town of Draco Noir, on Eros.* Otto drops the skidder to surface level and deploys the wheels and activates the skidder's ground engine. Tires screech as they touch the road off exit twenty six A and the skidder pulls into holiday ground traffic. The decennial celebration of the start of Naraji Ilkani's Uprising has kept the Singing Rock beach fronts open into October. What he wouldn't give for some quiet time with his family and a few neighbors, just like home.

"Activate skidder-com," Otto commands as he keeps his eyes on the traffic. "Call home page, Mari."

"Ozzie?!" answers his wife's soft contralto almost immediately. "Where are you calling from? I hear skidders in the background."

"If I tell you, will that give you time to get your lover out of the house?" Otto says smiling. There was a time when this used to be a joke, just as Otto means it to be now. The pause before she responds seems to take a little too long.

"Oh, don't worry. We had our tryst this morning when I knew you were at the spaceport," Marisol laughs. If only he could see her face, know whether the laugh is genuine.

"I just pulled onto Tolkien Road," Otto says, now frowning. "How are you settling in?"

"Most of the things we wanted sent to Earth have arrived. How long will we be here again?"

"We really won't be posted anywhere permanently. Being assigned to the next Emperor-Executor is a traveling job. Did you receive something from the studio?" Otto asks nervously. Being married to a galactic holostar has its own share of challenges. They'd met so long ago; then it had seemed only natural that they get married. But since then, Marisol Fitzgerald's career has continued to grow, and although Otto loves her more than his life, he often wonders if she is happy.

"Yes ... Yes," Marisol says simply, tiredly.

"What did you tell them?" asks Otto, now feeling literally hot under the collar.

"I want you to see it. They know how I feel but ... It's something special. It's written by Myichi Honda.

Honda is quite famous, lauded as one of the best screenwriters in decades, maybe centuries. His holos have won award after award. Marisol has also won an award—for best supporting actress in a Honda Holo.

"Ozzie, don't be angry. ... Let's talk when you get home. We have guests," Marisol says, breaking Otto from his concerns over how her career has affected their lives. (Otto hears a sliding glass door; Marisol must be moving inside because he can no longer hear the ocean.) "Be happy when you get home, okay? ... Agust is excited to see you." There is an audible pause, then Marisol says quickly, "I love you."

The channel goes silent as Otto wrings the steering wheel. Grass fields whisper silently by. *Damn, not again,* is all Otto can think. He missed the last eighth of Agust's life because she was on Eros shooting a music holo. Late afternoon and early morning sub-space holo transmissions weren't the same as actually being there. They'd kept her working until her pregnancy had made it impossible. Then, thinking that they'd give her time to adjust, she was almost working immediately after she had Agust. Otto found his expectations being challenged and the frustration difficult to articulate. How could he complain without sounding selfish? If he were anyone but a Bloodguard the answer would be obvious—quit. go wherever she goes. But he can't. He's been conditioned from near birth to be a Bloodguard.

Marriage was a difficult institution for those serving in the Corps. His parents had separated. *Don't be angry? How the hell not?!!* He feels that maybe he should pull over and go for a walk, but Mari expects him at home soon. She knows he's on Tolkien Road. Any delay would be misconstrued as his displeasure, plus he has to be back in the Capital by tomorrow morning. He may as well try to make the best of his time and not spoil it by being angry.

He turns into his driveway and slows the skidder to a crawl. As it moves down the driveway, he can hear the surf and the calls of gulls. He stops in front of his home—actually, her home, a series of Bron Ashton cylindrical towers in Erosi blackglass and granite. There are high-grav field warnings at the front walkway and skidder garage entrance. He grabs the long coat of his dress uniform from the back seat and tosses it over his arm, his other hand grabbing the thin metal attaché case.

"Daddy, ... Daddy, Daddy!!" shouts a young voice as Agust Buchanan bounds through the front door followed by the ever faithful Chike, a Rottweiler Pfizer had given him for graduation from the Bloodguard Academy in Neo Sparta. Both are wearing grav compensators in case they inadvertently cross through the grav field. The dog barely beats the boy to Otto and begins doing what Otto affectionately describes as the stubby shake. Otto has scratched the tail stub exactly once when Agust, still traveling at two gees, passes through the field, and although the compensators activate to put his muscles under two gravity restraint, there is the moment when he leaps with superhuman strength inside the one gravity of Earth and knocks his surprised father to the ground.

"Uh, ... No!" says Agust from atop his father's chest. "Sorry," he adds.

"How about a kiss?" says Otto smiling broadly, as the two-year-old leans awkwardly forward to comply. Chike has now begun to romp around them barking for them to get up.

"Well, look what the dog has found," comes Marisol's voice from behind a hedge that leads to the back of the house. Otto hears her footsteps and those of at least three others.

"How aw you, Daddy?" his son asks in his toddler lisp.

Otto looks into bottle green eyes just like his, and finds that at this moment lying on his back in the grass looking up at his son against a warm October sky, he is quite fine. "Excellent," Otto whispers. "How are you?"

"Fine, but bored. Comp'ny here. Have to be good," Agust says, wriggling off Otto's chest and nearly stepping on his face.

"C'mon Chike, Daddy," he says, turning and running towards Marisol's voice. Chike, however, having his master all to himself, watches the child leave and then launches into a fit of barking, trying to bring Otto to his feet.

"Okay, Chike. ... Who's this company? Do you like 'em boy?" asks Otto, getting to his feet and brushing grass and leaves from his uniform. Chike has retrieved Otto's hat and is now dancing mischievously just out of Otto's reach. Otto looks up and there rounding the corner of the hedge is Marisol Fitzgerald Buchanan. The gorgeous child star turned teen model, then recording star and accomplished piano player, now famous leading lady in three bestselling holo pics. Dressed casually in slacks of the Buchanan tartan and a black fishermen's sweater, not one curve had been augmented or biosculpted. The light breeze from the ocean plays with her famous shoulder-length rose-gold hair, like blonde fire. Marisol smiles at her son, at Otto and Chike and for a moment she is back in the past, when their future looked perfect.

"Daddy home," Agust shouts, as Chike, not to be outdone, drops the hat and begins another cacophony of barking.

Marisol laughs and to Otto it sounds like music. He feels his anger cooling to sorrow. He has not been this close to her in months and it is as if he is falling under a spell. He does not remember walking toward her, but he finds himself kissing the dusting of silver freckles on either side of her nose. He looks into her eyes and finds hers searching his as she looks for disappointment, or frustration, but in this instant all she sees is love and gratitude. She genuinely smiles in relief at his good mood and to Otto her smile seems brighter than the sun. "Ozzie, there are some people I'd like you to meet," Marisol says in his ear as she hugs him.

"Hmm? ... Oh," he says detaching himself from her.

CHAPTER 15

Both of these will overtake you in a moment, on a
single day: loss of children and widowhood. They
will come upon you in full measure, in spite of
your many sorceries and all your potent spells.

—Isaiah 47:9 Judeo-Orange Codex

Two of the visitors Otto recognizes. All three are wearing grav
compensators to negotiate the higher gravity of his home. The
first visitor is Fiona Shaw, Marisol's agent. Otto has always
considered her peculiar. In an age of genetic and eugenic
science, biosculpting and metabolic body design, Fiona has
deliberately chosen an unattractive appearance. The story as
Marisol tells it is that Fiona's parents are, or were, members of
the puritanical Restorer sect of the Aeon.

When the prenatal genetic technicians discovered a
recessive gene for obesity they had not removed it; instead they
had abandoned the child. So Fiona had been raised by foster
parents on the OuterRim. They had not cared about her size
and now neither did she. Marisol surmised that Fiona,
surrounded by the hyper-beautiful of the holonets, has kept
her appearance as if to say: "I am not a sex object, never was a
sex object, and will never be one. It is my mind that matters."
And, sure enough, Fiona has become one of the most sought
after agents in the Imperium, managing more than half of the
top box office draws in the industry.

The second visitor is Savoy Wiktor, from Pfizer's yacht.
Savoy had been the sole heir to the infamous Wiktor fortune

and now serves as CEO of The Wiktor Foundation, an intergalactic philanthropy organization. Pfizer met Savoy during Pfizer's studies with the Political Science Ministry. Savoy holds a chair on the CIMB, like the Ambros or the Hane. Savoy is tall, with the same fire blonde hair as Marisol, but his eyes are pale blue. His exploits as a playboy adventurer are well known in the scandal nets, and Otto feels a pronounced discomfort at finding one of the wealthiest bachelors of the Imperium at his home. Otto reminds himself to do a background check on the philanthropist.

"Otto," says Fiona, nodding to him. Savoy grins and shakes Otto's hand.

"Captain Praetor Buchanan, you and Marisol have a lovely home here," he says in his deep soothing voice.

The third visitor is none other than Myichi Honda, a tall striking man of Asian descent, with a mane of startling silver hair and expressive gold eyes. "Mr. Honda," Otto says, "I saw your reworking of Shakespeare as a boy. It's an honor, sir."

"This might not be so difficult, Mari," quips Fiona.

Marisol throws her agent a shocked and embarrassed glance. "Fiona," she says, indignantly chopping her hand for the large woman to desist.

"Uh-oh, Mommy's mad," says Agust, stopping his play with Chike and turning toward the adults.

"Actually, Captain, ... we stopped by in an attempt to get your wife to consider our proposal." Savoy interjects into the embarrassed silence.

"Which is?" Otto says warily.

"They're offering me the role of Julia Hane, in a reworking of My's earlier Honda and Verdanz rendition of *Gert and Julia*—," begins Marisol.

"It's the role of a lifetime, Otto. She'll be famous forever," interrupts Fiona.

"Please, Fiona." Marisol cuts back in. "It will be two and a half years in production, at seven different locations," Marisol says, quietly steeling herself for Otto's reaction. She watches his pupils dilate even further and it is not the sunlight. She sees the subtle clenching of his jaw.

"Two and a half years?" Otto asks making sure he heard correctly. *How could she?! By the Only God, how could she do this to us, to him?!* He feels his eyes burning in frustration.

"Actually, Captain, I apologize for coming at you like this. But I spoke to the Scion earlier. I know that you do not want to be separated from your family like this," says Savoy.

There is something in what Savoy says that suspends the surge of hurt in Otto. He can't help feeling that Mari has betrayed their plan to try to live as a family and work this out. But something in Savoy's eyes seems very sympathetic and understanding. But how can he understand?

"Do you?" asks Otto.

"Yes, I do, Otto," says Savoy. Otto hears the beginnings of bitterness in Savoy's voice, a carefully guarded pain Savoy is choosing to display, and feels sorry for his earlier outburst. "Yes, I do," Savoy continues. "I lost my parents when I was only a little older than your son. I've spoken to the Scion as I said. If this is what you want, he is willing to intercede with Bloodguard Corps Command and grant you an extended leave."

"Otto, it's not like you're asking for any favors. You've accumulated the leave time. We can be together," says Marisol.

"We're in the middle of something of a crisis—with Pfizer being on Earth, with the riots. Anyway, what's it to you, Mr. Wiktor? And I don't mean any offense ... I appreciate your sympathy," Otto says, glaring pointedly at Fiona.

"The Wiktor Foundation has agreed to be the principle corporate sponsor and producer," says Fiona taking up the challenge. "He recognizes Marisol's talents and what a loss she would be to this production and to the arts in general."

Savoy spreads his hands palm up before him to convey that he wants nothing to do with the conflict between Fiona and Otto. "I don't know about all that, Ms. Shaw. It's true we are financially involved, but Captain Praetor, I swear to you, we are not trying to undermine you—"

"We are trying to give you every possibility of having the

best of both worlds," cuts in Myichi Honda. Suddenly, there are three ear-piercing whistles from Otto's coat. He removes his omnipalm and sees flashing red and gold lights on his Bloodguard status indicator. "Excuse me," he says, stepping away and pulling the privacy com ear piece from the omnipalm and inserting it in his ear.

"Otto," Marisol says, taking three quick steps to be beside him; she has instantly recognized the omnipalm's noise and lights as a Bloodguard emergency. "Whatever you need to do … do your duty. This all can wait. I do love you," she says, stepping away again to give him his privacy.

There is a message on the Omnipalm screen which Otto reads as a voice says through his ear piece: "RE: Red One Alert. This is not a drill. All Bloodguard security units on duty are to deploy cybernetic battle armor and report to Corps Command Tactical. All security units off duty and in reserve duty have two hours to report to Corps Command Resource. All Praetor stats and those in the Diplomatic Protection Group are to report immediately to Corps Command Tactical. Those off duty and in reserve duty have two hours to report to Corps Command Resource. Message repeats."

Otto quickly recalls Pfizer's security schedule. Who are the Bloodguard personally guarding Pfizer? Who is in operational command while he's in Ellendale? Then Otto activates the communication window in the omnipalm and taps the secure com icon signaling his Executive Officer. Lieutenant Commander Praetor Mahoney.

Mahoney's dark face appears on the screen. He is in an office at the Pinnacle. Otto recognizes the view behind him, the Imperios and the Capitol Complex. Mahoney gives a thin-lipped smile and salutes. "His Imperial Highness is secure, sir. And we are secure here. All security protocols in effect are green," says Mahoney quietly and efficiently.

"Who is guarding His Imperial Highness?" asks Otto.

"Ensigns Conner and Teke," answers Mahoney from memory.

"Switch Teke with MacKenzie," orders Otto thinking of

one of the more promising Praetor candidates and an Aeon from Inferno, a deep range mining colony in the Erosi Alliance. "Does his Imperial Highness suspect anything?"

Mahoney frowns and considers Otto's question. "Maybe. I can't be certain. He's very proficient in the emoto-control."

"Tell him I'm on my way and will advise him of what I know. Buchanan out," says Otto. He turns to Marisol, intently watching him from the backyard near the pool. There is a fourth visitor, a tall, silver-haired, regal-looking woman wearing an omnipalm audvid link. He does not know her but she appears to be working with Savoy. Otto tries to smile at Marisol. All Marisol sees is a weak imitation of his smile. She knows something is wrong. Otto watches as she excuses herself and heads toward him, leaving them in her silent wake. *The Universe is unfair. No sooner does life come together than it starts to unravel faster than we can stitch it back.*

"You have to go?" Marisol says in that matter-of-fact way that Otto loves.

"Yes," Otto says, putting his arm around her. "What do you want to do?"

"What do you want me to do?" she asks.

"Love me. Whatever makes you happy. The happiest …," Otto says. "Even if that means leaving again. I mean, I've just been called away on alert. I can't ask you always to be waiting."

"I do. I am. I'm not going to take the part," Marisol says, brushing his cheek with the back of her hand. "At least not yet. Otto, I want this to work, I really can leave it all behind for a while."

"What about your fans?" Otto asks.

"I love and live with my biggest one," she replies.

A chuckle escapes Otto.

"Come on," she says, taking his arm. "Get in the pool with your son while I give our guests the bad news."

What the hell? A few minutes with Agust so he'll remember me spending some time with him. And after our guests leave some time with my wife, Otto thinks. They head toward the pool and he notices Savoy Wiktor has been watching him and Marisol, with that odd look of concern on his face. Maybe Savoy wasn't Otto what assumed him to be.

Savoy sees Otto watching him observe Otto's family. Savoy can remember so little of his life with his own parents. He does remember his mother's tear-streaked face as she urged him to stay hidden in the closet and no matter what he saw to stay there. What Savoy saw changed him forever, brought him to this place. Marisol Fitzgerald Buchanan reminded him a lot of his mother, what little he could remember of her. Even though Savoy's father hadn't been a Bloodguard, Otto in his friendly, country boy and straightforward way reminds Savoy of his kind, sincere father. It was ultimately that kindness and sincerity that was his family's undoing. When he was very young, Savoy swore he would do everything in his power to prevent others from experiencing his tragedy. And now, he's just been informed through his Takazhr contacts that some kind of interception of contraband drugs and weapons has occurred in-system and that the Bloodguard are on some kind of alert. He's known since he was a child that his parents had been closely allied with the Ambros and the Hane and that his father's Foundation had done something to infuriate the wrong people, and they had killed his parents.

All his life Savoy has played the role of a spoiled heir while becoming close to his father's allies and competitors. Always acting the part of the harmless playboy, while learning about them and their connections to the Wiktor Foundation twenty years ago. Pfizer is an idealist like Savoy's father had been, and the good-natured Savoy is certain that those who conspired against his parents' lives would soon turn against Pfizer and his family. Savoy just has to make sure he is in the right place at the right time to preempt catastrophe.

Otto watches as Savoy's silver-haired assistant breaks Savoy from his thoughts and passes along Marisol's invitation to stay for dinner. Savoy waves and smiles from across the pool. Otto turns toward the cabana to change his clothes when his omnipalm signals him again. The signal identification is the Tempellian Embassy, the identifying icon Counselor Luxvico's.

The breeze coming in off the ocean suddenly makes Otto shiver. He activates the omnipalm and Luxvico's face appears. "Lux? Excuse me, Counselor Luxvico," says Otto, noticing the Tempeler does not wear his normal stony emotionless expression and actually looks worried ... anxious. Otto discovers his normal hostility for Lux's callousness is absent; instead he finds himself concerned. "What can I do for you?" Otto asks. A look of surprise flicks across Luxvico's face. Otto is unsure why. Lux apologizes for calling him at home and then asks to meet him in public saying it's urgent. This unqualified emotional behavior from the normally reserved Tempeler has Otto's complete attention. "When?" Otto asks.

"I have a meeting with his Imperial Highness this afternoon in the Capital. I understand you live in a suburb outside the city—Forstar County, the borough of Ellendale. I can meet you there," offers the normally taciturn Luxvico.

No. There are too many people here. I don't want to alarm anyone unnecessarily. "No, I live a good hour from that part of the city. Why don't I meet you at the Cosmodome, by the reflecting pool in front of the Pax Monument?"

"I have access to a government TAV. I can meet you anywhere, Captain Praetor—," begins Luxvico. Otto notices Savoy making his way around the pool toward him.

"Good, we'll stick with the reflecting pool. One hour," says Otto closing his omnipalm and ending the transmission. He closes his left eye and checks his eyelid chronograph for the time. It will take a half hour to get back to the Cosmodome. He sighs deeply. So much for spending the time with Marisol and Agust.

"Something wrong, Captain Praetor?" asks Savoy now on his side of the pool.

Otto throws out his best version of what Marisol calls his "ain't nothin' wrong good ole boy smile." "No. It looks like I've overlooked some business in the city. It's routine. Listen, Mr. Wiktor, call me Otto."

"Savoy, Otto," says Savoy, tapping his own chest.

"Listen, Savoy, I'd like for you to hold that opportunity

open for Mari a little longer. I have to go in a few minutes. And I'd appreciate it if you'd point out all the pluses this could mean for her career."

"The way she tells it, you're the biggest plus in her career," says Savoy dryly. Otto feels his face coloring in embarrassment. He'll find some way to make it up to her. He does not know that he will never feel her breath on his face again.

CHAPTER 16

Knowledge is power. Power is Law. Law creates
Heaven. Live longer. Live stronger. Another
friendly reminder from AAG.

—*Profiles in Power: The AAG Monopoly*

"You've allowed things to degenerate into quite a mess,"
scolds the image of Balthasar Hane to the select group
Anastacia and Millian have gathered at the Pinnacle. "We are
under economic attack and vital off-planet chemical products
for our ocean farming industry are late. A half dozen planetary
governments are defaulting on their HaneBank loans. There is
severe rioting on Acheron, seemingly from out of nowhere.
Ana, I suggest you order a hold on interplanetary and galactic
stock exchange transactions until the holiday is over. As to the
situation with the Bank..."

"All your deposits and reserves will continue to be insured
by the Federated Reserves of the Imperium and the CIMB,"
says Anastacia to the image. Balthasar Hane is as imposing as
his brothers, with the same glacial eyes, and he is the oldest of
the children of the Widow.

Balthasar alone of Millian's family had supported her
marriage to Millian. The pragmatic Balthasar saw the economic
and political advantages to such an alliance. When the Hane
patriarch died defending Oriana from a mob, Balthasar alone
had told Anastacia that he did not blame her for his father's
death. However, if Balthasar had been compassionate when
she least expected it, he has also never hesitated to tell her

when he disagrees with her. He is used to saying whatever he wants to his brothers and he pulls no punches with her.

"Anastacia, I told you, asked you to wait with this Omnividome Project until after the anti-monopoly suit against AAG. Then a rival would have been removed from the field. My advice, had it been followed, would have been considerably cheaper to both of us than the financial aid you're requesting now." Balthasar pauses. "When both our houses are under economic siege."

Anastacia holds up a hand to keep Millian from protesting. "Balthasar, you were right; I was wrong. You can chastise us all you want ..."

"I had nothing to do with these finances," sneers Creed, attempting to remove himself from his older brother's disapproval. *Am I the only one who doesn't try to solve a problem by throwing money at it?* he thinks bitterly. *Oh, we have a situation! Don't worry, we'll throw money at it and it'll go away.*

Anastacia motions Creed to silence with a finger to her lips. "However you want it, Creed. *Millian and I*, Balthasar, we alone pushed for the Omnividome. In my anxiousness for a media coup I acted impulsively," says Anastacia, watching as this appears to satisfy the ruler of the HaneNation and the planets of the Erosi Alliance.

Balthasar's eyes narrow and he stares at Anastacia for a moment. "Charming and straight to the point. I am beginning to see why you married her," he says to Millian.

"Balthasar!" begins Millian in frustration, but Anastacia lays a restraining hand on his arm.

"Balthasar, stop antagonizing. Let us cut to the heart of the matter," says Anastacia calmly. She holds up an omnipalm. "I have here an executive order to the Imperium Federated Reserves to lower interest rates to two percent below prime for the HaneBank. Pfizer will be negotiating with the Wiktor Foundation to procure the products you need for Eros' ocean agriculture. As to the rioting on Acheron ..." Anastacia turns to Cato Ahren.

Cato looks up from the holographic schematic of New

Eden he's been referencing with Defense Secretary Goldshef at the conference table. "I have been in contact with Takazhr Command Eros and they report situation normal," he says, rising and approaching the image of Balthasar Hane.

"I am not about to report to the galaxy a little rioting on this planet's moon," Balthasar says. "Our stocks are being undermined and devalued enough as it is. No need to cause a sell panic. I never was fond of the idea of having one of the largest penal institutions in the galaxy on the moon above Eros, which happens to be one of the Imperium's financial centers. But what about my request to suspend trading until after the holiday?" petitions Balthasar deftly.

"Denied," Anastacia says flatly. "This would fuel opposition in the Imperial Congress. Besides, I want to initiate our joint take-overs here and now. There will never be a better time than now, with all the money you're going to be borrowing from this government," she observes shrewdly.

Balthasar appears about to protest, when a communication interrupts him. Anastacia turns as the iris behind her spirals open and her General Praetor Houka Jamal enters with Counselors Lozo and Romena, her Tempelers from the Academy's Economic Science Ministry. Millian leaves a heated discussion with Creed to meet them. Then the four of them approach her.

"Domina," says Houka reverently saluting. "Forgive the interruption but Counselors Lozo and Romena say they have urgent matters to speak with you about."

For nearly one hundred years Anastacia Ambros has had Tempelers or Tempellians on her Executive Council, and never in all that time has she ever seen more than the barest flicker of emotion from any of them. Now these two before her are clearly embarrassed and ashamed. Lozo has served her family for nearly three hundred years, acting as Chief Information Officer for the Terrax Corporation. Lozo has been one of the advisors since Anastacia's time as the Executrix of Terrax, the greatest of the Ambros financial holdings. Romena, the other Tempeler, has served Anastacia's administration as Secretary of

Labor and Industry.

"Your Imperial Majesty," they say simultaneously as they bow. Lozo smoothes his gold surcoat as he straightens. Romena merely stares at the carpet. "Your Majesty, I regret to inform you that unfortunately Romena and I have been recalled to Tempel. We will be resigning our respective posts immediately."

"You are what?" asks Millian. "What about your contracts?" he protests.

"If you check, you will find that our service to you was open-ended due to our status as members of the Academy faculty," says Romena. Tempeler women wear an elaborate gold headdress, a vestigial form of gender ornamentation. Romena adjusts the crown rather than look at the First Lord.

"Creed, contact your office and see if your Counselor-Advisor is still on your staff," asks Millian of his brother apprehensively. Millian notices Cato is using his omnipalm's private audvid link to contact his planet's embassy.

"He's gone Mil," growls the Lion. "He handed in an immediate resignation to my chief of staff, and with The Erosi Embassy." *Llwis taught me nearly everything I know about the art of warfare. The Tempellians have forgotten more about warfare than even we the Hane of Eros know. There can be only one reason for them all to want to leave planet ... only one reason,* thinks Creed.

"They know ... You knew ... And now you're just going to leave?" asks Anastacia her voice rising in anger. "Tell me, Lozo, how long have you known?"

Lozo's magenta eyes focus on Anastacia, eyes which appear childlike with innocence beneath his hairless eyebrows. "I know nothing other than the fact that my government has ordered me to return home. These economic moves against you and your allies were not suggested by any of our long-term strategic financial advisors. When I contacted the Political Science Ministry of the Academy I was told to return to Riffellon. I refused. Ten minutes later, Counselor Romena informed me she had been recalled and to tell me I was to return or face irrevocable exile." He stops and bows his head.

"This is difficult for me ... When I first took this assignment I thought of you as nothing more than very clever pets ... Forgive my arrogance ... Now I view you all as intelligent, compassionate people," says Lozo as he steps closer than the required three steps and puts his hand on Anastacia's. The minute he starts forward, Houka surges into action but Millian, recognizing the movement as non-threatening, stops him.

"You and the First Lord came to Tempel for the induction of my great granddaughter in the Musical Science Ministry," he says, shrugging off the glare off Houka.

"We could have simply palm notified you or used an audvid link but we wanted to tell you," begins Romena. She looks at Lozo and continues. "You are in danger, all of you. As Lozo says there was no indication that these moves would be taken against your aggregate fortunes. That these maneuvers were kept so secret until their deployment attests to the quasi-legal nature of this assault. We therefore advise extreme caution."

"If the Academy is having us abandon this planet, what more evidence do you need?" Lozo says. "I wanted to tell you in person and request that we be excused from service. Leave while you can, your Imperial Majesty. Take your families and go," advises Lozo.

Seeing the two Tempelers expose themselves defuses Anastacia's anger. *Besides, I have more pressing concerns than my anger. Clearly Creed is right: we need to get the children off planet. As soon as the Uprising Ceremonies are complete, I'll have them sent to HaneHome,* she thinks. "Lozo, Romena, return home with our blessing. May the hand of God keep you," Anastacia says, dismissing the two Tempelers.

"The Tempellians are leaving Eros as well," says Balthasar angrily as the iris spirals shut behind Anastacia's departing Tempelers.

"Excuse me, your Imperial Majesty, but my staff Tempeler, Lomin, has requested political asylum at the Titan Embassy," Cato says, pressing his aud-receiver into his ear to hear over the background voices. "Another Tempeler," Cato pauses and looks at Millian, "Prince Pfizer's, Luxvico from the Political

Ministry, is meeting Captain Praetor Otto Buchanan?"

"Buchanan is Pfizer's Bloodguard, Captain, for those of you who don't know," offers Creed. "If Pfizer is on his way here from the Imperios, we should divert Captain Praetor Buchanan here with the Tempeler. Why is this Tempeler so important, Cato?"

"I agree with you," nods Cato to Creed before continuing, "This Tempeler is carrying classified Academy information concerning—." Cato pauses to listen to his aud. "Repeat that," he demands. "Concerning this plot," he says finally to those present.

"Information and evidence. Now we can finally arrest them. Thank the Only God!" says the Lion victoriously. "Where is Buchanan meeting this Luxvico?"

"Lomin did not divulge the information. I trust him with my life," says Cato. "Contact your Bloodguard. Find out where the rendezvous is and we'll send back-up."

"I advise against it," says Defense Secretary Elaine Goldshef, the civilian and public face of the Ambros defense services. A long-time Ambros supporter, she is a retired Naval Admiral, a graduate of the Academy's Military Ministry, and has served on the board of directors with Imperial Arms Galactic, Allied Autotechnics Galactic, and the Munroe Corporation. She is a blocky athletic woman with iron gray hair and an iron demeanor to match. "I've been in touch with our intelligence services as much as I dare. Comm channels, especially omnipalms, are not to be trusted. We'll have to depend on this Buchanan being smart and coming to us without getting on the comm channels or using his omnipalm. We need—"

Secretary Goldshef is cut off as all attention turns to the main iris and Pfizer enters escorted by an armored Bloodguard. The looks of relief on Millian and Anastacia's faces are obvious. Millian actually rises and rounds the table to put a hand on his son's shoulder. "I'm glad you made it. Your mother and I are very proud of your speech at the Cosmodome," says the First Lord, trying to smile.

Pfizer raises an eyebrow in apprehension. "Your mother and I" his father says. *Not Her Imperial Majesty and I. First my meeting with the Executive Council cancelled, then my sister delayed for our interview. And now armored Bloodguards deliver me to Imperial Military Command, the Pinnacle. I should have taken Otto up on his offer to visit the coast.*

He glances around the room. They have gathered in the Defense Secretary's private, severely modern conference room. The table is made of highly utilitarian Erosi blackglass and there are comp terminals at each of the sixteen chairs. There is a large flat screen holo projector on the wall opposite the main iris. Next to the iris are a beverage and snack dispenser and a knot of waiting Bloodguard and Takazhr, armored and unarmored. The far wall holds a picture window looking out to the North Western Atlantic. The wall behind him is dedicated to the central projection bubble in which an image of his Uncle Balthasar, First Elector of the Erosi Alliance and ClanLord of the HaneNation, watches the proceedings. Balthasar smiles at his nephew and Pfizer reads the smile: *An idealist like his mother but I can see my brother in him.* Pfizer returns Balthasar's smile in a way that lets the older man know his thoughts are transparent. Balthasar chuckles.

"My favorite nephew," purrs Balthasar. "You have the emoto-subtleties of your mother's family. You spoke brilliantly. I could use you at the next Convocation of the Clans on Eros." He continues, turning to Anastacia, "Sister-in-law, you did a good job with this one. Hane Export and Import, along with our other affiliates, stands with you. I'll contact my corporate brokers." To Millian he says, "Update me as to the situation with Pfizer's Tempeler." To Creed he says, "You know what to do."

"I will, Balthasar. Give Mother our greetings," says the Lion saluting, looking every bit the recruitment holo.

"Very well. Take care little brothers." For just a moment the supreme confidence radiated by Balthasar dissipates. "Mother would like to hear from both of you."

"What's all this about?" demands Pfizer of no one in

particular. This is a very strange gathering indeed. He knows his mother can barely tolerate his uncles, least of all Creed. Yet here she is talking to them concerning some sort of alliance. It would be naive to believe that his speech has ameliorated a century of animosity. Something has occurred to bring them to this unprecedented degree of cooperation, and while he wishes it could be his doing ...

"Your speech was inspiring, son," says the First Lord, reading his son's face.

"Not so inspiring. These are your top military advisors," says Pfizer skeptically. He lowers his voice and leans closer to his father. "Mother is not exactly crazy about your brothers."

How do you tell a dreamer his dreams are about to be tested? How do you tell an idealist that ideals are sometimes not enough when confronted by reality? You must tell the truth. "Sit down," he orders. Something in the paternal way he says it makes Pfizer sit obediently.

Now that Pfizer has spent a few minutes in the room he has gauged the mood. His mother and father are clearly concerned. No, worried. They are doing a good job of hiding their angst but his years amidst the emotionally sterile Tempellians has made him uncannily perceptive to the smallest emotional nuances. They, like his sister, are hiding something of grave import. What do these people have to fear? Together they represent a vast portion of the Imperium's financial and armed might.

"Approximately four hours before your touchdown at O'Meara, a Tupolev CTS VIII freight racer was intercepted by Naval and Takazhr units in near Jupiter orbit. The racer was carrying more than two tons of refined tursapoi. Ninety-four fifty-megaton-yield a-mat warheads, one hundred and twelve ten-kiloton tactical nuclear warheads, and an assortment of advanced particle and fusion weapons including SAA suits." Millian pauses for a moment to assess Pfizer's reaction. His son waits calmly for him to continue. Pfizer merely seems to be itemizing what he has heard. Out of the corner of his eye, Millian notices that his wife watches the exchange intently.

"Most importantly, aside from the racer's crew of twenty eight, there were forty seven e-mortals enhanced for high-gravity and tursapoi addiction.

"Examination of their neural tissues has revealed nano and cybernetic adaptation for martial arts, small arms, and small group tactics through MentAmp biosoft programs." Millian pauses this time to see if Pfizer recognizes the profile.

"Deathmen," whispers Pfizer. He looks immediately at the Lion, who is now also watching him. "Deathmen?" This time it is a question. Like all of them earlier, even though he knows it to be true, he still questions the facts. They are too terrible to be true.

"Yes," says the Lion, surprised and pleased by Pfizer's cool assessment. At least he didn't liquefy into silence for twenty minutes like his mother.

"What is the possibility of it being a sleeper cell from the Wasting, Deathmen whose stasis or cryogenic support malfunctioned?" asks Pfizer, but the minute the question passes his lips he realizes that it is a long shot.

The Lion answers the question with another. "A sleeper cell in a Tupolev CST VIII?"

"Why not?" interjects Anastacia. "They could have stolen it."

Cato Ahren and Elaine Goldshef exchange glances. Elaine accesses the after-action reports with Cato leaning over her shoulder. "Forensic analysis shows little or no signs of stasis or any of the varying forms of cryogenics on the forty seven Deathmen."

"What are you going to do?" Pfizer asks his father.

"That was only the beginning. An hour and a half ago, a majority of Ambros-owned and operated companies, as well as those of our allies and associates, came under economic attack—"

"You are keeping us and our senior advisors on sight in order to calm our shareholders," Pfizer interrupts, turning his gaze to Creed, who nods in acknowledgement.

"Let me finish, son. There'll be time for questions and

speculations later."

Will there? thinks Creed.

"After the attack on our finances, it became obvious that whoever is behind this assault has intimate knowledge of our corporate emergency management protocols," Millian continues, again waiting to see if Pfizer will put it together on his own.

"They have an informer on the Executive Council, or someone who was on the Council," says Pfizer. He knows of only one person who was ever so dissatisfied as to betray the Ambros. "Do you have a list of suspects?" he asks Cato Ahren.

"You know who the most likely suspect is," interjects the Lion angrily. *There is no more time for vacillating. We need to take action.* "I'm sorry, Pfizer," he adds more gently.

"We need to contact them through Oriana, negotiate with them. Surely there is a settlement we can reach," says Pfizer preparing himself for the onslaught from his father, uncle, and Cato.

"What?!" thunder Cato, Creed, and Millian simultaneously. Millian is on his feet glaring down at his son.

"Explain yourself," Anastacia whispers into the tense silence. *He can't be a part of this conspiracy, can he? No. I'm crazy to doubt him.* "What are you thinking?" She quietly asks her son.

"Violence is the last option of the desperate—."

"Or the first of the insane," interrupts Creed.

"Let him finish," Anastacia says through clenched teeth.

"Whoever these people are they believe communication is no longer an option. They believe we are so rigid in our policy that the only way for there to be change is revolution."

"Revolution? ... *Revolution?!* ... You mean rebellion, conspiracy, and murder," says Millian glacially. "Your mother has always been willing to communicate. The Omnividome—"

"Backed them into a perceived corner. Conflict, all conflict, arises from differences in perception. We need to meet and look for common ground instead of holding such divergent perceptions. The Omnividome can work for both sides, and violence can only harm and set both sides back. I'm sure if we give them an opportunity for anything other than violence they'll jump at the chance to prevent it," says Pfizer, calmly looking up at his father. "Let me negotiate with them; it's what I was trained to do."

"Never!" roars the Lion furiously.

"Out of the question, your Imperial Highness. The Scion cannot be risked," says Cato.

"I agree with Creed and Cato," says Anastacia, rising from her chair and going to the window, "albeit for different reasons. The minute they chose violence as a form of policy they removed themselves from the realm of civilized discourse and into that of the terrorist." She raises a hand to keep Pfizer from interrupting. "Negotiating with them would set the human race back millennia. It would return us to a precedent whereby if you can't get what you want, you take it, coerce, force, extort. They would always believe they drove us to the bargaining table with the threat of force."

"What form of policy do the Bloodguard, Imperial Navy, and Takazhr represent, Mother?"

"The Domina is right, and such a question is sophomoric at best. When this all came to our attention, I begged her to let me arrest the possible suspects. She refused, stating something to the effect that it would make her no better than these terrorists. There is no doubt—"

"I believe what I said at O'Meara; it wasn't just for convenience. Why are you so sure that they intended to use these weapons in a coup d'état? How do you know they weren't trying to acquire them for defense if something goes wrong with the Fragmentation Initiative?" asks Pfizer remaining maddeningly calm.

"Deathmen for defense?" murmurs Anastacia. "I think not. Those weapons are illegal, outside government control. They sought to acquire them for the purpose of breaking or subverting the law. I respect the courage of your convictions, Pfizer, but evidence is on its way here from the Tempellian Embassy in Nevada. We will let this determine our course of action. In the meantime, Cato, have you managed to gather any information from the freight racer's destination point?"

"We should have information shortly. I've sent Basileus to coordinate with local Takazhr at Manhattan's Ellis Island Cosmodome Annex," says Cato.

"When you get your evidence and have your naval forces in orbit, what are you going to do? Arrest them? If they believe in their cause do you expect them to come peacefully? The course of action you're planning now may very well precipitate the violence you hope to prevent," says Pfizer as calmly and as pedantically as a Tempeler. "Why are you so afraid of talking? What is to be lost from communicating besides a little time? Isn't communication what the Omnividome is all about?"

Flawlessly logical but—"Son. everything you've said has definite merit, but you seem intent on ignoring the fact that they've broken the law. Do you intend to dismiss this?" asks Millian, attempting to remain calm in the face of his son's maddening pacifism. He can see that Creed is rapidly approaching the limits of his patience by the way he paces back and forth on the other side of the room. The Lion caged.

"*Allegedly* broken the law. No warrants have been issued. There's been no Grand Jury investigation. Your advisors are prompting you to act based on speculation."

"The Tene Thantos crucifix Cato's son found on that freight racer is no speculation, nor are the bodies in the *Bismarck's* stasis morgue, or the confiscated weapons. Answer your father's question! Why do you ignore the fact that the Unionists have broken several laws that are treasonable offenses?" shouts the Lion.

Pfizer sighs, marshaling his patience. "If Oriana has broken the law, then she should be censured, and suffer the penalties for her actions. I simply think the courses of action you've outlined, uncle, will lead to violence and we know you have not addressed the causes for their behavior. Without dealing with that, the problem will only occur again, and next time you may not get a heads up notice," says Pfizer, becoming even calmer in the face of Creed's ire.

"That's enough from all of you. Our decisions stand. We

wait for the information Luxvico and Captain Praetor Buchanan are bringing in. We wait for what Captain Ahren discovers at the Ellis Island Annex. Information will determine our course of action. Now we wait and pray," announces Anastacia.

"You have my chief Bloodguard and my Tempeler involved in this?" asks Pfizer, and even as he speaks he hears the anxiety in his voice.

Creed notices his brother's relief at his son's heightened emotion. "Cato's Tempeler, Lomin, has requested asylum at the Titan Embassy in Redwood, California," Creed says. "You may be unaware but Tempelers are being recalled from the Sol, Spica, T'ang, and Aquila star systems. Apparently, your Tempeler refused the order and contacted Buchanan. So it appears your advisors have taken action based on simple speculation, as have your parents. Maybe it's you who needs to re-examine your point of view towards events," says the Lion, his voice seething with recriminations.

Millian puts a hand on his son's shoulder, understanding Pfizer's concern for his friends, and what is undoubtedly anger at Creed's veiled hostility. Pfizer stares at Creed and for the first time he understands what he has considered his uncle's barely controlled emotionalism. Clearly, the Lion has friends and family that he is worried about, and he has to wait upon the decisions of others before he can take action.

"I understand," is all he says to Creed, but the impact of those two words instantly mollify the Lion, who drops into one of the chairs at the conference table. He nods in acknowledgement of Pfizer's understanding.

"We wait," says Pfizer to his mother.

"Only I hope it isn't too long," Anastacia says turning Creed.

CHAPTER 17

Thou shalt protect the Divine Purity of the
Human Race. Only Man is created in God's image.

—The Prophet Naraji Ilkani, 4081 I.C.

The cold rain that blew across the mall drove most of the
tourists running for safety, but it didn't last for more than ten
minutes. Luxvico supposes it could have been a glitch in the
planet's weather modification network. Rain on Tempel was
restricted to night time. Luxvico can't accurately recall the last
time he'd been caught in the rain. Foot traffic is beginning to
return to the mall that separates the Pax Monument, an
immense gold angel lifting a child toward heaven, from the
Atlantean Obelisk outside the Cosmodome. Luxvico glances at
his omnipalm and sees that the Captain Praetor should be
arriving shortly. He must admit to a strange anxiety since he's
been waiting. He's felt like everyone's been staring at him.
True, outside their professions at the Academy's chapters and
annexes, Tempelers are a rare sight. And now with all but a
handful of his people leaving the planet, they will become rarer
still. That his people can sit by and watch the rebirth of an
ancient atrocity fills him with dread. A world where everything
is defined has become uncertain and dangerous. An elderly
human male, leaning on a cane, watches him intently from the
pedestal of the Pax Monument.

"Councilor," whispers Otto's sandpaper voice from behind
Lux's shoulder, startling the Tempeler.

Luxvico turns quickly, and there is no mistaking the

amusement in the Bloodguard's eyes as he wipes rain from them. Otto is dressed in a heavy flannel shirt of the Buchanan tartan, jeans, and hiking boots. He brushes water from his hair with one hand.

"Walk with me. I have transportation in a lot just on the other side of the Obelisk," says Otto turning in that direction.

"I have transport on the Green, closer, about four hundred meters away," offers Luxvico, turning toward the Pax Monument. Where is the old man?

"Excuse me sir," says the old man but from the opposite side now, an arm's length away from Luxvico. Luxvico looks down into white, gold-flecked eyes and his heart freezes. Luxvico drops immediately to the ground before the thought of recognition enters his mind, *Deathman!* The swift chopping blow intended to decapitate him misses, instead grazing Otto with enough force to drop the Bloodguard to the ground. But fortunately Lux's reaction gives the much faster Erosi time to avoid most of the blow. Lux rolls on the ground and gets to his feet, his hand moving beneath his surcoat to pull out his omnipalm. But the old man is metamorphosing into a larger form and kicks the omnipalm away, shattering bones in Lux's hand. Luxvico manages to turn and flee as a second kick catches him in the back, sending him stumbling forward toward the reflecting pool.

"Run," Otto groans, trying to rise to his knees. Luxvico watches as the Deathman mimic turns toward Otto then stops and returns his attention to Luxvico. The mimic activates a stealth field, becoming invisible but for a hazy outline as the visible light is bent around the assassin.

Luxvico to his own surprise screams and runs into the reflecting pool, hearing the sound of running and splashing right behind him. *I am a dead man! I have no weapons, no communications, that creature was made for combat in two gravity environments. He is faster and far stronger than I, especially on Earth's surface.* He feels his heart pounding in his chest and his lungs burning with exertion, and insanely part of his mind begins calculating how many seconds it will take the Deathman to reach him. People are beginning to notice the commotion now, but all Luxvico can think is that it's too late. He stumbles forward panting and swears he hears and feels the air cook above him from a plasma burst. He regains his footing again.

I've got to do something! I can't let this monster get the information I have. "I wouldn't shoot again. You might damage the information you are looking for," Luxvico yells at the running wake heading toward him. Abruptly the running stops and the glow of a laser sight plays across Luxvico's chest.

"Fekking monster!" is all Luxvico can manage at the affront of the laser sight. He kicks water at the apparition in desperation and frustration. Water splashes upward and for a moment the barest outline of the assassin is visible. Suddenly three sharp blasts of light strike the water ghost with the *zhoff!* sound of super-heated air and water. There are blue flashes as the creature's shield absorbs most of the energy of first blast. Then with the second shot there is a multi-chromatic flash and the Deathman becomes visible. With the failure of his stealth field, the third shot knocks the Deathman off his feet.

"Keep running!" Otto shouts, charging forward discharging his blaster three more times. The Deathman never regains his feet. The fourth shot overloads his shield. The fifth and sixth take apart his head in flashes of white light and a burst of melted skull and flaming tissue.

The adrenaline surge passes and Luxvico drops to his knees in the pool, the headless corpse of the Deathman before him.

"Are you all right?" asks Otto, splashing up beside Luxvico and kneeling.

"Huh?"

"Councilor, are you injured? Did he damage you?" says Otto calming himself with deep breaths trying to sound as impassive as the inhabitants of Lux's world. "Councilor Luxvico, are you damaged? Do you require medical attention?"

"Uh?" Lux holds up his right hand. "I think he broke some of the bones in my hand." Luxvico says, feeling his vision clear. There is an odd smile on Otto's face, a relief concerning Lux's returning coherence. "What's so amusing Captain

Praetor?" Lux asks.

"Nothing, Councilor," says Otto, helping the Tempeler to his feet and still surveying the area. Four armored Takazhr are running toward them with pulse rifles.

"Get your hands up!" they scream with raw adrenaline. "Drop that weapon! Drop that weapon!" they blare through the voice augmenters of their armor. Otto raises his arms but does not drop his blaster as he continues to watch the area. Luxvico sees then that the blaster is attached to a power holster on Otto's wrist. All Otto has to do is hold his hand as if he were ready to hold the weapon and sensors in the power holster around his wrist and forearm would eject the gun on its power cable into his waiting hand.

"I am a Bloodguard, Captain Praetor Otto Buchanan, Special Services Division. I am wearing a power holster and I cannot drop my weapon." He stands away from Luxvico in case the Takazhr are trigger crazy, but the Tempeler seems aware of this and does not allow Otto more than an arm's length distance.

"Extend your arms and let the blaster go from your hand!" orders the first enforcer to reach them, his pulse rifle pointed at Otto's head. The second Takazhr swiftly and efficiently removes the power holster and blaster from Otto. The third scans and pats Otto down for more weapons, which to Luxvico's surprise he has ... in abundance. A Hephaestus, neuro-muscular biocircuitry, class five defensive body shield, even some kind of cruel looking knife in a calf sheath. The fourth Takazhr questions whether Luxvico was injured and what happened.

"The Captain Praetor saved my life. We are here on official business," says Luxvico.

"Where's your identification, Tempeler?" demands the first Takazhr, his weapon still pointed menacingly at the Captain Praetor.

"Over there somewhere," Luxvico indicates with a nod of his head. "My identification is on my omnipalm; however, our attacker may have damaged it."

The first rifle-wielding Takazhr motions for the fourth officer to look for the omnipalm, as the second Takazhr steps away from Otto with a retinal-verifier declaring: "You're legitimate. We're sorry, sir," she says.

"Give me back my weapons," Otto commands as he continues to sweep the area with his gaze. "You are to call your Watch Commander immediately. Have your commanding officer take charge of this crime scene and report only, I repeat, *only* to the Office of Takazhr Command. In fact, all investigative support is to come through OTC," Otto continues, while strapping on the power holster and replacing his Hephaestus. He salutes the officers. "Keep the media off our backs do not ... do not let them near the body," Otto adds, watching several teams of reporters and holo technicians hurrying toward them through the reflecting pool. Otto turns to grab Lux by the elbow but finds the Tempellian watching him intently. "Let's go," Otto murmurs heading toward the obelisk, at the end farthest from the gathering reporters.

They walk swiftly and in silence. Otto still vigilant watching everyone. Strangely, people ignore the sight of a Tempellian and a young man slogging through the reflecting pool of the Pax Monument, focusing instead on the Takazhr and the growing circle of media forming near the center of the pool. When they reach Otto's skidder, a modified Davini-27, Otto opens the front-facing storage compartment and offers him a towel.

"Unnecessary, Captain Praetor. Aside from the precipitation that fell on my face I am not wet. My bio suit's integrity was not compromised," Luxvico says staring at the towel.

The Captain Praetor looks at him strangely and says, "Well I'm soaked. But we'll worry about that later. How is your hand?" Otto asks.

"I have vital information, Captain Praetor," Luxvico says quietly, barely audible with the soft patter of falling rain.

"You think," chuckles Otto sarcastically while glancing over his shoulder back toward the carnage they barely escaped. Otto opens the passenger side door for Lux and then secures it after the Tempellian gets in. *I saw him scream, and I saw him at the tail end of the fear flight response. Now he's moving himself back toward the typical Tempellian desensitization,* Otto thinks, as he gets in his skidder and touches a thumb to the biometric ignition icon.

"I am not emotionless," Luxvico says, once again barely audible with rain falling against the skidder.

"Counselor, I do not appreciate telepath—"

"Before you continue your insult, I am not reading your mind. Your behavior is an incredible representation of your thoughts," Luxvico says, the disgust clear for Otto to hear. "Before you misinterpret me further, the anxiety is my own. In the last few hours I have experienced emotions I have not felt since childhood. I have made emotional displays and allowed emotion to influence my decisions. I apologize if I endangered our lives," Luxvico sighs.

Otto, with his attention on traffic as he raises the skidder through the climbs, says to Lux, "The feelings that *you* seem to want to dismiss saved our lives. Your fear gave me the chance we needed, when you ran and when you disrupted his stealth field with your desperate act of flinging water." Though dismissive when he began speaking Otto is consoling when he finishes. "You and I cannot afford to relive the issues between our two peoples, Erosi and Tempellian. We're going to need to work together.... I want—"

"Pay attention!" Luxvico exclaims, indicating a skidder dangerously in front of his.

Otto smoothly shift-climbs his skidder, moving over the other skidders and barely avoiding a collision. "You see, Counselor? Another useful display of you emotions." Out of the corner of his eye Otto catches the shadow of what could have been a smile disappear off Luxvico's face.

CHAPTER 18

In light of evil, seeing evil, knowing evil, be strong
and of good courage. Do not be afraid.

—Deuteronomy 31:6 Judeo-Orange Codex

Nasir Qamar removes the MentAmp from his head and the
world of three-dimensional numbers, charts, and multi-colored
graphs vanishes. The blinking servosphere before him waits
ominously. Nasir rises from his floater couch and beckons the
sphere toward him. He pulls a remote activator from a thin
neutronium chain around his neck and points it toward the
sphere and a holo-bubble of static winks into existence.

"Mimic Three went offline, less than five minutes ago. I am
moving our time table to z minus eight point four six mark,"
says a computer distorted voice from the holo-bubble.

Nasir smiles, *so soon.* "Finally, the twilight of the age," he
whispers caressing the sphere. "Flesh and perfection, matter
and energy, man and machine, one," says Nasir. He closes his
eyes and the Unionists' entire communications array appears
before him. With flicks of his eye he highlights the appropriate
icons and transmits the new strike times. Acknowledgements
flash at the bottom of his vision and sounds ping from his
auditory nerve.

"All units acknowledge new time for first strike," says Nasir
to the bubble of static. *We shall kill all the vermin,* he thinks,
viewing the city of High Orbit through the windows of his
office. The bubble blinks quietly before him, its connection
still active.

Dating back to the reclamation of the planet more than six thousand years ago, High Orbit is an interwoven amalgamation of space-factories, residential pods, orbital complexes, eco-domes and agri-spheres. Naval drydocks and space hangars form a ring around the orbital city. *Ironically, the city is older than any of the blasted or buried cities that have been restored below in the mud. From above is the only way to view the cesspool of genetic mixing that has occurred for millennia on the accursed planet's surface. But in less than nine hours' time, half the filth that inhabits this world will be scorched from existence.* Nasir looks forward to hunting the survivors in the cold nights that will follow the antimatter fallout.

The traffic of cargo-carriers, interplanetary hoppers, and deep-range passenger liners fills the space around the immense orbital city. Some of the ships were manufactured by Tupolev, some are AAG auto haulers and roboships, and some of them are carrying ingeniously hidden a-mat devices and strategic fusion weapons—weapons that will crash into Space Guard and Naval bases, detonate over cities.

"Dust thou art and to dust thou shall return," Nasir whispers. For so long the short-lived have hemmed in his kind, suppressed them in their cowardice, kept them from achieving true greatness. The short-lived have regulated his kind's genetic potential; they have tightly controlled his manufacturing and service industries.

"I am concerned with Pfizer Ambros," says the disembodied voice of the bubble. Nasir, distracted from his revenge fantasies, glares at the holo-bubble, his eyes narrowing.

"Why?"

"His speech at O'Meara, the statements he's been making to the media. He's already caused his sister to reconsider her position with us. He must not survive the assault."

"He will not. Oriana will be the only Ambros worth mentioning left alive."

"See to it he does not," says the voice from the bubble, and even though it is computer generated Nasir can hear the chilling threat. But this infuriates the Chosen. "What have we to fear from this pseudo Aeon? I will kill—"

"Nasir, I was like you once. I was so sure of the rightness of my cause. But Pfizer will be seen as the dreamer cut down before his time, the usher of a golden age stopped before his message could be received. It is a given fact that he will be made a martyr should he die. If he should survive, he will be the focal point of all organized resistance."

When the Master spoke so enigmatically, even Nasir wondered at their choice of leadership. But the Chosen have nothing to fear from mere halflings, especially the weakling Ambros. The real challenge will lie in defeating the Hane.

"The Hane are in love with money and their homeworld. They'll do anything to spare Eros the coming fate of Earth and Tempel," says the voice from the holo-bubble to Nasir's unspoken thoughts. *And Tempel?* These moments of the Master's omniscience give Nasir an almost sexual thrill. "I will teach you this and more Nasir Qamar, but it will require your absolute obedience. Now you will contact Rachel Tsimpo and tell her that she is responsible for insuring Pfizer's demise."

"You have set the standard, Master. I would not trust so important a goal to human scum," hisses Nasir.

The bubble silently crackles with color before him. "You use the tools available ... I had thought to wait before revealing this to you, but you need to know now to make contingency plans. Two of the Tempelers have gone renegade."

"That sophist Laurza assured us he could control his people!" barks Nasir. "The renegades, that's why the Mimic went offline. Did it succeed before going offline?"

"You are learning ... The Mimic failed. Security for the Academy's central computer was breached; that is what alerted us. Lomin, the Tempeler to the Grand Kurseg of the Takazhr downloaded incriminating evidence and observations for our plans going back before your birth. The data, should it come to light, would jeopardize my ascendancy, which is why I have advanced the strike time."

Suddenly Nasir is nearly overwhelmed by a sense of vulnerability. He looks at the iris to the office and imagines it liquefying under plasma beams from armored and tursapoi frenzied Bloodguards pouring through the still white hot opening, leveling their deadly Hephaestuses and burning him alive. There would be no other penalty. *None of his people or their followers will survive to go to trial. They will be eliminated as soon as the Ambros bitch has signed the termination warrants before the Executive Council.*

"Alarming as this is, Nasir, there is no cause for fear. The encryption codes on the data will require hours to decrypt. I believe you can use the AAG Central AI to spread a virus to their AI's to slow down the decoding. That will give us the time for our forces to strike." There is unmistakable joy in the artificial voice as it whispers, "At last."

Glorious, revels Nasir in his thoughts. *My God knows my thoughts as well as my fears.* Nasir walks quietly to his work console and whispers access codes to the AAG Central Artificial Intelligence code-named, Nemesis. An upload begins of a prefix code which arms the automated elements of the conspiracy. AI elements begin a countdown that will poison the CIMB. Nasir stands back and smiles. He ... *They* have passed the point of no return. All that remains now is to inform Rachel Tsimpo of her orders and then wait. He will watch the coming conflagration from his hyperzeppelin, Qamar One. "When will you reveal yourself to the others?" asks Nasir.

"Soon, after Oriana's ascension and the discrediting of the Bloodguard," answers the voice. "Nasir, see to the issue of Pfizer Ambros. Do not fail me," commands the voice, and Nasir knows that he is being dismissed. He bows slightly, touching the Tene Thantos crucifix beneath his singlesuit, and the bubble vanishes. He will have one of his agents contact Rachel Tsimpo with appropriate recognition cyphers. He cannot bear contact with her—slow, dull-witted as she is. The Nemesis protocols will do more than just attack the computer systems of the government and military; they will also attack those of his CIMB rivals: Hane, Ambros, Att, Merck, Sansom, Yoshida, and MicroSung. In the end they will all have to turn

128

to AAG to reinitialize and renetwork their systems. In the end he will be the one with a majority of the CIMB's shares. Politics will yield to economics, and in time he will become Emperor-Executor Nasir I.

CHAPTER 19

We were foolish, so sure in the righteousness of
our cause that we forgot that the Universe is
balance, and whatever our capacity for good, so
too there would be for evil.

—*The Luxvico Logs*

Otto finishes closing the last of the fast seals on his working
uniform. Luxvico has said nothing since their arrival at the
Pinnacle, other than that he does not wish to leave Otto. "You
know you're safe here, Councilor," says Otto, checking his
Hephaestus and holstering it on his right hip. His left hand
then checks the settings on the power holster around his right
wrist. The Tempellian has been staring out the window of
Otto's Pinnacle office since the debriefing officer brought
them here. Otto shrugs and contacts Pfizer's honor guard,
confirming Pfizer's location with his omnipalm readout.

"When will you be allowed to personally oversee the
Scion's safety?" asks Luxvico not turning from the window.
*Am I to spend the rest of my life under blue skies, never again to see the
red, moisture-barren sky of Tempel?*

"Any moment now. Why?" questions Otto.

Luxvico turns from the window and regards Otto with a
strange intensity. If Otto could attach a significance to the look
it would be incomprehension. "We are not safe," Lux says,
stating the obvious and then turning back to the window.

Otto takes a deep breath. *I have been babysitting this ambulatory
deepfreeze unit for almost an hour now. Earlier I saved his life, and ever*

since we arrived at the Pinnacle the only words out of his mouth are the utterly obvious. During Otto's debriefing the Kurseg of the Bloodguard, Creed Hane, had updated him on the current situation. Now, here he is, waiting with the enigmatic Tempeler, while someone else guards Pfizer.

Worse, he had not been allowed to contact Marisol, although the Lion himself had assured him that Mari would be notified that he was safe. The sheer magnitude of the weapons discovered on the Tupolev freight racer had shocked Otto. He'd suggested immediate retreat from Earth and its orbital environs, a move the Executive Council had apparently decided to reject. This has left them in a highly vulnerable immobile position. "What am I going to do?" he unintentionally asks aloud.

I have been asking myself the same question for nearly two and a half hours, thinks Luxvico. *I am exiled. I will never see my home tower, my family, the Academy. The only person I trust is an Erosi Bloodguard who definitely dislikes and distrusts me, and it is imperative that I gain his trust.*

"We have to find the Crown Scion and get him and his family off this planet," Luxvico replies.

"The Executive Council has refused withdrawal as an option," says Otto, dropping into a low leather chair before an equally low Erosi tea table that he puts a foot on.

"It was the freight racer. I know. Deathmen were on board. They probably carried tursapoi and a host of a-mat and fusion weapons," says the Councilor to the window.

"The Takazhr Councilor told you?" says Otto, his curiosity rising.

"No, Captain Praetor, he never told me the content of his meeting with the Takazhr Grand Kurseg, Cato Ahren. This is a logician prime projection based on miscellaneous but interrelated data. They are planning an assault using the weapons I mentioned. If they have additional weapons, then rest assured they'll use them. The only safe place to be if these weapons are used is behind them or nowhere near them," says Luxvico simply.

"While I'm impressed by your Tempeler deductive abilities, I'm supposed to do what?"

"Get us out of here. Protect Pfizer Ambros," answers Luxvico in the same emotionless deadpan.

"You're going to have to do better than state the obvious," snaps Otto unintentionally. He promised himself he'd try to go a little easier on the Tempellian after his close call, but Luxvico's tight-lipped, monosyllabic answers were wearing Otto's patience thin. *He's going to have to learn to trust me.*

"Yes. So it would seem," says Luxvico, taking in the shocked look on Otto's face. "Again, before you ask, I'm not reading your thoughts. Just using my 'Tempeler deductive abilities.' Dr. Tsimpo is a traitor."

"What?" Otto actually laughs. "You're joking." However, Luxvico's impassive face assures him it's no joke.

"On Ambros Two, before Earth orbit, he, the Prince, called us to discuss the Fragmentation Initiative—"

"And you managed to nearly unhinge him with your prophecy of doom and gloom," Otto almost shouts.

"It is unfortunate that I told him what he did not wish to hear. But his question initiated the events that have brought you and I here. Now the choice is whether you will confront the truth and act or leave our fates in the hands of others."

"Are you trying to provoke me?" Otto asks, astounded by Luxvivo's accusation and now his attitude. *Despite my feelings, Pfizer reveres this human computer.* In the back of his mind Otto hears Marisol's voice saying, *Listen to him.*

"You are ready to communicate?" Luxvico says to Otto.

"Why do you say one of the Vice Directors of the PPRC is a traitor?" Otto asks, resignedly activating his omnipalm's holograph digicorder.

"The Scion called us shortly before Earth Orbit," begins Luxvico, a faraway look coming over his face. "The Scion has always been a prize pupil; he brings fresh perspectives to observations he makes about a myriad of paradigms. He called me to review the factional alignment of the situation on Earth. My analysis must have seemed heartless in view of what has happened. It was only in his calling my attention to review the situation that I realized the high probabilities for violence." There is genuine sorrow in the Tempellian's voice and on his face as he pauses.

"Dr. Tsimpo was coming by for a prearranged meeting with the Scion as I was leaving. Her behavior during the interview is what made me suspect her—her passion for the Unionist point, her body language. She suddenly felt exposed and was prepared for violence if the Scion hadn't innocently defused the situation."

"And you didn't tell me this immediately because …?" Otto asks angrily, the sandpaper voice going lower.

Luxvico merely stares back at Otto. The Bloodguard's response should be its own answer. "I wanted to gather evidence. I knew, correctly, you would act this way. When I went to contact the Academy, further inquiries were forbidden, and I was ordered to return home. It was then that Lomin and I defected; the Ahren have granted us sanctuary."

He's given up everything he's known, rank, purpose—and certainly not on a hunch. Otto activates his omnipalm's communicator. "This is Captain Praetor Buchanan. I need to speak with Kurseg Hane immediately," says Otto reacting the only way he can.

"Captain Praetor?" comes the Lion's growl over the omnipalm.

"Sir. Pardon the interruption, Sir," says Otto at attention suddenly. "Sir, I have been interviewing the Tempeler Luxvico. I believe that it is imperative that the Scion be returned to my direct supervision, Sir."

"Granted. Report to the conference room of Secretary Goldshef. Hane out," orders the Lion and the communication goes dead.

"Let's go," says Otto, pocketing his omnipalm.

"Thank you, Captain Praetor," says Luxvico, mildly surprised as he follows behind the Bloodguard.

"I'm capable of a bit of deductive reasoning myself, Councilor," says Otto bluntly. Then he more graciously adds,

"We're going to trust each other where Pfizer is concerned." Otto turns partially as he extends his hand. Luxvico, though again surprised, shakes his hand briefly. *Who would have thought he actually has a firm handshake?* Otto thinks. *And his palm isn't ice cold.*

I have underestimated the Captain Praetor again, thinks Luxvico. *He is our best chance for survival. I must become more useful than threatening and judgmental.* Luxvico lowers his head. They move quickly through the corridors of the Pinnacle. The number of uniformed personnel is low, as befitting the holiday, but those that Luxvico observes are working at a near-frantic pace. *It's as bad as I might have imagined. I have been exiled, disbarred, attacked by a Deathman, and the Ambros have decided to entrench themselves over PR issues and economics.* They enter a turbo-shaft that speeds them upward toward the Pinnacle's top floor.

CHAPTER 20

Bare one another's burdens and so fulfill the law.

—Galatians 6:2 Judeo-Orange Codex

When Luxvico and Otto step out of the turbo-shaft, they find themselves in a sea of white-armored Bloodguards, white- and red-uniformed officers, blue-uniformed naval officers, and green or black-uniformed Takazhr. There are also a few civilians with credentials clipped to their persons. The two pass through this organized chaos into a substantially less crowded waiting room with a few more high-ranking military officers, one civilian, and the honor guard for each of the Aristos in Secretary Goldshef's conference room. The Captain Praetor stops before a mid-height, frosty-eyed Bloodguard with intricate black Chosen tattoos on the upper right quadrant of his face. Otto gives the Bloodguard a faint smile of relief and gratification.

"The Scion is safe inside with the Imperium Security Committee," says the tattooed Bloodguard in a voice younger than the Scion's. Houka Jamal, Her Majesty's Praetor appears in the iris to the conference room. "Captain Praetor Buchanan, Councilor Luxvico," he calls, and ushers the two into the conference room. The Scion seems to lighten visibly upon seeing them, as does Lomin, who is standing with Grand Kurseg Cato Ahren. The First Lord and the Empress-Executrix are regarding their son, and barely acknowledge their presence. Secretary Goldshef and the Lion, along with an Admiral from Naval Intelligence, review a holographic tactical display of the Sol System. "Councilor Luxvico, Captain Praetor Buchanan," says the Lion, straightening and excusing himself from the Defense Secretary and the Admiral.

"Sir," says Otto saluting. "Councilor Luxvico believes there is a spy on Prince Pfizer's staff." The background conversation in the conference room suddenly vanishes. Otto becomes aware of rain pattering on the windows.

"Who?" ask both Pfizer and the Lion at once. Instinctively, Otto turns to Pfizer.

"Dr. Tsimpo," Otto says simply. Even with Otto's limited degree of emp-psych, it is obvious that Pfizer thinks he is mistaken.

"Excuse me, Kurseg Hane, but shouldn't it be possible to pull the servosphere observation logs or the executive workroom's AI?" asks Luxvico. The Lion glances at the Naval Intelligence officer, who nods and says, "I'll contact the orbital shipyard at High Orbit."

"You believe this, Luxvico?" asks Pfizer, unable to keep the bewilderment from his voice. "Are you sure you haven't misinterpreted her disagreement with you as treason?" Pfizer adds softly.

Clearly, when he asks questions like this it's due to the Captain Praetor's anti-Tempellian influence, Luxvico thinks. The look on the Councilor's face is enough though, and Pfizer says, "Of course, you are. Rachel, Rachel, Rachel. I thought I knew her."

"She's PPRC, and an empathic-psychiatrist. They are masters of mask and illusion. People see and feel what they want them to," says the Lion, his face reddening. "I want her arrested."

Everything I said at the Cosmodome, swept away by the traitorous actions of a few. "Is it possible we could use her to ferret out the others?" Pfizer asks softly. He looks at his mother and father. *What about their dreams. My own sister is a part of this.*

"That's not a bad idea." Creed says, looking to Anastacia and Millian. Anastacia nods her consent. "Well people, it's time to make some hard decisions. We've only got a few hours until the Uprising Ceremonies begin."

CHAPTER 21

Personal Log: Classified Entry 102163 Captain
Basileus Ahren. They burned the warehouse.

—Cato Ahren, *Profiles of Courage*

"I arrived with a team from the New Eden Special
Investigations Branch at 1300 hours to find rescue and fire
units responding. The blaze spread to other warehouses before
they were able to contain it with force fields. There are
combustibles inside that continue to feed the fires. I know
there are three bodies inside. We could send in armored teams
to remove the bodies, but I'm concerned about damaging the
crime scene. I've been informed the warehouse owner is en
route."

Basileus finishes his log and turns off his omnipalm. Then
he frowns and replaces it to its shoulder clip.

The fire seems to burn out in one of the warehouse-sized
buildings only to flare back to life with two blossoms of black
smoke and geysers of flame. Gulls keen over the electronically
augmented voices of the Emergency Response Teams. The
spectacular vista of Manhattan from this part of the artificially
enlarged Ellis Island is obscured by the warehouse blaze and
gives the entire skyline an eerily apocalyptic effect. Basileus
shrugs off the dark vision. Reflexively, his right hand reaches
for the pocket where the security capsule had rested. But he
exchanged his clothing for armor hours ago, and he had turned
over the evil contents of his pocket to Lomin.

Two armored Takazhr are approaching him now with a

middle-aged human between them. The man is just shy of two meters and slim in build, with a thin, disdainful face. He is dressed in holiday finery. *An expensive suit of Erosi seal fur and leather, and an embroidered white shirt. It is clothing no Erosi would wear. Exports for the 'cosmopolitan' who reads the Erosi advertisements.*

"Mr. Chilken, this is Captain Ahren from the Office of Takazhr Command," says the unaugmented voice of the Takazhr to the left of Mr. Chilken.

Basileus retracts his face plate to reveal one of his best Court smiles and extends his hand. "Good afternoon, Mr. Chilken. I'm sorry you were pulled away from your holiday plans by the loss of your warehouses. I promise I'll be brief."

Chilken shakes Basileus's hand absently. His attention is fixed on the top of the burning warehouses. "No. No, Captain. What can I do to help?"

Basileus pulls his omnipalm off his shoulder and activates it. With a few adjustments an orbital cargo off-load manifest appears in 3D above the palm's projector. "Your firm was scheduled to receive off-load orbital cargo from a Tupolev CST VIII this morning," Basileus says, indicating the notation in the holo field with his free hand.

"That's just it. That ship never arrived. And the client paid in advance," says Chilken, his attention still consumed by the fire. "One of my associates, Larujic Birabel, had called me when they were three hours overdue and unlocatable on the space net—that was around eleven this morning. I told Lar I wouldn't worry, probably holiday delays, and besides, the client had paid in advance."

"Do you remember who the client was?" interjects Basileus offhandedly.

"No. Only that they paid in advance. Is the client under investigation?" Chilken asks with dawning suspicion. He pulls a gold cigarette case from his pocket and lights it. Basileus recognizes the sweet smell of the shinbar. Chilken takes several deep lungfuls before exhaling the thick blue cloud. Not everyone enjoys the smell, and Basileus notices one of the Takazhr activating his armor's filter. "I'm sorry," Chilken says, blushing slightly. "It relaxes me. Lar could identify the client. Have you been able to find him?"

Basileus turns to the Takazhr who dislikes the shinbar. The Takazhr shakes his head. "Mr. Chilken, I'm sorry to be the one to tell you this, but there are three bodies inside ..."

"Oh, my God! Oh, my God! Lar and Bethany ... Who's the other?" There are tears forming in the man's eyes. He desperately drags on the shinbar.

"You don't know?"

"Wha...? No ... How would I know? It's a holiday. Normally I would have closed us down, but Lar had agreed to meet the client's shipment. Beth ... Beth, she handled the records and client contacts."

He doesn't know anything. All this questioning is doing is breaking his heart. "I'm sorry about your friends. Officer Ardnez will take you through the cordon. If we have any other questions we'll contact you."

The warehouse owner nods his understanding, wiping tears from his eyes as he is led away.

Basileus activates his omnipalm to speak with his father but all he gets is static. He tries next to call his second, Bernard Al-Feza, but the comm channel is again dead. He checks his omnipalm's diagnostics and finds the machine functioning but a notice that the central Takazhr comm relay is down. Basileus waves another Takazhr over and asks to check the officer's omnipalm. He is met with the same frustrating static. Local communication is possible, but the picture is not clear and the sound is bad. The Manhattan office informs him that an intricate virus is contaminating the entire Takazhr communications network and they are trying to contact the Pinnacle. He considers logging into the Central Information Net, but fears that to do so may infect his omnipalm.

The fire, though diminished, is still keeping the firefighters busy. It will be several hours before they can enter the building and properly identify the bodies and examine whatever records survive. The ceremonies for the Uprising will begin in less than five hours. *If I hadn't found that Tene crucifix, this comm blackout wouldn't have me so on edge. But I can't help thinking now that everything is connected. In five hours the Imperial Family, a great deal of the Imperium's aristocracy, the Imperial Congress, and a majority of CIMB chairs will be gathered at the Imperios for the dedication of the Omnividome. This comm blackout could be the first step in undermining our defenses.* Basileus begins searching through the Takazhr officers to find the CSI commander, Major Cross. He finds the Major with the chiefs of the firefighters and the rescue teams.

"Excuse me, Major, sir," Basileus interrupts. The Major, a tall, dark-skinned man with the rich accent of the French district of the European precinct, turns to him. Soot from before the force fields went up has darkened his face even further.

"Captain Ahren?" says the Major. Basileus thinks momentarily how similar the soft French accent is to the dulcet tones of the Serd.

"I'm concerned with the comm blackout we're experiencing."

"Comm blackout?" says Major Cross, checking his comm unit to find the same static. Both the fire and rescue chiefs report the same thing. "My palm is giving me a virus warning."

"Probably university students playing a prank," says the rescue chief.

Basileus and the Major exchange glances, and Basileus wonders just how much the Major knows. "Major, I'd like to leave at once to report to the Pinnacle. I'll report to the Grand Kurseg and ask for the re-initialization protocols for the comm net, sir."

Although the Major is aware of who Basileus's father is, he is also aware of the anxiety in the Captain's voice. "Is there something else, Captain Ahren?"

"Sir, I think we need to recommend to command that we postpone the Uprising Ceremonies, sir," says Basileus slowly. *How do I warn Father without causing a general panic?*

"Not because of a comm glitch," says the rescue chief. Major Cross steers Basileus away from the other two. "What's going on, Captain?"

"Sir, as you know, I was attached to your command by orders from the Office of Takazhr Command. Those orders came directly from the Grand Kurseg. I'm not at liberty to divulge the nature of those orders, but I assure you, sir, it is a matter of Imperium security."

The Major studies him intently for a moment, clearly disliking being kept in the dark. "I don't like this, Captain. Go to the Pinnacle. Take my aide's skidder. Though I'm sure they're aware of the problem, report back to me as soon as possible. We're in the dark here."

Basileus salutes and nods his thanks and trots away, worst case scenarios filling his mind. He retrieves the key to the skidder from the secondary command post and rushes for the parking lot, which is empty but for the vehicles of those who chose to work during the holiday, the ERT, and the gathering media. He pulls off his helmet to better search for the skidder. The acrid smell of burnt ferrocrete and the polymers of cargo containers assault his nose. His eyes sting and tear slightly from the chemical haze, but over all this he smells the pungent odor of the shinbar. He looks around for Chilken, the hairs on the back of his neck stand up as a feeling of apprehension settles over him.

Basileus snaps back on his helmet and activates his defensive shield; soon ozone is added to the menagerie of smells, as the helmets filters clear the air. A shadow falls behind him and he hears the sound of steps through augmented ears. He turns his plasma blaster, ejecting it from its power holster into his waiting hand with a snap. There is a comforting whine as the weapon powers. He sees nothing through the right unenhanced side of the helmet. A verbal command activates the ocular sensor analysis over his left eye. Another command switches it to infrared and Basileus sees a figure charging toward him.

There is a flash of light from the red spectral image. Basileus twists his body, blinking the spots before his eyes away and there is a loud pop as his shield absorbs part of the shot and he is slammed onto the hood of the skidder behind him. Another verbal command activates adrenal enhancers. He turns and fires at the red blur that only his left eye sees. The figure ducks and spins out of the way with astounding speed and there is a burst of white fire and his ears ring with a loud boom! The enemy shoots again and Basileus is knocked head across heels over the skidder he just pulled himself from. He slaps the other side with a thud and the air is forced from him. He rolls away, under another skidder, as his pursuer scrambles over parked skidders toward him. *What I wouldn't give for a Bloodguard Hephaestus!* he thinks. He is about to give a verbal command for proximity sensors when he is pulled from his hiding space and slammed into another skidder, leaving an imprint dent. His shield flashes and crackles with the kinetic energy of the impact. Basileus instinctively attacks with his elbow. As he twirls away he shoots out his left leg to sweep his enemy off balance. Basileus then turns, aims down, and discharges his blaster furiously. There are blinding pyrotechnics from the close range assault on his assailant's shield and Basileus swears he hears a howl of rage through his augmented ears as the assassin is incinerated.

"Proximity scan for targets in stealth mode," he shouts inside his suit as he crouches down for cover. Though perspiration is occluding his vision, Basileus sees the holographic tactical display over the clear right side of the helmet; it shows the parking lot and a blinking receding form a dozen meters away and moving fast. Basileus opens fire but the figure easily sidesteps his attack and returns fire before continuing to flee with incredible speed.

"A-grav unit activate," Basileus commands, dodging two lightning-like laser attacks. He leaps up and begins firing as he passes over this second intruder. His blaster fires two shots before emptying its charge. His first shot misses, the second splashes harmlessly against the enemies shield, although for a moment the stealth field is overloaded and a black armored form is visible as it's knocked off balance.

"Takazhr down!" Basileus yells into his helmet link, correctly judging from his swift defeat of his first opponent that it was unarmored. However, he had glimpsed his new enemy's armor. It was black, Deathman black. Basileus's distress call is answered with static because the Deathman is already jamming him. Basileus points his left arm toward the Deathman's stealth field apparition, intending to use the pulse laser built into the forearm of his suit, but he is struck by what feels like dozens of tiny impacts as the arc of his a-grav assisted jump is abruptly terminated and he is thrown toward the ground. Alarms ping inside his helmet and he is presented with a series of flashing red and yellow damage indicators superimposed over his holographic tactical display.

"Divert all available power to shield," Basileus manages to yell even as he painfully slams the ground. Displays go dark as power is shunted to the shield. Basileus is knocked sideways as if a giant has kicked him in the ribs as a plasma burst detonates on his shield. He knows he is beaten as he struggles to regain his footing but there's yet another attack, and this time pulse lasers knock him down.

"Shield failure," warns his armor with the impact of the first strike. His armor manages to partially deflect the second shot but there is a burn-through and Basileus feels as if someone has poured molten lead on his right quadriceps. Strangely he doesn't cry out. The pain takes a distant second to the threat of the Deathman and the threat of his impending death. He removes a plasma grenade from his belt as the parking lot swims before him. The apparition of the Deathman is reloading the flechette blaster that knocked him to the ground.

Basileus smiles grimly. The plasma grenade will incinerate everything in a two hundred meter radius; hopefully the creature's shields are damaged enough that it won't survive the blast either. He dials for maximum blast but before he or the Deathman can act, the Deathman literally vaporizes beneath the distinctive blazing white beams of Bloodguard Hephaestus. Black spots ink Basileus vision and he thinks of Titan as he falls to the ground, wind blowing through leaves of perpetual autumnal color.

CHAPTER 22

"Our ability to communicate, to form
communities, to protect and provide for one
another is the source of our greatest power."

—Empress-Executrix Anastacia, extract from
Executive Council Minutes 16 06 21 I.C

Servospheres rise like air bubbles in water, lighting the twilight
sky. It looks like a scene from an enchanted faerie land.
Courtiers and Media laugh softly to the gentle tingle and ring
of glasses. The setting sun paints the horizon orange with great
mauve and amber clouds. The blackglass of the Capitol shines
gold in the waning light. The Pinnacle is a brilliant needle of
silver. The call of birds fills the rich salt air. Pfizer Ambros
inhales, deeply glad to be outdoors, if only for a moment. In
the hours since he was brought to the Pinnacle and told the
news of his sister's duplicity, his mother has entrusted him
with the Coventry Protocols. Coventry, a modern myth to him
until now ...

"I would prefer that you remain inside the foyer," Otto
says from behind him, interrupting his thoughts. Otto's green
eyes sweep the area around the Imperial Residence, the
manicured lawns and ancient Greco-Roman architecture so
synonymous with power. The Imperial Family has gathered for
the traditional procession to the Imperios, marking the
commencement of the Uprising Ceremonies commemorating
Naraji Ilkani's revolt against the Enslavers. This year's
ceremonies will begin with the opening of the Omnividome.

Despite the cool, off-shore breeze Otto feels the perspiration beneath his dress uniform collar. The Domina's decision has left him numb. The Takazhr Kurseg's son has been attacked ... *This is not good. Don't they see this?* Otto imagines sprouting wings and flying across the Atlantean countryside home to Marisol and Agust.

"I am sorry. I needed a minute of fresh air," Pfizer answers. He turns and acknowledges Luxvico standing beside Otto. Two armored Bloodguards nearby step away to a more discrete distance. "The skiddercade leaves in a few minutes, and it will be all holocams and interviews. What's the news from Manhattan?" Pfizer asks wearily.

"Captain Ahren has been released to his father and will attend the Uprising Ceremonies. The press is being told it was an aborted smuggling attempt," answers Luxvico, also watching the sunset.

"All these lies," interrupts Pfizer.

"A premature or invalid panic would be catastrophic. The planet's transportation infrastructure is already operating at above thirty-five percent capacity. The loss of life that would occur now could damage your mother's government almost as badly as an attack." advises the Tempeler. "Besides in view of the latest intelligence, it appears an evacuation at this juncture would be premature, as it does not appear that the opposition will strike for another eight days."

"I don't know if I believe all that. It's too good to be true," Otto mutters.

"It does seem strangely fortuitous," says Luxvico, apparently unfazed by Otto, much to Pfizer's surprise.

"You won't mind if I'm a little extra paranoid for the next few weeks. To be on the safe side?" asks Otto, still scanning the horizon. "I want to make Ensign-Praetor MacKenzie your honor guard."

"A Chosen! Why?" Pfizer demands, surprised by his own reaction. "It's because of e-mortals like him that this is happening; they should have been forbidden to breed and allowed to die out."

"MacKenzie graduated top of his class in special services and covert ops. And those marks on his face might buy you some time," replies Otto. "All of the Chosen aren't Tene, nor are they all corporate thralls of Nasir Qamar. He's a Bloodguard," says Otto irritated by Pfizer's racist outburst.

"Apologizing seems to be all I'm good for this afternoon," remarks Pfizer, turning to Otto. "Of course, whatever you think best."

"Look at it as more media spin. One of your Bloodguard is a Chosen," says Otto, his anger dissipating.

"You do not believe Secretary Goldshef's report from Manhattan?" asks Luxvico quietly.

For a moment Otto had forgotten the Tempeler was there. "It's very strange that the unarmored Deathman carried encryption chips in his skull, and that the codes allowed us to download the Unionist timetable," he answers.

"What about the raids in Dumenor and Memphis, the arrest, the uncovered weapons?" asks Pfizer hopefully, though he knows Otto's response, and deep in his heart he knows he agrees with it. But the joyous feelings of hope and relief he had felt earlier were hard to dispel. He would discuss this all with Creed and his father when time permitted.

Otto sees that Pfizer already knows his answer. "Sops. To lull us into a false sense of security before they strike.

A flight of Aurora fighters roars overhead, needle alloy composite arrowheads on engines of plasma. Fireworks explode brilliantly in their wake and the crowd around the Residence breaks into cheers, hollers, and whistles of appreciation. Then the spectacular transparent exploding spheres of antimatter displays—brilliant globes of sapphire, gold, crimson, and emerald that erupt with the sound of distant thunder rolling over the island continent. Pfizer hears people singing the Imperial Anthem. "I really think we need to tell the truth," he says slowly.

"Who do you truly believe the truth will serve right now? Your people who will die when they rush to escape this planet, or your conscience that you wish to salve?" asks Luxvico, somewhat cruelly Otto thinks. Pfizer's face actually shades; he's probably had just about enough questioning of his integrity.

"Actually, Councilor, none of those options occurred to me. I was thinking about saving lives. Saving people from being out in the street needlessly; some might be able to find shelter. Warning those who might be able to escape." Pfizer stops and looks at Lux with eyes that remind Otto of the Lion. "My greatest obligation is the safety of my people," Pfizer says with iron determination.

Otto feels a surge of pride in his friend. Pfizer turns and looks at him with the same steely determination. "As soon as the ceremonies are over, I'm making a press release," Pfizer says.

"The Domina has forbidden this. If you continue with such an action, I will report you," Otto answers, but he does not look Pfizer in the face. Continuing to stare at him, Pfizer says, "We'll both do what we have to, my friend."

"In the end, is that not all that people of good conscience can do?" Luxvico says barely above a whisper in the quiet between thunderous fireworks.

"I suppose we should be heading to the limos," Pfizer says, checking his eyechrono.

Fourteen kilometers from the Imperial Residency, in the heart of New Eden rises The Wiktor Foundation building. Aside from the Imperios, the Pinnacle, and the Hane Trade Towers no buildings stand higher, and perhaps The Wiktor Foundations building is the most impressive. The Imperios and the Hane Trade Towers are Erosi blackglass and the Pinnacle is ferrocrete and space alloy. The Wiktor Foundation however is silver- and gold-veined white marble. The top penthouse lot is covered almost entirely by deciduous forest, firs, pines and evergreens. This is the home and executive office for Savoy Wiktor when he resides on Earth.

From the windows of his office Savoy Wiktor watches as the high orbit antimatter fireworks illuminate the twilight city in dazzling spectral hues. Four three-meter holo-bubbles whisper and flicker behind him. The first shows revelers in the streets with Kate Fel of EWN covering the festivities, her sheer gown leaving nothing to the imagination. The second bubble shows the Imperial Residency, the Ambros and select guests as they prepare to make the traditional journey into the city. "This year instead of going straight to the Imperios, Anastacia will commence the Uprising Ceremonies at the new Omnividome site," reports the fatherly Walter Merrick of GNN.

The third bubble shows the great gold geodesic dome of the Omnividome, backlit by Einstein Bay, which is bridged by the Second Golden Gate. Within the dome are still more revelers, and the youthful Haight Rush and Imani Devereaux, who are interviewing pop stars, athletes, and local planetary politicians.

The fourth bubble contains currency bar graphs and stock evaluation charts following the tumult of today's markets throughout the Imperium

Katherine, who accompanied him to Otto's home earlier that afternoon, sits on the other side of the desk using an audvid link to the Wiktor AI. The holographic reflections of the bubble's numbers dance ghost-like across her face. Katherine raised Savoy after Tene Thantos Deathmen killed his parents. She told him everything would be all right, that he could always count on her support. She had helped him protect his fortune from the vultures that sought to devour the Wiktor Foundation assets in the wake of his parent's death. Aware of his attention now, Katherine pushes the audvid link away from her left eye and smiles. Savoy waves a hand for her to continue what she is doing. He gets up from the desk and goes to the windows where the fireworks continue to crackle and burst above the city in glorious celebration.

A high-level informant in the Takazhr has informed him that the smuggling attempt was traced to the Ellis Island Cosmodome Annex. And the media is calling this a successful arrest. *'Two Tene Thantos agents—one certainly a Deathman—attacked two Takazhr officers, killing at least one.' And of course there's been not a whisper in the news about the Tene Thantos, just as when they savagely killed his parents.* Savoy has been cultivating a relationship with Pfizer Ambros, the next Emperor-Executor, in hopes that Pfizer will prove to be the ally he needs to expose the Tene Thantos and crush them at last. Surely Pfizer must know what's going on. Savoy finds it difficult to believe that the idealistic man will remain silent.

Savoy has decided to confront Pfizer with his findings at the ceremonies tonight. He turns and picks up his black bow tie from the desk and ties it using his reflection in the windows. He runs a comb through fire gold hair and replaces it in his tuxedo's jacket pocket.

"Ready?" asks Katherine behind him. "You know, you could take a much younger companion, have more fun," she says as he helps her into a full-length coat of Erosi seal leather.

No. With all the Tene Thantos activity on Earth, Savoy wouldn't dream of letting Katherine out of his sight. And what could be safer than attending the opening of the Omnividome with the Imperial Family?

CHAPTER 23

My people have changed their glory for what does
not profit.

—Jeremiah 2:11 Judeo-Orange Codex

Princess Oriana Ambros watches New Eden beneath the glow
of incandescent fireworks. In less than two hours the city will
be under another bombardment. She has not been allowed to
travel with the Imperial Family to the opening ceremonies of
the Uprising at the Omnividome. She has remained at the
Imperios and will leave with her Bloodguards and a delegation
from the Ilkani Church. Through this same window she
watched the dawn on the day of Pfizer's speech at O'Meara.
Now she watches the sun slowly set as antimatter fireworks
make pale imitations in the twilight sky.

"They are beautiful," says Jovion Quiso beside her. She'd
told her Bloodguards to admit him without announcement,
and he'd quietly joined her while she was lost in her thoughts.
The Baron is dressed in a formal black tuxedo with a silver silk
sash bearing the Quiso crest.

Oriana finds herself remembering the first time she
watched antimatter fireworks. She had watched them from this
very window; it had been a New Year's celebration. Her father
had scooped her into his arms and leaned against the window
so they could feel the vibrations of the detonations through the
great window. They had laughed. And here in the now she still
smells the cologne he'd worn as he held her in his arms. She
bites her inner lip to distract her from the tears she feels

forming.

"Your family and their guests are boarding their limos and they are about to leave the Residence," Jovion says unobtrusively. He puts his hand over hers, the look in his eyes worried and compassionate.

"Jovion, I ...," she begins.

"I know this must be hard. But what choice did you really have?" he says slowly, continuing to study her with the same inviting warmth. "Did you really want to spend the next five hundred years on that rock?" He leans up against her and she can feel the heat emanating from him. She has been so lonely.

"You will never be alone again. You will be adored," he whispers to her unspoken fears, and his lips caress her ear. Oriana is suddenly overcome with passion, and she kisses Jovion.

The so-called First City of the Imperium, New Eden, glows and vibrates with celebration. When Millian and Anastacia board the limos the smiles on their faces are fixed, inspired emoto-control, but the sincere joy of the people is infectious. They stop outside the gates of the Residence much to the chagrin of Creed and Cato. School children serenade Millian and Anastacia, showering them both with flowers. Anastacia bursts into laughter amidst the rose, tulip, daisy, and orchid petals. Anastacia steps out into the crowd, accepting hugs and kisses from her adoring public. Millian restrains the Bloodguard when they surge forward to encircle her. This is what the Omnividome is about, connection to her people.

Back in the limo, Anastacia notices Millian's silence as he watches her. "What?" she asks, still smiling radiantly.

"I just like watching you," Millian says, feeling his cheeks color. "Especially when you are sincerely happy." Spontaneously, she leans over and kisses him.

"I have always been happy when I'm with you," Anastacia says and though Millian knows this cannot possibly be true, right now it seems as if they have always been happy. "It would have been better had the day begun now instead of the way it did," Anastacia says, turning to look at the coastline speeding by.

"I'm very proud of Pfizer," says Millian taking her hand. "He'll make a fine Emperor-Executor; he seems to have taken the best from both of us."

"Really?" asks Anastacia, turning toward him. "I'm not surprised Pfizer spoke of compromise and reconciliation, but you know he's usually much more adamant." *More like you, my love.*

Millian frowns. "Our son's not done with us yet. Did you see the grim looks on the Tempeler's and Otto Buchanan's faces when they got into the skidder? At first I couldn't place the look. Then when Creed and I were discussing evacuating—"

"Millian, I thought I—." Anastacia stops as Millian's face hardens. "That was the look you saw." He nods.

"We are leaving after this, Ana. A goodwill tour to see the Omnividome applied throughout the Imperium. It's good press."

"And safely aboard the Imperial Flagship, together, we win."

"We win," Millian says. He leans back in his seat. He looks at his wife and notices the smile on her lovely face has faded to one of sad contemplation. "What's wrong?" he whispers.

"I suddenly wonder if we'll ever reach the flagship," she responds.

* * *

Basileus and Cato have enjoyed a quiet ride together in the Takazhr Command skimmer. Sitting in the executive bay they can see the lights of the a-grav-powered entourage as it speeds under firework-dazzled purple twilight. Monitors continue to blink and hiss as the virus is cleared from the system. Basileus scratches around the bone healer braced partially over his right thigh and knee. He can walk without a cane or crutches and the only sources of discomfort are a few bruises and a burning itch in his leg.

Cato, at Lomin's prompting from Redwood, dispatched the

royal Bloodguard from the Embassy, a squad bristling with weapons and armor. They found Basileus under attack in the parking lot and responded viciously. The Deathman never stood a chance. Basileus's father was at his side when he regained consciousness and he has not left him since. Considering the crisis, Cato seems strangely serene. Basileus observes his quiet watchfulness. *Maybe he's just resigned.*

"You and Lomin will return to the *Bismarck* immediately following the opening ceremonies," says Cato. "I will follow with the Empress-Executrix and First Lord."

"What about the Scion and the Princesses?" asks Basileus, a feeling of dread pushing past the halcyon contentment induced by energy pills.

Instinctively Cato glances at the green lights of the bay's spy shield indicator. "Eros to HaneHome, we're here," says Cato, standing and adjusting his black dress uniform with gold piping. Basileus stands as the great geodesic Omnividome dominates the bubble view from the skimmer's bay. Skidders and TAVs hover around the dome like a myriad of fireflies. People on the ground with hololights make an Earthly reflection of the stars overhead. The Ambros' skiddercade, a red and blue river of stars, makes its way through the galaxy of people on the ground toward the entrance of the Omnividome. Suddenly the dome lights throw a great beam of light heavenward and above the dome, the clouds shine as though the Moon has just risen beneath them. Basileus adjusts the medals and commendations on his father's uniform and then Cato inspects his son's.

"Magnificent," whispers Cato, viewing the Omnividome, a monument to the Ambros credo: "Cooperation is superior to competition." Nearly a million planetary and system governments will have their electorates instalinked to the great dome. Legislation and referendum that had taken weeks can now be done in hours, another step toward the democracy the Ambros have sought to change the Imperium into.

The Imperial Family is moving up the front steps of the Omnividome entrance plaza—Empress-Executrix Anastacia and the First Lord, the Crown Scion Pfizer with his sister, the Imperial Princess Gabrielle. Following them is the Imperial Princess Zoe. Around them armored and decorated Bloodguard in white and red dress uniforms, the gold phoenix badge of the Imperial House on their right shoulders. As Anastacia enters the plaza more lights burst on and still more fireworks erupt into the sky. The Monarch's Herald plays as she and her family approach a podium. The crowd begins chanting her name, "Anastacia, Anastacia, Anastacia." Giant holo broadcast images of Anastacia began relaying throughout and around the crowd. The applause is thunderous. Cato and Basileus both activate subcutaneous aud-links and with quick adjustments mute the deafening background cheers. Anastacia seemed to be making adjustments to her own audvid link so she could hear herself speak. She lifted her arms and began to wave and still the thunder grows, "Anastacia! Anastacia! Anastacia!" they cheer.

"Noble citizens of the Imperium, Peace and greetings wherever you are." The voice of Anastacia rises over the crowd like the voice of God over the celestial choirs. "My family and I thank you for being here with us tonight as we usher in a new age. A new age of communication, understanding, and democracy."

"The Omnividome is already transmitting to households across the galaxy. In minutes it will be transmitting to your very omnipalms." Anastacia turns and enters the dome while the holo screens outside track her progress inside.

Assur-Banipal Orani, Magus of the Ilkani Church, waits near the entrance to the Omnividome with the Church's delegation. The Daakan has to keep pushing back the exuberant crowd. He speaks subvocally through a throat microphone; it is impossible to hear amidst the jubilant celebrants. "Must we really go inside that deathtrap?" he asks, addressing his son Reza-Fahd, who is adorned in full regalia as a Prelate of the Church.

"You must give a prayer of thanks before the Uprising Ceremonies ...," says Reza-Fahd looking heavenward. *In moments the first bombs will begin going off in military bases, aboard ships in orbit, and in government buildings here on the ground.*

"How much time will we have, my son?" asks the Magus.

"Twenty minutes after the Uprising Ceremonies begin. Come Father, it's our delegation's turn to enter." Reza-Fahd gathers his cassock so it doesn't gather dust from the ground, his other hand guiding his father's elbow as the Ilkani procession, every bit as regal as that of the Ambros, begins to enter the Omnividome. What began as a night to celebrate a New Age, will be remembered as one of the darkest in history.

CHAPTER 24

Virtue cannot exist, will not exist, without
violence.

—Oriana Ambros, *The Book of Sorrows*

Admiral Sir Nicodemus Von Haagen Zhao, Admiral of the
Black, Knight Commander of the Order of Saint Ekaterina,
watches the celebrations on Earth beneath him. The central
screen of his flagship the Dreadnought ISN *Guderian* projects
holo images from San Francisco, Tokyo, New Mecca, Pretoria,
New London, New Eden, Josephus, and Nova Roma. "Turn it
off, Julian," the Admiral says wearily to his communications
officer. "We'll be hearing their distress calls soon enough.
Switch to tactical displays."

Holopicts of Earth blink into digitalgraphic and VR
displays of the planet and its orbit, ships, and environs. It will
be easier to view them all as multi-colored symbols and
alphanumerics than as real-life images.

He has strategically reassigned or sent on leave every
questionable officer. At the appointed time all the crew
deemed untrustworthy will be locked down in their quarters.
When he handed Anastacia the victory in the Anangan Star
System, at the cost of fifteen thousand Naval lives, she had
made him a Knight Commander and then continued her
insane plan to dismantle the very Imperium he lived to protect.
All those lives wasted. How many more lives would the
Empress-Executrix waste, trusting in the nonexistent innate
goodness of Humanity?

I am no traitor. I am saving the universe I love. Even if I don't survive this battle, my journals will, he thinks as he closes his left eye in time to see the digital display on his eyelid count down to zero.

"Admiral, multiple fusion and anti-matter explosions in orbit and on planet," reports the Comm officer. Even though the man knew the detonations were coming there is still genuine horror in his voice.

"Red Alert. On screen!" commands Zhao. The blue-green, white-wisped planet below blossoms ugly sores of white that flare to orange and then boiling clouds of black. In orbit it is as if the very stars themselves have visited apocalyptic explosions as his fellow officers burn and die—all because of this misguided family.

"Alert all Naval Units. This is a planetary distress signal from the planet Earth ...," begins the tritone voice of the Imperial Fleet AI.

"Shut it off!" orders Zhao.

The voice of the Central Naval artificial intelligence goes dead, whether from the destruction of Luna Base or Zhao's order, he does not care. "Order all advance sensor drones to intercept or jam all transmissions from Pinnacle Command. Launch all interceptor and bomber squadrons," Zhao commands. "Order Orbital Bombardment to cover our ground forces and bring us in to orbit above the capital."

"Ground forces are launching. First strike command reports we have eliminated ninety percent of enemy assets in place. Transferring command protocols to your flag Admiral," reports the Comm Officer. The bridge is bathed in crimson light, white- and blue-uniformed Naval personal perform their duties as if this were an exercise instead of an invasion of the Home World. On screen Qamar Long Range Autohaulers begin launching ground forces.

* * *

With the first thunder-like explosion Creed realizes that his worst fears have come to pass. Instinctively, he turns his eyes skyward towards the location of the blast. Full-fledged a-mat detonations are going off in orbit and the light streaming through the dome truly makes it daylight. The ground rumbles and the very air shakes. His second glance is not toward his brother and the Empress-Executrix, but the family seats where Bloodguards of the Hane protect his beloved Kiritzia and his son Aaron. Already, as planned, they are shielding his family with their armored bodies and moving them toward an exit. Creed turns to his brother. Millian's eyes are still skyward, his eyes wide in shock. *He knew this could happen. I begged him, warned him*, is the only thing Creed thinks for a moment.

Millian's attention seems drawn by what looks like thousands of slowly descending red fireflies.

"High orbit a-grav parachutes," yells General Praetor Houka Jamal, drawing his Hephaestus and extending it to battle pike. "Close ranks, CombatMecha units, intercept. Royal and Diplo armored, remain with your charges," Jamal commands amidst the growing screams and shouts of the terrified celebrants. Armored CombatMecha Bloodguard and Takazhr in flyer mode take to flight toward the slowly falling red lights like angry bees. The crimson arcs of Deathmen Zeiss and the white arcs of Bloodguard Hephaestus begin intersecting and the electric blue of shield flares fills the air, along with what sounds like the groaning and cracking of a great sheet of ice. "The Dome!" Jamal shouts. The orange fusion of plasma guns and the green and red of lasers crisscross the night; explosions burst above the ground

Despite being shielded, Creed ducks and covers his head with his right arm but is showered with shards of polymer from the ruined dome. There are displays of blue pyrotechnics all along the ground floor as debris bounces harmlessly off those lucky enough to be shielded. Hundreds are not so fortunate. The Lion stands, shakes off debris, and grips his Hephaestus like a rifle, sighting down its axis. There are cracks of thunder and the white beam of antimatter plasma lances out each shot like a bolt of lightning. The shields of the falling Deathmen flash briefly before being incinerated by what the Bloodguard call, "the fire of heaven." The Lion tosses aside his spent Hephaestus and pulls another from his dress uniform. One of his personal Bloodguards pulls him down. Creed hears the fury of Zeiss beams hissing and crackling on the Bloodguard's shield. Helplessly, Creed is ushered away by armor-enhanced muscles. He twists his head desperately, trying to catch sight of his brother through the rapidly growing smoke and fire of the battle.

He'd last seen Millian staring up at the sky, a mixture of abject fury and despair on his face. *If they're trying to get me to safety, is it because Millian is dead?*

* * *

When the first explosion turns night into day and the screaming begins, Millian hurls himself over Anastacia, folding his body over hers to shield her from falling debris. *I must get her to safety.* As he pulls himself off her he looks into her gray eyes, but all he sees is concern for him. He pulls her to her feet.

"Love always. I love you," he says, hugging her and activating her body shield. With that he can no longer touch her, as they are inexorably forced apart by her shield. He sees the dawning realization of his intentions on Anastacia's face, and it's unbearable. A scream builds and builds in his heart. He activates his own shield.

"GET HER OUT!" he commands, pushing her into the arms of her honor guard. He glimpses her brief struggle measured in half seconds as she is surrounded by six armored Bloodguard. Over the noise of the battle, he hears her scream his name, but he must force such thoughts from his mind. *She will be safe,* he thinks desperately. Next, he turns to look for Pfizer, who he sees with Counselor Luxvico and Captain Praetor Buchanan, crouched behind a firing line of armored Bloodguard. *The girls, where are the girls?* Millian wonders franticly. He isn't sure, but he believes he hears Zoe call for him. Millian looks in that direction and thinks he sees his daughters being led by armored Bloodguards through an exit.

The growing battle smoke is making normal vision nearly impossible. He spots his brother angrily shooting invaders from the sky before one of the Hane Bloodguard knock Creed to the ground. Millian activates his subvocal but the tie to his brother cracks with static. Millian hears loud popping sounds from above him and suddenly he is showered by clear polymer from the collapsing dome. In the sky he sees armored landing craft. He tries another channel. "Anyone in the Hane Bloodguard, respond?" Bloodguard throughout the dome who receive the signal recognize the source. Multiple responses assault Millian's ears but through them all, he picks out one voice. "Major Battaglia, get my brother to safety. Retreat into space and crush this insurrection! That's a direct order. Tell Captain Buchanan to get my son out of here!" he shouts.

A perverse rage fills him as his Bloodguards try to move him toward one of the now embattled exits. "No! I must draw their attack here! Get them to concentrate here while my family escapes. Release me!" Millian roars. An armored Bloodguard with the red and blue of a Vice Regal House on his shoulders steps before him. "My charges are dead," he snaps bitterly. "I am General Praetor Jakob Meir, what are your orders?" he says with the amplified voice of his armor.

"Find heavy weapons. Those landing craft must not reach the surface. If you can't find them, have Bloodguard combine their Hephaestus fire and dispiks. And get me a proper suit of armor!!!" The First Lord commands.

As Bloodguard scramble to obey his orders, the first Deathmen reach the surface and many of the survivors later wonder why Millian DeHaaven Hane, first Lord of the Imperium, a General Praetor of the Bloodguard begins to laugh. But he is thinking, *My family is safe. My family is safe.*

* * *

Pfizer's eyes are blinded by tears with the first explosions. Dreams of reconciliation and peace die as he watches the first fusion- and antimatter-powered beams cross the sky. He moves instinctively toward his parents but is knocked down by the armored form of Heath MacKenzie, his honor guard. Heath pins Pfizer for what seems like an eternity, despite his cries that he be let up, that he must get to the Empress, his mother. Pfizer grows silent when he hears the first Zeiss beams and plasma burst sputter off Heath's armor. *His kind are responsible for this! Damn all Chosen to Hell!* he thinks, as he struggles and demands to be released. Heath makes no move to lessen his protective grip but over the deafening battle noise Pfizer hears his armored augmented voice saying, "You'll survive" over and over again like some crazy mantra. Suddenly the honor guard pulls him up like a rag doll and snaps a heavy combat shield on his forearm and activates it.

"Don't move," he commands, still keeping his body between Pfizer and most of the pandemonium that is the Omnividome. Pfizer sees his parents' emotional separation as his mother is sped off into the fiery night. He sees his sisters being ushered through one of the subground exits before the exit is destroyed in orange and red plasma explosions whose concussive blasts knock all but the high-grav'd down. His ears still ringing, Pfizer is lifted by Heath. Pfizer sees his father's heroic command of the Bloodguard before he is pulled back down, his shield crackling against the Bloodguard's. Pfizer remembers he has a subvocal mic and activates it. "Otto, we have to get my father out of here," he yells.

Otto, hunched behind a group of armored family Bloodguards shooting their Hephaestus, blasters, and dispiks skyward, grabs his right ear in pain. He turns quickly toward Pfizer and makes a sharp angry gesture. Luxvico, next to Pfizer with an armored Bloodguard of his own behind him, jams his face into Pfizer's.

"Let Captain Praetor Buchanan do his job. Our lives depend on it," Luxvico shouts.

"People, we are leaving," Otto's voice orders over Pfizer's

aud. Pfizer is jerked up by Heath despite his resistance.

"Otto, I'm not going anywhere without my father," Pfizer screams. Even though the shield allows him some movement he cannot escape the Bloodguard. Luxvico pushes up against Pfizer again.

"Listen," the Tempeler demands. "Activate your aud to multi-channel and for your father's sake, listen!"

Pfizer eases his struggle against Heath and adjusts the receiver below his left ear. Over the plasma burst and high-pitched whines of particle beams he hears embattled Bloodguard and Takazhr—

"... losing ground. Request permission to ..."

"Dead, all commanding ..."

"Pinned down. No..."

"We have no orbital support here. Do not fall back to this."

"We can't hold..."

—And between the desperate shouts of the forces of law and order Pfizer hears the far more numerous encrypted static of alien transmissions, enemy transmissions, the Deathmen.

* * *

They are trying to kill me! Damn me for a fool for ever trusting them! They're trying to kill me! thinks Assur-Banipal Orani, Magus of the Ilkani Church, as he flees madly for his life, his robes billowing behind him.

Homo Deus, the Chosen—Fek, they are Homo Nemesis, Homo Diabolicus. He stumbles but his son behind him rights him, urges him onward while the Omnividome dome collapses. Assur-Banipal turns his head for a quick glance to see the once beautiful gold geodesic broken like an eggshell, the sky above it alive with the polychromatics of weapons fire and bright exploding bursts of their targets.

God, I have sided with the devil. May Ilkani the Prophet intervene for my soul, he prays. Outside the ruined Omnividome the situation is marginally better than inside, but even so bedlam rules. The celebrants have become an insane mob frantically trying to seek cover. The great city of New Eden burns all around him. The Pinnacle looks like the flaming sword barring entry to the mythical first Eden. Another wave of remorse and guilt causes him to stumble once more. Amidst the screams and the chaos he realizes, *I have my answer*, and he is wracked with sobs as he runs for his life.

CHAPTER 25

Be careful what you wish for and what you believe in.

—Oriana Ambros, *The Book of Sorrows*

The concussion from one of the suborbital blasts shatters the picture window in front of which Oriana and Jovion were standing, knocking them to the ground. As the countdown neared zero Jovion backed her away from the window, but not quickly enough. Now, lifting her up from shards of high-density glass, he looks at the city outside. The Pinnacle, the Omnividome, the Hane Trade Towers, the Imperial Congress, Wiktor Foundation. They are all burning. A host of secondary fires burn from the initial attack on the primary targets.

The building rocks again and the lights go out as both of their armored Bloodguard squads burst through the iris into the room. Firelight from the smashed window eerily lights their shields and armor. Jovian begins a countdown in his head.

"Major? Aren't those blasts coming from above?" Jovion Quiso asks in his dulcet Serdian tone.

"My scanner is being jammed," says one of the armored retinue.

Weapons whine as they are powered up, shields flicker, flash blue into firmer existence. Quiso throws his body over Oriana as howling Deathmen wearing a-grav harnesses drop in through the broken window.

Oriana feels the air above her cook with the violent exchange of the combatants; the floor vibrates with the detonation of hand-held explosives. A charred chunk that sure is, or was, an armored Bloodguard's head rolls before her obstructed view and she screams. As quickly as it began, it is over, and she hears someone addressing Quiso.

"My lord, it is done," shouts a voice strung-out and crazed with the barely controlled frenzy of tursapoi addiction.

Oriana picks herself up and sees her first Deathman out of the histories she'd studied. The Deathmen wear stylized black battle armor. Cruel studs and sharp projections cover every part of the body that can conceivably be used as a weapon. They carry a Zeiss similar to the Bloodguard Hephaestus, plasma blasters and rifles, grenade launchers, and flechette hand cannons. They begin stripping the Bloodguards of their weaponry and other *things*. More Deathmen enter through the window, rushing like deadly screaming black shadows into the Imperios.

※ ※ ※

"We must leave for the *Bismarck*, Cato," states Lomin calmly despite the mayhem on the screens and in the holographic displays around them. Many of the monitors show static— their comm-eye relays to the command skidder destroyed. Anger boils in Cato Ahren. The Tempeler's cowardly suggestion for retreat to the command skidder initially seemed like the best strategic and overall tactically sound idea for survival. However, his own survival conflicts with his overall mission of defending the Imperial family, of protecting the rights of citizens and their property.

My friends, my people are dying, while I wait in the relative safety of the command skimmer with a full cohort of the Ahren Bloodguard and two platoons of Takazhr protecting it.

"I know you want to help your family and friends, help the Empress-Executrix, but the best way to do that is to remain alive, My lord," continues the monotone voice of the old Tempellian Counselor. Lomin's eyes urgently search Cato's furious aquiline features for some sign that he is getting through.

"There are still more than a thousand Aristos, thousands of Citizos in what's left of the Omnividome," Cato answers, trying to remain calm as he indicates a long-range passive scanner's holographics tactical display. Blue and silver dots wink out amongst an overwhelming number of red dots." The First Lord is still in there!" he says, pointing at a gold blip behind vanishing purple blips. "The Crown Scion just went off our scanner."

"Went off the scanner, Cato? It wasn't disconnected," says the small thin man quietly. He stands calmly beneath the mountain of volcanic rage that the Takazhr Kurseg is becoming.

"I could find him. With an active scan. I could," sputters Cato.

"An active scan would be traced, and the traitors in orbit would launch a strike," replies Lomin with his infuriating calm.

Lomin is right. Cato has seen several Bloodguard and Takazhr units suffer swift destruction from orbit for traceable transmissions or brief active scans. "How do you know the *Bismarck* is even still in orbit? Or do you think Fleet Grand Admiral Tanenov is hiding, too?" Cato snaps. The light of distant explosions flicker in the command skimmer's observation bay, several more of the relayed combat scenes turn to static, as if making Lomin's point.

"If she is hiding, my lord, that is why she is the Grand Admiral. Cato, can't you see?"

"Kurseg Ahren," interrupts a dark-skinned, uniformed Takazhr officer at one of the observation bay's stations. "Your Bloodguard Commander wishes to speak with you immediately." The Takazhr's brows are beaded with perspiration, his eyes wide in shock from the night's events.

At that moment General Praetor Pieter Hane-Mugabe Hamar, commanding officer of the Ahren family Bloodguard, barges in, shoving an armored Takazhr guard aside.

General Praetor Hamar is nearly as tall as Cato but has a heavier build. A native of Eros, he has the typical pale blue eyes of his Hane cousins. General Hamar is famous for his steadfast calm and deadly abilities, abilities he proved during the Anangan Insurrection. Right now he displays little more control than Cato. He breathes heavily having pushed his way past an armored Takazhr. "Grand Kurseg Ahren, I demand to know your intentions!" he shouts in his deep baritone, tinged with the guttural accent of the Ultima Thule Highlands. Distant explosions continue outside the dome, casting menacing shadows. The bay rumbles from the concussions. Never has the loyal Bloodguard addressed him this way, but given the circumstances ... "You have adequate protection here. Permission to take all but a phalanx of your Bloodguard to attempt to retrieve the First Lord!"

Lomin drops his head. "It will not make a difference; you will die as well," he almost whispers.

"Be silent, Tempellian!" yells General Praetor Hamar, turning on Lomin in his frustrated anger. "Your intentions, sir," he says whirling back to face Cato.

"As you were," Cato says icily, putting every bit of authority in his voice from a hundred years of being a Viceroy.

We are wasting time. This calls for desperate measures, Lomin decides. "General! Cato! Look at me!" shouts the ancient Tempeler.

The two men turn toward Lomin in shock at his display of emotion. To both of them the room seems to darken until there are only the three of them in darkness. Lomin also seems to fade becoming ghostlike except for his bird bright eyes. Suddenly the darkness becomes a panoramic view around them.

A montage of scenes appear before their eyes. First they are on the terrace of a skyscraper in a great city. Skidders and hovercraft zoom and flit through a brilliant blue sky. Suddenly there is a burst of white light in the distance and the city literally melts and withers before completely vaporizing. Then they see great forests and oceans, majestic mountains, pristine deserts, great flowering fields—indescribably beautiful vistas from what seem to be hundreds of worlds—fouled, polluted, and laid to waste in seconds by antimatter and fusion annihilation or endless particle beams, lasers, and bombs. They see enormous orbital habitats and immense drift

*cities burst and explode, exposing their inhabitants to the cold vacuum of
space. Great space fleets wage unremitting war and in the end battered,
charred, glowing hulks litter space.*

Cato realizes there is one thing all the tragedies bear in
common: senseless waste, death, and destruction.

*You see, Cato? You see the things I have seen. This is the way it
started before,* Lomin shows them in their minds.

Reality returns. Both men are swaying on their feet. Lomin
sags wearily in his a-grav accoutrements. "We've got to get out
of here," Cato mumbles, looking up at Lomin with awe
growing in his eyes.

"This Tempeler's telepathic tricks are not enough of a
reason to flee and abandon your Empress," grunts General
Praetor Hamar, shaking his head, trying to clear his thoughts
from the telepathic contact; he eyes Lomin with frightening
suspicion.

"Pieter, I understand your sense of duty to the Crown. I
feel it, too ... but we have a greater responsibility to the
Imperium. We must get off Earth, warn the other members of
the BloodCircle, anyone who can contest Oriana's claim to the
throne," says Cato, as another distant explosion shakes the
command skimmer and fills the bay with threatening light.

"You implicate the Princess Oriana in this?!" demands the
Bloodguard, his hand going automatically to his Hephaestus.

"Lomin is carrying data from the most recent session of the
Executive Security Committee. Look at it," Cato says quickly,
instinctively placing himself between Lomin and the angry
Bloodguard.

Lomin calmly goes to one of the static-filled bubbles and
merely touches it. Images and words pour from the display.

The Bloodguard Praetor General puts on an audvid link to
faster absorb the information. Within moments he sighs
heavily, taking off the link. "Your Highness, Prince Cato. I
apologize for my behavior. What are your orders, my lord?"

Cato clasps a hand on the man's shoulder, forgiving him.
"First we must find a way off planet. Then, only then, will we
attempt to locate the beacons for surviving members of the

Imperial family."

The Bloodguard shakes his head looking at the chaos on the relays. "How?" is all he asks.

"There are courier vessels at the Tempellian Embassy in Nevada, fast courier vessels," answers Lomin.

* * *

They had jumped through a broken window on the fourth floor of the Omnividome, all ground exits either destroyed or embattled. Pfizer saw half of the Bloodguards assigned to his protection killed in less than fifteen minutes after their a-grav assisted escape. Now he watches the Omnividome burning from behind the cover of shrubberies in one of the gardens outside. Civilian bodies litter the grounds along with dead and wounded defenders. Cries for help pierce the night, discernible only between the explosions and bursts of energy from weapons fire.

"We have to get out here!" Rachel Tsimpo screams on the verge of hysterics, snapping Pfizer out of his terror.

"You *bitch!*" Pfizer shouts. "You're under arrest for treason...," he begins, trying to crawl toward her before being restrained by the ever-vigilant Heath.

"Your Royal Highness, please be still," the Bloodguard whispers.

"I don't—," Doctor Tsimpo begins, her eyes wide in shock. *I am going to die in this miserable place,* she thinks.

"Spare us your fekking lies!" Pfizer snaps. "I'd have you strangled now if I didn't intend to use you as a witness," he says, surprising even himself with his murderous statement.

To Luxvico, Rachel seems like an animal, caught in a ground vehicle's headlights. She looks to each of them desperately for some sign of support, but all she gets are at best dispassionate stares, at worst unfettered hatred. Luxvico realizes he has allowed his contempt for her to display itself on his face. He suppresses the urge to carry out Pfizer's suggestion, his expression returning to its normal look of disinterested neutrality.

"How did you intend to escape?" he asks, and the night seems to grow quieter as whispers amongst them stop and many lean close to hear Rachel's response.

Sitting in the dirt, hiding behind bushes, her clothes and hair in disarray, make-up smudged and running, Rachel Tsimpo starts shaking. *It wasn't supposed to be like this. I was supposed to have had another twenty minutes before the attack began. What happened? Is there still a way out for me in Stratadeen Park?* she wonders.

At that moment Pfizer is aware of a new intensity generating from Luxvico.

"What is in Stratadeen Park?" Luxvico asks her.

Rachel tenses involuntarily. She hadn't said a word about Stratadeen Park. *Telepathy.* Her hand goes to the pendant concealing her T-shield, but the pendant is gone, undoubtedly lost in the fighting.

What's in Stratadeen Park?! Luxvico seems to shout inside her head, an intense migraine-like pain makes her cry out. Instinctively, she imagines the TAV supposedly waiting to take her safely into orbit.

"A TAV in Stratadeen Park?" Luxvico says to Otto, who watches both Dr. Tsimpo and him with a comprehending expression.

Otto nods. "It's too small. Counselor, I thought you said—" Otto begins.

"I never read your thoughts," Luxvico says quietly. This appears to satisfy Otto.

"Good, I am glad you two resolved that," Pfizer says with bitter sarcasm. "Now kill her! Kill her now, Otto!" Pfizer shouts pointing at Rachel.

"What?" Luxvico and Otto ask simultaneously, shocked.

He's gone mad, Luxvico realizes, and is surprised at his dismay and sorrow. *We don't need this now.*

"Domino, we still have to find some way off planet. We might need her," Otto says, before turning to check in with his perimeter guards. There are peals of thunder and the sky flashes with lightning.

"There goes the Weather Modification Network," someone says as a cold October rain begins to pour.

As rain flickers on shields, there is another swift, violent exchange of weapons fire as hidden combatants are revealed. Pfizer is again pushed into the dirt by Heath, who at least this time mumbles an apology.

"We're going to have to move again. Our left perimeter's being turned," Otto whispers.

"Where?" asks an armored Bloodguard, his armor scorched and burnt from shield burn-throughs.

"Nevada," offers Luxvico.

"What's in Nevada?" asks the tired voice of another Bloodguard.

"The Tempellian Embassy; there are three courier vessels."

"Nevada's practically on the other side of the planet, and what makes you think your embassy wasn't hit. Thirty-six cities are known to be under attack. Armstrong on Luna and even Nix Olympia on Mars," interjects the Bloodguard with the burn-damaged armor.

"The Tempellian Embassy wasn't attacked," replies Lux with bitter certainty, thinking of his world's tacit approval of this holocaust by their silence. "We can try taking the subsurface hyperrails to one of the Atlantic MerCities and from there we can make the eastern seaboard off the North American continent," he finishes, as the survivors draw near, gaining hope from his plan.

Otto, realizing for the first time that their chances of surviving are improving, finds his thoughts turning to Marisol and Agust. It was doubtful that the fighting encroached on any of the suburbs, and with any luck the Erosi Embassy will have warned its citizens of safe havens or evacuation points.

Please, let the Erosi try to evacuate their people, he thought, turning to check on Pfizer who sat huddled and shaking from the cold rain and who knows what else.

"The Counselor's plan works for me," Otto says, pulling his omnipalm from his pocket and activating it as he crouches down, trying to obscure it with his body while he scans through a series of preprogrammed holographic maps. He finally stops at one and motions the two Bloodguards with him to examine his find. "This is a map of the subsurface hyperrails. There should be a functioning entrance less than half a kilometer that way," Otto says, nodding in the direction of what appears to be heavy fighting.

* * *

In the chilly wet October night Anastacia's six Bloodguard including General Praetor Houka Jamal race her to an evac TAV outside the Omnividome. Before she can even be suited into standard Bloodguard cybernetic battle armor, Jamal decides the situation in orbit is too dangerous for the TAV. He wants at least a fighter or armored shuttle to get her into orbit. Bloodguards in GAV-mode CombatMecha armor who had made up part of the skiddercade try to escort the TAV to the Dumenor Bay government space port there, but they turn away because a fusion torpedo from orbit has just vaporized the area. In the TAV, Houka's armored head drops in dismay as he ·witnesses the destruction of their destination. *The Navy's been compromised; the enemy has orbital support.*

"Where to, General?" asks the armored TAV pilot.

"Orbit. We go for the *Bismarck*. Then we see if we can go back for the First Lord," Houka says, turning to see the CombatMecha Bloodguards outside the TAV windows reconfigure into flyers and follow the TAV up into the atmosphere.

All Anastacia can do is think of Millian. Millian waking in the morning and brushing her hair back from her face to kiss her. Millian holding Oriana or Pfizer. Millian in his workroom at the Imperios. Millian resplendent in his dress uniform on the grounds of HaneHome.

The memories threaten to overwhelm her and she sways in her seat attempting to hold back a tide of unbearable sorrow. When she takes a deep breath, trying to stiffen her resolve, she smells his cologne on her and she begins sobbing again. The harder she fights the ache in her chest the more the suffering that threatens to consume her. *Millian,* she thinks. *Millian, Millian.*

The TAV rocks and bumps as it clears the upper atmosphere and the pure star-spotted blackness of space fills the cockpit. Strangely, now Anastacia's thoughts turn toward Pfizer and she wonders, if he does survive, will the experience drive her beautiful son, her only son mad?

"General, we have multiple incoming!" announces the TAV pilot as the small pod-like vehicle lurches from evasive action. "Type and source?" demands Houka.

"Anti-fighter kinetic missiles! FOF identifier says it's the Dreadnought ISN *Guderian*!"

The TAV does another series of maneuvers. Then one of the Bloodguards launches his CombatMecha flyer into the path of an oncoming missile. In a fiery flash it disintegrates him and his CombatMecha. The resulting shockwave sends the other CombatMecha into another of the deadly missiles.

The TAV is thrown end-over-end, thrusters firing as the pilot tries to orient the tiny craft but cannot ...

"I failed you. Domina, I'm sorry, so sorry," Houka yells in the spinning craft.

Houka can't see Anastacia's tear-streaked smile beneath her armor, and as the fire and light of the TAV's destruction consume her, she whispers Millian's name and goes to find him in the Light.

One single thought from her childhood pervades her mind: *In the Beginning God said, "Let there be light."*

And to the Light, Anastacia Ambros returns.

CHAPTER 26

Oh, that they were wise ... that they would
consider their latter end.

—Deuteronomy 32:29 Judeo-Orange Codex

"The Empress-Executrix is dead, m'lord," a Deathman informs Jovion Quiso triumphantly. Jovion and Oriana quickly make their way down the length of the Desnay Arena's playing field; a landed marineguard transport waits. The only sounds in the cold dark around them are the thunder of distant explosions and the rustles and whispered communications of their armored escort. Search lights and strobes from the transport cut through the night, lighting their way.

"It was swift? She did not suffer?" inquires Quiso softly, for Oriana's benefit.

"Yes, m'lord. One swift strike from the *Guderian* and they were finished," replies the Deathman ·with far too much gloating for Quiso, yet the Deathman's enthusiasm mirrors his own.

"She didn't suffer," he says comfortingly to Oriana, hugging her close to him, trying to keep the building sense of triumph from making him burst into victorious laughter. Armored Deathmen disperse from the grounded transport as five more marineguard transports begin landings on the field.

"My father, my brother and sisters?" asks Oriana from Quiso's shoulder. She expected to feel some grief over her mother's death but curiously she feels nothing, so she asks about the rest of her family. Still, strangely she feels nothing.

No gratitude for safety or for her ended exile. Not fear in this apocalyptic night. No sense of victory. Nothing. She pushes herself away from Jovion and looks into his angelic face for an answer.

"Princess Gabrielle's escort was intercepted by the first of our arriving CombatMecha units. Your father is still holding ground in the Omnividome," Jovion answers with reluctant admiration. *What a Deathman he would have made*, he thinks. "The Crown Scion and your sister Princess Zoe are still unaccounted for," he says as they reach the marineguard transport ramp.

Oh, Gabrielle! I'd hoped you would survive. You'd have been safe under my coming Regency, Oriana thinks, but there is no emotion with her thought; it is just another piece of datum in her mind. *They would only have made me Regis until she came of age. Only The One knows what would have become of me then. Better for me this way,* Oriana thinks. She stops half-way up the ramp. The burning city can be seen over the top tiers of the Desnay Arena. "Order Admiral Zhao to nucleo the site," Oriana commands dispassionately.

Excellent! Quiso muses to himself. *I was just about to suggest that.* Aloud he says, "No civilian ground targets have come under atomic or a-mat attack since the initial sabotage bombs went off. Are you sure you want to compound the surface damage? Besides, we can still use the Omnividome to keep the Imperium together instead of tear it apart like our late Empress-Executive planned."

"Destroy the site. We may catch Pfizer in the blast. The Omnividome is nothing but the hub in a wheel; it can be rebuilt." Oriana answers regally, pulling her Ilkani cloak around her for warmth.

"Princess, I…"

"I gave you an order, Baron Quiso. Nucleo it!" Oriana shouts and whirls with a flair of her robes striding into the transport. *I am Empress-Executrix in all but name. Queen of a million worlds and Chief Executive of the CIMB. It's time I take up my part.*

As she strides haughtily up the ramp, Jovion Quiso thinks, *In the end how simply she has fallen, no willed herself under my dominion.*

"Admiral, we've received an order to implement situation Omega," the *Guderian's* communications officer reports.

Admiral Zhao looks up from the situation monitors and holo projectors of his command console. It had been a complete rout. The initial attack had neutralized more than eighty percent of the planetary defenses; Bloodguard and Takazhr casualties were higher than anticipated. They were ahead of schedule. The inevitable reinforcements from outside the star system would not arrive for hours. Only a few loose ends remained. The First Lord had directed a legendary defense of the Omnividome; however, his heroic action was merely drawing most of the surviving Bloodguard and Takazhr to his aid, gathering them all ... into one spot.

Admiral Zhao no longer considers the missing Crown Scion and his youngest sister to be threats and neither will the First Lord be in a moment. Omega situation calls for the orbital destruction of the Omnividome by matter conversion attack.

* * *

The *Bismarck* rocks again, but this time Creed manages to maintain his balance. Power conduits and over-stressed circuitry crackle and explode. More acrid smoke fills the bridge. Damage sirens blares and warning lights flash. Life support ventilators hum as they try to clear the air.

"Defensive Commander reports port shields are down to twenty percent and failing. The Battle Cruiser *Ajax* is moving to our port to exploit the situation," reports the *Bismarck's* First Officer. "The Battle Cruisers *Agamemnon* and *Lysis* are moving for a portside intercept."

"Cameron, do something!" Creed roars.

Grand Admiral Cameron Freya Elizabeta Tanenov lifts her blond head from behind the *Bismarck's* Weapons Commander's station. "Concentrate all port-orienting energy weapons on the starboard weapons emplacements of *Ajax* and open fire. All portside tractor beams stand by. All missile and torpedo tubes,

I want firing solutions on the *Agamemnon* and *Lysis*."

Creed turns his attention to the forward main screen where the lead of the three pursuing battle cruisers can be seen off to the *Bismarck's* left. A-mat lances, plasma cannons, and point defense quad-mounted laser batteries open fire from the *Bismarck*. The *Ajax's* starboard side shields flash briefly before failing under the fierce assault; then her starboard side weapons are reduced to little more than molten slag. Fires blossom into space along the *Ajax's* starboard side before the vacuum of space extinguishes them, leaving white plumes of frozen escaped atmosphere. Ghostly pale green tractor beams pull the crippled vessel alongside the *Bismarck*.

Now the crippled *Ajax's* still active portside shields can be used to cover the *Bismarck's* damaged side. The *Agamemnon* and *Lysis* seem to hesitate in space, their commanders seemingly afraid to fire on their compatriots in order to attack the *Bismarck*.

"ASM missiles and torpedoes fire," Grand Admiral Tanenov whispers grimly.

The deck rocks as the remaining one hundred and twenty light-speed acceleration tubes fire. Sixty-eight fire eight missile rounds per second; the other thirty-two remaining torpedo tubes belch five torpedo rounds per second.

The *Agamemnon* explodes after two seconds, her Tsasinov core erupting like a small blue sun. The *Lysis* begins to come about in a vain attempt to escape, but only outlasts her sister ship by another three seconds before she too explodes into nonexistence.

"Flight officer, inform fighters not on perimeter duty or dealing with the surviving enemy fighters to neutralize *Ajax's* remaining defenses. Kurseg Hane, I'd appreciate your commanding our boarding parties," Grand Admiral Tanenov commands, not missing a beat as she turns toward her Damage Control Officer.

"Cameron, all indications are that my brother and what's left of his family are still trapped on Sacred Home," begins Creed angrily.

Cameron glides from around the Weapons Commander's console and walks almost casually to her Command console, not taking her eyes off the Lion. She sits gracefully in her command chair and regards him, her right hand on her pointed chin.

"That was not a request, Grand Kurseg," Cameron says, her voice firming, her eyes locking on the Lion like a-mat lances. "There may be crucial data aboard that ship. We end this quickly if we escape with it," she declares quietly. The Grand Admiral leans toward him now. She smiles gently, almost motherly, though she appears to be the same age as he. "We cannot possibly return to Sacred Home until reinforcements arrive, and we will not live to see them if we allow the rest of Admiral Zhao's Dreadnought Group to catch us," she says.

Creed tries to check the fury growing within him. "Cameron, permission to take a Search and Rescue team back to Sacred Home," he allows the pleading not in his voice to show in his eyes.

The Grand Admiral regards him for another heartbeat. "Flight Deck Commander, I want three squadrons of volunteer fighter pilots and two volunteer SAR teams. Master-at-Arms, take command of the *Ajax* boarding," the Grand Admiral rises in a single fluid motion and glides towards the Strategic Ops Commander's console. The StratOps Commander, a tall gray-haired human with the rank symbols of captain, looks up from the multiple screens and holo fields of his console. The man's eyes are red with grief.

"Long-range sensor drone LRSD-12 has just recorded a massive thermonuclear event on the surface of Earth..., Atlantean Islands ..., the Omnividome..., approximate yield fifty megatons. Drone has been destroyed. Admiral, it looks like the *Guderian's* destroyed LRSD-12. One of her remaining cruisers is firing on LRSD-1. It looks like the *Guderian* and her battle group are trying to trace the drone's transmissions back to us.

Suddenly the *Bismarck* rocks violently and her bridge fills with a bright white light that makes everyone see spots before their eyes. Damage sirens blare as medical and damage-control teams rush onto the bridge.

"What—?," begins the Lion.

"The *Ajax* has self-destructed," Cameron tells him, looking at the rapidly expanding cloud of red-hot gases and debris that was the *Ajax*. "Helmsman, plot a course out of the star system. Damage Control Officer status?"

"This is Lieutenant Hidoshi. Captain Alonzon is in medical. We have fires on the starboard flight deck contained. There are several hull ruptures and bulkhead collapses starboard side, but emergency force fields are holding. Secondary starboard Tsasinov warp drive unit offline. ...."

"We can still get warpfold," the Grand Admiral mumbles to herself with grim satisfaction. "StratOps Commander, are we still receiving any Imperial family beacons?"

"The First Lord's beacon is no longer transmitting." The Captain swiftly gives the Lion a nod of condolence. "The Crown Scion's beacon still transmits—from North American Continent, Florida Subdistrict."

Creed feels his legs wobble beneath him and his breath catches in his throat. Some part of him tells him he knew this was coming, that his brother's stubborn defense could really only have one outcome. But another part of him had hoped against reality and logic that he would not hear of the death of yet another of his immediate family. Cameron guides him to an omniform chair that he wearily sits in. He hears her dispatching the SAR teams but the details elude him.

Momentarily the Grand Admiral leans over the back of the Lion's chair and whispers to him: "We can't stay, cousin. I've given the SAR teams rendezvous and contact instructions. I'm setting a course for home."

He looks up at her, the cold logical part of himself warning him of the folly of leading these traitors to Eros.

PART TWO

CHAPTER 27

With the measure you use, it will be measured back
to you.

—Matthew 7:2 Judeo-Orange Codex

The pre-dawn sky over Miami is soft gold with amethyst
nimbus clouds. The undersides of the clouds glow fiery red
and orange, reflecting the light of the burning city and space
port beneath them. There is a great flash in the east and Otto
watches the horizon turn to day from the relative safety of
the top floor of a Universal Parcel Service office depot. The
depot is closed for the holiday. The seven of them now in
the room are all that remain of thirty who had once made
up Pfizer's entourage. Behind him, well away from the
windows, Dr. Tsimpo and Lux huddle beneath a stealth
blanket, as Pfizer's honor guard Heath MacKenzie stands
watch nearby. MacKenzie has deactivated his armor to keep
from being tracked. Otto and the two other surviving
Bloodguards standing near the window assume that the
light on the horizon is the sun but something about the
immense burning in the distance seems hideously man-made.

"They've nucleoed Atlantis," the Bloodguard with the
burn-damaged armor whispers. The other Bloodguard pushes
him slightly and nods toward Otto, whose head has dropped
in dejection at what the terrible explosion must signify. The
nucleo is a mass energy conversion weapon, neither as
clumsy nor as radioactively unstable as antimatter or fusion
weapons. The nucleo is a clean weapon; everything within

range is just gone in one great explosion. "Maybe those murderers limited the blast to New Eden, sir," offers the indiscreet Bloodguard.

He's just trying to comfort me, Otto thinks. *But we can see the blast almost fifteen hundred miles away. To obliterate four hundred million people to get only a few? At least these butchers are running out of time. Maybe they'll think they got us in the blast, maybe those Deathmen didn't have time to report before we eliminated them during our escape from the Grodin UPS Center.*

"Look! Over there—to the right of where the spaceport scanning array used to be. There's some sort of armored mecha!" The three duck just as three black Deathman CombatMechas in flyer mode lift into the night sky and begin a lazy search pattern, slicing the dark with their search lights.

Maybe Mari and Agust got out before the blast, Otto thinks. He considers losing himself in the tursapoi frenzy, of throwing himself at the Deathmen in one last angry burst of defiance. Their plan to take the sub-surface rails had gone awry. In their desperate retreat from New Eden they had come across a UPS depot and taken a Class I UPS Courier Shuttle to Miami. The shuttle, damaged during their lift-off, could only be coaxed as far as here. *How would they ever make Nevada? It doesn't make sense to go on.*

"Captain Praetor?" Luxvico says, having moved from beneath the stealth blanket to crouch next to Otto. The Tempellian's pale violet eyes search Otto's face for a sign that the man has not lost himself to the despair Luxvico's seen claim so many this night. "We've got to start moving again. A blast that size has generated a tsunami that will inundate this area." *More unfathomable destruction. Their minds have been pushed to the breaking point,* Luxvico thinks.

"Tsunami?" mutters Pfizer, rising to his feet. He's wearing a brown two-piece UPS uniform, all they could find to replace his torn, wet clothing.

"A massive tidal wave," Otto whispers, staring at Lux who nods confirmation. "Damn it!" Otto shouts. Angrily, he pushes himself up and moves over to the stealth blanket, staying in the shadows all the while. At Otto's approach Heath pulls back the blanket and removes his helmet. He looks at Otto with icy eyes. "Sir?" he asks.

"I want the traitor," Otto growls. With one hand he effortlessly snatches up Rachel Tsimpo.

"Wha—?," she begins protesting.

"How are they tracking us?!" Otto demands, shaking her roughly.

Suddenly, the Bloodguard nearest the window yells, "The CombatMechas—they're turning toward us!"

"Don't activate your armor and weapons yet! It may just be a coincid—," Lux starts to warn. But it is too late. The room fills with the sound of activating armor and weapons. The two Bloodguards in the window shields flicker into existence. The lazy search pattern of the Deathman CombatMechas ends abruptly. They point at the depot and begin advancing with deliberate caution. Two of them begin reconfiguring into gladiator mode even before they hit the ground in the form of nine-meter-tall armored warriors.

Missiles launch from the still airborne flyer, and Otto thinks this is the end as he tosses Dr. Tsimpo to the ground and dives for his Hephaestus. The two guards at the window are raising their weapons but it will be too late. Two white-hot Hephaestus beams lance by Otto through the window, striking the incoming missiles. There is a blur of red and white as MacKenzie streaks by Otto, using the genetically enhanced muscles of the Chosen, augmented by powered armor. Otto's Hephaestus is snatched from his hand by the passing blur of Heath leaping through the window.

Pfizer begins standing and staggers. Otto grabs him and pulls him back down behind a desk. "Don't watch," he says simply as he shields Pfizer with his body.

As Heath lands on the ground, he activates the two Hephaestus in saber mode, one in each hand as he sprints forward. The two Deathmen mechas overhead attempt to strafe him with the rapid fire iso-kinetic cannons built into their arms. They pepper the area before them with the deadly rounds but he is too quick for them and slides in under their guard. At this range only neutronium can stop a Hephaestus, and Heath slices through their legs, toppling them. The armored pilots of the two felled CombatMechas eject from the vehicles in bursts of flame.

The Bloodguard with the burn-damaged armor raises his armor-powered dispik and fires at the mecha heading straight for him at the window in flyer mode. Even though his dispik is ineffective against shielded targets, the pulse from the weapon temporarily disrupts the CombatMechas' onboard systems, causing the craft to spin out of control. As it plummets to the ground the other Bloodguard launches two smart grenades whose EMP disruption fields disable the CombatMechas' shields just before the grenades detonate in low-yield nuclear pyrotechnics. The shock wave from the blast blows out the building's remaining windows as well as those in the surrounding building, showering them all with glass and masonry.

The blast knocks Heath nearly senseless. But having been trained for close-range combat with low-yield nukes in the burned waste of Sidonia, Mars, he's quicker to recover than the two Deathmen, who look staggered by the blast. Heath reaches for his one remaining Hephaestus and, switching it to lance mode, drives a two-meter-long beam of a-mat plasma through the head of the Deathman closest to him. Unfortunately the other Deathman has time to fire at him with a kinetic flechette blaster. With uncanny speed Heath leaps out of the way but is clipped on his right arm. His arm from his wrist to his shoulder feels suddenly mangled. He yells in agony and with pain-blurred vision aims and fires at the head of his assailant. The Deathman's head melts like hot wax and the headless body falls. Heath's armor is already feeding him painkillers and stims. His vision begins to clear. The Bloodguard with the fully intact armor a-gravs from the window to the ground and closes the space between them. "Good job, Chosen," the Bloodguard says without derision as he lifts Heath.

"Let's try to salvage some of their weapons," MacKenzie says, nodding at the fallen CombatMechas, a move that makes his vision swim again.

"No time," Otto's voice comes over the comm units. "Two more CombatMechas headed this way with support troops. I want you two back up here now!" Otto orders.

From the blasted-out window above Otto watches the two Bloodguards with Heath retreat toward him. Otto takes deep breaths, trying to marshal his rage and grief and turn the tide of negative energy that threatens to overwhelm him into some good. That's what Marisol would want.

"One last chance, Dr. Tsimpo," Otto says, turning to face the traitor. He does not care that she sees the tears on his face or the murder in his eyes. "How are they tracking us?" Otto's power blaster springs into his hand.

"I don't know!" Dr. Tsimpo cries in persecuted frustration. "I swear," she adds desperately. "Please believe me! They're trying to kill me, too," she pleads. She drops to her knees before Otto ready to beg for her life. "Maybe they are tracking us through Pfizer! I have no idea!"

"Fraznee!" curses the Bloodguard in the burn-damaged armor as he leans from the window to help MacKenzie and the other Bloodguard as they a-grav towards him. "We've got to cut and run, sir. They're almost on us." A high-pitched whine cuts over the Bloodguard's scanner. "Those CombatMechas are targeting the building," he says, turning up his shield and backing into the room with the others.

Otto points the blaster at Rachel Tsimpo's head and is about to pull the trigger when there is a tremendous sonic boom from above. The building shakes and they're all pelted with collapsing ceiling.

"Someone opened a warpfold in atmosphere!" Otto shouts incredulously, aware of the piloting and reflexes such a maneuver would require.

Through the blasted-out windows they see missile contrails streak out of the dawn sky, accompanied by the flashing burst of torpedoes and the lightning strikes of energy weapons.

The ceiling gives way completely and ten heavily armed and armored Bloodguard a-grav land around them. One of them, bearing the blue and gold patch with stylized dragon and unicorn of the Hane on his shoulder, bows his head to Pfizer reverently.

"Domino," the Bloodguard says.

Domino. Pfizer is now Our Lord, Otto thinks. The Bloodguard strap a-grav belts on all of them and attach quick-guide lines. Otto sees fighters hovering menacingly around the depot deploying ground effects weaponry, forming a perimeter.

"Leave her," Otto hears Pfizer command, with the same force he'd threatened Dr. Tsimpo with earlier.

Pfizer approaches her, grabs her roughly by the arms, and leans his head toward her until their faces are almost touching. "I am not Yeishua," he whispers, shoving her away. "Get us out of here!" he shouts over the marineguard transport's roaring engines.

"NOOO!!!" she pleads madly grasping at legs as Pfizer and the others are lifted into the air by the quick-guide lines to the giant mosquito shape of the marineguard transport hovering overhead. Its four weapons pods retract, the underside landing ramp closes, and the transport resumes its familiar shark-like appearance. Rachel Tsimpo screams and begs for them to come back as the transport lifts higher and higher.

Trying to gain his breath and composure, Otto turns to the rescuing Bloodguard commander, a Lieutenant.

"Reinforcements?" Otto asks.

"No." The rescuing Bloodguard commander answers, shaking his head sadly. "We're search and rescue from the INS *Bismarck.* "Now if we can just get out of this star system," he says, watching as the clouds out the hatch view port dissipate into the blackness of space.

"Taking evasive action, deploying counter measures," announces the Naval pilot over the ship's intercom.

The marineguard transport suddenly twists and Otto grabs an overhead handhold, keeping his attention on the rescue commander. "What happened?" he asks.

"Somehow they planted bombs or other ordinance in key naval and planetary ships or facilities. Then..."

Doesn't he realize I know this, Otto thinks angrily. Perhaps something in his face cued the reporting Bloodguard because a look of discomfort passes over the man's face.

"I was attached to Lady Kiritzia Hane's detail at the Omnividome," the Bloodguard Major continues. "We got her and her son to the *Bismarck* almost immediately. But we came under attack by an entire dreadnought group and were forced to withdraw. Grand Admiral Tanenov asked for volunteers. They knocked out one of our other transports on the way in and a lot of the fighters." The Bloodguard pauses. His eyes search Otto's face for something. "But he is Domino and he is also Hane—no matter what his last name is," the Bloodguard adds, looking at Pfizer being fitted into a suit of armor in case of a hull rupture.

What does he mean? Otto wonders as the ship takes more jolting evasive action.

Pfizer refuses to let them put his helmet on and instead places it under his left arm. He watches as two armored Bloodguards with medic symbols begin removing Heath from his armor and cybernetic bodymesh.

The ship rolls twice but all is kept in place by a-grav fields and inertial modifiers. Pfizer feels a lurch and instinctively he knows they have made the jump to warpfold space. "We're in Warpfold transit," announces the pilot over the intercom.

"Fek!" Pfizer hears one of the medics curse. "This guy's a Chosen," he says holding Heath's helmet in his hands staring at the Chosen tattoos around the right eye, face, and arm.

The other Bloodguard flinches, startled by the pronouncement, but then takes a look. "Fekking relax. Look at him! He's just a baby. It took balls for him to enlist."

"He just looks really young. He could be a thousand," the first medic whispers.

"He's a Bloodguard who saved my life," Pfizer says and for the third time Otto hears an unidentifiable but familiar forcefulness to Pfizer's voice. There is something very menacing, no—*wrong*—in it, and Otto feels a sudden surge of fear for Pfizer.

"Yes, Domino," the second medic says, embarrassed. Pfizer, helmet tucked under his left arm, follows the two medics as they insert the half-conscious Heath into one of the four surgo-op cylinders that serve as the marine transport's sickbay.

Pfizer allows another one of the rescuing Bloodguard to secure him in an adjoining seat. He looks up at Otto and the Bloodguard Major as they approach him. "Where are we going?" he asks with that force just lingering there in every word.

"Our rendezvous coordinates are in a dust cloud out-system. From there to Eros, I'd guess, unless you have other orders, Lord," the officer responds almost reverently.

"No," Pfizer says. "Not yet...Not yet. Thank you, Major Battaglia, isn't it? You may return to the bridge."

The man does a crisp Bloodguard salute—right hand over the heart, left hand extended palm up—then does a smart about face and departs.

"M'lord?" Otto asks.

Pfizer looks at Otto's weary, pained face. Despite all that's happened Otto is still looking after him. Perhaps it keeps Otto sane.

"All through the attack he tried to comfort me. Then he saved all our lives... And I hated him at first," Pfizer's voice almost breaks with his last sentence but he goes on with that strange forcefulness in his voice. "I hate the Chosen for their elitism. I hate the racism of the Tene Thantos, the wanton disregard for human life, and the Deathmen. But like you said, not all Chosen are Tene Thantos. No, my hate is now reserved for these traitors—mortal, e-mortal, Chosen—it doesn't matter. I've had enough. The Lion was right." *We sat there and talked while our enemies gathered.*

With those quiet forceful words Otto identifies the no-longer unidentifiable. *The new sound I hear in Pfizer's voice is Hate.*

CHAPTER 28

Only life is important.

—Gert Vespasian Xian Hammer-Hane (The
Great), as quoted in *The Hane Commentaries* by
Aaron Charlemagna Invid-Hane

The Hane's ancestral home on Eros sits in the ancient remains of a ten-kilometer impact crater that empties into the ocean. Their vast home boasts great palaces, monuments, and domed temple-like buildings of native blackglass and gold ivory. Marble mined from the quarries of Hecate crowds the center bay and works its way up the sides of the crater. Sun sparkles off towering stained crystal windows filling the crater with unimaginable rainbows that birds flutter serenely through. Waves pound like distant thunder and morning mist begins to retreat from the verdant lawns and thickly forested parks that dot the magnificence of HaneHome on Eros.

Spica rises gloriously white on the sparkling sapphire ocean. A warm clean breeze fills Balthasar Hane's office balcony with the scent of chlorophyll and sea blown kelp flowers. Here it has always seemed as if he could feel the planet's heartbeat, more than six thousand years after Magnus Haakon and Celeste Neuhaurer married and began the family now known as the Hane, the living heart of the Erosi Alliance.

Headlights of personal ground and air conveyances began shutting off with the coming of day. Despite the ambient tranquility Balthasar's mood is dark and troubled. In minutes the transmission from the Omnividome on Earth is scheduled to begin. The Hane descendent population empire-wide now totals close to six billion with nearly five percent, some three hundred million, on Eros alone. The Hane Nation, as the family is popularly known, is entirely Balthasar's responsibility. Aside from perhaps the Empress-Executrix he has more titles than any other individual in the Imperium. First Elector Of the Erosi Alliance, Stadtholder of Clans, ClanLord of the Hane Nation, Prince of HaneHome, Malva, Elad, Vey and Invid.

The softly tinkling bells of his mother's escort can be heard as they enter the reception salon to his office. Balthasar quickly checks his appearance in the balcony's sliding glass doors. Tall and muscular like all the Hane males, Balthasar's hair is raven black like his mother's people, yet he possesses the same b l e a c h e d icy blue eyes of the Hane.

That his appearance mimics that of an ancient mythical hero is no coincidence. His parents' gentechs had told them that his appearance would command respect and that Balthasar's character would also be shaped by his heroic physical form. While his brothers Creed and Millian always had feline, predatory movements, Balthasar's movements are clipped and precise. His movements are those of a man of powerful discipline and nervous energy.

He views himself, fists on narrow hips. Here on tropical Eros the inhabitants tend to wear flowing loose-fitting clothing. But today before the Omnividome transmission. Balthasar will celebrate with the other Electors of the great Clan Nations that comprise the Erosi Alliance. So now he wears the red and gold uniform tunic and jet black pants of a Coronal Regent, the Imperium's representative to Eros. Balthasar would prefer to have worn the loose green robes he would wear as First Elector, but today he wishes to demonstrate his loyalty to the Ambros. After all, the next Emperor-Executor, Pfizer, is a Hane by birth. His Crier, a distant cousin on his mother's side, announces his mother as she enters through the open double doors of his office: "Princess Fen Alona Anne Vey-Hane, Dowager Queen and Matriarch of the Hane Nation, Mistress of Vey, Elad, and HaneHome, and Sister of Peace."

The mother of Balthasar, Creed, and Millian is a woman of exquisite beauty. At first glance she could be taken for Oriana, but her eyes are even more luminous. The black silk and taffeta robes of the Sisters of Peace do little to cover her lithe but amply breasted figure. The right side of her face is tattooed in the black sigils and runes of the Vey, one of the Chosen Clans, a pure Aeon. Her marriage to his father Aaron Hane, The Great Hane, had caused a fair share of controversy back in its day almost two and a half centuries ago.

There are limits to the lengths most e-mortals will go to in modifying their genes. Most cannot afford to achieve true immortality or psionic powers. The advances made to *Homo Deus* evolution before the Wasting were largely the products of the advanced eugenics programs of many Aristo Families. Liesel Aeon of Eros had tried to advance the species even further by genengineering *Homo Dominus Deus,* the Master God Man, the Chosen.

Liesel was exiled from Eros but not before she'd experimented on some of the families there, some willing some not: The Vey, the MacKenzie, the Kellog, the Quon and the Invid. Liesel and her craft found a home in the court of Armingkon Quiso and his genetic purist on Anonjida. It was there that the Tene Thantos, the Deathmen, and the Wasting began. This made the Chosen, Tene Thantos or not, despised and mistrusted throughout the known universe. As much as many coveted the Chosen's Aeon genes many others went to great lengths to hide their lineage. Balthasar and his brothers were spared having their faces marked by the Vey denunciation of a Clan daughter, their mother. The Vey themselves had fallen, allying themselves with the rebels of Oriana's aborted Anangan Insurrection. Fen, the Widow, being the most senior *loyal* survivor of the decimated Clan, inherited all their lands and holdings.

His mother's smile of greeting is generous but confronted with the dark cloud of his mood fades quickly like the mist off the shimmering lawns outside. Her eyes quickly survey the large room paneled with polished native Noir Draco Pine. Intricate relief maps worked in rare and precious substances from the principle holdings of the Hane Nation adorn the walls. The office had once been her husband Aaron's; if she closes her eyes she can see him behind the desk smiling like the sun, rising to meet her.

"Mother?" Balthasar, the most ruthless and also the most sensitive of her sons asks, sensing her sadness.

"You are worried. I am worried," she comments, a family axiom. Her voice is deceptively shy and childlike.

It is useless to attempt to deceive her. He and his brothers always joked that she read their minds. Balthasar sighs, displaying a weariness he would never show anyone else, not anyone.

"Your brothers," she breathes, pinpointing the source of his dark mood as surely as he knew that memories of his long-dead father were what had troubled her. "Your aides sought to distract me with some nonsense about your being preoccupied by Alliance and Nation business," she says softly.

"Don't be angry with them. With this Tempellian exodus we've lost some very skilled and important personnel," he offers, trying to deflect her from the knowledge that more Hane may die violently.

"An issue with the Bank? Is this why my Bloodguard Commander informed me that all Hane Nation leaders are to be notified of a Condition Red? Our true strength is family, our true wealth is family," Fen says moving closer to her oldest son in a swishing of robes. Any more pretenses would be useless.

"It's Anastacia Ambros; she sets her sights up much too high. The Omnividome reminds me of the Tower of Babel from Pfizer's En'Zefi study," Balthasar mutters as he prepares to escort his mother to the Omnividome transmission. In the Hall Of Justice the other Electors and Clan Lords await. There he will tell her of the dreadful transmission from his brothers.

There is a commotion in the reception salon outside, raised voices, among them Cedar's.

Why is he here? He's supposed to be at the Hall of Justice in the Elector's Gallery, Balthasar thinks.

Tall, red-haired Cedar enters with three of the family's Bloodguard Officers and the ranking planetary Naval officer, Commodore Robus Nilz Hane-Fahey and the Hane Nation Press Secretary Zwen Tran-Hane carrying an omnipalm and wearing his audvid link.

"Robus reports contact with the central Naval AI has been lost," Cedar says in his deep baritone voice, indicating the Naval Commodore, as the uniformed officer gently closes the double doors which lead into the office. He pulls an omnipalm from his pocket and begins putting on its audvid head piece.

"Get the news on," Balthasar orders, detaching himself from his mother. Cedar is activating the room's six large holo screens, tastefully concealed behind the large wall map of Eros that slides up into the ceiling. Cedar rushes over to Balthasar's desk and finds the remote wand. The screens flicker to life.

Screens one and two: a GNN broadcast from Earth in front of the Omnividome, Haight Rush speaking with the Arch-Duchess of Pegasus. Screens three and four: Anastacia speaking to a madly cheering sea of humanity, a HaneNet correspondent, Amora Hane-Singo, speaking with revelers in the Erosi Alliance's observation gallery of the Omnividome. Screens five and six: local images from Eros, the capital city Avon, and media correspondents in the main entrance plaza of the Hall Of Justice waiting for gathering Electors and more media outside the main entrance of HaneHome itself.

"There doesn't seem to be any trouble," Cedar says with a sigh of relief, but when he turns to Balthasar, he knows as well as the Widow that Balthasar is not relieved.

"Those are delayed transmissions, maybe ten to thirteen minutes, depending on the warpfold relay beacons. We're still getting real-time financial information from the CIMB instalink network," the mahogany skinned Zwen says in his rich Serdian-educated voice, seemingly confirming Cedar's assessment. Balthasar feels some of the building tension begin to ease when Zwen's face takes on a troubled look. He makes several adjustments to his omnipalm and audvid link.

"What is it?" Fen demands, turning her piercing attention to Zwen. "The instalink data from Earth has stopped," Zwen answers incredulously.

"The dreadnought group in our star system is reporting difficulty... I think...," begins Robus, the naval attaché.

No. "What sort of trouble?" demands Balthasar.

"Balthasar, look!" Cedar shouts. The scenes from Earth show panicked reports of the news media as explosions go off in the distance. The room is silent but for the sounds of waves slamming against the cliffs below and the keening of gulls flying in the warm morning light.

"The bunker," Balthasar says, taking his mother's hand and leading her toward the floor-to-ceiling wall map of Inferno. "Robus, get me the Takazhr in charge of Planetary Defense Command. Zwen—," As the sun shines on his face he realizes he may never again witness another morning like this, that his world may become black with rivers of molten ore like the wall map of Inferno. Fen squeezes his hand.

"There will be other worlds," she whispers.

"None more beautiful than this," Balthasar replies, barely keeping control of his voice. "Zwen," he continues, "I want the status of planetary defenses. Then prepare to issue a planetary alert and distress call. Ask the Electors to return and help prepare their respective nations. Tell the Electors from off-planet nations in the Alliance they need to prepare for relief efforts. I will be making a statement shortly."

"I don't know if the Bunker is the best idea," begins Commodore Hane-Fahey. You'd be under siege and giving up your mobility. We should—"

Balthasar turns sharply and stares down at the shorter man, "How Robbie? The safest transportation in the star system is

... How did you put it? 'Having difficulty.' No. We will ascertain the status of the fleet from the bunker. Now, all of you with me," he says turning to join his mother who waits in an evac pod.

The inside of the evac pod is like that of a maglev monorail or airbus. There is room to seat at least forty passengers comfortably, with plenty of standing room and handholds for more. As soon as it was released from high-priority assignments, the pod would begin transporting civilians to other shelters. Now the pod whisks them along at nearly four hundred miles per hour through a superconductivity tunnel. As Balthasar sits next to his mother she gives him a brief disapproving stare. He bows his head minutely.

"Speak plainly, Mother," he'd deal with whatever it was that had annoyed her before he told her what may be happening. Of course, they may be one and the same. His mother's eyes shift slightly to the others. She is too old-fashioned to display her ire in public, but she has seen to it that he knows she is displeased.

Looking directly at Fen, Balthasar says, "I had an instalink with a special session of the Executive Council's Security Committee a little more than an hour before midnight our time. Creed told me that a ship from an aborted smuggling attempt had been found to conceal Tene Thantos Deathmen with a supply of tursapoi and illegal weapons of mass destruction..."

The pod goes silent; the others have been listening. Balthasar turns to acknowledge their attention, then turns back to Fen whose eyes are wide in shock as she understands what he tells her.

"We thought we had days to prepare or even preempt their strike. My last communiqué from Creed was that they already made two successful raids and the Ambros were preparing to file anti-monopoly charges against Allied Autotechnics Galactic after the Uprising Ceremonies. When I found out I ordered the security upgrade on family leaders and our key facilities, but I wanted to avert a general panic. I was going to fill in all of you and the Electors at the Hall of Justice." It is the closest thing to an apology he will give them.

The evac pod comes to a stop. Ever since the centuries-long Siege during the Wasting the Erosi have maintained an elaborate series of bunkers in the event anyone else tried to raid or pirate their world's tursapoi kelp or other natural resources. This particular bunker, DracoHold, some ten kilometers beneath HaneHome is the largest, designed to house a million Takazhr, one quarter of the planet's total Takazhr force and their weapons. In addition there is room for another two million members of the leading Aristo and civilian families. There are vaults for cultural treasures, and zoos and gardens with samples of the planet's natural flora and fauna as well as reserves of frozen embryos and seeds. There is a gene bank containing genetic profiles of the six billion Hane currently living; it has been updated daily in the hopes that the Hane people's talents would never be lost. Another gene bank is also maintained in a secret location off-planet. This vast underground city was designed to house everything they would need for many years.

The evac pod has arrived at the station outside the War Room of DracoHold. Awaiting them is an escort of five armored Bloodguard led by Balthasar's General Praetor Nikeon Blaze and Sir Pau Mouvalo, Commander of all Takazhr in the Erosi Alliance. With Sir Pau is Teresa Moro-Hane, the Takazhr General in charge of Eros' ground-based planetary defenses and Chief Operational and Resource Officer for DracoHold, and her staff. As Balthasar steps onto the brightly lit black platform, the military there snap to attention and Teresa and her staff bow. Balthasar acknowledges them all with his sweeping gaze and strides toward Sir Pau and the Takazhr, both of whom look grave. "Status of planetary defenses?" he demands of the two green-uniformed men as he leads them all into the cavernous electronic hive of activity that is the War Room.

Sir Pau, the senior of the two responds, "Automated and computer-controlled space and ground systems are online and responding one hundred percent, m'lord. As per your instructions, we wiped and reinitialized the entire system last night. We unfortunately did not get all of their sabotage devices. There was severe damage at the planetary Naval Command at Asgard, in the South Polar Region. One of the two monitors, massive orbital fortresses, has been destroyed. Over two thousands of the crew were still on board, but many were evacuated. The ships docked there were able to escape.

"What of the fleet?!" Balthasar demands, unwilling to wait any longer for news of the dreadnought group defending the Spica Star System.

"Mixed news. We lost half of the six battle ships and five of the twelve destroyers. INS Dreadnought *Gert* is undamaged and the INS Dreadnought *Napoleon* is at Cytheria Naval Orbital Star Base undergoing minor maintenance—"

"The *Napoleon's* complete Group is with it?" Balthasar interrupts.

"No they are on their way here but will not arrive for thirty-six hours," answers Sir Pau, unruffled.

With all this the loss of life Balthasar knows that some of them will have been Hane. But two dreadnoughts and a sizable support force still defend the Eros Alliance home system and the planet. Thank the Eternal, the planet has not yet come under nuclear or a-mat attack. "What of the other planets in the Alliance?" he asks.

"Safe m'lord, and their attendant forces. Some of their Electors decided to come here," the Kurseg responds, indicating a colorful knot of the Eros Alliance's elected royalty who are now standing in the command and operations pit of the War Room, which is a cocoon of screens and holo projectors manned by busy technicians. Balthasar allows himself a small sigh of relief. *Now for the really hard question, the one I'm afraid to hear the answers to,* he thinks, reading the Takazhr's expression.

"What is happening on Earth?" Balthasar asks. He's aware of Fen standing quietly beside him. He takes her hand, steeling himself.

"Our last warp relay signal was from the INS *Bismarck*. The flagship is being pursued from the Sol System with Kurseg Creed Hane, his wife Lady Kiritzia, and their son Aaron on board. They are running in stealth mode and will not send another transmission for two hours."

"Where is my son Millian? Where is his wife? Where are my grandchildren?" questions Fen in her calm childlike voice, but she squeezes Balthasar's hand tightly.

The Takazhr Kurseg, knighted by the Empress-Executrix herself, bows his head. "The Empress-Executrix is dead. Her evacuation TAV was destroyed. I am also sorry to report the Death of Prince Millian Hane, the First Lord, and his daughter Gabrielle. The entire Atlantean subcontinent was nucleoed. The death toll on Earth is already at more than two billion."

Balthasar finds himself shaking his head unconsciously. *My brother. My strong, gentle, wise brother. The fulcrum between Creed and I.* Innumerable memories flood Balthasar and he feels his eyes glass. *So many dead in mere minutes, more than the entire Hane population currently on Eros. How many of my cousins died in the destruction of Atlantis? The Erosi Alliance Embassy, the Hane Trade Towers.*

"What of my nephew and my other niece?" Balthasar asks, his eyes beginning to sting, hoping the man has left them out due to a shred of good news.

"The scion's last reported position was in the vicinity of Miami Spaceport, near—"

"My son knows where Miami Spaceport is, Kurseg. Where are my grandchildren?" Fen demands, more fearsome than the Lion. Fen pulls her veils over her face.

Sir Pau feels as if the woman is looking through him. Everything that he is seems an open book before her piercing stare. "Grand Admiral Tanenov is mounting a rescue operation to retrieve the Crown Scion; we won't know the results for another hour and fifty-seven minutes. There is no sign of Princess Zoe. She has not been seen since the nucleo."

"Balthasar, I wish to retire and meditate," Fen interrupts regally. Not even waiting for a reply, she turns and leaves, gathering some of the assembled Bloodguard in her wake. *I love her, Mother,* Millian had said when she had questioned his choice of a wife. As the words of her dead son echo in her mind she is thankful for the veil over her face.

For a moment Balthasar watches her go, relieved and anxious at the same time. He turns to Sir Pau. "They didn't just attempt to sabotage our defenses without cause. What could their motive be?" he turns to the others, inviting speculation.

A Takazhr with communications insignia and gear hurriedly approaches. The officer goes straight to Balthasar barely excusing herself as she weaves through the high-ranking crowd.

"Sire," she begins breathlessly. "A planetary distress signal from Tempel."

"It's about time—Balthasar stops. "Did you say *Tempel?*" He was expecting news from Earth, not from the Academy or the Tempellian homeworld.

"Yes, sir. Tempel, Riffellon IX," answers the young officer, clearly awed by Balthasar's commanding presence.

"Let us see it," the Erosi leader commands, gently trying to put the young woman at ease.

"Sire, it is very—" she begins.

"Now," Balthasar orders quietly.

Using the gear with her, the Takazhr officer overrides the central holo projection viewer. A static jumbled image of Arch-Chancellor Lurenga, his face familiar to most citizens of the Imperium, fills the viewer. The Tempeler's white surcoat is smudged and blackened. Behind him the red skies are dark and the great golden towers are burning, kilometer-high torches. There is a look of utter shock and disbelief on his usually completely emotionless face. "This is the planet Tempel in the Riffellon Star System. We urgently request any and all military assistance. Fewer than thirty minutes ago all our computer and automated defenses went offline. An intruder vessel we have identified as a Deathship has entered our star system and launched an attack on Tempel. I repeat: an intruder vessel we have identified as a Deathship has entered our star system..."

Numerous exclamations from those watching drown out the Arch-Chancellor's voice, but what appears on the viewer returns the room to silence.

The Deathship is black and eight kilometers long, its dagger-shaped hull covered with weapons emplacements. Radiation shielding is not necessary for its cyborg crew so the shielding space is used for even more power units. Deathships are the most dreaded sight in the universe, and with good reason. As a Deathship's radiation takes its toll, its crew finds a suitable world nearby with a healthy populace to rape and harvest. There they break down those unsuited for organ replacement into raw nutrients. Then they 'restore' whatever remains. As those gathered watch in horror, bright flashes like machine gun fire indicate that the Deathship has begun another missile barrage.

"... they refuse our unconditional surrender and continue their bombardment. This is the planet Temp—"

There is a burst of light, whether from the monitor or the scene it captured, no one knows but the screen goes dark, before filling with static.

"Navigational beacons in the warpfold network are no longer reporting the existence of the planet Tempel," the Takazhr comm officer says to the silence, evidently with no idea how momentous her words are.

The room becomes a madhouse of shouting and disbelief. The military want data. The Electors are shouting advice, demanding answers, trying now to push their way through the Bloodguard cordon that surrounds Balthasar. He is staggered by the girl's words.

"You're *certain?*" he asks, trying to raise his voice over the shouting. Though she cannot hear him, Balthasar's question is clear and she rechecks her equipment. She turns back toward him, her young eyes suddenly looking older than they ever should, and simply lowers her head.

For a moment Balthasar begins to contemplate the loss of Tempel, but only for a moment.

Our world may be next.

CHAPTER 29

One of the descendants of Cush was Nimrod, who became the first of the kings. He was a mighty hunter, blessed of God, and his name became proverbial.

—Genesis 10:8-9 Judeo-Orange Codex

Cato watches three scouts, visible only through the enhanced macro-viewers he holds to his face. The remnants of the Tempellian Embassy still glow red hot in the cold Nevada desert morning. Cato and his force from the Omnividome are fewer than one hundred meters from the entrance to the underground hangar that Lomin says contains the courier vessels. After a short search, the scouts find the hidden controls to open the secret entrance exactly where Lomin said it would be. Inside are three Hermes class ultra-warp transports, Tempeler Naval vessels. They will only need one and intend to scuttle the other two lest the technology fall into enemy hands.

Strangely, since Lomin had imparted the vision of his past to Cato and Cato's Bloodguard Piter, Cato had found his thoughts turning to his long-dead wife, Persis. They had met on a brilliantly sunny day, a Tuesday. It was the Mardi Gras festival. Every detail of the evening now pervades his senses: The fireworks, the music, the smell of Persis' hair. It is as if the telepathic contact with Lomin has allowed him to relive his own life in the same three-dimensional panoramic details. The perpetual autumnal forest of Titan, the smell of the great trees that comprised his ancestral home—cherry, pine, mahogany. Persis' laughter, Orion's birth and how the doves had been released and the trumpets blared. In this terrible night these memories sustained him.

"Yes, Cato. That is how it is. Even the sorrows and the terror bring us closer to the true blessings of life, the most precious treasure that lies beyond avarice."

To hear him talk like this would normally alarm me. Emotional philosophy from my Tempeler, but I understand. Cato smiles benevolently at the ancient mentor beside him before returning his attention to the three-man Takazhr squad making its way to the hidden entrance. *Why the Tempellians had felt the need for this hidden hangar and how it stayed hidden for so long are questions for later.*

"We are a people of secrets, Cato," the old man says quietly beside him.

On the fused, scorched desert surface before them the Takazhr in stealth mode are barely visible but for the occasional wind that blows sand into their stealth fields. With the macrobinoculars Cato sees three clearly defined figures clearing debris from the camouflaged entrance controls. Lomin has assured them that the entrance mechanism will produce a negligible power signature. The traitors in orbit seem to have problems of their own. Cato gleans from monitoring communications that perhaps the Crown Scion has escaped.

One of the Takazhr raises his arm and motions them all forward. Next to Cato, General Mugabe-Hane Hamar issues orders. Ten armored Takazhr and an equal number of armored Bloodguard surge forward, fanning out into a protective arc.

"It's our turn, father, Lomin," says Basileus' armor-augmented voice from behind the three. Putting his armored arm around Lomin, Cato lifts the Tempeler to his hovering position, keeping a hand protectively around the smaller man's arm. They move forward with their main force of more than a hundred, desert crackling underfoot. Static lightning flashes eerily light the horizon. At last they pass into an underground hangar and Cato hears Basileus heave a sigh of relief behind them.

Before them stretches the black spear-shaped courier vessel, two hundred meters long, with stealth capabilities and Tsasinov drive. The first men in have already extended the main gangway.

Cato strides up the gangway, Lomin and Basileus behind him. Bloodguard are marching in their wake as if on inspection. Basileus cannot help but feel pride in his father, who has brought them all safely through this sick night of terror.

The hangar fills with a roar as the courier's a-grav units are brought on line. A great rumble is heard as servos are powered up to operate the overhead canopy doors. They pass into the ship and then into a waiting maglev that whisks them and two Bloodguards to the bridge. There Basileus finds most of the astrogation stations manned by Bloodguard who are expected to perform naval tours. A dark-skinned Bloodguard captain approaches them and salutes Cato. "M'lord, the men are familiarizing themselves with the controls. The man I've put in charge of engineering tells me he has the conventional drives to full power and Tsasinov drive a-mat core will be to power in less than ten minutes."

"Good work, Captain," Cato says, clapping the man on the shoulder. "What kind of weapons package are we working with?"

The Bloodguard captain's face breaks into a wide bright smile. "Four heavy sensor drones, eight high-speed advance sensor drones, plus a manufacturing suite; five heavy a-mat plasma cannons, two with forward-firing arcs, one on the port side, one starboard side, and one astern; five forward-firing torpedo tubes including countermeasure launcher; two tubes firing astern; and, m'lord, there are eight missile launchers. We have six long-range Vikings with multiple attack a-mat war heads. We are cataloging the ordnance now." Then suddenly the man turns a hard stare on Lomin.

"My government maintained an agreement with the Imperium in which these vessels were supplied and maintained," there is a note of disdain in Lomin's voice for the Bloodguard daring to question his loyalty.

Cato puts a reassuring hand on Lomin's shoulder. "Well done, Captain, very good. Lomin tells me this ship can make it to Titan in one jump."

"Yes, sir. It's far. It's five, maybe six days. Can't be exact until we commence a warpfold," answers the Bloodguard giving Lomin an apologetic glance.

"M'lord, what about the Naval Base in Alpha Centauri?" questions Cato's Bloodguard, General Praetor Piter Mugabe-Hane Hamar. "We could be there in less than an hour."

Gently Cato says: "Piter, if there were help to be had then it would have arrived. More than likely they experienced sabotage as we did. But if we get a signal that loyal forces have regained control of the system we'll turn around."

"Thank you, m'lord," says the General.

"Sir, as far as I can tell we're clear of overhead air and orbital traffic. I estimate a six-minute window," shouts a Takazhr from one of two science scanning stations.

"Take us out, Piter," Cato orders.

Cato's Bloodguard Praetor General nods to the Bloodguard Captain who greeted them, and the Captain gives orders for lift-off.

Through the forward view port they see the roof canopy door's explosive bolts trigger and desert begins to cascade into the underground hangar. Immediately the courier begins lifting, falling sand and dirt flashing crystallized blue on the ship's shields.

In the arrowhead-shaped bridge, Cato, Basileus, and Lomin grab onto the railing around the command console occupied by Piter and the Bloodguard Captain standing behind him steadying himself on the command chair. The view outside tilts upwards as the courier clears the hangar doors and pulls its nose up and away from the desert's surface. The remaining two vessels are scuttled and the deck beneath them rumbles. None of them look back.

"They see us!" reports the Takazhr from the scanning station. "A drone is relaying our position to an orbiting battleship. Incoming fire!"

"Launch countermeasures. Evasive action," orders the Bloodguard Captain.

The courier sways gently, clearing the incoming fire without being hit. Already the view outside is space. Soon, stars streak by. There is a sudden flash and the stars now look like spectral comets as the ship enters the relative safety of warpfold. A cheer goes up from the bridge crew. Basileus embraces Cato and Cato allows himself a moment to return his son's affection.

"What's wrong, father?" asks Basileus, surprised by his father's spontaneous display.

"So many things, Basileus, but at this moment nothing is wrong," Cato answers. Cato turns to Lomin. "Lomin, we need intel. I want to use the ship's briefing room to view news broadcasts," he says.

"This class ship has no briefing room to speak of Cato, but we will use the chart room directly astern," responds the Tempellian as he begins floating toward the rear of the bridge. He has answered in his familiar mentoring voice, but his shoulders sag and his head is down, and Cato feels a sense of dread akin to the day of Persis' shuttle accident.

"Are you all right, Lomin?" asks Cato as the iris to the chart room spirals closed behind Lomin, Basileus, and him.

The old man nods and he and the others begin activating comm and holo screens.

The grandfatherly Walter Merrick of GNN, his well-known silver hair in disarray, appears in the holo field of the chart table. Cato, familiar with Earth architecture, knows the reporter is transmitting from New London in front of the Restored Parliament at Westminster. The sky behind the reporter is an ugly gray, obscuring the noonday sun.

"I tell you, this reporter has never seen anything like what he's seen this morning—the devastation, the refugees, the coastal damage, the intense relief efforts. For those of you just joining us on Imperium Standard Time, Good Morning. Tragedy on Earth, Sacred Home: last night at approximately 2038 hours during the Omnividome Uprising Ceremonies, fusion and a-mat attacks began on orbital and system colonies. Deathmen terrorists have assassinated Empress-Executrix Anastacia III and her husband, the First Lord, Prince Millian."

The announcer bows his head in genuine sorrow again. He has repeated the statement more times than he can count and each time he reports the news he relives the catastrophe.

"The entire Atlantean Island Continent was obliterated in a mass conversion attack by a weapon outlawed and forbidden since the Wasting. I want to warn our viewers that the scenes we are about to show are quite graphic. Discretion is advised."

"Change it!" Cato commands, not wanting to see what he already knows.

The chart table holo projectors change to a scene of explosions on the Highport Naval Yard but again changes to the EWN logo. The announcer is an unfamiliar woman w i t h black hair and harried brown eyes.

"The entire planet if not the entire Imperium seems in state of siege. The death toll includes Princess Gabrielle and apparently the Crown Scion Prince Pfizer. The Imperium is nominally under control of the surviving Scion, Her Imperial Highness Princess Zoe Anne Gertrude Ambros. There have been calls for a Regency that names the oldest surviving member of the Imperial family, Princess Oriana Fen Anastacia Ambros, as Regis. This has been confirmed by the Ilkani Church and several other major CIMB holders. With the chaos on Earth affecting the Imperium from the viceregal level to the priory, we have yet to hear from several levels of the executive branch. I am sorry to say that EWN's Military Correspondent, Cassandra Joss, was lost with the destruction of the Pinnacle and the ensuing obliteration of the Atlantean Island Continent. For Military updates, our correspondent…"

Out of the corner of his eye with his attention focused on the chart table's holo field, Cato sees Lomin suddenly slouch against the chart table. By the time Cato reaches him the Tempellian is lying face-down on the floor.

"Get help, Basil. Hurry! Lomin! Lomin, what's wrong? Speak to me!" cries Cato. The sound of desperation and anguish in his father's voice breaks Basileus' heart as he runs out the iris. "It would have been faster to use the communicator," whispers Lomin. as Cato turns him over and gently lowers him to the floor cradling the old man's head in his lap. Cato tries to smile at Lomin's jest but begins weeping like a child.

"I see the little boy I began teaching almost three hundred years ago. Do not be afraid," and there is gentle teasing in Lomin's voice. He tries to wipe the tears from Cato's face but he cannot even raise his hand.

Cato shakes his head emphatically like a small child. "Don't speak, Lomin, please. What will I do?" The great giant's head sags and he is consumed by his emotions.

Basileus and two Bloodguard medics practically leap through the iris. As Cato prepares to stand out of the way Lomin grabs him with surprising strength and holds him.

"You will do what I taught you. What was born into you." It is the first time Cato remembers seeing Lomin angry. "You will listen, you will look, and you will learn." The elderly Tempellian tries to smile but his face becomes a grimace of pain. "Something horrible has happened to Tempel. Cato, there is no time."

"No time? Wha—?" Cato begins but just then a violent seizure grips Lomin. By the time the medics reach Lomin his body is still.

"Save him!" Cato orders. The two medics begin working furiously, scanning Lomin's prone form, attaching cardio and encephalo stimulators to his chest and head. It is a scene all too familiar now to father and son.

"I'm sorry, m'lord. There is nothing we can do. He's on total life support and we're having trouble maintaining a sufficient level of brain activity. The best we can do is put him in a surgo-op set for stasis. Maybe more experienced doctors on Titan can do more," reports the Bloodguard medic as he stands up still looking down at Lomin.

"Lomin," Cato whispers sadly. The Kurseg of the Takazhr kneels beside his fallen mentor and places his forehead to Lomin's. "Until we meet on the other side where there is no pain," he says quietly. Suddenly the equipment keeping Lomin's body alive begins beeping ominously. Cato draws back more from curiosity than from fear as the medics begin rechecking the equipment. Basileus, standing, is the first to notice:

"Father? He's disappearing!"

Cato shakes his head to focus on the here and now. Truly Lomin's body inside his lifesuit is ghostlike, glowing with soft brilliance. There is an expanding flash that seems to pass through all of them, and suddenly the body is gone. Only the black lifesuit, Lomin's yellow robes, and the life support equipment remain.

"His body!" Basileus exclaims. "What happened?" he asks, turning to his father.

Once again tears fall from Cato's gold eyes. "Tempel has been destroyed."

"Father, do you know what happened? Is this how they die? Where is Lomin?" asks Basileus. now wondering if Lomin's death, on top of all the others, has pushed his father too far.

Cato, not bothering to wipe the tears from his face, smiles paternally at his son. "No,. I don't know. But Lomin...Lomin is here," says Cato, placing his hand over his heart. Basileus notices that his father's eyes have gained a bird-bright quality.

CHAPTER 30

Fool me once, shame on you. Fool me twice,
shame on me.

—Old Earth children's rhyme, En'Zefi File

Grand Admiral Sir Nicodemus Von Haagen Zhao knew he
should have left the orbital bombardment and destruction of
New Eden to his battle cruiser commanders. He should have
engaged Cameron and the *Bismarck* directly. But Jovion and
Oriana had insisted that he personally oversee the assault on
the Omnividome and assure their orbital superiority. When the
Bismarck had limped from orbit, in a desperate attempt to
escape the star system, he made the mistake of thinking the
battle cruisers *Agamemnon*, *Ajax* and *Lysis* were more than
enough to finish Cameron and the escaping Lion onboard the
Bismarck. Now he wishes he followed his instincts and
observed the ages-old adage:

"If you want something done right, do it yourself," Zhao
says aloud.

"Sir," says his first officer, an Erosi Invid, Commodore
Kristane Bodecia Invid-Zana. The right side of her face is
marked with the dark blue and hunter green tattoo runes of
her Clan. Like all Invid she is angelic in her beauty, her face
radiant with vitality framed by luxuriant rose fire hair. She
appears as a Valkyrie in the condition-red lighting of the
Guderian's bridge.

Before the Wasting the Family of Liesel Aeon and Lucent
Invid had sired The Invid Nation, which had rivaled the Hane

211

for control of the Erosi Alliance. The Invid had been ardent E-mortal and Aeon extremists and had sided with the Tene Thantos during the Wasting. Even after the destruction of most of their population and loss of much their territories to the Hane, they still maintained enough numbers and territory to send an Elector to the Erosi Alliance and a ClanLord to the Convocation of the United Clans. Still, the stigma that was on all Chosen was more on the Invid, so twenty years ago they had sided with Oriana. Jasmine was, after all, a planet of the Invid Nation and Oriana's lover had been an Invid. The Invid forces had fought fiercely albeit briefly to wrest control of the Erosi alliance from the Hane. After Oriana's defeat, Balthasar and the Hane had responded brutally, stripping the Invid of all their territories except for their ancestral home in the Acheron wasteland of Hecate. They retained their colonies on fiery Inferno on the edge of oblivion, and those on the cold waste of Ultima Thule. However, the relatively few Invid who survived still represented a power in the known universe, to be feared and desired.

"We should have ignored Baron Quiso's orders and gone after the *Bismarck* ourselves, Kristane."

"Sir, you followed your orders, sir," she says. "But I agree. I'm doubly to blame. We should have never underestimated a Grand Admiral and I should never have underestimated a Hane."

Zhao is tempted to ask his first officer why. He finds the racism behind her comment repulsive. But she is right albeit for different reasons. The Hane are not to be underestimated.

He never wanted all this senseless destruction. "Ship's status," he demands quietly.

"As you know, sir," reports Commodore Zana, coming to attention instinctively, "the *Bismarck* has gone to warpfold and headed for Eros. We are in pursuit at maximum warpfold and are only minutes behind in real time. According to our probes that survived the destruction of our battle cruisers, the *Bismarck* suffered minor damage to starboard side weapons emplacements and starboard conventional drive." "Have our

LRSDs reached Eros?" Zhao asks his first officer. More to himself he says: "Maybe I can get an idea of the coming battleground conditions, choose where to intercept Grand Admiral Tanenov."

"No sir, but we can receive naval audvid communications from relays in the Erosi Star System," Zana answers, while motioning from the Communications Control as she anticipates the Admiral's next orders.

"Let's hear it," Zhao commands and he watches, Julian, his Communications Officer, make an adjustment in his console's control fields.

"This is Admiral Kenda-Hane. All ships prepare to re-engage. Destroyers, attack pattern Shaka." The usually superbly calm and maddeningly self-assured face of Remus Kenda-Hane is animated with nothing less than tension and disbelief. There are fires on the bridge around him, explosions and crackling circuitry and the screams of the wounded and dying.

Is this an encirclement maneuver? Who are they fighting?! Are they intercepting Cameron? And re-engage? *The Bismarck should be no match for a fresh dreadnought group.* "Commodore, I want data," Zhao demands. *What is going on? Are the Tene trying to start another Wasting? Have they used me?... Played me like—*

"Strategic Operations Officer, I don't care how you do it but get us long-range telemetry from that battle site," Zana is already commanding from the console on the platform behind him. There is a flurry of activity behind the Strategic Operations Officer and down on the Command deck with communications personnel. Meanwhile, the communications interception continues:

"This is INS Destroyer *Arden* we have taken heavy damage. Captain Gerling is dead as is most of the bridge crew. I am twelfth in the chain of command, sir, Lieutenant Rosa, in Auxiliary Control. Request permission to disengage," begs the plainly terrified junior officer who to Zhao appears a young woman no older than his daughter or nieces. *Little more than a child herself.* Her face is blackened and streaked with soot from fighting fires.

"Negative!" Shouts Admiral Kenda-Hane as he yells into the holo's pickup, his face looming larger. "You will re-engage. If that thing gets through, our home will be destroyed. Now re-engage!"

"Yes, sir. Yes, sir," the young woman says regaining her composure. "Re-engaging at maximum speed, attack pattern Shaka."

"Sir? What's going on?" asks his First Officer. "I understood the Deathship was only to attack Tempel." For the first time there is alarm in her voice.

"Maybe they knew the Grand Admiral fled with the Grand Kurseg to Eros. The Deathship would be the only ship that could catch them besides us. Especially if the Hane navy officers in the sector defected to Grand Admiral Tanenov," she says, rationalizing her questions and doubts.

"No... No, they're not just here after the *Bismarck*. I should have known. Listening to Quiso's mad dog, Nasir, I should have known," Zhao says aloud as one of the holo monitors shows the young woman from the destroyer scream and die before the holo monitor goes blank. The holos showing the bridge of *Gert* show nothing but fiery wreckage being whisked into the vacuum of space by a hull breach in that area. "No, Kristane. The *Bismarck* is not even there, and they are destroying ships they could have used as allies. Their intentions are clear. The Tene intend to repeat their maneuver at Tempel here," Zhao says flatly.

"B...But our alliance. The epitome of the Human Race is in the Erosi Star System," the Commodore mutters, openly expressing her views.

"Apparently the Tene Thantos do not agree with you, Commodore," Zhao snaps, bitterness coloring his voice. "Communications Officer, I want you to signal the Deathship the minute we emerge from warpfold. Inform them we want to assist in neutralizing Eros' orbital defenses to facilitate planetary bombardment at their direction."

"Sir, you can't be serious," begins the Communication's

Officer.

"I am, Julian, but I have something else in store for our allies. Kristane get the Commander of Engineering up here," Zhao orders. *I will never be used again. No matter what, I will do the right thing.*

CHAPTER 31

Honesty, though a virtue, is dangerous.

—Tene Thantos Aphorism

Inside the ornate confines of his study at the Ilkanite Palace, in what had once been the ancient Vatican City, Assur-Banipal, the Magus of the Ilkani Church, wrings his hands in nervous anticipation. *A Deathship! Tempel has been destroyed by the Deathmen of the Tene Thantos, although it will be hours before the rest of the Imperium knows.* Dressed in his most formal silver robes and matching skull cap he is an imposing figure, even amidst the holy relics of the ages that adorn the walls and tabletops of his study. Today though, the Magus feels troubled and diminished. Usually upon donning his robes of office he feels buoyed by righteous convictions, yet ever since the harrowing flight from the destruction of New Eden and Atlantis…

The Magus walks to the large French doors that open out onto to the balcony overlooking what was once Saint Peter's Square, now the Plaza of Naraji. A great multitude of the Faithful, troubled and seeking spiritual solace, has gathered beneath a gray gently precipitating sky and the ancient and modern splendor of Nova Roma.

The far doors to the Magus' study, which lead into the ancient Vatican Palace proper, swing open and *they* enter. Jovion Quiso and Nasir Qamar, and with them their abomination, what appears to be a four-year-old girl, the exact likeness of the Princess Zoe Ambros. Never had the Magus

216

been so grateful for the presence of Bloodguards outside his door. Over the protests of his son and most of the Curia he had leased an entire division to augment the Ilkani Church's elite Swiss Daakan Security. He no longer believed the Daakan could defend him, even the two in this room, after he had seen what the Deathmen had done in New Eden. And now these monsters had destroyed Tempel. *Anastacia's stupid Fragmentation Initiative has died with her; there would be no more talk of democracy.* Although it seems obvious only to him, there are far worse things in the universe than the misguided Ambros idealism.

He has to be careful not to let his loathing for this Tene Thantos apparition of Oriana's sister to show. The girl creature smiles sweetly at him, but it requires all of his emoto-control to keep repellence and hatred from his eyes. *How dare these neo-human demons bring this unholy ghoul creature into the Sacred Precincts? They will seek to gain the Church's support in favor of Regency under Oriana for this Tene Thantos golem replicant. Then the minute they get this our days of usefulness to them will be numbered.*

"How dare you announce the Holy Church's support of Regency?" Assur-Banipal begins offensively, turning his back on them and striding in a swishing of robes to the French doors of the balcony. The view of the Faithful, so innocent, gathered, looking up at him gives him strength.

"Is your courage due to the Bloodguards outside this door? Or have you gone mad, old Human?" Nasir Qamar asks icily, the jewels and gold of his tunic glittering.

"If there were Bloodguard here, he would not dare speak that way to me," says the little Princess who is not a little Princess in the hideous voice of an old crone. The creature seems to delight at the horror in the Magus' face.

Oh yes you are horrible you miserable little beast but you do not scare me. "I say again, *how dare you*?! Answer me, Jovion!" The Magus shouts.

Jovion blinks and continues into the room, seating himself without invitation before the Magus' desk in one of two ancient high-backed leather chairs with actual wooden legs.

"Did you see the Princess Oriana's speech last night?" Jovion asks rhetorically in his dulcet Serdian tones. "She was magnificent: 'My mother, our Empress-Executrix, now belongs to the ages.' Half the Admirals there were ready to declare her Empress-Executrix. What's left of the Bloodguard High Command is spoiling for revenge and she's promised them they'll get it. The Takazhr want to round up any Aeon with suspicious connections."

"Good, let the Blood Wars begin," snarls Nasir, spit flying from his mouth as he stares at the Magus with glowering hatred. "The sooner we get the stink of these humans off us the better."

"Don't interrupt me, Nasir," Jovion, usually composed and civil, barks. Instantly Nasir comes to heel and stands quietly behind his master's high-backed chair.

"As I was saying, the shock seems to have catapulted all the high cards to Oriana's hand. We need to maintain some kind of hold on Oriana *and you,* lest the anti-terrorist wave that is about to sweep the Imperium gather us in its deadly grip," Jovion answers, once again pleasant.

"Oily devil!" bellows the Magus, and the second he utters the words the Magus knows they are literally true, that his visions have been real and this is Satan. "A Regency—in that monster's name?!" he says, pointing at the replicant. "The week she comes of age Oriana, I, and who knows how many others will die. You destroyed Atlantis! The entire continent!" *I do not care. My rage is right and true.* "You ravaged this planet, the birth place of the human race! Sacred Home! Tempel with a billion inhabitants. And the Only God alone knows how many millions of students and visitors perished at the Academy! The knowledge lost in the great libraries. Stop smiling at me, you inhuman monster, and answer me!" the Magus screams.

"We did not order Atlantis destroyed. We, the Tene, did not do it. Oriana did, and Zhao carried out her order. I have a recording of her order. Would you like to see it?" The Devil Baron says sweetly.

"As to the Tempellians," Jovion shrugs continuing, "knowledge is the most dangerous of weapons. They had far too much to go on living. They would have eventually been a threat. Now they're not. And darling Zoe here insures that neither are the soon-to-be Regis Oriana or you. You implicate or expose us and you will destroy yourselves. Ahh-ah, wait," says Jovion, seeing that the Magus is on the verge of another explosion. "The replicant will never reach the age of fifteen. Long before that age she could ascend to the Phoenix Throne. Instead, she will terminate due to a spontaneous allergic reaction. I will show you the medical files if you like," Jovion continues calmly.

"Uhh?" the Magus mutters, his fury foundering on this new revelation. He stares with pity at the replicant, who watches him with baleful eyes that appear a fiendish yellow. The Magus shakes his head marshaling his thoughts and his anger. *Do they think me stupid? Arrogant Aeon. Typical.* "What about the Deathship?!" he demands. "A Deathship! Right out of the Wasting! How many have you built, demon?! Don't lie! I'll know, and if you lie to me, I swear by the Only God I will expose us right here and now, agreements be damned!" finishes the Magus towering over the sitting Jovion like an a-mat warhead. The child-replicant's eyes are wide and Nasir surges forward but is stopped by an upraised hand from Jovion.

Well, well, what have we here? You've just forfeited your life, old fool, thinks Jovion, seething with rage at the Magus' threats, but he says: "Only three. An additional one is under construction. They should suffice for now." Jovion is the epitome of civility, watching with inner glee the impact his words have on the Magus. *Until Nasir can build more, many more! Then, old sow, we will slaughter you shorted-lived apes.*

So many? Already? What do they intend to do with them?! the Magus thinks.

"No more, Your Honor, Baron Quiso. Do you

understand me? I'm going to want Daakan Observers on those vessels with full access to communications," says the Magus calmly, addressing Quiso by his title.

Again, Nasir is about to protest but is stopped by Jovion with a simple raising of the hand "Agreed," Jovion says simply. "But we have other things to consider. Most importantly, the late Empress' Chief Nimrod is still alive, and the Lion is on his way to Eros with Grand Admiral Cameron Tanenov. We have therefore dispatched a Deathship to the Spican Star System."

"Are you insane? If you destroy the tursapoi then those Bloodguard and Takazhr who are addicts will go mad. It could start a civil war! The surviving Hane will not rest until they destroy those responsible," yells the Magus, losing his composure again at the hands of this wicked Baron.

"Be calm *Wise Man*," says Jovion, translating the Magus' title. "It will also cripple the last vestiges of Imperial authority. We've already discovered Naval Admirals can be bought. The people will have to turn even more to you, your Eminence. And as for the Hane, if Gert Hane had finished what he started we wouldn't be here now."

The Magus laughs inwardly to himself. *He truly thinks me stupid. Without Bloodguards the other Aristos and Magnates of the Imperium will once again build private armies for protection, or worse conquest, and with the Navy so obviously fragmented some may enlist Navy support. The ground is indeed being laid for civil war if not another Wasting.* For a moment The Magus considers ordering his Daakan to kill these three, conventions be damned, and perhaps the Only God would forgive him his past sins for ending this travesty. However, there are too many variables and more than likely it is he and his Daakan who would be killed.

"More than likely, much more," Jovion utters coolly to the confusion of the replicant and Nasir.

"You're a *telepath*? I thought the telepathic gene was expunged from the Quiso bloodline." *Oh, what a weapon he has just given me. If I let it be known that a male descendant of*

Armingkon Quiso, progenitor of the Wasting, is a telepath the crowd outside this building would tear the palace down to get him.

"M'lord, why have you revealed this to this gene muck?" Nasir asks, almost mournfully.

"Because I grow tired of hiding what I am. The time is almost right for full disclosure. I have allowed the Wise Man to see merely another piece of my enigma. I have also just bound us by chains of mutual vulnerability. Now we must protect each other's secrets. As I said, your Eminence, we have more important things to deal with. Cato Ahren and Creed Hane are still alive."

"Come now, Baron Quiso, let us be reasonable. There is no need to destroy Eros. Ravage it perhaps and lay to rest the insane notions of democracy the Ambros and Hane wanted. Convince the people we need a strong central authority to protect us from threats like this Tene Thantos re-insurgency," the Magus suggests and immediately regrets his words.

"Destroy them. Kill them all. Nucleo their whole pathetic world. They have to pay for what the Hane did to us—did to *your family*, m'lord. The Ancient Debt must be paid with blood," growls Nasir from behind Jovion.

"Never bring this monster into the Holy Precincts again, Baron Quiso. The Daakan will have orders to shoot it," the Magus says, calm again, sitting now behind his intricate carved mahogany desk. "I don't want Eros destroyed. Remember that our future Regis, Oriana, is by birth also Hane. I don't think she'll appreciate your exterminating her father's family, especially the family of the grandfather who died protecting her," the Magus says earnestly.

"It's too late, old fool. The Deathship is already on its way," Nasir says with delight.

"Send a message, change your orders," the Magus replies. "You can use the warpfold network that was part of the Omnividome project. And please Baron Quiso send Mr. Qamar away. I weary of his constant barking and posturing," the Magus says, this time refusing to be baited.

Jovion looks thoughtfully at the Magus. This is indeed a

wily old human. He just might be useful. "You make a good point about Eros. I will send a message. Nasir, you must leave, my friend," Jovion commands, though still politely, as the black Aeon Magnate looks ready to begin another rabid diatribe. Nasir glowers at The Magus once more and sulks from the room.

"You see, your Eminence, you and I can work together."

"Compromise is one of Satan's weapons and you wield it well, m'lord Baron. Now, please tell me, how do you plan to insert this other...comrade of yours?" the Magus questions, indicating the replicant with a nod of his head. "Many believe, rightfully so, that the real Zoe is dead."

"We've already leaked a cover story. Her Bloodguards, fearing they were being tracked, changed the Princess' clothing and deposited her in one of the marine lifeboat pods at the Grumman Bay Cruise Terminal. That's actually true, up to that point, Eminence. Then my people caught up with her and her Bloodguards and we eliminated them and disposed of her— once we'd taken what we needed from the child to make the replicant. I have informed Oriana already and she is on her way here to retrieve her "sister." You and the Daakan are heroes, providing little Zoe here with shelter after Red Crescent Red Cross Relief teams plucked her little pod from the cold Atlantic," Jovion says, gently stroking the child's honey hair.

Though he feels nauseated hearing this, the Magus maintains his dignity. "And the third Deathship is for Titan and Cato Ahren, I assume," he says, disgusted at how casually and easily this neo-human demon ordered horrific murder and destruction. "Excuse my thoughts, Baron, but your actions disgust me," he adds, drawing back in his chair.

"Of course, any good commander has contingency plans. Ordering death becomes an anticipated variable after a time, but in honor of our new understanding I will spare the planet Titan from complete destruction, provided our assault forces can find and eliminate Cato Ahren. After all, the planet yields valuable CIMB-level commodities and raw materials," answers Jovion, noticing how this seems to mollify the Magus and prevent yet another outburst.

There is a sudden buzzing and a holographic projection ring artfully concealed beneath the desk activates. "Pardon the interruption, your Eminence, but we have word the Princess Oriana and her retinue will arrive shortly. They are on their way here from the Ostia Cosmodome," says the disembodied head of the Magus' personal secretary.

"Thank you, Father Ferra. I'll be out shortly. Assemble a suitable honor guard of Bloodguard and Daakan so that we may take the Scion to meet her sister. Please inform the representatives from the Judeo-Orange Union, the Zen-Buddhists, and the Catholic-Islamic Alliance of our situation here. They may join us in meeting the Princess Oriana, and then we can attend to business. And Antonio, ask my son to join us as well," the Magus says standing. To Quiso he says, "I believe you have some counter-orders to make. After you're done, however, and provided that my observers are on board the Deathships, you may join me in recognizing Oriana Ambros as Her Imperial Majesty Queen-Executrix—this will make public your liaison with her." The Magus couches his additional demands in conciliatory tones.

"I appreciate the offer, Eminence," Quiso says rising and bowing his head slightly. "If you simply will tell Oriana I will contact her later, that will suffice for now. Go with the Magus, Eris," Jovion says to the replicant.

"*Eris.* You named it for the spirit of strife," the Magus whispers. *Was there no end to these Tene Thantos perversions?*

"I like my real name. I think it suits me," the replicant answers in the dead Zoe's sweet child voice.

Outside the *Camera Magus* Jovion joins Nasir and watches as the Magus forces himself to take the replicant by the hand and lead her away surrounded by Bloodguard and Daakan into a brightly lit passage.

"Nasir, give orders that Titan is to be spared. Find another planet for our Deathmen to feed on after they eliminate the Ahrens. Make preparations to receive Daakan observers on Board the Deathship and begin looking for a new star system for new ship construction facilities," Jovion instructs, knowing it is only a matter of time before Oriana and Assur-Banipal demand the destruction of the orbital and planetary docks designated Tartarus that circle the fifth planet in the Zaelon Star System. It is there at Tartarus that Quiso had initiated the construction of Deathships and it is where, even now, Deathmen are growing in number and force. He holds up a hand while he activates a spy shield surrounding the two in a cylinder of ghostlike red energy.

"What of the Erosi?" Nasir questions, oddly calm in the presence of only Jovion.

"Burn their planet, shatter it," Jovion hisses, a smile of utter contentment on his angelic face.

"What about what that gene muck charlatan said about alienating Oriana? What about his Observers?" Nasir asks pensively in his deep baritone.

Behind Nasir's rabid posturing is a sharp mind. He is, after all, one of the most powerful Magnates of the Imperium and an Aeon, the product of millennia of ambition. "He may be right…But who cares? It will be after the fact. We'll say our Deathship commander was over zealous. It will be simply: too bad, too late. And if the Observers attempt to interfere with our operation, what's a few more dead Ilkani?" Jovion replies. "Come, my faithful servant. I want to view Oriana's reunion with her 'sister.'" Jovion deactivates the spy shield. He turns and Nasir follows him down into the darker recesses of the Ilkanite Palace.

CHAPTER 32

While love can exalt, it can also ruin.

—Erosi Aphorism

"Warning: Airlock AP1 Emergency Venting," blares the marineguard transports computer as Otto is about to tell Pfizer not to give himself over to hatred. The ship rocks from a dangerous change in air pressure and Otto turns to look for Lux to ask him what can possibly be happening when he realizes he has not seen the Tempeler since they boarded. "Where is Counselor Luxvico?" Otto asks Pfizer, as calmly as possible.

Pfizer's electric gray eyes immediately go wide with worry. "I don't know," Pfizer answers, panic edging his voice. "Where's this airlock, Otto?" Pfizer asks, getting up from the seat by the surgo-op.

"Aft-port side, deck one," Otto says, remembering his naval training. His power blaster has already sprung into his hand and in his other is his Hephaestus. "Stay here," he says to Pfizer, charging out the iris. The Bloodguard Rescue Commander follows after him. Pfizer, who has no thought of staying, dogs on his helmet and runs after them. Usually he could never hope to keep up with Otto, but in the powered armor he is right on his heels when they reach the airlock.

They find Luxvico huddled in a fetal position, naked, shivering before the airlock inner door. The Tempellian is covered in some gold viscous fluid that to Otto smells faintly of chicken broth. "Lux—is he all right?" asks Pfizer, trying to push past Otto who has turned to hold him back.

"Please stay back, Domino," the Rescue Commander says, as he pulls out a scanner and begins diagnosing Luxvico. "No toxins, no radiological traces or biohazards detectable," reports the Rescue Commander, passing the scanner over Luxvico again.

In powered armor Pfizer easily struggles free of Otto's grasp and opens one of the emergency lockers beside the airlock. From it he pulls blankets and a towel from plastic seals. "Are you all right, Counselor Luxvico?" Pfizer asks again, handing Otto a towel to hand to Lux.

Otto nods at Pfizer's gesture and accepts the towel before handing it to Luxvico who immediately clears his bald head and face of what had been his lifesuit's nutribath.

"I realized...," the Tempellian begins through chattering teeth as Otto drapes a blanket over him "...that we ha-had tt-taken ss-so mm-many precautions not to be tracked and I w-was the only one logical choice to kk-keep a permanent fix on His Royal Highness. M-my lifesuit emits or rather emitted a n-negligible but identifiable power signature for those who w-wanted to find it. I could not trust the ship's shields to block the signal but by ejecting it there's a ch-chance they may think our ship destroyed. I recommend you j-jettison approximately twelve kilograms of a-mat plasma with a three minute-delay, and fuse the explosion to lay all doubt to rest."

"Do it!" Pfizer commands, before anyone else can react. The Rescue Commander salutes and moves to the side to use his audvid link to contact the bridge. "Will you be all right without the lifesuit, Counselor?"

"I am relatively certain I will be," says Luxvico, more normally now that the blanket has raised his body temperature "Though I will have to adapt as you do, eating,...sleeping." There's the faintest hint of disgust in Luxvico's voice as Otto helps him into a single-piece marineguard working uniform, dark blue almost black armored mesh. Whether Lux is disgusted by the prospect of eating and sleeping or by the standard issue Imperial cotton underclothing and armored mesh Pfizer is uncertain. Otto shows Luxvico how to fasten the quick seals in the front of the uniform. Luxvico scratches around his chest and neck but at least he is no longer shivering.

"There. How's that?" asks Otto, standing back to view his handy work. The muscular Tempellian does look every bit a marineguard in shipside duty uniform. Otto is about to tease Lux about this when he notices the Tempeler stiffen and go utterly still. Luxvico's eyes widen in shock and disbelief. He is seeing something in his mind, something horrific. After a few moments his body goes limp and he whispers, "No!"

"What's wrong, Lux?" Otto asks.

"Tempel is gone.," Luxvico says.

"What do you mean, Lux?" Otto asks. *It can't be possible. Tempel gone?!*

"Tempel has been destroyed." Luxvico says again, as if to make sense of the words. "I was just there with my family. They are no more."

"Lux?" Otto gasps.

Pfizer's jaw clenches but he remains silent. He understands.

Luxvico continues,his words flat and even, "My great-great-grandchildren were running in fields of red saw grass outside our solar farm. My wife Roelyn and my daughter Rexalla were watching them. Roelyn was the first to hear the sonic boom as the mass-drive weapons penetrated our defenses and entered Tempel's atmosphere. The children stopped running and they were pointing at what they thought were comets or meteors. Then they turned and ran back toward the solar farm. ... No!" Lux whispers again, as if he had the power to stop what had already come to pass.

"I'm so sorry, Lux. So sorry," Otto whispers as he takes in the magnitude of what he has just heard.

Pfizer just stares at Luxvico.

The three are silent. There is nothing to say.

After a few moments, Luxvico pulls himself up straight. His emoto-control is once again in place. His eyes are shaded by the bill of his marineguard cap, embossed with the transport's name, INS MGT-BI-1 *Vendetta.*

What an appropriate name, Pfizer thinks.

Otto's audvid link sounds, breaking the silence. Activating it he has a brief discussion with the Rescue Commander then turns to the other two. "We just jettisoned and denoted the Counselor's a-mat decoy package," Otto informs them. "Let's hope it works. We're almost halfway to our rendezvous point with the *Bismarck.* Why don't we go to the command and control bay?" he suggests.

"I'd rather stay with Heath," says Pfizer, pulling off his helmet.

"I agree with Captain Praetor Buchanan. If we go to command and control we can view news broadcast, ascertain what is happening without jeopardizing our position, possibly even find news of survivors," Luxvico says, looking pointedly at both of them. "It's very important that we find out the position of the rest of your family, Your Royal Highness, notably the Hane and my people," Luxvico adds.

Pfizer sees hope enter into Otto's face at the mention of survivors and knows his Praetor and friend would wait with him by the surgo-op out of duty but his heart would be in the command and control bay worrying about his family. "Okay Lux. Otto, the bridge it is."

The three take a maglev to the crowded dark red command and control bay, which is a flurry of activity when they arrive. But as Pfizer steps into the cramped cabin the Master at Arms by the maglev iris shouts, "Attention on deck: Emperor-Executor Pfizer Ambros!"

The command and control crew snaps to attention, *Emperor-Executor I am? ...Aren't I?*

My investiture is merely a formality, Pfizer thinks. "At ease, Major Battaglia. Until my formal investiture, Prince Pfizer will do," Pfizer says, addressing the Rescue Commander.

"My aides suggested we come to the command and control bay for a situation update," Pfizer says. As he nods toward Lux and Otto, Pfizer sees a look of extreme distress on Luxvico's usually emotionless face. The Tempeler puts a hand to his head and sways on his feet but Otto steadies him and guides him to an empty chair for observers in the command and control bay.

"Luxvico?" Otto inquires cautiously.

"Something has happened," Luxvico groans as if struggling for air. "I have tightness in my chest and stomach and there is a lump in my throat," Luxvico says sniffling and Pfizer notices there are tears in the Tempellians eyes. "Tempel has been destroyed and now they are killing the survivors," he whispers looking at Pfizer. Pfizer is desperately sorry that these are the first emotions he has ever seen Luxvico evince.

"Impossible!" interjects Major Battaglia, the Rescue Commander. "It would require the effort of half the Imperial Navy. You must be suffering the effects of removing—"

"Please verify Tempel's position in the warpfold navigational net," Otto directs, interrupting the Rescue Commander, who immediately signals the marineguard transport's navigator to follow Otto's request.

The navigator, an officer in the white and blue uniform of the Imperial Navy, checks his station's instruments, a holo projection chart table in the middle of the bay. A look of consternation comes over the man's face and he appears to double- and then triple-check his findings. When he turns to face them, the blood has drained from his face. "I can no longer verify the position of the planet Riffellon IX, Tempel," he says. "I am sorry, Counselor."

"Communication, start running through all passive comm intercepts and let's get some help up here to monitor news broadcast," Major Battaglia orders immediately.

"Gone… My whole world, the Academy, the Ministries, the great libraries, more than fifty thousand years of human knowledge, the brightest young minds of the Imperium— Gone," Luxvico mutters.

Pfizer can feel a scream building inside him. He loved the Academy, so much knowledge there for the asking. It would only have been a matter of time before every problem faced by the Human Race could have been solved. Or so he had once thought in his youthful naiveté. *These monsters respect nothing—not life, not knowledge!* In mere hours they had destroyed so much of what he loved and revered. His vision swims with red.

"Excuse me, Praetor Buchanan. Something you should see," a Bloodguard says, the one from Pfizer's retinue with the burn-damaged armor. He sits at one of three communication terminals and repeats, almost shouting, "Something you should see!"

In two steps Otto is behind the man. There on a holo with the GNN logo, a stylized image of the god Mercury, is Walter Merrick still reporting from New London, about to enter a Wiktor Foundation Hospital. Following him are Savoy Wiktor, wearing a heavy-hooded black cloak against a driving rain, and Marisol in a cloak of white Erosi seal edged in contrasting black Erosi mink. In her arms is Agust, in a yellow rain slicker.

"Mari, Gus," Otto says, reaching out his fingers to touch the tiny screen images.

"...with Savoy Wiktor is the equally famous Marisol Fitzgerald. Both are survivors of the Atlantean Holocaust. Is it true, Mr. Wiktor, that you've been asked by the PPRC to be Impgov Liaison?" Walter Merrick asks.

"Please, not now, Walter," says the image of Savoy Wiktor, putting his hand and then his body between the reporter and Marisol. "Mrs. Fitzgerald-Buchanan has been through a great deal. Her husband is among the Bloodguard missing. My office will respond to questions..."

"Marisol, your husband was Captain Praetor Otto Buchanan of the New Canaan Freehold on Eros, assigned to the late Crown Scion Prince Pfizer Ambros. Do you have any comments?" the GNN reporter presses.

"My office, Walter. Call my office and ask for Katherine Nielson," Savoy says, more insistently, before escorting Marisol through sliding glass doors and into the building.

Blue-uniformed Wiktor Foundation guards with actual gold badges and license to carry firearms bar entry to the reporters.

Otto, in shock, overwhelmed by the joy of seeing restored that which he had thought lost has to hold back tears of happiness. His knees are shaking, and Bloodguard and Naval officers in the cramped bay are congratulating him and patting him on the shoulder. He is not really distinguishing what they're saying. Then he hears Pfizer say: "I am happy for you, Otto. I'm glad they're safe," but Pfizer's voice is emotionless. Pfizer puts his hand on Otto's shoulder and squeezes, trying to give some emphasis to the words he knows were hollow and passionless.

Otto turns and looks into Pfizer's face—it's full of anger, grief, and barely masked hate. "I'm sorry about your mother and father, Pfizer," Otto says sadly. "Tempel, too. We both had a lot of friends there."

Pfizer gives Otto a quick hug. He actually smiles, brilliantly, handsomely. "I *am* happy for you," he says and the old light is almost there in his eyes. "Now if you'll excuse me, I'd like to use the head," he says almost jokingly. But as he turns Otto sees the light in his eyes vanish to be replaced again by the cold, hard stare.

Black spots now flicker in Pfizer's red vision. His head and heart ache and the latest display of emoto-control has left him exhausted. His family are gone. A wave of nausea grips him and he stumbles against the iris of the command and control bay's head. He opens the iris and practically falls inside. He slams up against a dual unit sink, turns on the water full blast, and begins vomiting. There is a buzzing from the ship's intercom. "Excuse me, Domino. Could you return to command and control, please sir?"

"I'll be right there," says Pfizer, toggling on a wall comm by the sink. He splashes his face with cold water, rinses his mouth. His vision begins to clear. He sighs deeply and glances at himself in the mirror, a black eye and split lip are all he has to show for tonight, yesterday, whenever it was. Billions dead in hours, including his immediate family, his parents and sisters.

One planet, Earth, savaged—many cities wrecked by terrorist attack, even more flooded by the deluge that followed the destruction of Atlantis by nucleo. The environmental damage was catastrophic and would take months to clean.

Another planet, Tempel, utterly destroyed—nothing but rubble circling a core of molten gases. Most of his friends had lived there; he had even considered living and teaching there until it was time to become Emperor-Executor. The burning behind his eyes has returned by the time he steps through the head's iris into the command and control bay.

"Over here, Domino, please sir," calls a Bloodguard two uniform seats down from the one who summoned Otto. "I was monitoring GNN. They just broke for news in Nova Roma. Look, Your Royal Highness—your sisters," the Bloodguard points enthusiastically.

"We're switching to Nova Roma on Earth where our probable new Crown Scion, Her Royal Highness the Princess Zoe is being reunited with the Princess Oriana," says the voice of an unseen announcer. The image shown on the holo screen is one of awesome splendor even for Nova Roma: Oriana's conveyance leading a procession of a thousand armored Bloodguard, with a hundred more in one of three CombatMecha armor modes—flyer, gladiator, or hover tank.

Rome has not seen such an Imperial force in untold millennia. The holo screen switches to the steps of the Ilkanite and the Basilica of The Messiah Naraji, once the old Vatican's St. Peter's Basilica. Princess Zoe runs down windswept steps to embrace her sister Oriana, who stands regal and beautiful, her own robes billowing in the afternoon breeze. The assembled crowd breaks into thunderous cheering, a moment of the best of humanity amidst such chaos.

"Major, I thought Zoe was dead?" Pfizer asks, finding he begins to shake. There's something wrong about the way Oriana holds Zoe, about the way Assur-Banipal, Magus of the Ilkani Church, watches them.

"We heard the Bloodguard defending her die," says Major Battaglia. "We saw the readings when she expired as well. I'm truly sorry Domino. There are records on the *Bismarck*," the man adds softly.

"Excuse me," Pfizer mutters, reaching over the Bloodguard to operate the holo zoom controls. Out of the comer of his vision he sees Luxvico rise slowly and head towards him.

Oh my God, no! Pfizer staggers back from the holo screen. Otto is beside him in a moment. Pfizer's mouth is open and all he can do is point at the screen. Luxvico has moved the Bloodguard operator aside and is now operating the holo screen himself.

"And it is our most reverent wish that our sister's exile be commuted and the Princess Oriana be allowed to serve as Regis until we come of age and claim our birthright," says the child's piping voice, a voice Otto takes to be Zoe's.

Pfizer groans.

"Luxvico, what's going on?" asks Otto. "What's wrong with him?"

"Not him, Captain Praetor," Luxvico says, handing the Bloodguard operator back his audvid link. "But *her*," Luxvico says, pointing at the tiny image of Zoe. "It's a replicant. A good one. It would take a family member or Temp—," suddenly Luxvico pauses and turns to Otto. "It's an impostor," Lux says simply.

All eyes turn to Pfizer with Lux's startling revelation.

"I'm okay," Pfizer says sitting up.

"Let's go back to the surgo-op. Let the Counselor have a look at you," Otto says, but Pfizer knows it's no request by the determined look on his face.

"Lieutenant Battaglia will record any relevant news for you," Luxvico adds.

Pfizer walks back quietly, through two compartments, between Luxvico and Otto, aware of the side-long glances each is giving him. "What? I give up," Pfizer says cautiously.

"Do you remember screaming in the head earlier?" Otto asks just as cautiously.

"I remember vomiting. But that was before I was on the intercom," Pfizer says, stepping through the iris into the surgo-op compartment. Pfizer finds his honor guard Heath MacKenzie sitting up while a Naval officer with medical caduceus on his collar passes a hand scanner over him. "At ease," Pfizer says, turning to face Otto and Luxvico coming through the iris behind him. "I said I'd be right there. Then I splashed my face and walked out."

"No. That's not what happened, Pfizer," Otto whispers, his bottle green eyes nervously searching his friend's face.

"Then what happened?!" Pfizer shouts angrily.

"You turned the intercom on and began screaming unintelligibly. Then you walked out as if nothing happened," Luxvico answers, actually hoping to deflect some of this uncharacteristic anger of Pfizer's away from Otto. "We Tempellians have words for everything," Luxvico continues. He heaves a great sigh and taps his chest. "But when this hurts, how does it speak? The heart has no tongue."

Otto finds himself moved by Luxvico's intimate confession. Pfizer, however… "That's not what happened!" Pfizer snaps, turning toward Luxvico.

"Hey! Hey!" Otto says, raising his sandpaper voice. "Let's forget about it," he says, looking pointedly at Luxvico. "Domino, please get some rest."

The way Otto says this touches something deep in Pfizer and he hops up on one of two examination beds. He swings his legs up and lays his head back on his hands behind his head.

"Happy now," he says to no one in particular. He looks up to see Luxvico looking down at him, the Tempellian's eyes shaded by the naval cap. Pfizer feels the coolness of a dermal match against his neck and then is suddenly very drowsy.

"What are you doing?" It's Heath's voice, menacing, threatening, and suddenly very close.

"At ease, Ensign Praetor," Pfizer hears Otto's voice calling for calm again. "How is your arm?" his voice asks. But then Pfizer hears Otto add, "Put your uniform on, Praetorian."

"Yes, sir," Heath's voice replies, moving away.

"How long will he sleep, Lux?" Otto asks, his voice more weary than Pfizer's ever heard it sound.

"Not long," Luxvico replies. "We have a little over an hour

to the rendezvous with the *Bismarck*. Why don't we all get some rest," he suggests.

Pfizer loses consciousness.

* * *

"I can help you. Will you let me?" It's Heath. He's standing in the dark wearing Bloodguard boxers and a t-shirt with the sleeves removed.

"Help me by staying here and protecting him," Otto whispers sharply in the dark. Pfizer can see him going over a Hephaestus before handing it to Luxvico. "If anything happens, or we're not back in twenty minutes, get armored and get to an escape pod," Pfizer hears Otto say.

"Respectfully, Captain Praetor, I don't think the four of us should separate," begins Heath.

"You have your orders, Praetorian," Otto hisses forcefully. There is a flare of light as the iris spirals open to the next compartment and Pfizer sees Otto's and Luxvico's silhouettes pass through before the iris just as quickly blinks shut.

"You're awake, Domino," Heath says.

He knew his disagreement with Otto woke me, Pfizer thinks. "Yes. What's happening?" Pfizer asks sitting up and only now realizing they'd left him in his armor. In the dim light Pfizer can see Heath pulling on cybernetic bodymesh. He winces as he pulls his left shoulder through, but he answers. "We've arrived at the rendezvous coordinates with the *Bismarck*, only it's not here, just a Heavy Long-Range Sensor Drone in slave orbit around the coordinates. They're bringing it on board now. The Captain Praetor and your Counselor went to go see it firsthand."

Pfizer calls for the lights in the compartment. "Why isn't the *Bismarck* here?" Pfizer asks. The moment he does so, he knows the young Bloodguard knows the answer. "Tell me Heath. I am your Domino," Pfizer says.

Knowing he's been found out and a lie would be an

unimaginable breach of conduct, Heath blurts out the truth: "The *Bismarck* left the rendezvous to respond to an emergency. Eros is under attack."

CHAPTER 33

Because they do not possess the evolved
extended family of the Hane Nation many people
must depend on a 'state' or 'government' to
protect them and care for their welfare... Pity
them.

—Randoval Hane, as quoted in *The Hane
Commentaries* by Aaron Charlemagna Invid-Hane

He could not believe it yet there it was on their screens, more
fearsome than any holo or model he had seen as a child: a
Tene Thantos Deathship. "I want confirmation,
Commodore. Is it the same ship that attacked Tempel?"
Balthasar demands. *Mother, where are you?* "Sir Pau, I want you
to prepare for the evacuation of the gene bank and essential
Nation members. Cedar, go and find my mother. Take her to
an evacuation point."

The Takazhr General salutes and moves to carry out
Balthasar's orders.

Cedar moves up behind Balthasar. "I'm not leaving you.
Send one of your Generals to evacuate your mother."

Balthasar sighs, "Cedar, I will function better if—"

"Balthasar, Intel confirms it's the same Deathship that
destroyed Tempel," announces Commodore Robus Nilz
Hane-Fahey down in the holographic command pit. The
holo model fills with ghostly holographic images of the Spican
Star System, where Eros is located, and the star system's
defensive satellites and starships. Behind Robus a long black
dagger shape enters the scaled-down holographic model of

the system. The ship, displayed in intricate detail, begins encroaching on the asteroid belt at the edges of the star system.

"Computers are attempting to plot her optimal firing solution for Eros," says the Commodore quietly, ominously. Already missiles represented by strobing red holograms are probing system and planetary defenses. Even Balthasar can see that if the System Defenses of Eros had been offline as Tempel's were, then Eros would already be in flames.

"I have the data," the Commodore calls as he begins walking toward the blue green jewel of the holographic Eros. "Here," he says, stopping several feet beyond the orbit of Hecate, Eros' smoldering sister planet. "Computer, project the Deathship terminus line, defensive endpoint," he orders.

A flashing yellow circle cuts through the giant display. "This is it people. If it reaches this point it will be able to overwhelm planetary shields and countermeasures. Eros will be obliterated sixteen minutes after first firing," Robus says.

"It will never make it there," says a soft yet confident voice.

"Romula...," Balthasar hears Cedar whisper.

Balthasar turns to see his father's younger brother's daughter striding toward him. The slim woman appears little more than a teenager but Balthasar knows his first cousin to be ninety-seven. Romula Salome Kenda-Hane, Marshal of the Hane Pax Force, wears the black mesh uniform and body armor of the HPF. She salutes Balthasar.

"Stadtholder," she says in her young voice, addressing Balthasar by the Hane family title for Supreme Commander of the Eros Alliance. Then, her pale blue Hane eyes sparkling, she stands on her toes and kisses Balthasar's cheek.

"I'm sorry about Millian and his family, *cher,*" she whispers to him softly. She turns and addresses the others confidently, boldly.

"My brother, Remus, is in command of the joint task force consisting of the dreadnoughts *Gert* and *Napoleon*. He will stop the Deathship with the aid of a long-range missile barrage from the monitor that's orbiting Cytheria. We will stop the Deathmen nearly twelve astronomical units from the terminus line in the Cytherian orbit."

Romula strides down into the holographic command pit. She places an audvid link on her head. "Display INS *Gert* Task Force," she commands.

"Displaying Apocalypse Class dreadnoughts INS *Gert* and *Napoleon*. Displaying Eclipse Class battle cruisers INS *Hector* and *Mars*. Displaying Nova Class destroyers *Hood*, *Potemkin*, *Wellington*, and *Arden*. Displaying Aurora Class Space superiority fighters. Displaying Thor Class Space bombers," says the tritone voice of the DracoHold AI.

Tiny white ghost images, though exquisite in detail, are hard to view in the scale model of the star system. The wedge shapes of dreadnoughts, the shark shapes of battle cruisers, the sleek beetle forms of destroyers and swarms of pinhead-sized holographic fighters and bombers are added to the holographics. Hundreds of missiles, represented by strobing blue lights, launched from the Cytherian Orbital Monitor on the far side of the star system streak into view, passing the task force. As the long-range missiles of the Monitor pass they are joined by the additional missiles fired from the task force. In the final minute before the missiles strike they break apart in multi-targeting individual warheads. The space around the Deathship fills with thousands of lightning flashes from point defense lasers and the red bursts of countermeasure missiles and intercepts. The storm of attacking missiles is reduced to a light though impressive pelting of fewer than a hundred against the Deathship's shields.

"Enemy shields reduced eighteen percent. Warning: Enemy shields recharging, eighty-four percent and rising," informs the tritone voiced AI.

"Don't worry. Remus is just getting warmed up," Romula says, *almost* as confident as before, as another barrage of attacking missiles from the Monitor is joined by those of the task force. Balthasar notices that his cousin Robus, the Naval

Commodore, and several of the Electors see Romula's dip in confidence. The results of the second barrage, although ending with a fiery assault on the Deathship's shields, are much the same.

"Enemy shields reduced to sixty-four percent and recharging," informs the AI. Warning: Twenty-eight minutes to terminus line," the artificial intelligence adds ominously.

"We've still got one barrage left from the Monitor," says Romula, striding toward the image of the Deathship. Everyone in the War Room knows, however, that another barrage fired from the Monitor will not reach the Deathship until after it has crossed the terminus line. Even so, true to human nature, another barrage bursts from the Monitor, its Commander hoping these missiles will break the laws of space and time. Meanwhile, the third barrage is joined again by even more fearsome fire from the task force. This time there are actually shield penetrations. Two plumes of green fusion plasma burst from the Deathship and the great ship actually lists for a moment.

A cheer goes up in the War Room, but the victory is short lived. The Deathship soon rights itself.

"Target shields reduced to thirty percent and recharging. Continuing to advance. The missiles from the Alamo Class Monitor *Invictus* will not reach the target in time," the AI tells them, devoid of emotion.

"That's why we're going to smash it into bits," shouts an electronic voice from overhead. Vice Admiral Remus Kenda-Hane is as maddeningly confident as his twin sister. "I'd hoped our combined assault would have done the trick, but as usual the Navy has to finish the hard work."

"Negative. Do not engage," Balthasar commands, thinking of his impetuous brown-haired cousin in command of the task force.

"Balthasar, that thing is less than twenty-seven minutes from the terminus line," Remus replies. A hologram of the Vice Admiral winks to life. Remus has Romula's youthful features and annoying boldness. So much like Creed, their cousin, his brother.

"Maybe if they could just slow it down we could use the quantum disruption mines," suggests Cedar. In the chaos Balthasar had forgotten his companion was a civilian weapons consultant and military strategist.

"Tell ... tell Cedar that the quantum mines are after the terminus line. Standing by to engage. All ships attack pattern alpha one," the Vice Admiral commands to someone off-holo.

"Damn it, Remus! I gave you a direct order. This is gross insubordination," Balthasar growls.

Balthasar watches the holographic representations of the task force begin their assault. Pale blue a-mat lances strike out, flaring with fury against the Deathship's shields. Orange plasma lasers strafe even further. The magnetic fireballs of plasma and a-mat torpedoes flash against the Deathship's shields followed by another burst of weapons. Enemy shield collapses lead to explosions along the Deathship's hull. Overloaded plasma conduits on the Deathship's port Tsasinov engine send energy arcing like lightning along the Deathship's rear quarter. A significant portion of missiles manages to break through this time and a-mat and fusion warheads detonate across the length of the Deathship. Still, the enemy ship moves relentlessly deeper into the system and begins launching its counter attack against the task force. The pale red of Zeiss beams fills the sky along with kinetic energy weapon intercepts and point defense plasma lasers.

"Apocalypse Class Dreadnought *Napoleon* disabled. Eclipse Class Battle Cruiser *Mars* disabled. Eclipse Class Battle Cruiser *Hector* destroyed," the AI tells them, but they can see clearly in the holopit the task force strength has already been reduced by half.

"Eclipse Class Battle Cruiser *Mars* destroyed," the AI continues relentlessly. Balthasar watches in horror as the disabled battle cruiser spinning out of control literally vaporizes in an expanding globe of white anti-matter fire.

"Apocalypse Class Dreadnought *Napoleon* destroyed. Nova Class Destroyers *Wellington* and *Arden* disabled," the AI announces. Balthasar turns his head in time to see the fading light of the *Napoleon's* destruction.

"Take evasive action. Fall back to these coordinates with best possible speed. Attach record buoys to homing beacons and stand by to eject," the voice of Admiral Kenda-Hane is heard commanding his surviving ships. The image of the *Gert* in the holopit shows the ship blackened horribly in several areas due to shield burn-through. Angry fires dot her wedge-shaped hull. Uncontainable hull ruptures bleed atmosphere to vacuum. Her starboard conventional drive vents fusion plasma. The *Gert's* shields flash with repeated assaults from the Deathship.

"Balthasar, please listen to me," Cedar implores. "The quantum mines, when placed in position, were all equipped with conventional drive in case they needed to be repositioned. We can move them!"

Balthasar suppresses anger at Remus' arrogant dismissal of Cedar's suggestion earlier. If Remus had listened, this might not have happened. He turns to the young Takazhr communications tech still beside him.

"Get those codes, young lady," he orders. At least Remus left a battle cruiser and two destroyers in orbit, but it is clear from the holographic model that they are busy taking on essential refugees and material. At best maybe a million ... a million might be saved from a planetary population of ten billion. What will become of the millions of innocents on Hecate? And the thousands of prisoners at the Acheron Penal Facility there? The millions on Libra and hundreds of thousands working the gas giant Cytheria? If the Deathship follows its historical pattern, once it has destroyed Eros it will eliminate the other worlds in the star system—or do far worse.

At least I won't live to watch the destruction. Balthasar pushes past the sense of depression bought on by impending doom. He can see civilian space ships, cargo haulers, freighters, star liners, and ore and garbage barges taking on evacuees. The ships in orbit will wait until the last possible second before retreating to safety. Balthasar drops his head. Never has his position weighed so heavily upon him.

"Sire, Defense Command is moving some of the quantum disruption mines. It will take twenty-three minutes before they intercept the Deathship moving as fast as conventional drive can, at sublight speeds. That will be twelve minutes after the Deathship crosses the terminus line. The AI tells us that while the planet may survive the bombardment, all life on Eros will ... be terminated," reports the communications tech.

"Balthasar, I'm sorry. We'll try to buy you your time. All ships prepare to re-engage attack pattern delta three," the voice of Admiral Kenda-Hane is heard to say.

Balthasar remembers his father saying: "No matter what, in the end a Hane will always do the right thing." *Sadly, for some of the Hane it took until the very end.*

"Remus, wai—," Balthasar begins.

"No time, Bal. Romula, I love you. Tell Mother and Father I love them, too," the Admiral says. There is the distinctive click of an ended transmission.

"Remus, no!" Romula shouts, her lovely face contorting in anguish as the damaged dreadnought and its escorts turnabout to face the Deathship.

"May the Eternal guide them," Balthasar whispers.

The remaining two destroyers flanking the dreadnought move even further to the very flanks of the Deathship. The *Gert* opens fire with beam weapons first followed by a hail of missiles but the great ship is a shadow of its former self. The Deathship's shields flare incandescently. Balthasar watches in angry helplessness as the Deathship's counter fire blazes against the *Gert's* shields. He watches as it begins to rip apart the *Gert* with missiles and torpedoes, dissect it with energy weapons.

Get out of there, get out of there, Balthasar thinks hoping the crew will head for escape pods, but then again, escape to a pod would leave a fate far worse than death. The Deathmen would undoubtedly retrieve the pods after they destroyed Eros and what they'd do to the survivors does not bear thinking of.

"Apocalypse Class Dreadnought *Gert* disabled. Escape pods launching," the AI continues its tragic commentary. Balthasar closes his eyes as escape pods begin to jettison from the charred hulk of the *Gert*. He feels the light of the explosion through his closed eyes.

"Apocalypse Class Dreadnought *Gert* destroyed," the AI reports, informing them of the obvious.

Balthasar opens his eyes to see his Bloodguard General Praetor Nikeon Blaze and his mother approaching him. He has to suppress unmentionable rage that she has not been evacuated. He looks at the terminus line and the Deathship, perhaps ten minutes remain. *And the mines are still nine minutes short of the effective intercept mark. I am going to have to order Cedar and Mother dragged aboard the remaining battle cruiser. Goodbye, my beloveds,* Balthasar thinks as he steels himself. He is dimly but grimly aware of the destruction of one of the two remaining destroyers.

"Nikeon," Balthasar commands, "as Coronal Regent of Eros and your employer I order you to take Princess Fen and Mr. Wills to the battle cruiser taking evacuees."

"Balthasar, please don't," protests Cedar as two Bloodguards begin approaching him.

"Your men will have to drag me, General Praetor Blaze, if they intend to remove me from my home," Fen says in her quiet childlike voice.

"Take them!" Balthasar roars thinking even Creed would be proud. At least Creed and his immediate family are safe. The Hane Nation would continue, but as what? Hunted refugees without rank or succor.

"Nova Class Destroyer *Hood* destroyed. Target is attempting to regenerate shields. Eleven minutes to terminus line. Warning: Large scale warpfold event in system. Confirmation The Apocalypse Class Dreadnought *Bismarck* is three light minutes from intercept of Deathship," the AI tells them.

"Cameron and Creed are here!" Cedar exclaims jubilantly, wresting loose from the two Bloodguard.

Even the brilliant Grand Admiral and my audacious brother Creed might not be able to buy enough time—and if so, at what cost? The lives of Creed and his family onboard? Balthasar thinks. "Nikeon, I gave you an order. Why are they still *here!?*" Balthasar demands.

The Deathship has begun firing on Eros, probing, plotting the planet's defenses, seeking a way to overwhelm them.

"Son, don't do this," Fen implores quietly, but emphatically.

"Mother, please go. Take Cedar with you. In moments the places I love will be obliterated. Don't let me die knowing those I have loved dearest will perish as well," Balthasar says quietly, no tricks, no emoto-control.

Fen bows her head, allowing her tears to fall freely. Another of her sons! The most ruthless and sensitive of her sons. Every instinct in her screams: *Protect Your Child!* She is too old, too disciplined to break into open sobs but the effort of not doing so leaves her feeling dizzy and sick. "Please do not do this. The Hane Nation needs its leader. The Clan Nations need you to hold the Erosi Alliance together. They need you now more than ever!"

"There are still three hundred million of my cousins here, nearly ten billion other citizens on this planet alone. Even if I had not taken my oaths of office I could not leave," Balthasar declares. Not once has he raised his voice.

"And I cannot leave my first-born son!" she rages at him.

"Creed will have desperate need of you, Mother, and he has a son, the next ClanLord of the HaneNation."

"Warning: large-scale warpfold event in system. Confirmation Apocalypse Class Dreadnought *Guderian*." The AI interrupts them with this devastating news.

"The traitors that Grand Admiral Tanenov reported!"

Commodore Hane-Fahey exclaims. And he like everyone else shivers at the thought that another Wasting has begun.

"Mother, you have a duty to Creed, your grandson, to Millian's children. Yes, even to Oriana. The Hane Nation and the Erosi Alliance outweigh any obligation to me. Now please go. I intend to make certain these abominations pay dearly in the attempt. Regardless of the outcome, I will see you again. On the other side if need be. Where there will be no more tears," Balthasar kisses her cheek gently, and hugs both her and Cedar to him. "Now *go!*" he commands, pushing himself away from them and walking down into the holographic command pit.

"Please come with me m'lady," Cedar says, offering his arm as Balthasar walks away. Fen takes his arm and before Cedar can take a last look at Balthasar he is being ushered out surrounded by a cordon of Bloodguard.

"Commodore, report," Balthasar demands the moment Cedar and Fen are gone. The Commodore stares back at Balthasar with hopeless eyes. "Grand Admiral Tanenov and the computers say we need to hold the Deathship for another four minutes before the mines are at intercept point, but with the traitors here we don't stand a chance."

CHAPTER 34

There is a moment in each day that Satan cannot find.

—William Blake, Old Earth poet, c. 19th century A.D.

Grand Admiral Cameron Tanenov stands calmly almost proudly behind her command console, hands folded behind her back. While the bridge of her flagship is usually the epitome of efficient naval discipline, it now swarms with harried activity. She knows that it is vital that she remain poised and composed. Her people are depending on her to keep things together, keep them alive. Seeing the Deathship has been more shocking then any intellectualization or rationalization she could have imagined. The Deathship continues its relentless advance, leaving behind the wrecked burning bits of the *Gert's* task force. Then, to make matters worse, Admiral Zhao, has indeed pursued them from Earth.

"My God! Those traitors," she hears Creed whisper behind her.

"It's not over yet, Grand Kurseg," the Grand Admiral says with nerve-steadying calmness. "Strategic Ops Officer! Those are the quantum disruption mines. Confirmed?"

The naval officer only has time to nod an affirmative before the Communications Officer interrupts: "We are receiving combat telemetry between the *Guderian* and the Deathship. Admiral Zhao is requesting firing coordinates on Eros!" the Comm Officer reports in disbelief.

"Four minutes. All we need is four minutes," the Grand Admiral says to herself as she sees the *Bismarck's* computer confirming her math. Even as she turns to, Creed standing behind her, she runs scenarios in her mind.

"Take Kiritzia and Aaron to a marineguard transport," she says. "We will provide a fighter escort and cover fire. Get to one of the transports fleeing Eros. Find a civilian transport. These traitors will pursue the military ones," she says, and for the first time since he's known her Creed hears defeat in her voice.

"Cameron, look!" says Creed pointing at the main holo.

The Grand Admiral whirls about to see escape pods madly ejecting from the *Guderian*. The *Guderian's* Tsasinov drives flare as the ship prepares to warpfold. Suddenly the *Guderian* accelerates forward to pierce the local space time, but the space between it and the rear of the Deathship is catastrophically and deliberately close. The *Guderian* slams into the Deathship at near light speed. Not only does the *Guderian's* self-destruction tear a hole in the Deathship, but it gives the Deathship additional momentum, pushing it forward into the waiting quantum disruption mines.

Blindingly intense blue disks of light erupt before the Deathship and everything—everything—the light touches seems to disintegrate and vanish. After three such attacks the leading edge of light touches the Deathship's Tsasinov cores, which have been building to overload since the *Guderian's* suicide run. The cataclysmic and spectacular destruction of the Deathship is like the birth of a small white star sucking in the unfortunate escape pods. Doubtlessly visible on Eros, the small star created by the Deathship's destruction will give them one of the most impressive memorials in the Imperium, since the explosion will continue to bum for several days until it exhausts itself.

The cheering that fills the bridge of the *Bismarck* is deafening. Cameron allows herself a relaxed moment and hugs Creed triumphantly, a radiant smile on her face. She laughs heartily and with relief. Admiral Zhao had come to his senses, no doubt upon seeing the Deathship and the murderous forces he had aligned himself with.

"Signal from Eros, ma'am. First Elector Hane from DracoHold," says the Communications Officer.

"Well done, Grand Admiral Tanenov!" a holo image of Balthasar Hane winks into view before them. "Come home! We are waiting to fete you like heroes and honor those who have made the ultimate sacrifice in the safeguarding of so many. On behalf of all Eros, if I may be so bold, Humanity: Thank you for your courage. I know your first priority is to see to any possible survivors, but we all eagerly wait to hear from you."

At the first appearance of his brother's image, Creed nearly runs forward with joy. Then Balthasar starts talking, making another speech. *This is no time for speeches, Balthasar!*

The holographic image of Balthasar turns toward the Lion, his right hand directing Creed to *wait.* Balthasar seems to be listening to someone off the holo's pick-ups. The image seems to jump.

"*Shalom, frère,*" Balthasar says in the Hane language. "Very good. This channel is secure, but even so, *Hane shal truduch.*" Cameron, thank you for bringing home my brother. Creed, I have honestly never been happier to see you. Is our nephew with you?" Strangely, Creed can sense his brother's sincerity even through the hologram, and despite their differences he is happy to see Balthasar. The Lion nods. "I understand: *trust only Hane.* Our nephew is safe, but I'd rather not get into his location. I'm coming down. We'll talk then. I'll have to tell you how our brother died and I will have to face Mother."

The holographic Balthasar studies his brother intently and then nods. Balthasar now wears the inscrutable, cold expression the Hane are known for. "Very well. Landing coordinates are being sent." Balthasar's expression softens minutely. "I will be waiting. DracoHold out," and with that the image blinks into nonexistence.

As if reading Creed's mind, the Grand Admiral says, "We have time before we need to rendezvous with the Scion. Let's go down and see what your brother wants."

He's going to come here making demands, Balthasar thinks,

leaning against the railing of the holographic pit. *"You don't know that,"* *Mother would say. She's always had uncanny insight into her children.*

"Do we have a casualty update since this all began?"

"It's ugly, Bal," answers his cousin Zwen, the Hane Nation Press Secretary. "Military fatalities: seventy-one thousand six hundred thirty-seven and rising. Civilian fatalities: including accidents attributed to panic and suicides: By the Only God, seven hundred—"

"Stop. I want the most up-to-date numbers on the death toll on Earth and from Tempel as well, Zwen," Balthasar says to his mahogany-skinned cousin. "Transmit the data to Cedar—" He pauses, recalling that Zwen's wife was at the Hane Trade Towers. "And then take some time," he adds, in a softer tone. He is silent a moment. Then he turns to Commodore Hane-Fahey, who has come up from the holographic command pit, and claps his hand on his shoulder. "Commodore, tell everyone here how proud I am of them. I want you to coordinate with Cameron." With that, Balthasar exits the War Room and heads back to the platform, gathering others in his wake: Electors of the Clan Nations, Military Officers, HaneNet and Eros GNN Correspondents, Bloodguards, Erosi Alliance and Hane Nation Officials.

"My son," Fen cries out as soon as she sees him. Balthasar stops and she gracefully crosses the short distance between them. She has to stand on her toes to caress his cheek with one hand while she lightly kisses him on the other. "Greatness is often dismissed in the young, mistaken for pride in maturity, ignored in the old, and only recognized in death," she whispers in his ear after the kiss. "You are as great as your father," she says, and she allows him to see the tears of pride in her eyes.

Whatever doubts Balthasar has about meeting Creed evaporate with her approval. He places her veil over her face and bows his head. Perhaps to hide his emotion from her? "That means so very much, Mother."

* * *

Kiritzia D'Invid-Hane, wife of Creed Duran Goethe Hane, waits serenely for her husband in the flight ops center of the *Bismarck's* main hangar. Like all Invid she is compellingly beautiful, radiant. She seems an angelic light amidst the bustle of the ops center. Dressed in a dark blue full-length wrap and shawl adorned with luminescent gold Hane Dragons and crushed Erosi Vendam micro-pearls that complement her pale gold hair.

She is unaware of the attention she commands, even from disciplined Navy and Bloodguard, men and women alike. Perhaps only her two-year-old son standing attentively beside her is aware of it, for he glances up at his mother with his father's bleached glacial blue eyes. She smiles at him and the equally beautiful boy, Aaron Charlemagna Invid-Hane, smiles eagerly back at her. The twinkle in her mercury eyes is only for him. The soldiers in the room spring to attention, unless involved in essential duties, as her husband the Lion enters with Grand Admiral Cameron Tanenov.

"Ritzia," Creed says, embracing her tightly. Not since they were parted at the ill-fated Omnividome ceremonies had he seen them. He'd known they were on board with him, but to see his wife and son with his own eyes, touch them with his own hands! The Lion sniffles once, scoops up Aaron, and embracing them both bows his head between them. When Creed lifts his head his eyes are red but his face is composed.

Kiritzia feels the anguish in her beloved's heart. The raw emotion of the loss of his younger brother, Millian and all those he was charged to protect. She reassures him with a steadfast gaze and touches his mind. *You did your best. Many are alive.*

Creed smiles weakly and takes her hand, still holding Aaron in the crook of his other arm. She is an empath like Fen and in cases of deep emotional rapport like the love she has for him or their son she can actually communicate her thoughts. With him it is one way, with his son Aaron, he knows it is something much, much more. "We're going home," he says, following the Grand Admiral and her escorts and aides via a ramp in the rear of the flight ops center to the hangar below. Three marineguard transports wait rumbling and pulsing in standby mode.

Knowing Creed's mind well from their long family association, Cameron breaches the subject she knows has been on Creed's mind since the Deathship was defeated. "We have sixteen hours before we must leave for our rendezvous. I'll give you twelve hours to convince Balthasar to join us," she says slowly and as inoffensively as possible

Creed's eyes narrow and Kiritzia feels him stiffen. "Pfizer is our nephew, your cousin. Cameron. There is only one thing Balthasar can do," Creed says bitterly. *Everyone senses Balthasar, my brother, would deny us.*

"Is there? We shall see, shall we not? I mean no offense, *cher*, but Balthasar's first priority will be to protect Eros. He is First Elector of the Erosi Alliance," the Grand Admiral replies with the Serdian-like poise for which she is known.

"Then, why say it?!" Creed begins angrily.

"My love, Cameron," Kiritzia interjects, "This is something that can wait until you actually see the Balthasar. Yes?" Kiritzia's tone is gently scolding.

Cameron nods her white blonde head. "I have always appreciated your sagacity, Kiritzia."

CHAPTER 35

In every man, there is something not of dust or
earth or flesh or time, but of God.

—Abraham Heschel, Old Earth theologian,
20th century A.D.

Balthasar and his staff, Fen, and two phalanx of the Hane
Bloodguard in full armor wait on the top landing platform
of the Haakon-Neuhaurer Palace. The palace overlooks the
massive HaneHome crater that spills into the ocean at the
center of the crescent. A vast, multi-tiered colonnade gives the
palace more the look of a temple than a building of state. Giant
Hecate gold statues of the Hane progenitors crown the
apex of the palace, gazing past the landing platform and
inland toward the capitol city of Avon.

In the minutes following the defeat of the Deathship,
some three million Hane family members and others had
gathered around the perimeter of the great crater to
volunteer and to welcome home two of its most favored
citizens. Barely audible above the frantic cheering is the
thunder clap of the marineguard transports as they enter
atmosphere and sweep into view. At the first sight of
Balthasar on the landing platform, the crowd grows hush, and
for one infinitesimal moment all that is heard are the
pendants of the Erosi Alliance snapping in the warm
afternoon wind.

"Glory to the Only God who has delivered us!" Balthasar
shouts triumphantly. All of the Erosi, with the exception of

Fen and the Bloodguard, cheer with praise. Bells ring and music blares, first the *Anthem of the Hane Nation* followed by the *March of the Imperium*.

At last Balthasar continues, "Let us also remember our fallen heroes who made the ultimate sacrifice. Let us pray for our brothers and sisters on the stricken Earth and let us find the strength to deliver them as we have been delivered!" More cheering erupts and even with his words being transmitted around the crater Balthasar is momentarily drowned out. He raises his arms again and again, inciting the masses to an even higher pitch.

"Yes! Yes! That's it! Let—It—Go! Remember WE ARE EROS!!!!" The people are screaming themselves hoarse now, stamping their feet, clapping their hands, blinking lights, waving flags, crying, singing, and dancing. Balthasar is grateful their attention is focused on their own revelry instead of on him, for finally his powerful figure shudders and all the emotions he has tightly checked he releases. *Creed is coming, Creed is coming*, he thinks. He takes a deep breath, rolls his shoulders, and arches his back stretching. The high winds swirling around the platform will dry his face. He clears his throat and with that he is once again Balthasar Gilead Cicero Hane, First Elector, and Coronal Regent.

The marineguard transports are circling, making their final approach. Creed watches the triumphant, jubilant Erosi and he is certain they are mostly Hane. He hears his older brother's words over the intercom. He hugs Kiritzia and Aaron closer to him. Perhaps this wouldn't be so hard. Maybe Balthasar does understand. He feels the gentle rocking of the marineguard transport landing, like an elevator reaching ground floor. He hears hatches hissing open and almost immediately smells the sweet salty scent of the Vendome Ocean. He is home on Eros.

Cameron enters the embarkation bay from the command cockpit. She wears the spotless white uniform with gold buttons which bear the eagle of the Imperial Navy. Somehow ingeniously she has coifed her luxuriant white gold hair, to keep it from blowing in the platform winds. Kiritzia lifts her luminescent blue shawl over her pale fire hair.

"We are ready, commander," Cameron says to her Bloodguard Praetor, a powerfully built sepia-skinned Commander Praetor. The officer nods and calls their escort detail to attention. At the Grand Admiral's previous instruction, the three marineguard transports play *Taps* as they idle. Then the *Dirge of Fallen Heroes* is played, as Bloodguards and Navy officers disembark from the other two marineguard transports and stand at attention. When the second chorus begins, Cameron and Creed, Kiritzia and Aaron, the officers and guards, some twenty in all solemnly disembark. No sooner do their feet touch the Erosi blackglass landing platform than the multitudes of assembled Erosi resume their rapturous revelry.

It takes a full minute for the procession to cross the landing platform, but at last Creed and Balthasar stand face to face. The music has stopped. Suddenly, the crowd falls quiet. The brothers' differences are no secret, as they are public figures. But the keen perspective gained from a shared near-death experience overrides all else. They are brothers. They embrace, prompting renewed waves of cheering from the Erosi.

* * *

The brothers meet in the late afternoon at the Dome of the First Elector, a stadium-sized geodesic solarium situated on a large star-shaped artificial island in the center of the crater's bay. It is here that the Robes of All Power and the Stadtholder Mace have been presented as the symbols of office to the First Electors of the United Clan Nations of the Erosi Alliance for more than six thousand years. Here too inaugurations have taken place on a vast disk of Erosi blackglass shot through with veins of gold. Only from above can one discern that their unique shading forms a map of Eros. The disk, surrounded by gently splashing waters, presents a stark contrast to the surrounding landscape,, as befits a site where so much power is conferred. To one side HaneHome, the past and present glory of Eros. To the other, an open view of ever-changing sky and endless ocean, a seemingly infinite horizon.

Balthasar is regally dressed in a dark blue tunic embroidered with gold Hane Dragons. He wears the Robes of All Power like a toga and cradles the mace in the crook of his left arm, its base in his palm. He is more imperial than any Caesar there can be no doubt to his authority. Knowing this Creed does not come dressed as the Grand Kurseg, the Commanding General of the Imperial Corps Bloodguard. Instead Creed wears the clothes he would wear if he were home, earth tone light weight linen shorts and a hunter green short sleeved shirt. He smiles seeing Balthasar's expression and the smile becomes a grin. Despite his formidable emoto-control he knows Balthasar is reassessing the situation.

"I think after all this time you forget I am a general," Creed says amicably.

"No, I don't. I do forget how subtle you can be—When you want to be," Balthasar says with equal friendliness in his deep baritone.

"Balthasar, will you aid Pfizer?" the Lion asks simply. No posturing, no demands. His expression is open, allowing Balthasar to see how difficult this is for him.

Taking a cue from his younger brother, Balthasar allows his guard to drop as well. "Creed, I appreciate the way you chose to broach this subject. I really, really do—"

"It's what Millian would want." Creed interrupts.

Balthasar sighs deeply and regards Creed intently. He places a hand on his shoulder. "I know. It's what makes this much harder," Balthasar replies, feeling Creed's shoulder muscles tense beneath his palm. "Please, Creed. Wait. Hear me out first. The last thing I need right now is a fight with you. Our world barely escaped the fate of Tempel."

"Oriana must be stopped!" Creed says forcefully but without anger.

Balthasar cannot be pushed. "Without a doubt. But by all our ancestors the conflict will not take place here."

"Why not? The Alliance will support Pfizer and the Hane

admirals cannot be bought. Cato is alive somewhere. This will draw him out. And Cameron is here."

"You are not thinking like a general now, little brother. The first rule of military engagement is know your enemy, is it not? Accurate intelligence is crucial. Yes?" Balthasar says softly. Creed nods and he continues. "How many Deathships does the enemy have? What if we allow Pfizer to declare himself openly here and a half dozen Deathships warpfold into this system? The quantum disruption field would be overwhelmed and this planet vaporized in minutes," Balthasar says. "I need time to bolster our system defenses, and gain support in the CIMB and the Imperium Congress. I'm sure other magnates and Aristo, hell the Citizo, want answers. I will be their voice," says Balthasar boldly. "Pfizer has been invested with the Coventry Protocols," he continues, referring to the failsafe contingency plan to rendezvous at coordinates known only to the Imperial rulership and a select few. "So I know either you or Cameron must have the coordinates. Take him there and when you're ready we will put him on his rightful throne."

CHAPTER 36

Tomorrow is not promised.

—Creed Duran Goethe Hane, as quoted in *The Hane Commentaries* by Aaron Charlemagna Invid-Hane

Six black helio-jet pods bearing the WiktorCorp emblem weave through the upper climb traffic that approaches Nova Roma, Earth's provisional capital. In one of the helio-jet pods is Marisol Fitzgerald-Buchanan. The landscape is gray and blighted and what began as cold rain has turned to ashen snow. The amount of dust thrown into the atmosphere had been tremendous, causing temperatures to drop worldwide. Fields of semolina and durum almost ready for harvesting are suffering from the unseasonal frost. Robo-farmers frantically work the farmlands surrounding Nova Roma attended by their fearful masters. It had taken the Terrax Corporation hundreds of years to restore Earth after the Enslaver bombardment of 2273 AD, and in a matter of hours humans had once again scarred the planet horribly.

The leaden skies reflect Marisol's mood. Although she has entertained princes and potentates, her impending audience with the newly crowned Regis Oriana has her feeling like she hasn't felt since her first auditions. Added to her dread of meeting Oriana is the desperate hope that the rumors she's heard circulating may turn out to be true—*Pfizer alive!* This is what consumes her, what drives her to go along with Savoy Wiktor. If the rumors turn out to be true, then she has all the more reason to cling to the fierce hope that Otto, too, is alive.

Marisol glances at Savoy Wiktor seated next to her in the armored helio-jet. She had tried to get him to comment on the rumors, but he had remained mysteriously close-mouthed, causing her to suspect that he has his own agenda surrounding the throne. Reliable information has been so hard to come by. The Imperium has been in a panic. And too many things have been happening. The Deathship that destroyed Tempel moved on to attack her homeworld, Eros. When it was in turn destroyed, Marisol had been glued to the holonets watching as they burned the metal monstrosity to ash. Grand Admiral Cameron Tanenov was known to be in-system during the Deathship's destruction. *Did she escape Earth with the Crown Scion? Why hasn't she reported in?*

"You don't have to do this, you know," Savoy Wiktor says interrupting her thoughts.

Katherine casts a sharp, disapproving look at Savoy. *Katherine's right to be angry,* Savoy thinks. *I'm using Marisol's concern for her husband's well-being for my own inside-track into Oriana's circle.* Savoy feels shame. He's adopted more and more of his enemies' tactics. If only he had gotten to Pfizer sooner. Now it is a certainty that Pfizer's sister Oriana is in league with the very same people who had murdered his parents—the Tene Thantos.

For much of his life Savoy thought, as most Imperial citizens did up until now, that although based in historical fact the Tene Thantos were extinct like the KKK, the Nazis, the Humanity First League. But he now knows, based on years of discreet observation, that the Tene Thantos, those Aeon racial supremacists, those Restorers as they are sometimes called, are alive and well. And based on the intelligence Wiktor has gathered, the Tene Thantos leadership culminates in two persons: Nasir Qamar, the CEO and Majority Shareholder of Allied Autotechnics Galactic (AAG), and Baron Jovion Quiso, Coronal Regent of Anonjida and a respected Imperium diplomat. Jovion is a celebrated negotiator, having trained at the Serdian Diplos at Raga and having settled disputes between some of the Imperium's most adversarial members. Quiso also happens to be the current advisor to the new Regis Oriana.

What Savoy knows about Qamar, Quiso, and the Tene Thantos has taken years to glean. But when his parents were killed, Savoy swore that he would find out who had done it and why. Savoy's father had been a pioneer in the resurgence of artificial intelligences and cybernetic applications such as the MentAmp. Some of the technicians at WiktorCorp had been studying the possibility of creating biosoftware that would literally overwrite or amend the users personality to whatever the designers purposed. Kennedy Wiktor, Savoy's father, had immediately stopped the research and ordered the collected data destroyed. Within the space of nine days, Savoy's father, mother, and several WiktorCorp execs and researchers had each been assassinated. And now Savoy's agents in the AAG, Nasir Qamar's corporation, have informed him that the biosoftware his father destroyed, the biosoftware he lost his life over, Qamar has revived and renamed Project Black Ware. If such biosoftware were deployed over a place such as the Omnividome, those using MentAmps could be destroyed or worse, enslaved, by the Tene Thantos.

Marisol watches Savoy's eyes turn inward as he is consumed by his private thoughts. Katherine, his ever-present assistant, is as always engrossed in an audvid link, whispering numbers and dispersing orders throughout the Wiktor economic empire. Not knowing if Otto is dead or alive is the worst hell Marisol could ever have imagined. She senses ambivalence from Savoy over her role as the Imperium Government Liaison. Why the Regis Oriana requested her in favor of the more experienced PPRC members gnaws at her. Did Savoy make the suggestion to Oriana? Oriana feels like a pawn in a very dangerous game. At least Agust is safe. Right now, Fiona is taking him to the Erosi Alliance Drift City, Renewed Valor, where Marisol has family.

They can now see the great green domes of the Imperial Preservation Society that cover most of the Ancient City. Inside the domes, archaeologists, historians, and architects labor to restore some of the splendors of the legendary first Rome. Despite the protest of the Military that the surviving Imperial heir would be safer in space, Oriana and Zoe have chosen to remain on Earth, Sacred Home. Marisol sees it for the shrewd public relations move it is. Many of the official Ambros residences were lost in the destruction of New Eden and Atlantis. Marisol still has to suppress trembling at the thought of so much destruction. Oriana and the surviving Imperium Executives have taken up residence in the Restored Domintan Palace, a marble monstrosity that rivals even contemporary architecture in its ugliness. Oriana finds its historical and political symbolism appropriate.

The domes also wisely provide controlled access, though in the two days since the attack the entire planet has become an armed fortress. Bloodguards and Takazhr in battle armor and their counterparts in CombatMecha gladiator mode scan and pass Wiktor's entourage. The weather inside the climate-controlled dome is a stark contrast to the fallout winter outside. Filters in the dome show a blue but cloudy afternoon sky. The area has been cleared of sightseers and tourists. Official helio-jets and skidder limousines dot the streets and sky, some escorted by CombatMechas. There are soldiers everywhere.

* * *

Oriana Fen Anastacia Ambros has exhausted every calming regimen known to her.

Murderous bastard, she thinks, glancing at Jovion, who is seated calmly at a conference table of Erosi blackglass, while she herself paces the room. She still seethes with rage at Jovion for the Deathman attack on Eros.

They are alone in a small conference room off the main press conference suite of the Impgov holo studios in Nova

Roma. In order to welcome the soon-to-arrive Eros Alliance delegation, the room has been decorated in jade and lime greens. A row of transpari-steel floor-to-ceiling windows lead out to an interior garden of date, pomegranate, and fig trees. The beauty of the garden is lost on her now.

Everything the Magus conveyed to her concerning Jovion and Nasir Qamar has turned out to be true—including the monstrosity in the shape of her sister. There are those reports that her brother Pfizer escaped but they could turn out to be nothing more than wishful thinking. In any case, the Ambros family's shares in the Combine of Internetworked Mercantiles and Banks have been frozen. And Oriana's tenuous hold on political power will be further eroded by that severe economic sanction. The Emperor-Executor or Empress-Executrix, through the Terrax Corporation and Ambros Antimatter, controlled nearly fifty-nine percent of the CIMB voting shares. *Even children know that politics follow economic wealth.* If Oriana does not produce the access codes in sixty standard days, her position could be contested by any other surviving Ambros. In that event, a vote would take place within the Ambros Corporation and the victor would receive authority over the voting shares and thus control the Imperium.

Most of the Ambros Press and Public Relations Corp on Earth had been destroyed in the attack on Atlantis. Gone were Rachel Tsimpo and her mother's PPRC Director, Safar Howe. Oriana had readily agreed to Savoy Wiktor's suggestion of installing Marisol Buchanan as the new face of the Impgov Liaison.

"What do *you* think of Marisol Buchanan as Impgov Liaison?" Oriana demands of Jovion harshly.

Not seeking to provoke her further, Jovion wisely does not look at her but sits silently staring down at his hands for a moment.

"Why do you still keep me as an advisor?" he asks her quietly.

"I don't know anymore, Jovion. Probably so that I can keep an eye on you and rein in your treachery," Oriana answers coldly. *I could have loved him.* She had loved him, and he betrayed her. Did he think her so consumed by her lust that she was not an Ambros and a granddaughter of the Great Hane in her heart? She could have her Bloodguard arrest him now. But her complicity in the assassination of her family would lose her the throne she wanted and then plunge the Imperium she loved into civil war.

Still not looking up he says, "Don't trust Wiktor. He should be euthanized. The woman?" Quiso shrugs. "I don't understand why you don't simply use me."

Her uncle, Balthasar Hane had sent her an instalink voice memo. It was unmistakably his voice. She immediately suppresses the emotion lest Jovion sense any weakness. *The seeds of corruption bear only ashes,* Oriana thinks, quoting Naraji Ilkani. Pfizer had been right: her allies are worse than any enemy she could have fathomed. *Who can I turn to?* She had embarked on this course thinking that she might be able to assure her Regency with the sanction of the Hane Nation, her family, and therefore the Eros Alliance, but Quiso's stupid brutal attack had pointed her toward an abyss. Balthasar had sent her three terrible words: "You are damned."

"Do you know that there are reports from Eros that Creed Hane survived the attack on New Eden?" she snaps.

"Consider them confirmed," Jovion answers in his soft dulcet tones. "I have seen a holo feed from an agent on Eros. Balthasar Hane received his brother and Grand Admiral Tanenov several hours ago."

That explains Balthasar's voice memo. He knows. They all know, she thinks. "And you were going to tell me this *when?*"

"I assumed by your agitated behavior that you knew," responds Jovion.

Oriana comes to a decision. "Jovion, answer me as if your life depends on it because it does." Even Oriana is surprised by the unchecked venom that colors her voice. "Do you have a plan?"

"I don't want to upset you any further," Quiso says, though what he thinks is, *Bitch.* He stands and looks directly at Oriana for the first time since they entered the room. "The attack on Eros was necessary. When Admiral Zhao reported that the *Bismarck* had broken orbit, I suspected that the only reason Grand Admiral Tanenov would do so was that she had either vital personnel or vital information. I ordered Zhao to pursue them. We cannot afford any loose ends at this juncture. I sent the Deathship to make sure."

"A Deathship. A *Deathship*! Allying ourselves with your neo-Deathmen was one thing. But a Deathship? Did you really think a knighted Imperial naval officer, ally or not, was going to sit by and let one of those things survive? It was one thing, Jovion, to let a few thousand Deathmen ravage one world. But you started destroying worlds, *worlds* Jovion. Did you really think Zhao would stay loyal to us once that happened?"

"I never considered his loyalty, Oriana. My only consideration was protecting you, and I would destroy a thousand worlds, a thousand thousand if I must," *At least that part is true. I don't care how many human infested worlds I destroy, and it is what I know Oriana needs to hear.* "After you ordered the Nucleo detonated over Atlantis," he continues, "the Bloodguard and Takazhr High Commands, the cream of the officer corps, were eliminated. What is there left to fear, Oriana? I thought I could operate without sanction to destroy our enemies. I knew you would never approve of an attack against the Hane. I regret you are angry, but I don't regret what I have done," Quiso says, moving toward her.

Pointed toward an abyss, she thinks. *The Bloodguard and Takazhr High Commands based at Pinnacle were the elite command officers of the Imperium's armed forces, my forces. How can I defend myself now against my traitorous ... love?*

"In the future I will approve all military plans," she says, the 'or else' threat implicit in her voice. "Balthasar has sent me a voice memo condemning me. Now we have no choice but to find a way to destroy them," she adds wearily.

Jovion checks his smile, covering it with a cough. But inside his black heart roars with laughter.

CHAPTER 37

I wish I had remembered that it is darkest before
the dawn. Something so simple and yet I forgot
that ancient wisdom.

—Pfizer Ambros, as quoted in *The Book
of Sorrows* by Oriana Ambros

"The Scion needs help," Luxvico says flatly to Otto as they
rush again to the Marineguard transport's aft port airlock.

"We could all use a little help right now, Counselor," Otto
mutters.

Let him focus on the task at hand, Luxvico thinks to himself.
Otto's continued functioning matters to their survival but
Pfizer is the linchpin and if they lose him, in the end everyone
will lose. The two are at the airlock of the marineguard
transport, where two Bloodguards are overseeing the final
stages of the sensor drone retrieval. Otto and Luxvico watch as
the cargo armature lifts and sets the sensor drone inside the
airlock. Warning strobes go from red to green and there is the
hiss of pressurization. Luxvico studies the lock's scanners over
the shoulder of one of the Bloodguard. *Nothing hazardous,
radiological, chemical, biological, nano.* He nods to Otto, who orders
the airlock open.

Luxvico goes to the drone's main maintenance access hatch
on its top side. In storage mode it resembles nothing more
than a large shiny black four-meter lozenge.

Otto watches Luxvico expertly and deftly retrieve a black
military encrypted crystal data chip. The Tempeler scans it with

his ubiquitous omnipalm.

"There is a cypher called the Coventry Protocols," Luxvico says, turning to Otto and holding out the CDC and an Hephaestus.

Otto accepts the CDC but refuses the Hephaestus. "You keep that," he says. He turns the shiny black CDC in his fingers before shoving it in an arm pocket of his working uniform. "He'll be okay, Luxvico. He's just been through a lot. We all have. Let's wait and see."

"Adequate," Luxvico says emotionlessly, then adds as a polite afterthought, "Of course, Otto."

"I know this is specifically for Pfizer, but I wish I knew what was on it," Otto says hesitantly, rhetorically.

"You and I both know the Crown Scion is the only one who can access that crystal. But I, too, am concerned how he will react."

"What if Eros has been destroyed?" Otto whispers darkly, and his eyes are those of a small child who wants his nightmares wished away.

"Even if the Tene Thantos have reached Eros, the star system's defenses are some of the best in the Imperium," says Luxvico reassuringly.

"So were Earth's and supposedly Tempel's," says Otto bitterly.

"We have to give that crystal to the Crown ... to Pfizer. There are undoubtedly instructions from Admiral Tanenov. We are wasting vital time." *Have Otto and Pfizer both lost their minds?* Luxvico wonders. "Otto?" Luxvico prompts.

Otto sighs deeply. "I'm okay. I have to remember that it's not a question of what's lost but what I can ...we can save."

* * *

Cato Ahren dreams of verdant Titan and the gentle misting rain through thick perpetual autumn forest of Glythsphr, Titan's capital. A flock of Erosi dartwing gulls soar over the great Dome of the Elector at HaneHome. Hecate rises full, bathing Eros in twilight night.

He sees Pfizer, wearing the Domino uniform, ascend the golden Phoenix Throne in a vast chamber lined with blue crystal marble and Erosi fire silk tapestry. A woman kneels, swathed head-to-toe in the fine black lace of the Sisters of Peace. Cato sees a tattooed face beneath the black veil, and thinks of Fen, the Widow of HaneHome. HaneHome has many widowers and widows now, orphans and worse.

Tempel bubbles and gleams like an overheated marble, its atmosphere burnt away before it shatters completely in a titanic explosion. A parade of men stampedes in the ghastly armored black of the Tene Thantos. A cascade of symbols and numbers fill his thought's strange yet intimately familiar. A river of knowledge roars in his mind and every drop is a fact, an experience. The current threatens to drown him in visions of what was, of what is, and what could be. He can feel himself slipping away, losing his sanity and then, Cato Ahren dreams of Basileus...

* * *

Cato awakens violently, staring about the courier ship's computer core. He is thankful he is alone. He has spent a great amount of time here since Lomin's death. The crew and even Basileus mercifully left him to his self-imposed isolation, after all he'd lost a friend and mentor of almost three hundred years, hadn't he? He has used most of his time alone to try to sort and collate the vast knowledge of Lomin's experiences and the frightening changes in his own awareness since his possession, no his sharing with Lomin. The metaphysics of this undertaking exhaust Cato but he is driven by the conviction that he can access the knowledge required to save Titan.

* * *

Otto and Luxvico find Heath watching the iris as they enter, Hephaestus in his right hand. Pfizer sits on the edge of a surgo op bed in the med bay. Pale blue circles of exhaustion have formed beneath Pfizer's eyes, now granite gray, their lightning gone.

Otto hands the CDC to Luxvico, who inserts it in his omnipalm. The Tempellian, his eyes on Pfizer, hands the omnipalm over to Pfizer.

"There was a heavy sensor drone with this at the rendezvous coordinates," Luxvico says in explanation. "The cypher reads Coventry Protocols."

Pfizer wipes his suddenly perspiring brow and looks down at the omnipalm with dread. He inputs the codes impressed upon his memory by MentAmp before the procession into New Eden, which seems like a lifetime ago. They all watch as the omnipalm holo emitter sparkles, ghostlike polychromatic beams fan out before coalescing into images of Creed and Grand Admiral Cameron Tanenov.

"Domino," the image of the Lion begins, bowing, "I regret that we must leave you to answer the distress call from Eros. Cameron and I both believe your chances of reaching Coventry are better if you do not remain with us." Even in the ghostlike hologram it is clear the Lion is having difficulty continuing.

The image of the Grand Admiral steps forward. "Majesty," she says saluting, "the Gunship *Callahan* will rendezvous with you at the secondary coordinates. It is my hope to meet you on Coventry Prime in five days' time. The Grand Kurseg and I believe we can enlist Balthasar Hane's support in moving for a vote of no confidence in Terrax Corporation and Ambros Antimatter. This will force Oriana's supporters to reveal themselves."

"Brilliant," Luxvico mutters.

"I will have arrived by then and you may declare yourself openly and take what action you deem necessary against your adversaries, Majesty." The Grand Admiral stops and turns to Creed.

"Domino, I speak to you now as the brother of your murdered father and I swear to you, Cameron and I have agreed that whatever the vote, the Hane Nation does not abandon family. I have a message from your parents," Creed says.

The holographic images reinitialize into images of his parents as they were just a short time ago. The orange light of a setting sun burns the white marble of the Imperial Residence gold and red. The shining silver spires and towers of New Eden, dominated by the Imperios and the gleaming needle of the Pinnacle, fill the background, lit by the light of a fading day. The holo pickups catch the October wind rustling through the ripe lemon and lime trees and Pfizer can almost smell them. Involuntarily he moves toward the images of his parents. His father stands, hands folded behind his back, resplendent in the black uniform with red piping of a retired Bloodguard General Praetor. Pfizer's mother wears the elegant black suit she'd worn to the cosmodome to greet him. Tears drip down Pfizer's face as the ghost images shatter whatever calm he had achieved and the screaming in his mind grows louder.

"Pfizer, your mother and I are so very sorry we must leave you this message. There is so much we want to say, and as always never enough time." The lump in Pfizer's throat is now choking him; he feels the veins in his head and neck pulsing hot.

"That is why," Anastacia begins, "you must try always to let those you care about know of your challenges. Do not let this stop you from giving, Pfizer. We will always live through you, and you will see us in your actions as we see you in ours. Pfizer—," Anastacia stops, bowing her head and covering her face with a black-gloved hand. The holographic Millian puts his hand on his wife's shoulder and continues.

"Protect the people to the utmost of your abilities. This is your duty. *Noblesse oblige.* But beware of the exploitive nature of mankind. Son, I bequeath all my rank, titles, and privileges as a Prince of the Hane Nation. But most of all—," the image of his father's handsome, boyish face twists with sorrow. His deep voice cracks. "I give you all the love I have. I am so very proud of you."

"Remember, Pfizer," his mother finishes, "beware of pride. Were it not for our pride, we would now be able to hold you in our arms and tell you that we love you. Farewell." Pfizer drops the omnipalm, trying so hard not to cry that his ribs hurt.

Pfizer doesn't even notice the image change back to his uncle Creed and Grand Admiral Tanenov. Pfizer has his head buried in the crook of arm as he suddenly gives way to sobs. Otto instinctively steps forward and hugs his friend. *What else can I do for him now?* The Lion says: "Similar messages were left for your sisters, had they survived. Cameron and I are aware of the hideous abomination pretending to be Zoe. Take heart, Pfizer, keep faith. An entire Nation of your family is behind you."

CHAPTER 38

This is not the end. This is not the beginning of
the end … But it is the end of the beginning.

—Sir Winston Churchill, Old Earth statesman,
20th century A.D., En'Zefi File

We are not going to make it to the rendezvous, Luxvico realizes,
having calculated the coordinates of the *Callahan* as Otto
attempts to console Pfizer. *The antimatter we jettisoned would have
made up the difference.'*

"Is there something wrong, Counselor Luxvico?" Heath
asks from behind Luxvico. *How could he know?* Luxvico turns
his eyes, searching the young Bloodguard with intense scrutiny.
Luxvico's amethyst eyes look into Heath's white blue irises. *I
can't read him. How did he read me? He's an Aeon pure breed. Who
knows what abilities he has?*

Heath pushes the heel of his left hand against his head as if
fending off a headache. "There's no need for that, Counselor.
You got suddenly quiet. That's all." The sincerity in Heath's
voice is evident even without Luxvico's abilities.

Luxvico feels shame at his paranoid and offensive action.
Otto had selected this man as Pfizer's personal bodyguard.
Luxvico studies the intricate blue-black and dark green tattoos
around Heath's right eye. *MacKenzie, Vey, DeHaaven, and Invid,*
thinks Luxvico, reading the lineage runes.

Heath lowers his head.

*He's ashamed of his lineage? Such impressive bloodlines, but only the
MacKenzie had remained loyal during the Anangan Insurrection. How*

did he come into Bloodguard service? "I'm sorry, Ensign Praetor," Luxvico says.

"What's going on here?" Otto quietly demands, irritated. He's just gotten Pfizer to sit down at the sickbays system ops console.

"Nothing, sir," Heath says, instinctively coming to attention.

"Lux?" Otto prompts turning his attention to the Tempellian. *If I didn't know better, I'd think I just missed an embarrassing moment for Luxvico.* "At ease," he says to Heath, waving his hand dismissively. Though the youth relaxes, he stays by them.

"We have a problem," Luxvico answers, despite the honor guard's presence.

"Say it, man," Otto insists.

"I think we should discuss it on our way to the control cockpit," Lux says turning.

"No! I think you should discuss it right here, now!" Pfizer says rising angrily.

"M'lord—," starts Luxvico.

"Domino—," begins Otto.

"Enough!" Pfizer shouts, glaring at Otto "No more lies—counselors, advisors!" he yells with derision. "You will tell me what affects me out of friendship and simple courtesy if not out of duty to me as your Emperor! How am I to make effective decisions when those I trust most keep secrets and coddle me?!"

Otto is unsure whether he reacts from Bloodguard conditioning or just never having seen Pfizer so enraged. "You're right. Forgive us," he says. But in the back of his mind he hears a whispered echo of Luxvico's warning.

Doesn't he see what he's encouraging? Luxvico thinks, but to his own horror he says, "We meant no disrespect, Lord." *I surely do not. But am I the only one who can see the change in Pfizer's behavior? Otto doesn't want to see it.*

"By the Eternal, Lux, what is it?" Otto rasps.

"When we jettisoned antimatter as a diversion we also made

it impossible to make this kind of a rendezvous."

"What about reprogramming the heavy drone to return and report our situation to the *Callahan*. I know we don't know where it is now, but we know where it will be later," volunteers Heath.

Not a bad idea, Otto thinks. "Lux?"

"Reprogramming the drone will be simple and we can employ the Coventry Protocols as a secure cypher to ensure positive identification."

"That's a start," Pfizer says in his quiet voice. *I've got to get out of here.* "But what if the probe is intercepted? I don't relish the idea of waiting without fuel. It limits my ... our options. I think we will send the drone but we will also acquire additional a-mat."

The three begin to protest but Pfizer stops them with an upraised hand. "I know the three of you don't like this, but consider: If for some reason the drone fails or the *Callahan* itself encounters some unknown variable, we will have options and a means of getting even closer to Coventry. Now it's a question of finding an a-mat facility. Otto, can you access the ship's navigation charts from here?"

Luxvico watches Otto access the Marineguard transport's computer. Holographic star patterns begin appearing and disappearing as he inputs search parameters. "I don't know if this is a good idea. All it takes is the wrong person asking questions. Antimatter is a controlled energy source. Too many questions are going to be asked," Otto abruptly stops his search and leans back against the wall.

"I'm not going to sit here and wait for Tene Thantos assassins to find me," Pfizer growls, but his voice is tinged with a note of hysteria that draws the attention of all of them. For a split second there is only the humming of the ship's a-mat drive.

Pfizer suddenly has to shake his head to clear it of the images of his Bloodguards dying to protect him as they flee the Omnividome. *My dreams have betrayed me and become nightmares. If only I were a comet and could blaze away from this; better yet, if only the*

273

Only God would hear my prayers and release me, Pfizer thinks bitterly and his resentment is like an acid that threatens to choke him. *My little sister was used as a template by my killers and they want me to wait here!*

"No. No. No!" Pfizer shouts.

"What, Domino?" Heath asks innocently, and Otto wonders if he himself were ever so innocent. He thanks the Eternal that he chose this particular man as Pfizer's honor guard. Otto feels as though he, like Pfizer, has lost his faith.

"What if we took the drone's a-mat reserve? Would that get us to the rendezvous?" Luxvico interrupts, and begins doing calculations on his omnipalm.

Otto shakes his head to clear it, exhaustion nearly catching up with him. Despite the light gravity of Earth and this ship he has been more than three days without sleep. How Luxvico has maintained his composure, with the exception of the incident with the Deathman and Tempel, is remarkable. Calmly always pressing them forward, keeping them from falling apart. Otto's earlier apprehension about the Tempeler has been replaced by a frustrating sense of his own inadequacy.

"Well?" Pfizer demands. He abruptly rises from his chair and begins pacing like a caged animal.

"It can be done," Luxvico answers.

"Then, SEE TO IT!" Pfizer roars, causing all of them to jump. Luxvico, having never seen Pfizer like this, is momentarily frozen into inaction even though he'd calculated this as a possible outcome. It was the outcome he didn't want to consider. *This is one of my finest students.* A sad and heavy sense of guilt fills Luxvico. *My people knew, we foresaw this coming and did nothing. I have lived centuries and the dreams of this child and his family deserved more respect than my dispassionate analysis. Now most of my race is where there is no shadow.*

With Luxvico lost in thought, Otto is the first to recover. He pushes himself away from the wall. "Counselor, walk with me please. Ensign Praetor remain here with the Domino," Otto orders, quietly staring at Pfizer in disbelief. Pfizer returns his stares but seems to see through him. Grabbing Luxvico gently by the arm Otto steers him out the iris. Once outside, Otto shakes his head sadly. "He's crazy, isn't he?" He immediately regrets his words.

Luxvico thinks about the question and considers a myriad of answers, intricate and complex, most of which would only burden Otto's troubled soul more. He decides to speak the man's own language and says with a compassion that surprises him, "I am afraid he's headed there." Then quickly he adds, "I have studied psychology and psychiatry—in fact I hold the equivalent of a doctorate in each. However, I need a proper analysis and I don't think His Majesty will cooperate." *I should not have said that.*

"So you're not sure either?" Otto asks.

Luxvico senses Otto trying to control his temper.

"It's just you're opinion? Huh?" Otto asks.

Luxvico, realizing where the conversation is heading, merely stares at Otto calmly.

"Then keep it to yourself," Otto snarls, roughly shouldering by Luxvico and taking off down the corridor.

"You and I cannot stop communicating Captain Praetor," Luxvico says calmly, quickening his pace to keep up with Otto.

Otto turns angrily, breathing deeply in a partially successful attempt to regain his composure. "I know. Just not about this. Not right now. We'll deal with this once we've dealt with the fuel situation."

"I am already dealing with this. I am concerned whether you can," Luxvico begins, at first oblivious to Otto's mounting frustration and anger. "Your friendship ... Perhaps your Bloodguard conditioning—,"Suddenly he catches himself. *Why am I being so insensitive? Is this some irrational response to the cultural rift between Erosi and Tempellian?*

In a blur Otto goes to shove Luxvico against the bulkhead, maybe to drive some compassion and feeling into this automaton. But although he moves with incredible speed, Luxvico reaches out and grabs his hands abruptly, easily. Otto instinctively tries to twist and counterbalance the Tempellians grip but finds himself unable to. Luxvico apparently can resist him effortlessly.

"Enough," Luxvico mutters and casually pushes Otto away.

Otto slams against the opposite bulkhead, grimacing and looking at Lux in disbelief. *How many secrets does this Tempeler have?*

"We are a people of secrets, Otto," Luxvico whispers.

CHAPTER 39

Returning to Titan often brings to mind these
inspiring words from Jeremiah 33:3: "Call to Me
and I will answer you, and show you great and
mighty things, which you do not know."

—Cato Ahren, HaneNet Interview 25-10-6323 I.C.

When seen from space Titan resembles a gleaming green gem.
The planet orbits the giant yellow star, Ekoz—a g-type star like
Earth's Sol and millions of others. Located on the very edge of
one of the spiral arms of the Milky Way Galaxy, Titan is one of
the Imperium's frontiers. The star system holds twelve planets,
of which only the fourth, sixth, seventh and eighth planets are
habitable. Titan, the seventh planet is almost ninety percent
land mass covered with lush jungles and forest fed by vast
underground fresh water aquifers.

A botanical treasure house, Titan had been settled by Cato's
ancestors more than eight thousand years ago. Unlike so many
of the other older worlds, the Ahrens had done their best to
preserve Titan's beauty. Archaeological research on Titan had
led to the discovery of the En'Zefi, a mysterious, non-
humanoid race, older than any humanity had encountered.

A once thriving civilization of trillions, the En'Zefi had
explored the farthest reaches of the universe, far beyond where
the Imperium's expeditions ventured millennia later.
Everywhere they had gone they had encountered worlds with
the potential for intelligent life but no such life was yet there.
Then through the millennia they waited and watched as

intelligent life forms did slowly develop on these countless worlds. They studied and recorded the awakening of sentient life in the primeval sludge of infinite worlds. Civilizations rose and fell, each one trying to explain in its own way the nature, meaning, purposes of life—their relation to the Eternal.

The En'Zefi had watched the Earth more than a billion years before the existence of *Homo sapiens*. Then mysteriously they vanished, all of them, and so became the stuff of legend.

So much of En'Zefi technology is beyond human comprehension even now. However, it is clear that they were very different from the alien races who enslaved Humanity from 2273-4082 A.D. In fact, had the En'Zefi still existed when Mankind overthrew their alien Enslavers, it is likely that much of the wholesale retaliatory slaughter against all aliens, hostile or no, may have been averted. Humanity might have learned from the En'Zefi the wisdom of peaceful coexistence. For the En'Zefi never interfered, they only watched and recorded. And what they had discovered—oh, what they had discovered! Only three people in the universe now know this.

Or is it four now, Lomin? Cato wonders, as the courier ship nears Titan. If only the Ambros Omnividome project had been initiated and we had the chance to spread this great knowledge. *'All of us were afraid. The minute it was discovered it should have been disclosed.* Lomin seems to whispers in Cato's mind. Cato shrugs, drawing a curious side-long glance from Basileus, who stands beside him at the holo screen. Basileus attempts to cover his curiosity with a smile.

"It's good to be home, father," Basileus says, turning back to the screen.

"M'lord, Titan Planetary Defense Command is hailing us. They are sending fighters to escort us to the Glythsphr Spaceport," announces the courier ship's Bloodguard Captain.

Through the view ports and on the main holo screen more than thirty of the aurora class space air superiority fighters flash into view and assume a defensive formation around the *Hermes*, sleek gray double-engined needles powered by C-drive thrusters and engineered for air and orbital superiority. They fly close enough that Cato and Basileus can see the pilots.

Titan's atmosphere is denser than Earth's, and when they finally pass through the thick roiling cloud layer they behold an arboreal world of lush Jurassic beauty, lit by the brilliant yellow light of Titan's sun. The canopy of the massive forest is a blend of deciduous and rain forest growth. The foliage ranges through the entire spectrum of green, from the palest lime to an almost black that glistens like emerald. Other trees and groves show colors more autumnal than any Cato has ever seen on Earth, or any other world for that matter. Then of course there are the great woad trees. which can grow a kilometer high and hundreds of meters across, and which, once their inner cores rot away, offer more than ample living space. Each woad could be grown to a family's specifications and, its wood could be treated to make it as fire retardant and durable as permacrete. The planet's cities therefore resemble nothing so much as a great forest by day, and by night faerie cities from legend.

Now the courier ship approaches a great stand of at least fifty woad trees, many of which vanish into the clouds. It is spring on Titan. In the northern hemisphere, the woad trees blossom with aquamarine and pale ruby blossoms that will yield amber and bloodstone red petals. Lights that weave through and around the massive interconnecting branches like a million fireflies are projected from the various airborne conveyances of the inhabitants of Glythsphr, the capital city.

The lights flicker creating a mood of jubilance.

The people of Titan know that Cato, their Coronal Regent, has returned. *If only Lomin were truly here with me, as he always was before*, Cato inwardly laments. He feels the ghost of Lomin within him evince a similar sorrow.

Kilometers outside the city, well hidden from view, the Titans joke, sits the Glythsphr's Spaceport, a stark metallic contrast to the lush growth surrounding it. The gleaming silver needle of the spaceport's subspace communication and flight control is encircled by fusion-welded topsoil that is marked with landing pits and flats. As they approach, shuttles, cargo haulers, star liner excursion launches, in-system transports, and freighters open a path for the *Hermes* and its fighter escorts. Cato loves the sight of his planet from orbit—to see the great forest that stretches from horizon to horizon, the great woad cities, their woods polished in shades of chestnut, pine, teak, and mahogany. Static lighting flashes in the humid atmosphere as if in anticipation of the fireworks that will be set off later.

I will lay you to rest here, old friend, Cato thinks and another wave of visions assaults him.

Cato sees Pfizer dressed in the plain brilliant white uniform of the Bloodguard Domino, chips of the Phoenix Star on his collar, standing on a balcony, paned glass behind him. Lightning flashes here too, and Pfizer's short hair blows in the wind before a storm. A look of sorrow and resignation marks Pfizer's features.

Bloodguards menacingly stalk forward through the rich halls of a palace Cato has never seen.

Oriana lies curled in a bed draped in gold silk, her bed linens tossed off her eyes wide open. She is unable to sleep.

Balthasar Hane is in the center of the great gold geodesic dome at the center of HaneHome. The Electors of Eros Alliance gather around him in all their glory, kneeling.

The Magus of the Ilkani Church, his face panic-stricken, runs for his life.

Looking up from an AI workstation, Nasir Qamar suddenly bursts into flames. Rage and surprise cross his face before Hephaestus beams incinerate everything.

Cato sees himself cradling a body. He sobs with unchecked grief. But he cannot see a face!

* * *

"Father!" It is Basileus' voice. Cato opens his eyes. The *Hermes* has settled on a landing flat close to the center of the port. Skidders and Takazhr CombatMechas begin pulling up to *Hermes*, their warning lights strobing. Media vehicles like vultures begin to circle in the skies above.

This is a mistake. They will know you are here, the Lomin within seems to say.

They already know, Cato thinks. He is thankful he has not spoken aloud. Then he wouldn't be alone in questioning his sanity.

"The preparations for Lomin?" he asks Basileus, putting a hand on his son's shoulder.

Lomin? Basileus thinks. *There is no Lomin, Father, only clothing, metallic conduit, and some nutrient fluid.* Nonetheless Basileus gives orders that what remained be placed in a sealed surgo-op tube, the exterior opaque, shrouded with the Academy crest and Cato's personal coat of arms. The great woads of Glythsphr in the distance draw Basileus' attention. Lights twinkle in the sky as Ekoz sets above the expanse of the emerald forest Basileus calls home.

Basileus felt a terrible loss at the death of old Lomin. Although it was Cato who adopted him when he was four, Basileus had loved the Tempellian like family, too. "All of Titan will mourn him, Father. He has been with our family for twelve hundred years," Basileus says feeling sympathetic grief for the impending sorrow of his adopted aunts and cousins below. *Sorrow for all of Titan,* Basileus thinks.

"Sorrow for the universe, for the Imperium, my son," Cato says softly, before turning to look his son squarely in the eyes. Basileus betrays momentary startlement. His face composes quickly but not before Cato sees the suspicion, the...fear—not of him but for him.

"Father, what is happening?" Basileus asks, deliberately but in a whisper. His father raises a hand swiftly, an indication to wait. Then Basileus hears in his mind, *Trust me. Wait, my son,* in a voice that is clearly that of his father and Lomin speaking in unison. The *Hermes* sways as it moves to a docking slip on the great needle that juts up at the spaceport's center. Basileus realizes this is no time for questions. More CombatMechas have joined the star fighters that protected them from above. Basileus hears the change in pressure as the courier's main hatch decompresses and opens. Almost immediately Takazhr and Bloodguard bearing the Ahren eagle crest swarm on board the ship. His aunt, Cato's older sister, Vice Princess Novia Dole-Ahren enters, followed by her entourage.

The Vice Princess is nearly as tall as her brother, with a pile of red hair coifed with pearls and diamonds above her hawk-like features. Her skin is pale and freckled, her eyes the dark clear blue of their father. Cato possesses the darker skin and gold eyes of their mother. Standing together, they resemble the opposing king and queen on a chessboard, Cato dressed in the black of the Takazhr Grand Kurseg and Novia dressed in shimmering white samite, her long, graceful arms bare. The Titans call her the "Iron Queen."

Cato's sister Novia acting as seneschal, has ruled over Titan and the hundreds of neighboring worlds in Cato's name during his frequent absences fulfilling his duties as chief officer of the Takazhr. She is almost a hundred years older than her brother, well into e-mortal middle age, though her fierce freckled face still looks like a young woman's. As she sweeps toward him now there is a look of anxious pleasure on her beautiful face. Then Cato sees her features change as she perceives a difference in her brother. It is more profound than even this crisis could have wrought. Even as they embrace Cato feels her stiffen against him, as if she'd gone to hug her brother and instead found a stranger.

"Cato?" she asks, her eyes searching his.

"Novia," Cato merely whispers and hugs her again. A little brother with his older sister. Cato feels the tension in her ease, the questioning in her eyes recedes. He knows Novia has seen the cortege of mourners for Lomin and he also senses that there is some greater, more immediate concern weighing on her.

"What is it, Novia?" and before she answers, Cato knows. A Deathship. Another one.

"A Deathship," Novia Ahren mouths the words her brother seems to know.

For the first time Cato truly sees that even if the Tene Thantos are fronting for the traitors, they have their own

282

agenda. If more than one Deathship exists, then Lomin's fears of another Wasting seem all too warranted. Armageddon has chosen his world as its next target.

"Coming here," Cato says, and he begins playing a part that Lomin within has warned him he must in order to keep his family's trust, even the trust of Basileus.

"Minutes before you entered atmosphere. Long-range sensor drones from our naval defense taskforce verified the suspicions you transmitted to us. How did you know?"

"Not now, Novia," Cato says, taking her hand and searching the faces of those gathered with his sister. "Where is Vice Admiral Lynch?" Cato asks, eager to speak with the commander of the Viceroyal Naval Forces.

"Outside. Waiting with your people," Novia answers softly.

"Novia, there isn't time for this—," Cato begins to protest.

Novia turns and looks at the black surgo-op bearing Lomin's remains.

"There will always be time," she chides Cato, imitating their deceased teacher with sad poignancy.

CHAPTER 40

Evil begets evil and the seeds of our sins blossom
into the fruit of our own destruction.

—Oriana Ambros, *The Book of Sorrows*

Oriana cannot bear to look at more holographs of the
devastation on Earth below, of the millions of refugees—or
hear the reports of Tempellian survivor convoys being
attacked. She sits with her Impgov military advisors at a large
blackglass table in the briefing room off the bridge of her naval
destroyer, *Alabama*, which serves as her mobile command post.
Dejectedly she gazes out one of the windows. She struggles to
control her grief and guilt but the carnage she conspired to
unleash numbs her and her eyes burn. Abruptly she stands,
scattering CDC's from the table's black mirror surface, and
turns her back on the holo images.

She has seen suffering that seems to rival the atrocities of
the Wasting. The Wasting, something she had sworn as an
Ambros to prevent from ever happening again. *Perhaps I am
damned.* Not just the hundreds of millions vaporized instantly in
the nucleoing of Atlantis but millions dead in the undersea mer
cities and many more in the Atlantic coastal regions. The list of
stricken areas is overwhelming. She had no idea there
are…were so many cities on Earth. The entire planet had been
brought to its knees. She views the flood-devastated districts of
Old Washington in the North American Precinct now
hovering nearly a mile above the devastation. Dark green
Takazhr CombatMechas swarm in and out of view escorting

284

the destroyer above flood ruined land in the dying light of late afternoon.

The tsunamis that followed the destruction of New Eden have caused catastrophic flooding in many of the Atlantic Ocean's coastal regions. Entire cities along the eastern seaboard were subjected to massive kinetic bombardments, New Boston, Neo New York, Old Philadelphia, Nova Charleston, and Novia Atlantia. Gone are the greens of the beltway and the glittering skidders and helio jets beneath the weather modification network's once blue skies—now the skies are toxic gray.

Ashen snow falls from the sky, fallout. *What have I done? Billions are dead. I have gone against everything both the Ambros and the Hane believe. I gave the order to deploy the nucleo! They are waiting for me to order a planetary evacuation except for the few surviving domed cities.* Confronted by the dreadful consequences of her decisions—defiling her homeworld, obliterating another— Oriana wishes she'd never left the peaceful confines of Nova Roma. But even more, she wishes she could escape the presence of the replicant impersonating her sister. *I need allies.*

And they will see your sorrow and remorse and feel sympathy for you, side with you. Jovion had whispered those words to her. She had once made love to him and now she wonders how she can stand the touch of him. *What is wrong with me?'* She wants to weep and scream.

Creed, her uncle, was reported to have been on Eros with another powerful Hane, her cousin Grand Admiral Tanenov. She knew they would refuse any contact with her, yet she had held onto the hope that they would. They had not. And now her surviving Admirals, Kursegs, Praetor Generals, and the Takazhr High Command are wondering why their surviving commanders—Elizabeta Tanenov, Creed Hane, and Cato Ahren—seem to be making moves of their own. It is exactly as Jovion had told her it would be. Oriana sees no choice now but to alienate her mother's military survivors and the Hane even further. All this suffering because she selfishly wanted to live her life her way. *I am damned and if there is a hell I am in it.*

Forever.

"Tell the Citizo it is an Aeon conspiracy of the highest order," Jovion had said to her. "Think of the irony: You, exiled for breaking prohibitions against genetic manipulations, are the only Ambros to protect your sister. You discover the plotting of Balthasar and his brother along with Cato and Tanenov to insure an Aeon Empire. A place where normal humans, have no place! Tell them the script that Marisol was supposed to read. Tell them that it was the Hane not us who allied with the Tene Thantos and deployed the nucleo. They killed your mother, father, and sister. They tried to kill you and sweet Zoe."

Oh, how he's played me, Oriana seethes. The Magus had warned her that Jovion and Nasir wanted nothing less than all-out civil war, and now that seems more and more inevitable. The Magus—another member of their conspiracy whose motives she no longer trusts.

"Take her!" Oriana hears her father's voice shout. She looks up at the conference table's central projection holo and to see her father push her mother into the protective arms of the Bloodguard—the looks of pain on their faces. Her eyes blur and she lowers her head.

In the holo projection, a-mat and fusion weapons begin detonating over Earth's cities. "Enough!" she nearly screams. So casually she had justified her violent acts: *You have to break some eggs to make an omelet.*

"Your Majesty?" a thin blonde man in the black uniform of a Takazhr Marshal says, startled. Oriana finds his voice soothing and calm. It conveys both concern and purpose with Serdian diplomacy.

Like a poisonous, dark addiction Jovion's presence and advice clings to her. When Oriana raises her eyes to address the Marshal, whose name she can't recall, her guilt is so palatable that his simple question seems an accusation.

"Shut it off," Oriana commands, turning from the window and indicating the holo with a sweep of her hand. Her voice is too sharp, too brittle. It only adds to the questions she reads in all of their faces.

"Excuse me. Marshal," she mumbles as she gathers her pale fire silk skirts and glides back to her place at the table. For a moment, just a moment, she considers fleeing from the room. She sees no choice but to follow Jovion's advice, but a quiet voice that sounds like Pfizer's tells her it does not have to be so. Taking her seat, Oriana announces: "We must consider the possibility that Cato Ahren, Grand Admiral Tanenov, and others have betrayed us." The room explodes with angry disbelief and flat-out denial but doubts and suspicions hang in the air, too.

It's exactly as Jovion said it would be, Oriana thinks.

"Believe me," she continues, "the irony does not escape me. But Secretary Goldshef has information that indicates that the Executive Council was aware of this plot and the 'conspirators,' she says, with emphasis, "had to move up their timeline in order for some chance of success."

More explosive speech detonates in the room.

"Creed Hane is many things, but he is no traitor!" declares the Marshal forcefully but with the same calm as before.

Marshal Iago Ngumo. Oriana remembers him now. Marked for termination, he had nevertheless survived the assault on Earth. Ngumo is Grand Admiral Tanenov's protégé and very dangerous—because he knows her, knows the family, the Hane. And in the absence of Grand Admiral Tanenov, Cato, and Creed, Ngumo is the senior member of the Joint Chiefs of Staff. He is a Hane wunderkind and a contemporary of Pfizer's Captain Praetor Otto Buchanan. *How did Jovion's briefing miss this very dangerous man's survival?* Iago is a pure breed Aeon, but like most Hane, he has been indoctrinated to accept the fact that although they are superior in many ways, the Hane are still modified, augmented *Homo sapiens* genetic stock.

Oriana had never believed the Citizo needed to be destroyed. She was no rabid Aeon racist, but mortals simply had no right to determine the genetic potential of the Aeon or other e-mortals. They were interfering with the true potential and awesome possibilities of the human race. And that had been exactly Pfizer's point when they'd spoken before the Opening of the Omnividome, when he had gone on about the potential of the Human Race—*Homo sapiens, Homo Deus,* and *Homo Dominus Deus*—all humankind. Pfizer had tried to get her to see that the relationship, even down to the individual level is symbiotic, synchronistic. Although human beings are not created equal, they must be given equal chances to achieve their potential.

"Rubbish," she had told him. "*Homo neanderthalensis, Australopithecus,* are extinct because they failed to adapt to the universe. Failed to shape it to their will as the Only God had commanded in Genesis." Yet despite the religious conviction and pragmatic cynicism of her words, she had been struck by that simple look on Pfizer's face that said: *All life human life is precious and to be appreciated.* It had paralyzed her prepared statements of evolution and genetic determinism. And then he'd gone on to talk about tolerance, forgiveness, understanding, and in her heart she had agreed. Oriana had known in the core of her being that Pfizer was right. Yet hours later she had ordered a matter conversion device detonated over an entire continent in an effort to kill him.

Oriana had made mistakes before as everyone does. But even when Pfizer and the rest of her family had offered her their complete forgiveness, she had failed to forgive herself. So she had not accepted their forgiveness. Instead, she had betrayed those who had truly never meant her any harm. Those who had tried to protect her from herself. In the willful attempt to declare her own independence, she had failed them and ultimately herself.

The lines are drawn, Oriana tells herself now. *Jovion's prophecy of this meeting, although it could turn out to be nothing more than perverse wish-fulfillment, leaves me no choice.* Her ideals will be forever compromised. Suddenly, in a soul-shaking moment, she understands her mother, how her mother, too, had to compromise her ideals. The others in the room have seen the consternation and doubt on her face. She must tell them something and certainly not the truth.

"My father's family has long harbored resentment due to the great sacrifices they made at Anangan and during the Wasting. They want control over the Imperium because they consider it their due." *Truly, Jovion's advice is so close to the truth that it will deceive even the most adept emp-psych. Why wouldn't it? I almost believe it myself.*

More demands of proof, evidence, and facts burst forth from those gathered.

"None of you has any reason to trust me. When I was younger, I did try to—I did reject my heritage and obligations. I regret I thought I was a law unto myself. But, consider this: I understand the Hane's motives better than anyone. Exiled to a barren rock in the orbit of a black hole, I have had more than enough time to consider—"

"Creed and Millian Hane are Bloodguard. In six thousand years has any Bloodguard betrayed his Regis' trust?!" shouts the senior Bloodguard present, nominee for Creed's office of Grand Kurseg.

"Excuse me, if Balthasar Hane is a traitor, why did the Deathship attack Eros?" Marshal Ngumo interrupts. "Or for that matter, why did it not attack Titan? That planet is not nearly as well defended." There is an edge to his voice now, and his pale blue eyes shine in the darkened conference room.

CHAPTER 41

In those difficult times it felt as if a strong wind was
blowing—and was blowing everything in my direction.

—Balthasar Hane, as quoted in *The Hane Commentaries*
by Aaron Charlemagna Invid-Hane

Balthasar Hane takes his time walking through the Sisterhood
of Peace Arboretum, outside his mother's retreat. The
Widow's Nest, the Hane call it. It's located on one of the
northernmost and highest reaches of the HaneHome crater.
Balthasar's father, Aaron, and his mother had begun building a
retirement home here. Then came the disaster of Oriana's
Insurrection at Anangan.

In the beginning, even Balthasar and Cedar had sided with
Oriana. Her call for a deregulation of the GenTech Board's
strict protocol had meant more than just unrestricted
genegineering and augmentation. It meant also that same sex
couples such as he and Cedar could at last have legitimate,
biological offspring created in vitro through the gestation
matrix. But Oriana had played the wrong hand. Sadly she had
appealed to the extremist and the fringe.

Everyone had someone in their family like he and Cedar.
Still, many extremists called for genes such as they possessed—
genes long associated with creative and spiritual genius—to be
removed from the human gene pool. Genetic Evolutionists, on
the other hand, argued that nature had created the non-
breeding members of the pack to defend the breeding core,
citing the fact that some of the greatest warriors in history,
male and female, were as the Hane said, "sexually artistic."

Hence the Bloodguard secret of admitting those such as he and Cedar—some of the fiercest and most brilliant military genius—into their ranks. However, the Hane Nation would not accept pathogenic nor cloned descendants in the family and certainly not its leadership. Oriana's movement had spoken of a legal means against this restriction… if she had won. But Oriana's insurrection had failed. And so it remained that no child of Balthasar and Cedar would ever rule the Erosi Alliance. Creed and Kiritzia's son, Aaron, would become First Elector and ClanLord. Or Pfizer would.

Balthasar shakes his head to clear it. He supposes it is natural for his thoughts to dwell on Oriana. That is undoubtedly why his mother wishes to speak with him now. Only for Fen would he have left his office at the Aerie, the building that serves as the ClanLord's residence. But he knows that Creed and Cameron will also be here with his mother. Their Bloodguard escorts were clearly visible when he entered the arboretum. Balthasar understands that whatever his family wants to say needs to be discussed away from the many eyes and ears of the Aerie.

A warm breeze blows off the ocean and Balthasar turns toward the tinkling bells of his mother's escort. "Wait here," Balthasar commands the two Bloodguard who had followed him to the arboretum's enclosure. Purple clouds from setting Spica fill the twilight sky, patches of which can be seen through the green expanse of the arboretum. Cicadas begin their discordant chirping and fireflies blink in the gathering evening. Balthasar takes a moment to enjoy the scents of Delphian Amethyst roses, Titan lilacs, and Xanadu blossoms. He remembers with sadness how much Anastacia had loved the purple jeweled petals of the roses.

"Over here, Bal," calls Creed's voice from the darkness. Balthasar sees his brother's outline in the shadows of an opening through the exotic foliage. Balthasar moves silently toward Creed, who still wears the comfortable civilian clothes he had worn the prior evening. Balthasar himself has changed to normal Erosi clothes. He wears a sleeveless midnight blue tunic, the Hane Dragon in gold over his heart, and his feet are bare except for soft-soled sandals like Creed's.

"What is the meaning of this, Creed?" Balthasar whispers. Not being a whisperer, however, his question sounds more like a demand. Even without being able to see Creed's face he feels his brother tense.

"Your mother thought it better that we meet in private." It is Cameron's soft contralto voice this time. Her dulcet Serdian-inflected tones smooth the tension between the two brothers. With her are three others, two Imperial Naval Officers, both dressed in the spotless white of Admirals, and a Takazhr Field Marshal in black. Cameron Tanenov, Grand Flag Admiral, steps from behind Creed.

"Cousin Balthasar, forgive us," continues Cameron. "Your brother said you'd resent this. But your mother and I thought this needed to be said in private."

Balthasar turns his head toward his brother. His eyes have adjusted now to Eros' bright starlit night and he can once again discern facial nuances. Creed watches him silently, an unfamiliar neutral expression on his usually passionately animated face. *Something else is wrong,* Balthasar realizes, *something worse than the impending Deathmen attack on Titan.'*

"I did not mean to sound harsh, Creed." Balthasar says, in his way apologizing but without ever actually saying that he is sorry. "But I was pulled away from an important staff meeting." He glares angrily at Cameron. "Are you aware, Grand Flag Admiral," Balthasar hisses angrily, "that a Deathship is targeting the defenses of the planet Titan as we speak? Where is my mother?"

"Yes, I am," Cameron replies, and for the first time since she's spoken Balthasar hears anger in her voice, or rather impatience. Then she adds, "Your mother told us." Only her great discipline prevents her from saying it vindictively. *All the men of my family are so arrogant. Look what Millian's and his father's arrogance has caused. Creed is the only one whose agenda is clear, but he's always perceived as the most stubborn. Since when was speaking the truth considered* hubris? *Is my family suddenly afraid of the truth?*

"No, Cameron." It is Fen's childlike voice that startles them all. No bells announced her presence. She is alone. Her wimple and veil removed, she stands as gorgeous as Kiritzia, as commanding as Cameron, as regal as Oriana. The black, dark green, red, and blue runes and sigils that cover the right side of her face are plainly visible. There are no gasps from the three others present. This tells Balthasar they are Hane. After the Wasting the Aeon, the families that had allied with Tene Thantos, those whose genes had been manipulated for fantastic and fearsome abilities, had been tattooed on the right side of the face to indicate their house and abilities. Many abandoned this to avoid the obvious stigma but some chose to interbreed, and their descendants were forced to carry the mark of the Chosen.

Fen's soft raven black hair frames the childish face in soft ringlets that seem to shine even in the dark. Her eyes are bright blue. She has given Balthasar the same sun-fused eyes of sky blue, not the bleached, glacial-white blue of the Hane. But tonight Fen's eyes are different, tonight they glow bird bright.

"You've used the Sight…," Balthasar tries to whisper again, and once again he cannot. There is great apprehension in his voice. "What…What have you seen?" Balthasar begins the regimen he uses to check his emotions. *She has used the Power for others. The entire known universe is going to know what I have never really known but only suspected. The Hane possess a powerful telepath-clairvoyant at the very heart of our family. They will suspect all of us now of mind reading and mind bending. We will be dragged into the courts and in front of the media. Agreements are going to be abridged, or worse, annulled. We could have done this my way. Now Oriana has a weapon to use against us. I know everything they know. My agents and spies discovered everything their costly reckless gambit has uncovered. How will I control the Invid once this is known? I rule this family, not anyone else, How dare—*

"Balthasar," Fen says, gently yet sharply. "I have nothing to hide. Don't you think 'the universe' already knows what lies beneath the black lace and veils of your father's wife? Oriana is my granddaughter. How much can she play this card without playing it against herself?"

"And now all the stories of your spies and our sycophants can be confirmed," interrupts Creed, without the growling sneer that would normally have accompanied such a comment from the Lion. His disapproval of Balthasar's methods is nonetheless evident.

Fen looks sharply at her middle son, silencing him with a mere glance. She turns her attention back to Balthasar. "You, Creed, and Kiritzia, with their child's help, will control the Invid. If we are challenged in the courts, Balthasar, you will do what you were bred to do. Your father, the Great Hane, recognized this, as everyone here does. That is why you are permitted to rule. You love your family, the Hane Nation, Eros, and our Alliance more than yourself—more than Cedar or any one of us," Fen quotes her late husband and the strength of his character carried in her voice causes everyone to bow their heads.

"Don't you hate it when she does that," Creed says ever so softly, nudging his brother, a smile in his voice, trying to diffuse the mounting surge of anger he senses from Balthasar.

"Mother answered the questions in my mind out of order." Balthasar's face remains neutral but there is obvious anger and hurt in his voice.

"Balthasar—"Fen begins.

"Stop this," Cameron interrupts. "Forgive me, ma'am," she says, immediately apologizing to Fen. She turns to Balthasar and takes a deep breath. "I'm sure you're busy, cousin. But if you're angry with us now it'll be worse when I inform you of what we know, and what our intentions are." Cameron continues holding out a hand to keep Balthasar from speaking. "Creed and I are announcing that Pfizer is alive—"

"Cameron wait," Balthasar cuts her off. "I've been in touch with several high-ranking surviving Ambros. They've got suspicions of their own concerning Oriana—"

"Are they ready to divest her of her current interest in CIMB and Terrax?" Creed interrupts, and this time there is a sneer.

"No, not yet, I think," answers Balthasar. "And rightly so. They're afraid. Earth ... Earth is like an abattoir, I hear—"

"Then there's no point in talking to them," Creed interrupts. "Your inaction is allowing the suffering of billions. Do you know," he adds, pointing an accusing finger at Balthasar, "that Oriana is refusing off-planet aid, saying that remaining on-planet insurgents are hijacking them?"

"Ridiculous. Surely the Navy controls orbital space?" Balthasar says questioning Cameron.

"It's Oriana's Navy, Balthasar," she replies. "Creed and I are taking Pfizer to Titan, along with every Navy warship I can muster, every Takazhr we can carry. I'm going to be asking all groups with militia—The WiktorCorp Guard, the Daakaan, the Hane Nation Pax Force—to send volunteers."

"You'd strip your home world and your family of its indigenous defenders?" Balthasar asks incredulously. Abruptly the idea of having his Bloodguard arrest them all passes through his mind. He is still ruler here.

"Don't start the wrong war here, Balthasar," Fen says gently. "Choosing to fight the Deathmen at Titan means the first engagement won't be here. This conflict may never touch Eros again, and isn't that what you want?"

Balthasar sighs. They'd out maneuvered him. They knew he'd have to agree now. But still, he had to know. "What have you seen, Mother?"

Fen walks quietly to Balthasar, a radiant smile on her face as she looks up at him and whispers with childlike wonder: "The Tempellians, my son! The surviving Tempellians are gathering."

For a moment Balthasar is caught in the sense of wonder and expectation his mother is trying to convey, but soon the cool, pragmatic side of the Hane exerts itself. "And?" He asks.

Cameron answers before Fen can. "And they are the epitome of logic and rationalism in our civilization. Would they take refuge on Titan if it weren't safe to be there?"

So they gather on Titan. "Take the ships and the volunteers but no tursapoi. Not one gram," Balthasar says firmly. He looks angrily at Creed but he thinks: *Is this going to be the last time I see him alive?*

Fen sighs with exasperation. Cameron simply stares at him, and Creed steps forward and for a moment just a moment Fen thinks he and Balthasar will come to blows.

"Why don't you just offer our capitulation to the Regis!" Creed shouts.

"Selling tursapoi or commerce in it is illegal without government sanction!" Balthasar responds with equal anger. "I'll not give Oriana the opportunity to send the Bloodguard against us!"

"Our nephew is the legal government!" Creed continues shouting.

"Then let him declare himself, and yes, you can have your tursapoi. But you bring this war to my doorstep, to our home world, you jeopardize our family that I've sworn to protect, and I'll kill you!" Balthasar exclaims, his voice venomously soft.

Fen raises her hands, about to advise calm and moderation.

"No!" Balthasar shouts. "I swear, Mother, by the Only God. I have sworn to protect this family and our world, my people, from suffering, and I will consider every contingency, every plan, before I decide whether we implement it. Father chose me—Me! I am Stadtholder, military leader of the Hane Nation Pax Force and the militias of the other United Clans of the Alliance!"

"We know all your titles, Balthasar. And only Mother and Cameron stopped me from issuing the Hanekar against you," Creed replies, referring to an ancient and violent ritual by which Hane Nation rulers could be replaced by members of direct family.

"Declare it, Creed! Say the word! Your interference has gone on long enough!" Balthasar shouts, eager to show his arrogant brother once and for all who is the superior.

"STOP IT!" Fen's voice rings in their minds as well as their ears. She fills their minds with a sharp pain that causes all of them to clasp their ears and shake their heads. When they look up, there are tears in the eyes of the ancient woman who still looks so very young. "Forgive me, all of you. But, please, that is what our enemies want. More than anything they want us to fight amongst ourselves. Creed, Balthasar is right. He will give us the tursapoi after Pfizer's revelation. Balthasar, you will give Cameron everything else she has requested and do it now."

"No! I won't do anything until Pfizer's revelation. And don't try any of your tricks, Mother. I'll know," Balthasar says, firmly redirecting his rage to form a mental barrier.

"Balthasar, wait." It is Creed and this time he does not shout. He sounds as mild as Millian. "Little Aaron...my son...he—"

"Your son. The next great Bloodguard Warmaster, the first since Gert. The union of all the Aeon Nations: Invid, Vey, Hane. Our father's plan. My replacement!" says Balthasar.

"No, Balthasar. He is like you. Like you and Cedar," Creed says with an effort that nearly drains him. He sees Balthasar stiffen and he continues. "When the gentechs came and told us we could have his genes resequenced, we thought about it, how hard it will be for him to bear the stigma. But because Kiritzia and I love him, he will be what he is. My son is what the Only God has wrought and I will love him as I love you. The loss of our brother is part of the same plan, a plan beyond our comprehension. Having Aaron has taught me this. I'm sorry, truly sorry, that at this place and this time you are the one to have to make decisions by which thousands, maybe millions, of our family will die. Let me ask you this brother: Is it for the sake of your pride or your family's safety that you keep from acting?"

"You sound like our brother," Balthasar says sadly. "Declare Pfizer," he adds, his strong voice now as resigned as Creed's. "I will swear our allegiance."

Silver light reflected from desolate, rising Hecate fills the clearing. The night becomes what seems an overcast day, all bathed in gray, Eros twilight night when Hecate is full. There is a cool breeze redolent with floral scents and charged with ozone static. The sound of thunder rolls from inland, approaching the ocean.

"The wind is growing strong," Balthasar says to no one in particular. Softly it begins to rain.

CHAPTER 42

When analyzing the multiple factors that led up to
the Vengeance War and shaped its outcome, any
realist must not lose sight of the influence that the
triumvirate behind Pfizer wielded—and I'm
referring now not to Balthasar Hane, Cato Ahren,
and Cameron Tanenov but rather to Otto
Buchanan of Eros, Luxvico of Tempel, and Heath
MacKenzie. Who better than these three to rein in
the Emperor's wrath and contain the war? And in
so doing they averted far greater slaughter and
ultimately assured the solidarity and diversity we
enjoy today.

—Aaron Charlemagna Invid-Hane,
The Hane Commentaries

*I'd give almost anything to hear Mari's voice. Thank the Only God, that
she and Agust are safe. But how safe is Earth, really? And why is she
staying there? Surely Fiona had fled with the first off-world transport, but
why hadn't she insisted that Mari, her money maker, come with her?*
These thoughts leave Otto in angry bafflement. Some deep
instinct, though, tells him that Marisol waits on Earth for some
news of him. That she has taken this position so he'll know she
is alive.

Otto had gone with Luxvico in angry silence to see to the
diverting of the drone's a-mat fuel. Then, while Luxvico was
absorbed in garnering news from the nets, Otto had slipped
away. Otto needed a moment to regain control of his far-too
turbulent emotions, especially the frustration and dismay he

felt at Luxvico's easily tossing him aside in the corridor earlier.

By now Otto has wandered the length of the relatively small ship. It was never meant for this kind of deep range travel. Otto comes to the evacuation hatch that contained the pod Luxvico had ejected earlier. He checks to see that the corridor is empty and the outer hatches are sealed. Otto opens the empty pod bay and practically staggers inside, sealing the hatch behind him before slumping down, his exhaustion finally catching up with him in this private moment. He takes several deep breaths and begins a Bloodguard calming exercise similar to Tai chi. He is just beginning to relax when the shipside hatch hisses open behind him. Even before he opens his eyes he knows it will be Luxvico.

The Tempeler stands silently in the open hatch looking very much like any other naval crewmen in his borrowed uniform. Even with the uniform cap pushed down over his bald head his violet eyes seem to glow beneath it with an inhuman intensity. Luxvico hesitates then turns to leave.

"No wait," Otto says quietly as he ends his regimen.

"I am sorry to have intruded on your meditation. Please forgive me," Luxvico responds still moving to leave.

"It's okay, Lux. I know on Tempel you take your privacy, and especially your meditation, seriously; I lived there for almost ten years. We're stuck on this tiny ship, so it's all right. What did you want?" Otto says this with a calmness that surprises Luxvico. The moment of peace seems to have done Otto more good than he would have imagined.

"This can wait," the Tempeler says. "But I have been monitoring naval comm traffic. Grand Admiral Tanenov is calling for all available ships and militia to rendezvous at Titan. The Deathmen have sent another ship against that world—," Luxvico says, abruptly stopping to gauge Otto's reaction.

Otto seems to know there's more Lux wants to say, "And?" he prompts.

"The First Elector of the Erosi Alliance and the United Clans has declared that Crown Scion Pfizer is alive."

Finally! Otto thinks with a sigh. "The Bloodguard have

turned against Oriana?" Otto asks this hoping that at last all of this might be over, that he might at last return to Earth and his family.

"That is unclear. Information concerning Earth is extremely difficult to come by. I'm still organizing what data we have."

Keeping any sign of exasperation from his voice and matching the Tempellian's tone, Otto says: "Please, Luxvico, speculate." Otto suppresses a smile as the Tempeler's right eyebrow arcs in what is now to Otto a characteristic display of surprise. *You are not the only one with secrets, Tempeler,* Otto thinks.

"It is strange. I actually anticipated swift retribution and her immediate ouster by the Corps Bloodguard. There are disturbing rumors that Oriana has said that the 'Pfizer' that the Hane have declared is a replicant, or worse, a soulless clone. There are reports that Oriana has gone to great lengths to establish her legitimate genetic identity. And that the Hane contrived the entire attack on Eros with their Tene Thantos allies—"

"She really wants to risk civil war?" Otto interrupts. "The Hane despises the Tene! Most Erosi do."

"All of her actions indicate a predilection for self-preservation. Not the survival of others. She will risk civil war if it means she can live another day free." Luxvico says this with a hardness that Otto now interprets as disgust and contempt. "She keeps saying the first Aeon were created on Eros and it was the Chosen amongst the Aeon that began the Wasting. Indeed, some Aeon supported Oriana's aborted campaign twenty standard years ago."

"Not all Aeon are Tene!" Otto shouts in frustration and though he is not yelling at Luxvico the Tempellian frowns and his eyes gain a hooded look. Quickly Otto follows with: "Forgive me, Luxvico. I allowed my frustration to speak. Continue."

Luxvico nods. "Otto, the average Citizo of the Imperium has long been distrusting of the genetically engineered, especially of those whose chromosomes are configured in gestation matrices like the Aeon. People have watched the home world of our species ruined. The greatest learning center in all Human history…Obliterated."

Once again Otto feels a palpable sadness emanate from Luxvico.

"So too the world of the first true human immortals," Otto adds, voicing the first of his speculations concerning Tempellian secrets.

Luxvico face reveals an amazing gamut of emotions, most plainly surprise, loss, and rage.

Otto suppresses his instinct to move into combat stance. His experience earlier in the corridor dissuades him from further provoking the Tempeler. In his calmest voice, he says. "It's okay. The Bloodguard have long suspected. We do keep some of the best records in the Imperium."

"How…?"

"I'll give you two examples. Lomin of the Ahren has served for six centuries. Before that he was known as Lomix, Ambassador to the court Emperor Executor Anton II, Pfizer's great-great-grandfather. Prior to that you were Luxam, aide to Marshal Kata Hane of the Hane Pax Force and elementary military instructor to the child James Caesar Americus Hane who would become the father of Aaron the Great.

"The Bloodguard suspected all this, but there was never any conclusive evidence. Your bio suits leave no stray genetic material for analysis. You could have been descended from one of these people—a son, a nephew, who knows. The Tempelers have never given the Bloodguard reason for suspicion, yet it is a well-known fact that you are the longest lived of the Imperial population."

The rage has vanished from Lux's face and he now watches Otto in stunned surprise. *I've gone further than hinting at a revelation of one of his secrets,* Otto thinks. *I have to let him know that the Tempelers' secrets are safe with me.*

"We never had a reason to reveal what we suspected but were never sure of. But when you disposed of your bio suit, I got a skin sample reading while I helped you dress. I was concerned for your health, and when going through the medical database to find your normal readings…," Otto leaves the rest unsaid.

Luxvico nods in respect and appreciation at the Bloodguard's deductive reasoning. "Well done, Captain Praetor. Of course, now you want to know how old I really am."

"I already know," Otto says, catching the Tempeler off-guard again. "And it doesn't matter to me—except how all the knowledge and experiences you've accumulated can help me fulfill my duty of insuring Pfizer's safety and my desire to be with my wife and son again."

"And you'd use me for those ends," Luxvico says coldly. *And perhaps reveal my secret? Thereby making the remnants of my race the most hunted prizes in the universe?*

"This is the second time you've insulted my honor. I'm asking for your help. If these rumors you speak of are true, I need you. *We* need you."

"And what do I get out of this except for being next to the Regis' prime target? No offense to your honor."

"I know your value and I swear to you, insofar as it does not conflict with Pfizer's direct safety, Heath and I will—any other of the Bloodguard on this ship will—give our lives to protect you," Otto says, dropping the emotional mask he'd been wearing to make himself unreadable to the Tempellian. *You've got to trust me.*

"I do. It is not often that one sees the capacity for true self-sacrifice and wisdom in one so young. You are a fine example of all that is truly noble in humanity, Otto Buchanan. This is the second time in as many hours where Bloodguard honor has shamed me. Of course I will help you. The first thing we have to do is inform Pfizer of the Hane Declaration. Are you ready? If you'd prefer, I will tell him. You appear as if you could use some rest."

At first Otto's best response is a weary, sarcastic chuckle. "I wish I could sleep. The best I could hope for is meditation."

"Then meditate. I will speak with Pfizer."

"I tried. You know, it's funny. I can always relax to the

sound of rain falling against the roof or a thunderstorm. You know like night back home on Eros," Otto says, visibly pulling himself together. "Of course we're stuck on a spaceship," he mumbles, more to himself than to the Tempeler.

Luxvico crosses the remaining distance between them until he is standing face-to-face to with Otto. Uncomfortably, but not threateningly close. "May I?" Luxvico asks, and Otto is not sure whether he hears this or receives it telepathically.

"Wha—?" is all Otto manages as the Tempellian leans forward and their foreheads touch.

"Eros Otto *schickshen shaanav shishaa,*" Luxvico whispers.

Otto feels the warm night breeze rolling over the plains of Draco Noir, his home on Eros. The wind rustles through verdant grasslands and thunder clouds roll like cobras ready to strike with hisses of thunder and static lightning. He lays his head back on the pillow, which obscures his view of the window. But he smells Marisol's hair as she sleeps beside him, their little son nestled quietly between them. As the rain begins to patter gently against the roof Otto closes his eyes and falls peacefully to sleep.

Luxvico gently lowers Otto to the deck. The Bloodguard adjusts himself as if sleeping blissfully in a bed. Luxvico sets the airlock's operating indicator to display active and occupied to prevent a venting, and then silently departs. *I could just as easily vent him to space,* his pragmatic heritage reminds him. *I could dispose of them all,* he thinks clinically. *The price I could pay to have Oriana spare my race?* Luxvico berates himself for such thinking. It was the same silent complicity and involvement with Oriana and her traitors that had destroyed Tempel.

He sighs deeply as he moves along the corridor back toward the sickbay. Perhaps now alone he may be able to reach Pfizer without Otto's over-protective interference. Mentally preparing himself, he steps through the iris into sickbay.

Pfizer stands before him showered, shaved, wearing the spotless white uniform of the Domino of the Corps Bloodguard. The uniform's only adornments are the fire-jewel-eyed golden phoenix emblems at his collar. Pfizer smiles slightly at what can only be the surprise that flashes across Luxvico's face. This was surely unexpected by the Tempeler.

"Your Majesty...," is all Lux manages.

"You've heard?" Pfizer asks, his voice resonating the confidence of his Hane lineage. Luxvico is grateful to see Pfizer restored to at least a semblance of his former self. *But how...??*

"I was coming to tell you—" Lux replies.

"Where is Otto?" Pfizer asks, having expected Otto to follow Lux through the iris.

Luxvico notes that the hysteria that had tinged Pfizer's voice is gone. "He is resting."

"Good. You and Heath come with me. We're approaching comm's range of the gunship. It is time for my Bloodguards and the universe to know that the Imperium is no longer leaderless."

Pfizer strides through the iris as if it's not just armored-Heath escorting him but an entire cohort of Bloodguard Praetors and this small marineguard transport is an Apocalypse Class dreadnought. When Lux hesitates, Pfizer turns with regal calm:

"What is it, Luxvico?" Pfizer asks.

Pfizer's voice is that of the man who was his student and yet now Pfizer stands, his shoulders straight and gaze direct just like his father the Emperor Executor would have liked to have seen. Even the Bloodguard uniform seems to compliment Pfizer more than anything Luxvico remembers. It seems appropriate. No delusions cloud Pfizer's eyes. He merely waits patiently for Lux's answer. Pfizer's practiced unreadable emoto-mask is in place. *How did he effect this transformation?* Luxvico wonders. *Why is that it that I question the fortuitous? The young student seems to have become a man before my eyes worthy of his Cardinal title in the no longer existent Academy.*

"Luxvico?" Pfizer prompts. The Counselor is relieved by his behavior but he still seems unsure. "You told me some decisions require immediate attention, and both time and choice are limited," Pfizer says with a benign yet chastising smile. Then Pfizer says simply, neutrally. "You can always stay here…"

Lux considers. "No Majesty," he says, falling into step. "I will go with you."

* * *

Marisol Fitzgerald-Buchanan cannot explain the sensation of Otto's presence that overtakes her. She hears him whisper her name in her ear and smells his scent, the thunder of Eros rumbling in the distance. "Otto," she says to herself.

Marisol is thankful she is alone in the rooftop garden, as her emotions overcome her outside the PPRC compound. *He is alive! If Pfizer is alive Otto is alive.* No Tempeler would agree with such logic but she knew. Marisol had been privy to some of the fierce discussions between knots of various officers— Naval, Bloodguard, Takazhr, Savoy's WiktorCorp Guard—that is, until they noticed her.

"It couldn't be a replicant. Did the Tene replicate his Praetor and Counselor?"

"Captain Buchanan selected the only Chosen Bloodguard in the Corp as Pfizer's honor guard. These recordings clearly show the individual listed as Ensign Praetor Heath D. F. MacKenzie."

"I don't care what they tell us. My unit's leaving for Titan once we're clear of Sol."

It's time for me to leave as well, Marisol realizes. With the communications blackout due to the Tene Thantos terrorism, the lies that she has told make her sick to her stomach. At first she'd been naive enough to believe the PPRC would be reporting honest news to the Imperium. But the organization had been decapitated during the vicious attack on Earth. This is why Jovion and Oriana said they needed her. *They've just used me,* she thinks, as she picks up her omnipalm and rises from bench. She has to get out of here now.

"A moment please, Marisol."

It is Oriana's soft voice from behind her. Marisol had been

so engrossed in her thoughts that she didn't notice the Regis and her party—Jovion Quiso, assorted PPRC staffers, and an armored Takazhr squad—approaching. *Where are the Bloodguard?* Marisol wonders. "Your Majesty," Marisol says, executing a graceful curtsy. "Forgive me. I was lost in my own thoughts," she apologizes, keeping her attention focused on Oriana. In their brief association she feels that she has established a rapport with the Regis. Oriana has seemed open to her comments and suggestions.

"Is there something wrong, dear?" Oriana asks, extending a hand and bidding Marisol to rise. *In another life she and I might have been good friends,* Oriana thinks. But there is no life other than the one she has chosen …

"Nothing that can't wait, Your Majesty. I—"

"Good," interrupts Jovion briskly. "We need you to make an important announcement. We are suspending the Bloodguard Charter," Jovion announces, watching her with crushing scrutiny.

Marisol cannot control the muscles in her legs at Jovion's statement. She sways but Jovion catches her. She pushes herself politely away and turns to Oriana. "Your Majesty? Sus…spend the Bloodguard?"

The amicable concern in Oriana's eyes never wavers but something harder and more penetrating enters her gaze. Oriana grips Marisol's hands. Her eyes moisten with tears and Marisol realizes *She is a far better actress then I will ever be.*

"Your husband is … was my brother's best friend, his Praetor," she says. Then, turning to Jovion to explain the woman's reaction, she begins, "Captain—"

But Marisol interrupts her. "D…Does this mean you've determined that it is a replicant impersonating Pfizer?" Marisol directs her question to Jovion, forcing herself to look at him.

Does this woman believe us or not? Jovion dares not use his telepathy to scan her mind. Oriana now travels with an Ilkani psi-sensitive to alert her to any unanticipated psi-forces. A sign of the widening gulf between them. *No matter, Queen of the Ambros, you shall not be of use to me for much longer.* Every world the

Deathships infest mean more Deathmen, more Deathpods, and eventually more Deathships. Nasir Qamar had managed to keep the majority of the Imperial Navy "protecting the space lanes and frontiers from acts of depredation and piracy during this crisis". With the Naval Command in disarray many ships were choosing to defend their home systems instead of responding to Cameron Tanenov's "mutinous orders." Even with the unforeseen variables of Pfizer's survival, a Hane rebellion, and the Magus' and Oriana's vacillations, he has managed to keep his enemies and adversaries from uniting in common cause. Jovion has fed the fires of their mutual distrust; Hane against Ambros, Aeon against e-mortal and mortal, Aristo against Citizo.

Divide and conquer. The saying was far older than he but he understood it better than all those before him. *And now if I can turn public reaction against the Bloodguard...*

"There are questions as to whether they responded appropriately to the 10-21 attack," Jovion answers coolly in his dulcet, Serdian-inflected voice. "There is evidence that the Bloodguard were aware of Tene Thantos activity in the Sol System more than forty-eight hours in advance but deliberately chose not to act."

That's a lie! Marisol thinks. "For more than five thousand years the Bloodguard have—" she begins angrily before the smooth sounding Jovion interrupts her.

"This has all been difficult for me to accept, as well. I, too, have depended on the Bloodguard for special protection and I've known many of outstanding character. But there is corruption and it must be rooted out. This is only a suspension during this time of emergency."

"Suspend the only one of two forces in the Imperium allowed to deploy tursapoi? Why? When an enemy that uses the drug is attacking Imperial worlds?! Majesty, the public will certainly question your judgment," Marisol says to Oriana, trying to keep the desperation from her voice and knowing she will fail.

Oriana smiles at her maternally. "Their charter is being

suspended, not revoked. I want you to assure the public of this. We don't intend to shut off the supply of tursapoi to those addicted; we're just going to place stricter controls on the distribution to high-level officers and enlisted," she says soothingly, pedantically.

"Who will protect the Aristos? What of the safety of your Imperial person?" Marisol asks, still not believing Oriana is allowing this to happen. "The Bloodguard have insured the continuation of your family for thousands of years."

"My dear," says Oriana. *You've raised good questions,* she thinks, realizing how this will compromise her own military position. She looks warily at the female psi-sensitive dressed in Ilkani robes similar to the ones she'd worn...until she became Regis. Had the Church abandoned her as well? Was this woman letting Jovian manipulate her? The fear that surges through Oriana is as close to paranoia as anything she has ever known, but the vice-like control she maintains on displaying her emotions in Jovion's presence does not fail her. However, such emotional control comes at a physical cost and her legs begin to shake beneath her. Marisol, being closest, catches her and guides Oriana to the bench she'd been sitting on minutes before.

Oriana realizes that the Takazhr had actually allowed Marisol to touch her. This would never have happened had Bloodguards been protecting her. Yes, the Takazhr had advanced in alarm when she staggered, but they had allowed someone else to touch her person. And if Marisol had not been such a loyal citizen or if she'd had some other agenda, like those who now surround Oriana, she would have been at her mercy.

"Regis?" Jovion looks questioningly at the Ilkani psi-sensitive.

When Oriana sees this the fury that grips her is unmanageable. "Leave, all of you! Mrs. Fitzgerald-Buchanan may remain," Oriana says rising. "You!" Oriana shouts at a PPRC executive emerging onto the rooftop garden from the executive suites. The startled man turns and bows deeply.

Hurriedly, he begins walking toward Oriana. "Stop there," Oriana calls, the studied sweetness returning to her voice. "Go back inside and find the ranking Bloodguard and tell him that I am unattended," Oriana orders. Even at this distance there is a look of horror on the man's face as he turns to rush inside.

"Oriana, please don't," says Jovion, still standing there within the squad of attending armored Takazhr.

"Get out of here, Jovion, and take her with you," Oriana says pointing an excusing finger at the Ilkani psi-sensitive. The woman evinces surprise as if her features are made of clay. Summers she'd spent on Eros in the company of her grandmother Fen had taught Oriana to recognize the telltale signs of telepathic possession.

"M'lady," one of the armored Takazhr says, but his voice is too raspy, too artificial. The distortion is more than the augmented electronics of a human voice even if addicted to the tursapoi. Oriana realizes that there are Deathmen beneath the armor of the Takazhr. "Your sister, the Crown Scion Zoe, gave orders that you are not to be left unattended..."

They are taking orders from the replicant!!! Infestation! "Jovian, what have you done? You f—," Oriana begins.

"I've had enough," Jovion says, his once angelic face made diabolic by the evil of his thoughts. For the first time in their association, Oriana realizes she is seeing the real Jovion. "You and this Erosi bitch are going to make that announcement *now*—willingly or after my Takazhr remove the T-shield this human female is wearing," Jovion commands. "And I promise you," he adds, glaring at Marisol malevolently, "after possession you will never be the same."

He sounds as sick and dangerous as Nasir,' Oriana thinks as she looks desperately to the entrance into the PPRC complex, hoping the exec had been wearing a T-shield. *But would it be enough?*

"He wasn't, and he's sitting in his office right now wondering if there is somewhere important he should be going," Jovion says darkly but there is strain in his voice.

"Baron Quiso, please," Marisol says, surprising even herself with the beginning of her greatest performance. "I'll make the broadcast," she says with dejection. With a trembling hand she removes her T-shield disguised as an earring and hands the device to Jovion.

"You should take a lesson from the wisdom of this woman's cooperation, Your Majesty," Jovion says mockingly. "You and you," he says to two of the armored Takazhr, "escort Her Majesty and Mrs. Fitzgerald-Buchanan to the holo studio inside and tell the Director we are going to pre-empt all broadcasts for an important announcement. Don't let either of them say anything until I return. I'll be there shortly after I've dealt with this," Jovion says, grabbing the Ilkani psi-sensitive roughly by the arm and leading her away.

When Oriana turns to look into Marisol's eyes she finally sees she has an ally. And even in the midst of a hell of her own creation her burden no longer seems so great. It was something Pfizer had been trying to tell her.

* * *

"Are you certain, Katherine?" Savoy demands a second time of his aide and confidant, pulling on his suit jacket as he moves toward a waiting TAV surrounded by a full squadron of Bloodguard CombatMechas in flyer mode. They are in a landing area outside a Wiktor Corp executive plantation retreat in the Georgia sub-district of the North American Precinct.

"Yes, Savoy. Marisol's T-shield went inactive fewer than five minutes ago," Katherine says.

"Do we have any of our people on site at the Nova Roma PPRC complex?" Savoy asks, raising his voice to be heard over the idling engines and a-gravs of his escort.

Katherine removes her ever-present audvid link to stare directly at Savoy, stopping their progress toward the waiting TAV. "They can't do anything to help her Savoy except get themselves killed," Katherine says with emphasis, realizing that when it came to his vendetta against the Tene Thantos his normal consideration for the lives of others evaporated.

311

Savoy stops his red hair blowing in the preflight wind. "I know what you're thinking, Katherine," he says, once again regretting his decision to have Marisol involved. He so clearly understood why Otto Buchanan loved the woman. Had he met her before Otto had, he would have wanted to share his life with her. In his life Savoy has dallied with many Erosi women, their charms could not be denied. They were strong physically and emotionally, and they were beautiful. But Marisol was also talented, kind, and gentle. It was to her credit that he never made overtures to her because he knew that would ruin the friendship he had achieved with her. Although he had lied to her and used her as Katherine's hard stare reminds him, he stilled cared about her, loved her.

"We have to try," he says. "Watch Commander!" he shouts as he steps on the first rung of the armored Wiktor Corp heliojet.

* * *

"Summon my Bloodguard, General Praetor," Balthasar orders his attending honorguard, who immediately departs, leaving him and Fen alone overlooking the harbor docks at the Aerie. Fern and dwarf evergreen surround them on a black flagstone patio overlooking the Bay of HaneHome, which sparkles like diamonds. Far below them the tiny figures of dock workers move spoiled bails of shinbar for burning. In the aborted evacuation much of the shinbar had been crudely ejected to make room for evacuees. Now no longer suitable for off-world consumption it was being burned. As a public official, Balthasar has avoided all connection with the shinbar. The core worlds had a history of recreational drug intolerance and even on hedonistic Eros the ever-pragmatic Hane consider the drug's consumption a negative for their off-world business interests.

"I was surprised to find you here," Fen says with a sly smile.

"Really, Mother?" Balthasar says sarcastically, inhaling

deeply. Smoke from the shinbar fires below has just begun reaching the patio. Memories assault him of Creed, Millian, and him laughing, singing, playing,...dreaming of the perfect future.

Fen smiles. Of course she knew. She takes Balthasar's hand and inhales deeply herself. Balthasar appears to be accepting the turn of events and she is relieved he is returning to a semblance of himself. The special relationship she has with him as her first-born has been strained but not broken.

"Where is Cedar?" Fen asks as a way of showing concern for Balthasar's needs, even though she knows the answer.

Balthasar sighs and turns to her. "He is one of my civilian military advisors. He's back up there," Balthasar nods toward the spires of the Aerie with regret. "He and I agreed we'd keep our relationship a low-profile while I attempt to lead the United Clans and persuade unallied Clans to join us in open rebellion." The sheer layers of Balthasar's sorrows and loneliness tug at his mother's heart.

"We are not *rebels!*" Fen hisses fiercely, tightening her grip on his hand. "You have the courage to fight for the legitimate ruler of our Imperium. Oriana is the rebel, the traitor."

Suddenly from above them they hear the alarmed voices of their Bloodguards and aides calling for them. Their audvid links begin beeping urgently. *Damn Cameron and Creed. It's another attack!* Balthasar thinks.

Cedar bounds down the flagstone steps surrounded by a brace of Bloodguard. "Balthasar, Fen. News from Earth. You've got to see this."

* * *

"An Impgov message from Earth, Domino," Major Battaglia says, as the iris to the marineguard transports closes behind Pfizer, Heath, and Luxvico. Pfizer can sense the relief in the Bloodguard and naval officers, seeing him on the crowded bridge of the marineguard transport. Heath had been right. Pfizer will forever be more than a person; he is now a symbol.

"And as your spirit drifts, so rise and fall the spirits of your people," Heath had reminded him.

Pfizer pushes back the black tide beneath the carefully constructed facade that has fooled even Luxvico. It is not over. His enemies will give him an opportunity he has only to wait for it. Find it and he will make them pay, destroy them. He checks himself. "On central holo please, Major," Pfizer says smoothly. The holo-bubble winks into existence.

"Greetings from Earth. This is Impgov Liaison Marisol Fitzgerald-Buchanan coming to you live from the Sol System Earth on November 3, 6323 I.C. In minutes Her Most Royal Highness Princess...Excuse me, Her Majesty Queen Regis Oriana will be making an announcement...." Marisol's face changes from that of a calm, self-assured commentator to that of a woman overcome by hysterical terror. "No!" she screams, "It's all been a lie. They've been killing us...killing us...stopping food and medical aid...suppressing—"

Zhooff! Zhooff! They hear the sounds of air being super-heated by a plasma weapon and Marisol Buchanan's head explodes on holo in a burst of red light and skull fragments.

"We are sorry, but this broadcast has been interrupted due to technical difficulties. Please stand by," begins scrolling through the holo.

CHAPTER 43

God grant me the serenity to accept the things I cannot change, courage to choose the things I can, and the wisdom to know the difference.

—Reinhold Niebuhr, 20th Century A.D. Theologian (words inscribed on the Viceregal Seal of House Ahren, Northern Spiral Frontier Ekoz, Titan)

Cato Ahren is dreaming. Bright light beyond description fills Cato's vision. It seems to fill his very soul. He sees his mother...so young...so beautiful. All his weariness dissolves and he feels renewed as if he is reborn. He stretches out his hand toward his mother.

"Cato, no. Stay away from the light." It is Lomin's voice, more demanding than ever.

"Cato, my beloved," Cato hears another voice say. It is her voice.

"Persis?" Cato calls, and his wife stands before him. He can smell her and all he needs do is reach out. "Where is Orion?"

"Here, Father," Orion appears before him. Not frozen and bloated, drowned beneath the icy water of Akel, but strong and whole. Cato wants to touch his son's short copper hair.

"My son...my son, my beloved son." Tears well in Cato's eyes and he can only hope that tears are not falling from his eyes for all to see. *"Cato, no! Come back!"* It's Lomin again, shouting.

"Not now, my love. Go back. Please, my love," Persis says and Cato feels his heart break into pieces beyond number, but he thinks: *I have been too long away from home.*

* * *

Cato gazes at verdant Titan through the tall, paned windows of his wood-paneled conference room, where his family and advisors are gathered. Gold light pours through the windows set into the living tree's wood. Here, near their home's rim, the wood has a tendency to be lighter but this was the only room large enough and with the proper technology to host this emergency session of Cato's Viceregal Council.

His experiences with Lomin and the planes of reality opened to him have drained him on every level. The news offers no relief. Flat screen monitors set into the wall to the right of him show frantic reports as the Tene Thantos encroach further and further into the Ekoz Star System. Most of Cato's advisors, gathered around the table with him now, were thrown into angry resentment when he invited members of the Remnant, the Tempel Government in Exile, to sit in on this session. Basileus had already left the meeting, seething with frustration. Cato's sister Novia appears on the edge of rebellion as she stares at him in angry disbelief. In fact every face at the computer inlaid mahogany conference table looks frustrated, shocked, dismayed or a mixture of all three.

"Cato!" Novia demands, her voice shrill with suppressed rage. "They have destroyed the monitor station on the outskirts of this star system and taken the survivors for conversion into Deathmen! The mining and science colonies on Tarna and Amphitron have been overrun and the Tene are constructing another two—*two!*—Deathships right in our star system."

"Stop pleading with him, Novia," interjects Cato's youngest sibling, Ashton. "Remind him of his duty to defend Imperial citizens and property. He's chosen to hide behind planetary defenses that are already being probed. We have more than twenty Imperial dreadnoughts at our disposal. We have ten times the number of ships the Erosi engaged the Tene at Eros with. I don't need to wait for Cameron Tanenov to tell me how to destroy them!" Ashton is shouting now. Like Novia, Ash has the fair hair of their mother, but like Cato he is dark-skinned and heavily muscled. *How much like Orion he looks, except for his hair, and he wears the camouflage greens of the Foresters.* With sorrow Cato remembers his lost son.

"What difference does it make?" Cato's Minister of Information asks. "The Tempellians have already told us that without the quantum disruption mines that defended Eros we don't have enough firepower to adequately defend this planet if all three Deathships strike at once. We need to be considering a planetary evacuation while we can still save our most important citizens and cultural treasures," says Mobotu Genza, the Minister of Information, a heavy-set black man wearing archaic spectacles. Many of Cato's family and Titan's advisors echo the Genza's sentiments.

"Who decides who is important?" Cato hears himself ask, but it is Lomin's voice. He ignores the stares from the increasingly suspicious Tempellians and his advisors. The thunder of freighters packed with fleeing Titans lifting off from the distant spaceport sends tremors through him as the bright light from a clear day on Titan continues to stream from the windows. The others don't know the nuances of his voice well enough to be aware of the change. Cato stares outside the tall, paned windows. The brilliant spectrum of greens that are the forest cities of Titan stretches before him all the way to the snow-peaked Akhnar mountain range. It is beneath Mount Akhnar that the En'Zefi had stored their inscrutable technological treasures. In his mind's eye, he can see this mountain range charred and smoldering, the forest cities aflame; he hears the shrieks of his people as the Deathmen infest Titan. Cato rests his head in his right hand only for a moment as visions of what could happen if he were to make one misstep fill his mind.

"You cannot divert ships from the perimeter," he hears a woman's voice say. It is the Tempellian Admiral Rowen. "As it is, you are barely stopping the Tene from their firing solutions directed at Titan. Evacuation is no longer an issue we have to stay and fight." As she speaks, multiple holographic projection monitors show Tene Thantos tactical a-mat warheads being intercepted by the brilliant neon flashes of particle beam cannons from Titan's orbital defense network. Rowen wears the red sarong of the Military Ministry over her black Tempellian lifesuit. From his sharing with Lomin, Cato knows her rank is synonymous with an Imperial Vice Admiral. Cato also knows the woman that looks younger than he is over three thousand years old. So many of Cato's questions have been answered but so many more remain.

"Why did you keep secrets from us...me?" There is no anger in Cato's question.

"Cato," the voice of Lomin is filled with scolding derision. *"Do you really think the people of the Imperium would have let only a few keep the secret of immortality along with our other powers?"*

"You told so many lies. Yes you...to me...I trusted you and you deceived me."

"Cato, if you'd known I could read your thoughts, would you have trusted me...loved me? My child, this is not the time for recriminations. You now know my mind and you know I have loved you as my own child. I have made the decision every parent does. What is my child ready to handle? You know the truth now. I'm sorry for the circumstances, Cato, but we will be together for as long as you need or until I pass on."

"Lomin, no!," Cato hears his mind's voice plead.

* * *

"...fight...*fight!* A Tempellian speaks to us of fighting." Novia slaps the mahogany table with her right hand. It is the slap that draws Cato back to the now. "You saw this coming for more than half a century and one of your damned ministries decided it was nothing but observable events in political science? How dare you?!" The angry voice of Novia once again distracts Cato from his mental digression.

"That's enough, Novia," Cato begins. But before he can continue, a brown-skinned Tempellian wearing the rare black robes of the Intelligence Ministry interrupts him in a preternaturally thunderous baritone. "You waste time Vice Princess Novia," It is Luchek, the Chancellor of the Ministry itself.

"*We have just begun.*" *Where did that come from?*

"*How obvious and ironic that Luchek should survive the destruction of Tempel,*" Cato hears Lomin within say. "*He was one of those who suggested we observe the impending crisis, but I swear to you if we'd known the Tene Thantos where rising again perhaps—*"

"*You knew, Lomin?!*"

"*I tried, Cato. I tried to tell them,*" Lomin within says. Cato is brought to the edge of what seems no less than a murderous rage. A supreme effort is required for Cato to contend with emotions that have been held at bay for thousands of years.

"*Don't Lomin. Please don't,*" Cato stops himself in horror. He has spoken aloud. The room erupts in a pandemonium of questions. Cato's mind reels with telepathic questions from the Tempelers but the presence of Lomin within is like a filter and despite the ferocity of the questioning from the motionless glittering-eyed Tempelers, Cato finds he…and Lomin remain in command of their thoughts. In no time the Tempelers and Cato come to their decision.

"Forgive us…Knowledge must have noble purpose," Luchek whispers.

The non-Tempellians are not so easily mollified. Cato feels Lomin within recoil at their venomous accusations. The Bloodguard that serves as Novia's honor guard immediately draws a plasma blaster into this hand, but it is slapped aside by the telescoping Hephaestus of Cato's General Praetor, Piter Mugabe-Hane Hamar.

"No, wait! Listen to him!" the General Praetor demands amidst the activation whine of half the weapons in the room. Most of the Tempellians in the room have managed to thrust their bodies between Cato and the drawn weapons of the Takazhr, Bloodguard, Foresters, and Naval officers.

"You possessed my brother, after all he's done for you," Novia shouts at the Tempellians. *Mind reading. How emotionless, deceitful, and manipulative—human AI. I should have known. He was different the moment he touched down at the port.* "You knew!" Novia hisses aloud at Cato's General Praetor.

"It's me Via. It's still me. It's just that Lomin is here with me." Novia is startled by the intrusion into her thoughts. The voice is a harmonious diatonic blending of Lomin and her brother Cato's voices. *Lomin, is that you?* she thinks.

"Lomin, I thought I'd never see you again," Novia says to the handsome young Tempellian in black lifesuit, wrapped in the gold of the Academy Psychological Ministry, just as Lomin used to wear. But this apparition is far too young, except for the bird-bright eyes. It is Lomin, but as he sees himself.

Tears well up in the Vice Princess' eyes. *"My mentor, my sage, my wise friend, my confidant since I was a baby. You have returned to me,"* Novia says to the vision. In her earliest memories, time-dimmed recollections; Lomin had always been there, patient with every question. He had taught her children and Cato's. Instinctively, she goes to embrace her revered teacher whom she thought she'd forever lost. When she grasps empty air she returns to reality.

"Stop! All of you!" she commands to the Titan advisors hurling their suspicions at the silent Tempelers. She walks over and stands beside her brother, touching his arm to confirm he is no mental ghost. "This revelation is the first good sign in a while. Both Tempellian and Titan have regained a…a hope?" she asks looking at her brother questioningly. Cato uncharacteristically shrugs but reaches to wipe a tear from her face.

"You'll all have to forgive me. I wasn't sure how to tell you," Cato says. He looks at his family advisors and Viceregal administrators. The room is now quiet. The only sounds are those coming from the frantic lifting-off of freighters skyward. "Or you," he says to the Tempellians gathered there. "But whatever his reasons, Lomin knows we still need his help, and I for one am pleased to have it."

"Father!" says Basileus as he bursts through the double doors into the conference room. "There's news from Earth that you—that all of you—have to see right now."

* * *

The command cockpit of the marineguard transport is silent. The static of Marisol Buchanan's aborted transmission from Earth fills most of the screens and holos. *That planet is cursed*, Pfizer thinks. "Major Battaglia, verify what we just saw. See if you can get something from GNN or EWN," Pfizer says, the first to speak. He turns to Luxvico, who still stares at the main holo in disbelief.

"I thought it would help," Pfizer hears Luxvico say to himself. The Tempeler bows his head and adjusts the visor of the baseball-like cap over his eyes.

What would help? Why is he crying? He didn't even know Marisol. I did. Why aren't I...? Don't I feel anything? Pfizer wonders.

"Domino, they are showing the same transmission on the other galactic networks. According to reports, Impgov has not issued a statement," reports the Bloodguard Major Praetor.

Of course that bitch hasn't made a statement yet, Pfizer seethes. *I'll channel this rage as Heath advised. There would be no more talking, no more listening, no negotiation.*

"Poor Otto," Heath mutters behind Pfizer. "Should I go and get Captain Praetor Buchanan, Domino?" Heath asks of Pfizer.

Pfizer considers this for a split second. It would certainly be the easiest way out. But he was no longer remotely interested in any simple conclusions. "How much longer until our communication with the *Callahan*, Major Battaglia?" Pfizer inquires calmly despite the agitation of those around him.

"Less than twenty minutes, Domino."

Pfizer purses his lips before speaking. "Very well. Maintain position here and signal me only if we receive a transmission or the *Callahan* has received the drone and adjusted its speed to meet us here. I'll be with Captain Praetor Buchanan," Pfizer orders smoothly.

"Counselor Luxvico, I'd like you to come with Heath and

me," Pfizer says quietly to the silent Tempeler. Though Lux's face maintains his normal stoic and unreadable expression there is an unmistakable feeling of dread emanating from him. *He can't possibly know what I intend,* Pfizer reassures himself. Having lived among the Tempelers for most of his life Pfizer is quite capable of at least being aware if his mind is being read and in most cases shielding his thoughts, an ability he certainly owes to his grandmother's genes. *But what is absorbing Luxvico so, if he isn't reading my mind? Is it something between him and Otto?* Although Pfizer sympathizes with what he senses to be Luxvico's desire to remain in the command cockpit, Pfizer needs to observe Otto and Lux together. This is the only way he can tell if there is a problem between them that will interfere with his plans. Luxvico merely nods and follows Pfizer and Heath through the iris.

When the iris to the airlock begins to spiral Otto's eyes snap open and cat-like he is on his feet before the iris is completely open. A blink of his left eye tells him he's only been lying down for a little more than a quarter hour. But he feels better, not so much rested but balanced. Lux's telepathic gesture has soothed him. He smiles warmly at the Tempeler and his smile broadens when he sees Pfizer clean-shaven and dressed in the uniform of the Domino of the Corps Bloodguard. *Things are finally turning around,* he thinks. Then he sees the solemn look on Heath's face and the sad resignation in Pfizer's electric gray eyes. Otto turns toward Luxvico. "Marisol?" he whispers.

"I am sorry, Otto...," Luxvico begins. Otto's bones seem to turn to gelatin and he melts to the deck beneath him. A boiling heat fills his chest and head. Otto's vision swims and the room bursts to the pounding of his heart in his ears. The dream Luxvico had pulled from Otto's memories had seemed so intense, so real, as if Marisol had been here seconds before.

"What happened?" is all Otto manages to say. His sandpaper voice is choked as he looks at Luxvico with pleading eyes. The sounds of Marisol's music, her holovids, play through his mind as a tumult of emotions assaults him.

"Marisol!" he cries, and the ache in heart becomes unbearable. With blurred vision he moves toward the airlock.

"Otto! No!" Luxvico shouts. "You will kill Pfizer, too." Luxvico's plea is both verbal and telepathic…The second he reminds Otto of Pfizer's safety, he halts Otto's impulsive suicidal thoughts.

Otto hesitates and Heath, quicker than he, is able to get between him and the outer door. Heath's Hephaestus springs to staff mode in a swift grating metallic *shink*.

"Otto, Agust needs you. I need you. This is not what Mari would want," Pfizer says into the quiet.

Luxvico smoothly walks around Pfizer and with surprising gentleness says, "Come to sick bay, Otto." The Tempellian steers Otto toward the inner iris with what Pfizer can only call uncharacteristic compassion.

"She was assassinated on holo trying to warn the rest of the Imperium about the truth of what is happening on Earth," Luxvico explains, sparing Pfizer the need to do so. Pfizer now merely nods in affirmation of the grim news.

Otto loses his composure briefly as the pain of Marisol's death strikes him again. He staggers against Luxvico to check his emotions.

All this suffering, Pfizer thinks. *What can men do against such capricious, relentless evil? No one I know has been left untouched by the misery the Tene Thantos have wrought. By the Only God they're going to pay.*

Otto is asking to see the recording of Marisol's murder. "Go to sick bay with Luxvico," Pfizer says sternly and before Otto can protest adds, "Consider this an order from your Domino." Then, more gently, "Heath will go to the command cockpit and bring back a CDC if you truly wish to see it. But I'm telling you now, Otto, her actions were no less than heroic and she will be avenged."

"Vengeance…revenge is for the immature or insane," Luxvico observes instinctively, pedantically.

* * *

Savoy is walking toward the PPRC Rome main holo studio listening to the broadcast in progress when Marisol's calm voice becomes a desperate shriek confessing the atrocities being committed on Earth. He breaks into a sprint through the corridors, hears the sounds of super-heated air from a plasma weapon, the shouts and screams of the holo studio's crew. He sees a ghostly pale Oriana escorted through the double doors of the holo studio surrounded by Takazhr in battle armor and accompanied by Jovion Quiso, his face an emotionless mask behind her. *Where are the Regis' Bloodguards?!* Savoy wonders in alarm.

"Where are the Bloodguards?!" Jovion Quiso demands for the benefit of the gathering crowd of PPRC and other news network personnel equipped with flickering holo recorders and audvid links.

Oriana gazes desperately at Savoy, swaying on her feet. There is obvious relief on her face when she sees Savoy's Bloodguard. Then she looks at the growing mass of reporters from which her Takazhr shield her. No, they are Jovion's Takazhr. She would never get another chance. She bolts away from Jovion toward Savoy and his retinue.

"Oriana, please don't—" Jovion begins ominously.

"Mr. Wiktor, would you have your Bloodguard communications people establish a direct link with my General Praetor?"

"Regis, please, the facilities here are more than adequate," Jovion purrs, advancing toward her.

"No, Baron Quiso. The facilities here are compromised at best. Mr. Wiktor, I hate to impose upon you again, but after we contact my Bloodguard I'm going to need immediate transportation," Oriana says regally to Savoy, whose gaze shifts between Oriana and Jovion with obvious scrutiny.

"Of course, Your Majesty," he replies. "But that may not be necessary. I've brought my own Bloodguards." Savoy gestures to the six heavily armed and armored Bloodguards, all Praetorian rank with a Colonel Praetor in working uniform.

The Colonel Praetor Oriana recognizes as one of the survivors who had protected the now decimated Aristo families that had been related to her on her mother's side. Colonel Praetor Luke Byrons. Savoy would have to have paid dearly to employ such a prized Bloodguard officer.

This is something she had not considered. If she suspends the Bloodguard Charter, eventually the revenues garnered from the Aristos they protect will dry up. This is further erosion of her already fragile economic position. It is only her fear of a murderous firefight here that keeps her from ordering Jovion's arrest.

"Regis, I must speak with you," Jovion demands outright, trying to reach her past Savoy's restraining Bloodguards.

"Oh, we're going to talk, your Grace," Oriana replies coldly. ...*In an interrogation chamber with a Bloodguard Inquisitor-Surgeon taking your treacherous mind apart!* Oriana thinks, the bitter taste of raw rage filling her mouth. There is actually an expression of fear on Jovion's face, not for himself but for his cursed precious plans to deploy the BlackWare. But instantly, Jovion's features recompose to serene angelic handsomeness. For a moment Oriana wavers, but she has seen the real Jovion, or rather the one she suspected but never had any proof of. He bows his head seemingly humbled before her. The whirring, humming, and ghostly light of audvid recording devices distracts Oriana from her thoughts of terrible vengeance.

They killed my mother and father, killed that innocent woman just now, and they will try to kill me, Oriana thinks, ignoring the flurry of questions being directed at her.

Savoy's feet crunch over shattered glass as he makes his way into the holo studio and stands over Marisol's shrouded body. A pool of blood coagulates around the head of her covered corpse. Savoy stifles an involuntary gag reflex and turns to face Jovion Quiso who now watches him with owl-like inquisition.

Savoy drops his head and recites the words of the Tempellian Last Rite: "May we meet on the other side where there shall be no pain." He stands and faces Jovion, who has begun to direct the crowd of PPRC officers. A blind rage begins to possess Savoy as he stands there, his hand balling tightly into a fist. He knows there will be blood. He can envision himself attacking Jovion and in that moment he knows that Jovion is using his supposedly secret telepathy to amplify his perfectly normal degree of anger. ... *To make it look like I'm behind this?* Savoy suddenly makes a conscious decision to let the fury possess him. *Fine, you Anonjidan murderer, if I can kill you now, so be it.'*

"Savoy!" Katherine shouts. Savoy knocks aside her gently restraining hand, but the mere touch of her flesh startles him enough to shatter Jovion's influence. He directs a withering look of hatred at Jovion, who appears momentarily shocked. *Probably because he's not used to having his telepathic snare fail.* Savoy turns to Oriana, who is now watching him, a look of consternation on her face; it's obvious to Savoy that life and death visions must be running through her mind.

"We should leave immediately, Your Majesty," Savoy tells her emphatically.

"I don't think that's a good idea," says Jovion.

For the first time she can remember Oriana hears desperation in his voice, and she is pleased. Perhaps she has an ally in Savoy; maybe she can make things right.

"Your ideas are questionable at best, Baron Quiso," Oriana says witheringly. Immediately, the gathering press barrages her. She inhales deeply. *Everything is spiraling out of control. I have to get away from here so I can think. I have to compose a statement.* But all Oriana can do is stare at Jovion, desperately trying to conceal the feelings of hate and betrayal that seethe in her.

Finally, as the reporters from GNN, EWN, HaneNet, and even the PPRC continue to shout their questions at her, Oriana says in exasperation, "Please all of you, I am as stunned by this tragedy as you are. As soon as the Bloodguard have a chance to do a forensic analysis I will share with you what I know."

"What about the reports that you called this press conference to announce the suspension of the Bloodguard

Charter?" shouts a woman from HaneNet managing to raise her voice above the others. The accusations and hostility in her voice are evident for all to hear and Oriana knows instinctively that Balthasar and the Hane have begun their assault to replace her. *I am lost…Finished…I can only beg Pfizer to spare my life.*

"Your Majesty," the Bloodguard Colonel Praetor intrudes on her thoughts. "I have a deep-range transmission from interim Commerce Minister Qamar."

The wind is blowing. Oriana thinks, remembering a Hane saying. *What has gone wrong now? Has Jovion's mad dog gone on to destroy more worlds?* she wonders. Oriana doesn't even want to touch the omnipalm that the Bloodguard Colonel Praetor holds out to her.

Tired of being the pawn of others Oriana decides to go on the offensive.

"Ladies and gentlemen," she says sharply. "I am trying to establish a transition government in this time of crisis. I have appointed Nasir Qamar of AAG to act as interim Commerce Minister."

"The known Aeon supremacist?" asks the damnable woman from HaneNet. Oriana casts a gaze of patronage upon the woman, something the reporter had not expected.

"Now is not the time for further dissention. Wouldn't you agree? The press release you are about to receive will be relayed to your various networks. It concerns the formation of an interim Executive Council. I assure you I am as disturbed as you are with Marisol Buchanan's comments and her brutal murder. However, at this time, with so little information, we cannot make any further comment. Rest assured, we will keep you informed."

CHAPTER 44

"We continue to have confirmed GNN reports of
planet-wide devastation on Earth in the Sol
System. The planet's a-mat power grid was
apparently sabotaged prior to yesterday's Tene
Thantos attack. PPRC officials stated that the
immediate planetary death toll from the
destruction of the a-mat grid has been estimated at
three billion. That number has grown, however,
and will continue to grow as more bodies are
recovered, EEC officials report. The destruction in
near orbit habitats has been equally catastrophic,
with the death toll of the High Port drift city alone
totaling four million."

—EWN news report 21-10-6323 I.C.

Luxvico floats in the zero gravity of the marineguard
transport's astrogation blister, an anachronism, but included on
all naval and marineguard star craft. Pinnacle Command
considered them useful training tools. Luxvico wants to verify
the navcomp readings. *I don't want to depend on computers right now.
And the people I'm stranded with? How much can I depend on them?*

A small modification of the astrogation system's
transceivers and sensors allow him to pick fragments of news
being relayed over the galactic hyperlinks. Mostly just voices,
there is insufficient equipment in the astrogation blister to
receive and display holo images. The very network that should
have been their target is still intact. Only the center is
destroyed and they are going after the other possible sites—

Tempel, Eros, and now Titan.

Luxvico returns to the cobbled hyperlink audio as there had been news of heavy fighting in the Ekoz Star System. *But has it reached Titan yet?* Luxvico feels the urge to reach out telepathically for other Tempelers, even another Tempellian. Now that his people are endangered, no on the edge of extinction, he finds oddly that his greatest consideration is for the well-being of a few humans. The growing feeling of exhilaration Luxvico began experiencing when...when he removed the lifesuit, continues to grow. Whether this is an unwelcome component of his mental link with Otto crosses Luxvico's mind. He decides to report back to the command cockpit. He deactivates the murmuring audio link and restores the settings and components of the astro-blister back to its original configuration. Strange that he feels he is still wearing the lifesuit here in the zero gravity of the blister. Only as he leaves, floating toward the iris, does he realize that he had not pushed himself out, simply willed it.

Luxvico finds himself hovering above the corridor but below the astro-blister's iris. The ship's gravity should have sent him slamming to the deck. *What is happening to me?* The thought is unguarded as if he were still wearing the lifesuit and attached to the Academy Ministry Nexus. Luxvico gently lands on the deck. The very sounds, sights, and smells, the very feel of the transport is riotously amplified. He is grateful no one witnesses his discomfort as he brings his senses under control. The banging of footsteps, the trumpeting sounds of voices, the thunder of the transport's a-mat core brings him to his knees and he covers his ears with his hands. Suddenly cacophony subsides and he opens his eyes, only to be sent reeling back to the deck in pain. The bulkheads, conduits, and hull of the transport show in glaring transparent detail, the crew members' insides rendered visible through clothing, tissue, and bone. He is about to scream in pain and frustration when he is aware of Otto's voice. "Luxvico? It's Otto. I'm here to help."

* * *

Curled in his bunk in the transport, Otto suddenly awakens from a nightmare of Marisol and people and places he somehow knows well even though he never laid eyes on them before. *Something is wrong with Luxvico. Something.* Otto lurches from the bunk with a burden of years he cannot possibly possess. Bloodguard training forces Otto to move and the weariness that could only have taken centuries to gain, that seems to belong to another body, eventually passes. A feeling of desperation pervades his senses. Otto knows it is better that he moves quickly. There is an unexpected clarity to his thoughts. *Thinking, moving.* Otto recalls the mantra for cybernetic battle armor training and he feels the *other's* thoughts lifted from his consciousness—the flashes of memories and blurred visions of battle armor, alien and familiar, frightening weapons worse even than Tene Thantos machinations. Otto exits the lift to the transports top deck, a dark metallic corridor with a ladder in the center leading to the astro-blister. Lux is in front of the ladder in the lotus position and floating. *Floating?* Otto tells Lux that he's there to help.

"I am right here, Otto. There's no need to shout." Luxvico says, opening his eyes.

"I wasn't shouting Lux," Otto finds himself saying with equal calm. The Tempeler seems composed. "I had the definite impression you were in distress."

"I was Captain Prae...Otto." Lux stands. "Something is happening to me. Something incredible. There is no need for us to use speech, Otto. Maybe you've begun to suspect this?"

Otto nods, the images, sights and sound that had been thrust upon his mind have begun to coalesce into memories. *How old are you?* Otto thinks clearly, knowing that Lux is reading his thoughts.

"You already know. The answer is in the lifesuits, Otto. Consider the Erosi colony that originally settled Tempel. Aeon every last one, genetically, eugenically adapted for survival. Then the Wasting and the lifesuits, bio-nanotech to further enhance our longevity, our physical and psionic abilities. Four thousand years of bio-technic-enhanced evolution. A

culture of secrets upon secrets. You didn't realize the long-term implications."

Otto feels a wave of remorse, and he knows Luxvico has considered the consequences. "I'm sorry. But we have a weapon now," Otto says, knowing Lux's decision has already been made and that the surviving Tempelers know what Lux knows.

"It has already begun, Otto."

CHAPTER 45

If only I could close my eyes and make the things
I've done become undone.
　　　　—Oriana Ambros, *The Book of Sorrows*

The reports coming in from Titan seem unreal to Nasir
Qamar. Deathmen are dropping dead at their posts. A-mat
magnetic locks are collapsing, the loss of an entire Deathship
has been reported. Then the most disturbing and unbelievable
report: Tempellians soaring through space in hoards literally
tearing ships apart, the crews and Deathmen microwaved.
Nasir watches holo images taken just hours before showing
Tempellian civilians without suits tearing the gantries apart on
the Deathship construction facility.

The entire vengeful host had seemed dedicated to the
destruction of everything Tene Thantos. "Terror to the
terrorist," they had screamed, sending telekinetic pulses
bursting blood vessels in the enemy, and causing hard
nanotech fibers to pierce every soft tissue of their skulls. The
Tempellians had telekinetically caused weapon misfires and
equipment failures. They had seemed impossible to stop. In
desperation a low-yield gamma weapon had been detonated
using the Deathship spacedock's core. The Tempellians died as
all things should, but the lethal gamma waves had vaporized
the spacedock and killed every living thing on the exposed side
of Amphitron.

Amphitron was the first planet in this entire operation that
the Tene Thantos had actually managed to occupy with the
exception of Earth. The Deathmen's plans to harvest the

population on Earth had been suspended while Jovion and Oriana continued their transparent manipulations to usurp whatever power remained in the Impgov. While Jovion and Oriana debated and schemed, those daring enough to invest and trade had thrown their wealth in with the Eros Alliance. After repulsing the Deathship attack on Eros, Hane Technologies stocks had skyrocketed. Tupolev, AutoDyn, and all their known subsidiaries had been purchased in a crushing display of Hane solidarity. Generations of wealth, property, and mineral rights were spent, and still they acquired blocks of CIMB shares.

Somewhere Cameron Tanenov is protecting Pfizer Ambros, Nasir thinks. *Perhaps all our forces should fall back and regroup here at Earth, hold the system, its population, and its multicultural treasures hostage. Either way the nest of short-lived dirt genes would be ravaged, maybe wiped out.* Nasir moves away from his console, turning to a half circle of windows. A cold, hammering mixture of ashen sleet continues to fall over the smoldering pit that is the ruins of New Sydney, Australia Precinct. Hovering high above the devastation in an AAG hyper-zeppelin, Nasir sends a signal using his Nemesis link. He dispatches Cross and Crescent rescue transports, encrypting a message to Jovion requesting removal of their forces from the Ekoz Star System. Three newer and larger Hane Pax hyper-zeppelin hover above the radioactive cauldron that had been the restored Sydney Opera House. The search lights of the zeppelins and landing craft converted for rescue appear like so many gleaming fireflies obscured by the smoke and destruction of the city beneath them. *More Hane altruism!*

Nasir reaches into the holo fields of the desk before him. The hyper-zeppelin's captain blinks into a holo field above the desk. "M'lord?"

"Begin orbital ascent procedures," Nasir commands.

"Excuse me, m'lord, bu—" begins the visibly startled captain.

"You have your orders, Captain. Follow them or I will find someone who can," Nasir says softly. The words have the desired effect. His ability to find someone else is a frightening AAG tale. *Hane altruism.* He would detonate the blasted city's a-mat power core. Power across eastern Australia and its sub-ocean colonies would go out. Those in the undersea colonies who had survived the initial attack and were now taking on refugees would find themselves without air and power and hundreds of thousands more would die. He would suggest that off-planet aid cease and no more off-planet volunteers risk their lives until the situation on Earth could be stabilized. *The Hane and their allies must be driven off planet while we have time to consolidate our position here.*

CHAPTER 46

And when they came for me, there was no one left
to speak for me. For I had spoken for no one, and
I was all that remained.

—Martin Niemoeller, Old Earth theologian,
20th Century A.D.

The blast on the monitors and holo fields causes them all to
turn away or shield their eyes. Immediately, shouted expletives
of anger and grief fill the room. Balthasar blinks, clearing his
vision and stunned. *Twelve hundred more Hane and more allied people
dead.*

"I want reports on deep-range extragalactic colonization
efforts," Balthasar commands. "Concentration on planets
where we can grow the kelp and feanospawn. Tell PPRC,
GNN, HaneNet, all of them left on Eros that I will be making
an Imperium-wide press release at sunset Avon local time."
Hane Pax and Clan Liaisons rush to fulfill his orders. Balthasar
turns towards his office windows taking in a spectacular view
of the voluminous clouds and the vast turquoise Vedan Ocean.
He motions to Cedar and the Naval Commodore Fey-Hane.

"Cedar, we are going to go to DracoHold protocols. We
need volunteers. Start coordinating anyone with military
experience. Speak for me here. I need some air," Balthasar
says, handing Cedar his audvid link and walking outside.

Spica shines behind luminescent blue clouds over waters
gleaming sea green and gold with reflected light. This is sunset
on Eros, the Clan Dome shines beneath the keening of circling

335

dartwing gulls. Geysers, waterfalls, and ancient statues dazzle tourists passing beneath, reflecting tiny prisms of light. *I am so grateful,* Balthasar thinks.

His father Aaron's words. "We have visited more than a thousand worlds; none has been or will be as beautiful as Eros."

Balthasar takes his attention from the vista of HaneHome. His mother, Fen, stands silently before him comforting a weeping Romula. Moments before, during an emergency meeting that Balthasar had called with Hane Pax officials, they were watching rescue efforts from New Sydney on Earth when their monitors and holo fields were filled with light brighter than the sun. The explosion they witnessed vaporized the Hane hyper-zeppelins and their converted landing craft. Those watching had to turn their heads away or shield their eyes. The room dissolved into expletives of rage and moans and gasps of grief. His cousin Romula, still stricken from the loss of her brother, rushed out onto the terraced portico outside his offices. Balthasar asked his mother, "Who better than Romula to deal with this?" Silently he thought, *Who else to coordinate with the Hane Pax officers for incoming intelligence of the deaths of more of our family? Twelve hundred more Hane and thousands of other Erosi obliterated. I am going to have to order a general evacuation of all the Erosi Alliance. How long until this war comes back to Eros?*

Fen turns her head skyward and tells her son. "Something is happening out there."

CHAPTER 47

This is the comfort of friends, that though they
may be said to die, yet their friendship and society
are, in the best sense, ever present, because
immortal.

—William Penn (Old Earth), *Some Fruits of Solitude*

Pfizer is not the friend I've known. Otto shakes his head, trying to make some sense of his observations, the change. *I've tried to blame it on the telepathic bond with Lux.* If only he could keep focus and remain concentrated on the peace that the sharing with Lux had begun. But it is so much to take in—the burden of time from so many shared years, the lessons learned over and over again, and the acceptance that life changes like the flowing of a river, never to be mastered but merely traveled. Otto's consciousness barely avoids drowning in the flow of Lux's memories. Skidding through the gas plumes of Jupiter or Inver—these experiences from Otto's own life ease the torrent of time from the Tempeler's memories. The questions that Otto spent a life-time confused by melt away, solved by hundreds of years. And then time moving in different realities and the ghosts of losses like world-ending comets drop him to depths of sorrow he could never have imagined. *I'm here still and if I could live this long, imagine what I could do? I understand the secrecy now. What life could those with immortality and actual super powers expect to have in a universe full of those without those gifts? My prejudices seem immature and ignorant.* Otto finds his anxiety easing, *The Universe would answer his questions, though not in the way he would ever expect. There would always be more to learn.*

In the days since they were stranded, the Tempeler has continued to wear and recycle the naval utilities Otto had given him. In order to keep the crew at ease, Luxvico continues to wear the cap, its bill shading but not hiding, the glittering amethyst eyes. Luxvico's growing ash blond eyebrows remind Otto of how Pfizer's hair had regrown when Pfizer had taken off his own lifesuit.

"Lux, what has this done to Pfizer?" Otto asks as the two walk towards the bridge of the marineguard transport. "And I know your people…our people are coming. What are we going to do? The Remnant intends to remake the universe." Otto is surprised at how calm he speaks despite the storm of words and thoughts he does not comprehend but must trust his Bloodguard heart.

"I do not know. I am very concerned, however, about the Crown Scion," Luxvico says, while thinking: *How could he already know about the Remnant?* Luxvico is surprised and pleased that Otto seems to be dealing with the physics of telepathy, apparently discarding his anti-psi feelings. "Otto," Luxvico says aloud, "I do not want to share our location with other…telepaths or Tempellians because my people know what I know about what we can become." Luxvico shakes his head. The disappointment Otto senses is not directed at him or the situation but at Luxvico himself.

Why? Otto wonders sadly.

Luxvico stops in midstride. A shock seems to pass through him. *Millions of us have taken to the sky.* He experiences a moment of profound joy as the human dream to fly floods his heart. And then those who are coming open hyperspace windows and all Luxvico can sense is the burning fury in their hearts and the certainty that they intend to change the Universe. "Pretend there is a wall in your head, Otto, , a barrier, the best you can conceive of!" Luxvico says, pointing with his index finger into his palm as if he is explaining something to Otto. *The Remnant is coming! My people. How will the rest of the Universe be able to stop us? Feelings of joy and dread almost sexual bring him close to shuddering. Such power, such POWER! My people are coming!*

"Do not use our telepathic bond unless absolutely necessary. Speak aloud. I know it may be hard to comprehend but in many ways my people may be more dangerous than the Tene Thantos," Luxvico warns. "Here we are at the bridge; guard your thoughts."

Otto and Luxvico enter the marineguard transport's bridge to find a scene of turmoil, with officers shouting for confirmation, Pfizer sitting stone-faced but calm behind the command console, and Heath at attention behind him.

"What has happened?" Luxvico asks quietly, thinking, *What part will I play in this?*

Although Otto is sure the question was meant for him, it is Pfizer who answers, not taking his eyes from the holo monitors in front of him.

"Relief efforts on Earth are being hampered," Pfizer says dispassionately. He turns to face the two of them. "The Australian Precinct a-mat power core has detonated. Initial death toll estimates are over twenty million, including the off-world rescuers. Counselor, estimate time to our rendezvous with the *Callahan*."

"Approximately forty minutes and—. Excuse me—" Luxvico stops in midsentence and turns toward the main viewer. "There are multiple hyperspatial contacts approaching."

"How could you know this?!" Heath blurts.

"Major, maximum long-range scans," Otto orders. *Have the Tene Thantos found us?* Otto thinks.

I do not think so, answers Luxvico, the faintest of smiles turning up the corners of his mouth.

"There are more than two hundred contacts detected. Long-range scans are picking up the lead ship FOF signal. Your Majesty, it is the *Bismarck*!"

There are bright flashes of white light as the very fabric of real space is torn open and Imperial Navy starships begin exiting hyperspace. Wedge-shaped dreadnoughts, shark-shaped battle cruisers, the elongated manta forms of destroyers, the blunt triangles of assault carriers, and hammer headed security transports. From over the marineguard transport's speakers comes the voice of Grand Admiral Cameron Tanenov: "MGT-43 *Bismarck*, this is INS *Bismarck*. Welcome home."

The marineguard transport's bridge erupts into cheers and applause. Otto turns to Pfizer, a triumphant grin on his face. Pfizer, seated at the command console, manages the barest of smiles. His eyes are the cold gray of a tombstone. "Otto, when were you going to tell me about the Tempellians?' Pfizer asks with the same menacing whisper he had used to tell Rachel Tsimpo he was abandoning her.

CHAPTER 48

So as it is in War, the same can be said in Politics:
The first mobilization begins with the young. By
reaching out to those of pre-electorate age before
they have any real political identity, it is possible to
convert them against their own best interests. It is
for these reasons that I want to stress that it is
absolutely essential we keep control of information
and discredit any point that does not agree with
ours as untrue, insane, or even traitorous.

—Oriana Ambros, as quoted in *The Hane
Commentaries* by Aaron Charlemagna Invid-Hane

Oriana views an old holograph of herself with sad distaste. In
the holo she is stressing how necessary it is to keep control of
information at all costs. *Was it comments like these that had led
Nasir and Jovion to think that I cared nothing for the laws of the
Imperium or my honor?* Oriana wonders.

Gazing out of the bridge's briefing room she sees the rough
gray toxic Pacific Ocean beneath her destroyer. The dead and
dying sea creatures and sub-oceanic colony refuse float
ominously. Something from a prophecy Pfizer had tried to
share with her gnaws at her consciousness; if only she could
recall. The fact that she cannot troubles her most of all.

*I was genengineered to have eidetic memory and enhanced recall, so why
can't I remember? I remember the first taste of solid food to pass my
lips... sweet potato every detail like it was yesterday, Erosi sweet potato.
And I can't remember what my brother said less than two weeks ago? Is
Jovion influencing me telepathically? Have I been drugged? Or is this some*

emotional and psychological wall I've constructed? Oriana wonders.

She dares not even use a surgo-op for fear the information may prove detrimental to her ambitions. The lack of advisors she can trust and the increasingly limited options she is being confronted with are keeping her from sleeping or eating. *They want me to be cut off, to be dependent only on them.*

Here she is on a naval destroyer half a planet from Assur-Banipal, the one person who had actually nurtured her and advised her spiritually for almost a quarter of a century after she'd been exiled to Pandarata. She is still being kept continually isolated while she travels from holocaust to holocaust sight. Every asset in her control—the Bloodguard, access to CIMB, even her innate abilities—was being neutralized. Jovion had demonstrated he would kill any that might be an ally. When Jovion had suggested Marisol as an advisor, was he already preparing to kill her and make Oriana the enemy of every one of Pfizer's advisors?, *I couldn't step foot onto Eros without being immediately attacked, murdered.*

How could I have been so blind? Oriana thinks for the umpteenth time. *Why did I once love Jovion? ... No, now is not the time to go down that path,'* she decides.

Oriana still has some surprises for her enemies. Twelve WiktorCorp a-grav carriers move through the cloud layer beneath her, dispersing gold plumes of bioengineered algae that will metabolize the various atmospheric toxins, leaving oxygen as waste. Her destroyer begins firing torpedoes loaded with Terrax Corporation nanotech elemental converters, NECs. Powered by the lethal radiation, the microscopic machines will manufacture even more nanotechs until they run out of sufficient radiation and then they will decompose into a mist of sodium, nitrogen, and simple carbons. Even though the swath of blue sky created is quickly occluded, the effect is obvious for all to see. *I have done something worthwhile. And I have demonstrated to others that something can be done. Wiktor and I can tell them there are more on the way.*

The old holograph of Oriana continues to repeat itself as she walks away from the window. "Alabama," Oriana says, softly calling the destroyer's AI, "Please ask Mr. Wiktor to join me in the bridge briefing room when it is convenient for him." Oriana realizes she should turn off the holo recording of her; there is no sense in antagonizing Savoy. She waves her hand through the holo, deactivating it and glances at her reflection. She looks like a younger version of her Grandmother, Fen. She wears a black suit similar to the one she'd seen her mother wearing when Anastacia had greeted Pfizer at the cosmodome such a short time ago.

The bridge briefing room iris chime sounds, "Enter" Oriana says. An armored marineguard enters and salutes. Oriana merely nods in response, resisting her Naval training to return the salute.

Oriana allows her eyes to glance down at the blue swath of atmosphere that the union of Terrax and Wiktor technologies accomplishes. The blue of the salvaged sky causes her to recall the sky above HaneHome. The regret that shades her face will be sufficient to convince the uninitiated of her sincerity.

"Regis, Mr. Savoy Wiktor and Ms. Katherine Nielson of WiktorCorp are here to see you," the marineguard announces. He quickly adds, "Is there something the Regis requires?" He is concerned that the last known member of the Imperial house appears so distressed.

"Thank you, no, Sam," Oriana says, continuing to observe the effect her chosen demeanor is having on those around her. *This is not what I wanted,* Oriana laments. "Please send them in, and close the iris on your way out." She manages the briefest of smiles and turns quickly away. *This will not be easy,* Oriana considers. *The costs keep adding and adding up.*

"Regis, excuse us. You appear to have other concerns. But I was told you wanted to see me." Savoy's Serdian-taught inflections and word choice convey concern, disdain, and anger all at once.

"Sit, please," Oriana says, extending her hand graciously, dispensing with protocol. "I am sorry to disturb you in what must be a difficult time for both of you," Oriana adds. Savoy's facial expression softens. The woman, Katherine, turns her attention to Savoy, her ubiquitous neutral gaze unchanged.

Unreadable is all that comes to Savoy's mind. The desire to turn to Katherine for answers is almost irresistible; but keeping his attention on the Regis is far more important. *This is Pfizer's sister. Can I trust her?'*

"Mr. Wiktor, I want to speak with you about acting as Impgov Liaison—" Oriana begins saying.

"Pardon me, Regis, but that didn't work very well for Marisol Buchanan," Savoy interrupts. "Besides, my obligations to WiktorCorp would make it difficult to say the least."

I thought you'd say that, and that will make ignoring my second request all the more difficult, Oriana thinks. "I understand, but please consider my position.... However, that is not exactly why I asked you to join me," she says. "I am not sure how to begin. Shall we start with the most obvious? My Communications Minister, Sir Nasir Qamar, was overseeing the New Sydney evacuation and relief with the Hane Pax—"

Genuine grief pushes the limits of her emotional control and she cannot stop a single tear that falls from the corner of her right eye. "As I've said, a difficult day for all of us. Cross and Crescent and Qamar Auto Technic relief vessels began lifting for high orbit more than three minutes before the city's a-mat sphere's detonation—"

"Regis," Savoy interrupts. "Excuse me, but I am aware of this. WiktorCorp lost people and had substantial interests in the region." Savoy regrets his anger. *I should have let her keep talking.* Savoy thinks.

He is so angry that he's having trouble controlling himself. There was a time when I could have used this, but no good will come of more anger now, Oriana observes.

"I need to be reviewing the rescue efforts in three star systems that include dozens of planets and colonies. The twenty eight billion survivors in those star systems—out of a population that once numbered seventy billion—are my people. The Imperium is fracturing."

"The late Empress-Executrix, your mother, wanted the Imperium to fracture," Katherine says dispassionately.

Oriana swears the woman's gestures seem so much like the Erosi Sisters of Peace so very reminiscent of Fen, her mother. *How dare she?* She feels the anger she hoped to use against them well up and threaten to burst from her like bile.

"Perhaps, Regis, if I dare suggest—these strategies were put in motion by various factions years ago; there is nothing you can do to stop them," says Katherine.

She sounds like Pfizer's Tempellian, Luxvico, Oriana thinks. Things she'd said to Pfizer after the landing at O'Meara float just beneath the ice that blocks off some of her memories, making them untouchable.

"This was going to happen either by smooth transition or violent spasm. Do you want to do what is best for your people, as Pfizer would have?" Savoy asks gently.

Katherine, however, is relentless. "Working with us to begin consolidated relief efforts has probably been the best move you could make to ensure your survival and political freedom," Katherine observes frankly, without malice.

"What can you offer me, considering my mistakes?" Oriana asks Savoy. She looks at a swath of blue, regenerated sky. The gold of WiktorCorp algae makes her think of Spica reflecting gold off the blue green oceans of Eros. *Now I sound like Balthasar. Balthasar, who would refuse to speak to me now.* The thought brings pain. Centuries of emoto-control and genetic and eugenic breeding cannot help Oriana contain her response. She gasps, quickly lowering her head to try to hide the emotions that Savoy and Katherine have clearly witnessed.

"We...No, I have allowed Nasir Qamar to betray the best interests of the Imperium. I believe...I know he is a traitor." *There, I've said it and I have probably begun a civil war. For I have broken the Eleventh Commandment.*

CHAPTER 49

Pray for us, for we are sure that we have a clear
conscience, desiring to act honorably in all things.

—Hebrews 13:18 Judeo Orange Codex

The crooning voice and soft instrumentals of Roland
Maldine play as Creed gathers sugar cubes for Erosi
absinthe and watches Coventry coming into view from
Cameron's ready room off the *Bismarck's* CIC. Cameron's
voice singing to the music from another room causes him to
smile as he places one of the sugar cubes in a spoon. Creed
glances down at the cube and in a flash he sees the carbon
and hydrogen molecules come into view. They dance as he
summons the fire just as his mother had taught him to do.
The sugar cube bursts into flames and just as he's inwardly
smiling with self-satisfaction, he realizes the music has
stopped and he hears Cameron laugh behind him. "Show off."

"My mother would say so, too," Creed chuckles. "And she
would be angry with me." Creed turns, dropping the heated
cube into the glass of the glowing green Erosi absinthe. Then
he straightens Cameron's blue shoulder brassards, tapping a
few of her ribbons into place.

"The Widow," Cameron sighs and brushes the shoulders
of her cousin's dress uniform, gleaming white like hers
except for the blood red striping. *The same uniform that Pfizer
will wear but with the shards of the Phoenix Star...Domino of the
Bloodguard.*

Cameron takes one of the glasses and raises it to her lips,

then pauses. *There must be some way to get through to my cousin.* "Tactical projections of Sol and Ekoz star systems," she commands the AI softly. The two star systems immediately blink into view. The first thing Creed observes is the Sol System infested with the red highlights of hostile ships and worlds; while Ekoz still shows the blue of loyal assets, the other star system is clearly in a life-and-death struggle.

As Creed stares at the projections, shame floods his heart. He turns and looks at Cameron. *She is so much like mother.* "Cameron, I—"

When she raises her beautiful eyes, with their long, white-gold eyelashes, Creed sees the same terrifying resolve of his brother Balthasar and his nephew Pfizer. "Cameron, I—," he tries again.

How can he tell his cousin what he wishes he himself didn't know?

He had discovered it by chance. He had come upon Pfizer's Bloodguard, Heath MacKenzie, outside the *Bismarck's* Bloodguard training area. The young man was sitting on the floor with his back against the wall, waiting to use the showers. He wore a military MentAmp with the clear glass goggles for real-time holographic non-neural interface. He was holding an omnipalm awkwardly in one hand, obviously favoring his injured arm, which was still covered in the white mesh of synthflesh gauze. As Creed approached, Heath recognized his superior and began to scramble to his feet. Creed immediately motioned for the lad to sit, saying, "At ease."

At that moment Creed sensed an intense wave of embarrassment, anger, frustration, even grief emanating from the seated man. "Bloodguard?" Creed asked, frowning.

"I'm sorry, sir," was all the Bloodguard said, indicating his state of undress, only shorts and t-shirt. "I was waiting for the showers and studying," Heath said, trying to keep his head down.

For a moment, Creed thought that perhaps Heath's brooding was due to some bullying from the *Bismarck's* Bloodguards. But then he sensed that something far worse than that was weighing on Heath.

Staring intently at the young man, Creed asked, "What's wrong, Bloodguard?" Heath sat frozen. As Creed watched fear and confusion cross Heath's face, his own frown deepened, "As Commanding General of the Corps, as your Kurseg, I order you to tell me."

Still Heath hesitated. Normally, Creed would not have tolerated a Bloodguard's less than swift response. But the grief on Heath's face coupled with Creed's concerns over what would drive one of the elite of the Bloodguard to behave so, had inspired him to caution. The hairs on the back of his neck rose. "Tell me, Bloodguard," he repeated, quietly this time.

And then Heath told him what he never imagined he would ever hear.

Now, turning to Cameron, Creed relays what he learned. "Cameron, Pfizer plans to nova the Sol Star System."

At last, he tells me. Waves of anger and bitterness wash over Cameron, sending her into a fugue state. Flashes of data and experiences are catalogued in her mind and as she compartmentalizes her emotions, the anger she intended to vent and even punish Creed with dissipates. "Pfizer's gone mad with grief. I think—no, I know—we all went mad with it."

"Camer—" Creed begins, but his cousin sighs heavily in a way that's so reminiscent of Balthasar that he stops. She glares at him. She appears even taller than he in her dress uniform. *How does she do that? She's worse than mother,* Creed thinks.

"Not just our Domino, but Balthasar and you want this mad plan to attack Earth." She finishes her drink and hands the glass back to him. "And don't think I didn't know. I know *everything* that happens on my ship, especially among my Bloodguards. "What's next, Creed? Will we descend into another two thousand years of bloodshed?"

Her words hit home. Creed knows what he must do. Abandoning all pretensions, he removes the Kurseg star cluster emblem from his brassard and lays it on the table before them. The hyper-dense neutronium easily cracks the table.

Cameron's sudden smile assures him that she understands and wants to listen. "Go on, Creed," she prompts.

"I formally announce my retirement from the Corps Bloodguard," Creed says solemnly. "I, as a Bloodguard, have no property, no title other than Kiritzia's and she is an Invid," Creed says, a look of such utter acceptance on his face that Cameron realizes she has underestimated Balthasar's influence grossly.

Creed removes the last of his medals and sits in front of Cameron's work desk. "I hope Balthasar is right, Cam. Not just the Erosi Alliance but the Hane Nation, our people, are going to have to do a lot, defend our worlds, supply tursapoi to the...defecting Bloodguard and Takazhr. What have I done? Millions of armed forces personnel have died. I am not just talking about my Bloodguard," Creed says with a sadness she did not think he could or ever would express. "There are fewer than six billion Hane in the universe now. I think I finally understand Millian and my father. And I will not help Pfizer burn more worlds."

Cameron, used to anticipating every contingency, shakes her head in a combination of disbelief and amazement. *A man that had always been so fanatical, so utterly sure that he was right, and so superior—more like his father and his brother than he would care to admit—now seems defeated and broken. Is he going to rebel?* The Hane know well the consequences of inter-family strife, civil war.

Cameron sits down behind her desk dropping her Grand Admiral mask. She is just Cameron Elizabeta. "Is there any way out of this?"

"There always is. You are going to have to listen to them. Captain Buchanan has a plan, he and the Tempellian," Creed says with a calm she finds not only unexpected but unnatural.

"Pfizer's advisors, his friends, may be the only people who can avert catastrophe."

"You don't think— 'Give them enough rope and they'll hang themselves'?" Cameron asks wryly, quoting the old Hane aphorism.

"No, Cameron. You are still not listening. They may be the only ones who offer hope."

Cameron's work desk chimes and the tritone voice of the *Bismarck's* AI informs them: "Representatives from the Tempellian Remnant are on board, Grand Admiral."

CHAPTER 50

"...I lost the last of the best of me."

—Pfizer Ambros, as quoted in *The Hane Commentaries*
by Aaron Charlemagna Invid-Hane

Pfizer squats in the waste outside Golgotha, a refuse heap outside Jerusalem. The cacophony of jeers and shouts from the mob is staggering and he questions what brought him back to this study of Yeishua. Pfizer is amazed by this remarkable human's idealism. It is not going to end well for this Yeishua. *I have no intention of even thinking of suffering.* The En'Zefi technology is incredible; Pfizer wonders whether he is witnessing the scene through the mind of one of the Aramaic people at the site or if he's sharing consciousness with an actual En'Zefi. *I used to find so much solace in having all this knowledge and wisdom at my fingertips, and now it means nothing. What will I say to them? To the Tempellian Remnant? I am a Cardinal of the Templers and I will therefore have to address the Curia and my family...I will eventually have to go to Eros to HaneHome to Avon...Where will my capital be?...Will I be an Emperor of never was and maybes?* He looks up at the dying man nailed to a tree.

Pfizer jerks the MentAmp from the back of his head and he is back in the reality of waiting alone in the INS *Bismarck's* auditorium style pilot's briefing room. The MentAmp dangles in his left hand; his right hand is clenched in a fist behind his back. Pfizer wears the white and red uniform of the Bloodguard, with the shards of the Phoenix Stone on his collar, pieces of the great jewel found by his grandfather on

Eros. In moments he will be named Kirin, Stadtholder, and First ClanLord of the Hane Nation—and more important, he will be vested with a controlling interest of CIMB shares and be named Emperor-Executor of the Imperium.

He sits down at the briefing room's command console. His Artie is gone, lost in the Battle of 10-21, as they now call the massacre at Sol. "Rotate console face view port," Pfizer orders and the circular section of floor on which the console and its chair sit rotate to face the view port.

The planet slowly turning beneath him appears to be another E-type world, with blue oceans, white clouds, the green and tans of continents. But this planet appears on no star charts. Its coordinates are known only to a select few. The planet is called Coventry and it is the planet the Ambros have always retreated to in times of danger. Pfizer knows that Grand Admiral Tanenov has ordered a fleet, no an armada, of ships assembled on the far side of Coventry. He is certain there are at least a thousand dreadnoughts and their attendant battle groups. *This is a planet I hoped never to see. But there are a million Bloodguard down there and even more navy and Takazhr.* As he continues staring at the planet, his mind darts from thought to thought. *Otto and Lux are coming. I'm going to have to deal with them... Are Cameron and Creed really behind me? ... Why is Balthasar sending Cedar as the Hane Nation Representative? ... Without my Artie there is lot of data I am going to have organize myself. I admit I miss that machine more than some of the members of my staff. ... Rachel, you bitch!*

Pfizer has been unwilling even to meet with his PPRC reps, so he pushed the task of intelligence-gathering off to Luxvico. At least at Coventry there is a backup of the government records that had been stored on the Imperio-Intellect, the massive Impgov artificial intelligence that had been destroyed in the nucleoing of Atlantis. However, all of his personal data and studies had been lost forever in the destruction of Tempel. They had been stored on Archon, the Academy's mainframe and possibly the greatest artie ever.

Pfizer pushes back another surge of rage over his loss and

begins to activate holographic fields. News feeds and official reports from Sol and Spica flicker and murmur around him. The mass driver bombardments of the planets Venus, Earth, and Mars orbiting Sol caused catastrophic damage to all three biospheres—tsunami damage, impact firestorms, and the attendant blast wave damage. Due to the resulting loss of sunlight, the solar satellites that had microwave-beamed power to the surfaces of those planets for centuries are now gone, and without power there is no weather modification, agro development, or food distribution. Most of the automated planetary infrastructure has collapsed, transforming all three worlds into frozen hells where sulphuric rain falls from the skies.

The screams transmitted from those planets are too much for Pfizer to bear and he mutes the Sol system holographics. The news from Spica, where Eros orbits, is different. Pfizer leans forward and pulls the HaneNet News closer to him. He taps his ear to increase volume and the *Bismarck* AI responds. He recognizes the voice of Iliayna Hane. He actually sighs with relief to see the background of Avon behind her. The Erosi capital city appears to be going through a November day, but on Eros near Avon it is mid-springtime in November.

"...Yes, David. I am still waiting outside the Clan Elector's Capitol building, where heads of the United Clans of the Erosi Alliance are gathering for an unprecedented meeting. Not since the end of the Wasting, according to our archive resources, has there been such an enclave. For the first time ever we understand that Tempelers will be allowed in this chamber. I hope by now you have all heard the amazing reports of the surviving Tempellians gaining what in the very least may be called extraordinary powers. For the first time on HaneNet we will have a live interview with a survivor of what is being called the Tempellian Remnant, made up of those few survivors who were off Tempel when it was destroyed. Tragically, we have received information that the number of survivors is continuing to drop and is now speculated at less than one million. There are reports of extreme fighting in the Ekoz Star

System, where a large portion of the Remnant has apparently gathered to protect that star system. Latest news from HaneNet indicates that—. Wait please, one moment. I think they are here."

In the background, the holo operator is turning his projector skyward and the majestic view of the otherworldly architecture of Avon comes into Pfizer's holo field. Suddenly, there is the thunderous sound of a hyperspace window opening in atmosphere, and the wind begins blowing fiercely on the ground. Trying to maintain her intricately styled hair with one hand and holding her audvid link in the other, Iliayna looks for the disturbance. As she does so the holo projection follows her view, shifting skyward.

Pfizer's eyes wander towards holos from GNN and WiktorLink, which are also covering the same location but from different vantage points. Impgov News and the decapitated PPRC continue their coverage of the Sol Star System with Impgov News being little more than propaganda for Oriana's Regime.

"There they are! Are you seeing this?!" Iliayna exclaims, her finger partially occluding the holo lens view.

Pfizer estimates that no fewer than one hundred Tempelers are moving through the closing hyperspace window. Their precision is military and the coldness in their eyes is even more chilling than Luxvico's. Pfizer has seen military Tempelers all his life, but now their black suits are red and their outer garments are gone. They carry only what seem to be bladeguns, and Pfizer shudders. Bladeguns, frightening hand weapons developed on Eros long ago, before the Hephaestus, are regarded as a proud artifact of Erosi heritage. That the Tempellians are now bearing the artifacts of the homeworld they revolted against is a gesture not lost on the Erosi or Pfizer. He pulls the HaneNet holographics even closer until he seems to stand next to Iliayna and he can hear the horns playing and the Clan Banners fluttering in the wind. A profound sense of longing overcomes him and he knows this is an important moment in space and time. Two Tempellians, a male and a female, approach the holo pickup. They appear to be little older than teenagers. The male has eyes of gleaming walnut, the female has eyes like Ambros gray; it cannot be coincidence.

As if on cue the iris to the briefing room chimes. Pfizer manages a smile and an appropriate chuckle and orders the iris open. *Luxvico I will have to deal with first.* Pfizer looks down instinctively at his chest; he will need a T-shield if he has any illusions about trying to deceive Luxvico. He clenches his teeth a moment before he can force the smile back on his face as he turns toward the iris.

Heath, ever vigilant, escorts Luxvico and Otto in. Otto strides through the iris first and his concern is written all over his face. A first-year empa-psych could read the consternation in the pale lime eyes. Pfizer stands a little taller and pushes more reassurance into his smile; it seems to calm the expression on Otto's face. Pfizer glances up at Luxvico and just as he expected he meets the Tempeler's cold glittering stare. Pfizer recalls Otto's earlier pokes about stones falling from Lux's mouth and the smile Pfizer manages is more than sincere enough. What is odd, however, is the sudden shift of Otto's attention back toward Luxvico. *There is something going on between them, but what? I must keep focus but be utterly honest.*

Once upon a time we were all great friends. Pfizer thinks briefly of a short argument the three of them had the evening in New Eden. He can hear the laughter and the clinking of glasses and see the fireworks bursting behind them, and the glowing servo-spheres of the city—a city on an island continent that was burned by a nucleo just hours later.

He makes his decision, but not in a thousand lifetimes would he ever imagine that the words would spill out like this.

"I wanted you both to know I intend to nova the Sol Star System," Pfizer begins. "The minute—"

"Nova the star system? That will destroy—," Luxvico interrupts moving to stand next to Otto.

"All life in the star system," Pfizer says, finishing the sentence. "And wiping out the Tene Thantos and their allies," he adds quickly with an edge to his voice that warns them arguments will not be tolerated.

"Pfizer…," is all Otto manages to say. *What has happened to you?* Otto thinks.

Reading Otto's expression and turning toward him, Pfizer responds, "I intend to be as ruthless as the Tene Thantos. This should drive them toward the Ekoz Star System and Titan. And we will be waiting for them there to end this."

"You'll kill fourteen billion of your Citizo—the people you and I swore to protect?" Otto says surprised by his calmness.

Miscalculating Otto's composure, Pfizer interprets it as a sign of acceptance, and he continues. "Exactly. My responsibility is to the Imperium, to all of my Citizo and Aristo," Pfizer declares. "Trillions of lives are at stake," Pfizer adds, turning to meet Luxvico's stare. "If I let the Tene Thantos infest the Sol Star System think of the resources they will rob us of—organic, tech, information. They will strip mine that star system," Pfizer says, fighting to contain his rage. "What will the Tene Thantos do, Counselor Luxvico, with an army of billions and all the mineral and strategic resources of one of the oldest and most developed worlds in the Imperium? "Look what they did to Tempel, Counselor. How can you disagree with me?"

That was too much, Pfizer knows.

"I didn't mean for our discussion to go this way," Pfizer says, indicating the tiered seating of the room and walking toward the first row of chairs. When Pfizer sits they have not moved but continue watching him, the view port behind them.

"Regent, please reconsider. There is no sign of outright infestation in the Sol System," Luxvico says. "There are at least fourteen billion survivors on Terra…Earth alone; there are close to four billion on Venus—"

"Spare us the count, Luxvico. We all know the numbers and so do the Executive Council. And my decision will be approved," Pfizer pronounces, with all the Tempeler certainty he can muster. *They have got to see it!*

"No, Pfizer. You are supposed to be our Domino. That is

not how they should remember you. Do this and they will remember you as a mass murderer, one of the greatest in history. Is this what you spent all those years on Tempel for?" asks Otto.

When Otto says this Pfizer has the vague sense of a Tempellian contact. He can feel the fire burn and hear the screams as it sucks the air from billions of lungs and the screaming rage from the thousands of survivors. *The reports are true...By the One God.*

Pfizer shrugs visibly in his chair. "Otto, I don't know what he's taught you. But you...Et tu?"

"Please, are you kidding me?" Otto asks incredulously. "The only point where the Tene Thantos have gathered in force is Titan, Basileus and Cato's home. There they are building the Deathships we all fear. As your ranking Bloodguard—"

Pfizer raises a hand. He is ready to retort, "My ranking Bloodguard is Kurseg Creed Hane," when Otto's comments finally resonate. *The Deathships are there.*

"You are right, Otto. The Deathships are at Ekoz; that is where we need to strike," Pfizer says, raising his hand again before they can voice more opposition. "Don't worry. I won't nova Ekoz. I want to keep Mount Akhnar intact," he adds rising. "It's time for us to meet Grand Admiral Tanenov, Grand Kurseg Hane, and the representatives from the Tempellian Remnant. Counselor, it will be good to see more Tempellians. I hope there are some of them that we know. I have questions if there are," Pfizer says.

Pfizer's voice seems distant to Otto. Suddenly Otto has the sensation of being in an immense crowd. It is no other than his Bloodguard School on Tempel. But the faces of the teenagers he sees now are not those of the companions he remembers. There are girls here, and while the room is exactly as he remembers it the glittering eyes surrounding him give it all away. Tempellian Presence. Luxvico had warned him about this. Lux told him that they all perceived their mutual telepathic contact differently and that above all he should not allow himself to be recognized by them or attempt contact with them. His Bloodguard training warns him that there is a danger to Pfizer, or the family he was conditioned to protect. There is an argument among the students in Otto's vision; he hears Oriana's name shouted with a derision and a malice that cause him to shiver.

"Otto, are you all right?" It is Pfizer's voice. *I am on the Bismarck. Reality.* Otto turns instinctively to Luxvico and finds the Tempellian staring back at him intensely.

Say nothing Otto, Luxvico warns Otto telepathically. Pfizer watches them closely and clearly senses something. Perhaps it is the Vey in him.

"Sit down, Otto," Pfizer orders and Luxvico guides him back into his seat. The Tempellian appears uncharacteristically agitated. He stares continually at each of the auditorium iris. *Something is definitely wrong. I have had enough of this. It's time for some answers. If I command it, Otto must answer me,* Pfizer thinks.

"Otto, right now I am ordering you to tell me—"

Cameron's voice booms from the work desk. Clearly she is breathless from running: "Pfizer—Regent, switch to the news from Eros—The Tempellians! Creed and I are on our way—Secure your Tempellian!"

The iris to the briefing auditorium spirals open and Heath steps in followed by a squad of armored Bloodguard. "Counselor Luxvivo, please, you are under arrest." Pfizer realizes that they are afraid. *Of what? Of Lux? No…*

* * *

From her workroom on board the *Alabama* Oriana looks down through a fallout filled sky at the massive refugee camp with its prefab barracks and barbed wire that sprawls like an ugly lesion around the burnt wreckage of Nuevo Dallas. Oriana turns to the now omnipresent Bloodguard and the female psi-sensitive from the Ilkani church that has not left her side since Marisol's death. Her work desk is cluttered with holo fields that spew audio-visual data around her , just as the MentAmp she wears spills data through her mind. *Never what I wanted,* Oriana thinks. She sighs and resists the temptation to smack the view port in front of her.

"Madame, if I might suggest—," the Ilkani standing behind her interrupts, with a civility that poignantly reminds Oriana that *that* was what she had wanted: A life of gentility, fertility, civility, and the never-ending springtime of the weather-modified core worlds of Sol and the other stars of the Draco Constellation. *But that isn't what happened, was it? The core worlds are now on fire or in open rebellion.'*

"Yes?' Oriana turns, hoping with a naiveté she knows is born of desperation that this woman's suggestion will somehow start her on a path out of the hell her decisions have led her to.

"Perhaps Madame should rest? No human woman could be everything to all people and be everywhere at once."

Another dead end, Oriana thinks. She smiles at the woman, trying to keep the disappointment from her voice when she says, "No, you are right. No human woman could, but I am no human. I am an Aeon," Oriana sits down at her desk. "You may both leave me, thank you," She says with a confidence she is not sure she believes herself. As they nod and back out of the room, Oriana returns her attention to the MentAmp spilling data through the neurons of her brain.

In the brief time since October, the Impgov debt has doubled and now with just the rumor of Pfizer being alive, the CIMB has suspended trading. The Bloodguard and Takazhr have begun defecting. The addiction to tursapoi she'd been told would control them is being subverted by the Erosi. The Hane have turned on her as promised—'Murderer!' The thought intrudes into her mind like a sledgehammer.

Oriana recoils from the holo fields, covers her eyes with her hands. The lessons on how to contain her emotions spill through her mind but they are not enough and she screams. She stumbles against her console as she tries to get away from the images of fire, death, and suffering. Above all else the Tempelers now whisper in her mind. Not merely some of them but all of them, the raging million survivors, and they carry with them the curses of five billion Hane. Oriana slaps futilely for the holo feeds to stop, all of them.

"GNN will continue to monitor the many memorial

services still taking place outside the Sol System. As many of you know with the destruction of our head offices in New Atlanta and New Eden, Alpha Centauri is the closest system we have—

"GNN will continue to monitor the many memorial services still taking place outside the Sol System. As many of you know with the destruction of our head offices in New Atlanta and New Eden, Alpha Centauri is the closest system we have—."

Each news feed repeats the same news over and over.

Oriana's mind is able to concentrate long enough for her hand to spastically move up her chest so she can activate her T-shield. She sighs with relief for a moment until her head ignites once again in agony.

We invented the T-shield. We are coming for you. Oriana sees the great school planet of Tempel as it once was—the gleaming gold spires of the chapter houses, the greens and crystal of agro-domes, and the sprawling and intricate arenas and amphitheaters. The ancient Tempellians and the millions of students are all gone now.

She had had no idea.

"I am so sorry," Oriana whispers. And then she feels her eardrums burst and her clothes and the world around her catch fire again and she hears not only the cries and screams on Tempel but all over the Imperium.

We are coming, Oriana.

The holo field in front of her blinks on. Instantly she recognizes the Hall of Justice in the Erosi capital of Avon,, where the Clan Lords of Eros Alliance gather. She desperately wishes she were there with her family now. She is consumed by a staggering sense of dread. *We are in danger. All of us are in terrible danger,* Oriana thinks.

* * *

Balthasar, Fen, Cedar, and other Hane Nation delegates sit in the central box of the Stadtholder, with the midnight blue

THE ELEVENTH COMMANDMENT

banners and the golden dragon symbol of the Hane. All the
Clan Nations' leaders have assembled in the Hall of Justice.
Their crests and colors are on proud display—the hunter green
and white stag head of the Sullivan, the scarlet and gold fleur
de lys of the Invid, even the grass green banners of the Qamar
with their graceful Old Islamic script. The great magnates of
the Eros Alliance, all descended from families that Liesel Aeon
had experimented on.

As Fen watches the Tempelers, a growing sense of dread
and anxiety begins to consume her. Everyone's attention is
focused on the monitors around the Hall of Justice. Fen looks
at Balthasar and Cedar but like everyone, their eyes are riveted
on the male Tempeler who is standing on the center platform
and whose imagine fills the monitors.

"Greetings. I am Lucien, War Leader of the Academy
Military Ministry," the Tempeler proclaims in a surprisingly
deep baritone voice that rings through the hall. "Centuries ago
a small group of Erosi left Eros and settled on Tempel. Today
we return home to Eros!" His words are met with thunderous
applause. Fen feels as though his glittering gray eyes are
looking directly through the holo pickup and at her. It is the
same on every net covering the feed from Eros.

That's not possible, unless—? Fen wonders. *They wouldn't dare!
Not on Eros,* Her fear and apprehension rise to the point where
she starts to tremble. She fears telepathic compulsion or
worse—the possession of the most powerful leaders of the
Eros Alliance. The Tene Thantos machinations had not been
so Machiavellian as that. Fen draws in a deep breath and turns
back to the holo fields, almost mesmerized by the Tempelers's
voice and eyes. *Balthasar, Cedar we have to leave now!*

Fen is relieved when she sees the two men turn to her in
shock. She knows the telepathic compulsion has been broken.
Balthasar, familiar with both possession and compulsion, is
clearly about to explode in outrage. *No. Not here. We have to
leave. Look! The Invid delegation is leaving,* Fen tells them
telepathically.

One by one, each of the Hane and Invid delegations rises

and begins to leave. Even so, the Tempeler continues his address. "I have come to Eros and this august chamber because the Ambros Imperium has failed! The Usurper Oriana has broken the Eleventh Commandment and lain waste to worlds. Her brother hides and vacillates while more atrocities continue! I am therefore going back to the Ekoz front to wipe out the Tene Thantos and their Deathmen myself." Lucien rises up from the platform, his hands outstretched. "But before I do, we will proclaim a new Empire, an Erosi Empire. E Pluribus Unum, Out of Many One. And we will lead this Universe out of darkness forever and we, the children of Liesel, will take our rightful place as the apex of human evolution. Hail Eros! Hail Aeon! Out of Many One! Out of Many One!" Lucien shouts, raising his fist in the air.

To Fen's utter horror most of those remaining in the Chamber of Justice take up his frightening slogan, leaping to their feet and shouting: "Out of Many One! Out of Many One!" The other Tempelers in the Hall rise into the air to join Lucien, their eyes all glittering.

TIME LINE

1969: Man sets foot on Earth's (Sol III's) moon (Luna).

2022: Luther Rawlings isolates anti-graviton particles during super-conductivity research and creates a-grav (anti-gravity) systems.

2036: Ozone Breakdown causes massive ecological damage. Mutations and illnesses plague general populace. Millions resort to cybernetics due to ultra-violet poisoning.

2052: Eugenic Preservation Act passed by United Nations Security Council. Mutated and cyborged made second-class citizens.

2214: Ivan Tsasinov invents the Tsasinov Warp Drive at the University of Nix, Olympia, Mars (Sol IV).

2230: Mutant-cyborg revolt put down; more stringent control laws passed.

2271: First extraterrestrial contact. Aliens are hostile and ally with dissident mutant cyborg factions. Invasion of Solar System.

2273: Battle of Callisto. Destruction of Solar Armed Forces. Earth bombarded by asteroids and rendered uninhabitable. Humanity surrenders.

2273–4082: GREAT HOLOCAUST. Humanity is enslaved.

4041: Birth of Naraji Ilkani in Sidonia, Mars (Sol IV).

4082: Naraji leads successful revolt against the Enslavers. A Church forms around his martyrdom and adopts the Eleventh Commandment: "Man alone is created in God's image." Ilkani Church is founded.

4097: Tursapoi (war drug) discovered on Spica V (Eros).

4113–5267: The Jihads (Naraji II) and the Church begin the systematic elimination of all sentient alien life, hostile or not. Tursapoi assures Humanity's victory. Alien technologies and artifices deemed useful are appropriated.

5270: Genetic experimentation on Eros results in the conception of the *Homo Deus* E-Mortals (Engineered Mortals).

5310: Joseph Ambros (*Homo Deus*) forms the Terrax Corporation, specializing in terraforming uninhabitable planets.

5320: Terrax Corporation successfully revitalizes Earth. Earth is repopulated and designated Sacred Home on all star charts.

5331: An attempt by Joseph Ambros and his Aristos (*Homo Deus* and *Homo Sapiens* Intellectuals, Military and Corporate Entrepreneurs) to gain greater access to CIMB (Combine of Internetworked Mercantiles and Banks) profits grows into a movement against the Church's political power.

5348: Civil War for political and economic supremacy between Church and Aristos.

5364: Aristos accept the Church's capitulation and Joseph Ambros acquires the majority of the Church's CIMB shares after the battle of Muladoon (Opuchi II).

5365: Joseph Ambros crowns himself Emperor-Executor of Man and moves his capital to Sacred Home.

I.C. (Imperia Commencia)

1: Founding of the Imperium of Man.

68: Formation of the Imperial Takazhr (Peace Keepers).

74: Emperor-Executor Joseph II orders the dissolution of the Aristo families' private armies after near assassination. He offers the Aristo families the protection of the Bloodguard (Warrior-fanatics loyal solely to the Crown).

721: Tsiamenus Ahren awarded viceroyalty of Northern Spiral Frontier. Formation of House Ahren.

759–1127: AGE OF ENLIGHTENMENT. Founding of the Great Schools.

925: Logician Midori Zorel founds the first school of Empathic-Psychiatry on Bellerophon (Deneb VIII).

1107: Empress-Executrix Josephine III founds the Academy on Tempel (Riffellon IX), a hedonistic arts colony attended by dissident Erosi. It will eventually become the greatest learning center in the galaxy. Liesel Aeon begins her first-known experiments into the evolution of the *Homo Dominus Deus* on Eros (Spica V).

1160: The Tene Thantos, a secret society of *Homo Dominus Deus* and *Homo Deus* racial supremacists, is founded on Anonjida (Balan IX). They begin a campaign of class, gender, and ethnic intolerance.

1183: Ethnic clashes and rioting break out in the Rim Regions.

1184: Viceroyalty of the Greater Magellanic Cloud (Rim Regions) request additional Imperial support to stop fighting in the Geryon Star System. In the Battle of Geryon the Imperial Seventh Fleet is routed by Tene Thantos forces.

1185–1608: THE WASTING. Populations in the Rim Regions stirred into frenzy by Tene Thantos subversion begin a series of anarchistic-nihilistic crusades. Entire star systems are destroyed, planets sterilized, natural and engineered plagues ravage the known human universe.

1198: Erosi moon of Halcyon captured by Tene Thantos forces, renamed Acheron. Nuclear bombardment of Eros in Tene Thantos attempt to take only known source of tursapoi, Siege of Eros.

1265: Emperor-Executor Felix I slain along with Bloodguard and Takazhr forces attempting to break Siege of Eros. Bloodguards remove surviving heirs to the planet or planets known as Coventry [Location (s) Unknown].

1537: Tene Thantos attempt an assault on Sacred Home. Battle of Titania, Empress-Executrix Magdelene I leads Imperial and allied star forces to complete victory over invading forces. Death of reigning Tene Thantos Shadow Pope Malvos Quiso. Tene Thantos begin retreating from galaxy.

1608: Gert Harre of Eros pursues remaining Tene Thantos beyond the Boundary (past all explored areas of the Wild Space Regions). The Wasting ends at last.

1617: Declaration of Aristos on Sacred Home: "To prevent the horror of and scourge of intergalactic war from being inflicted on future generations, all Humanity must be united under one government."

1620–1729: With the Unification Wars, the galaxy is brought under Imperium control.

1729–2201: GREAT DARK AGES. Piracy and brigandage isolate many worlds from contact. As a result, when these worlds are rediscovered some of them have regressed to stone age culture. These areas of cultural anachronism are designated Back Zones and access is highly restricted to stop cultural shocks on native Back Zone populations.

2201: Effective end of the Dark Ages. Ambros Terrax Corporation has revitalized most areas. Back Zones are established and the population is beginning to rise again. Aristos make attempts at democratic reform but the Citizo (Imperial citizens) refuse, citing the terrors of the Wasting as rationale for maintaining the constitutional autocracy.

2488: Period of Intergalactic Exploration. Colonies are established in Andromeda Galaxy. Evidence of earlier Tene Thantos presence discovered but no living signs are found. Exploration continues.

4115: Sorenson Rhys develops the first Artie (Artificial Intelligence) on the Academy chapter planet Thaos (Bernard VIII). The Ilkani Church places him under interdict for breaking the Eleventh Commandment.

5921: Kennedy Wiktor completes the first artificial gestation matrix; female pregnancy is now no longer necessary for child birthing. The Church places him under an interdict.

6191: Birth of Crown Scion, Princess Anastacia III.

6224: Crown Scion, Princess Anastacia III is invested with a majority of the CIMB Company shares and coronated Empress-Executrix Anastacia III. Declares Second Golden Age.

6278: Birth of Crown Scion, Princess Oriana II.

6298: Birth of Prince Pfizer I.

6303: Anangan Insurrection (Revolt on Ferros, Anangan VII). Oriana exiled to Pandarata on the Boundary. Pfizer invested as Crown Scion.

6321: Contact with Humans not under Imperium hegemony. Riots reported in several star systems protesting the alleged breach of the Declaration of 1617 and the Eleventh Commandment. Rediscovered humans are called the Outlaw, since they live outside Imperium law.

6323: Tensions mount due to Empress-Executrix Anastacia III's pacifist policies. Crown Scion, Prince Pfizer graduates from the Academy of Tempel a Cardinal in the Political Science Ministry. Lord Basileus Ahren discovers Tene Thantos artifact on board smuggler ship in Jupiter (Sol V) orbit.

About the Author

Richard Van White, Jr. has long been fascinated by space travel and the mysteries of the universe. His love affair with science fiction began while watching *Star Trek* on a black and white television in 1969, the same year that man landed on the moon. He soon developed a voracious appetite for all things sci-fi—from classics by Robert A. Heinlein and Frank Herbert to *Doctor Who*, *Space 1999*, and the *Star Wars Trilogy*. This is Richard's first science fiction novel. He resides in Philadelphia, Pennsylvania but also spends considerable time in Maryland with extended family.

A portion of the proceeds from this book will go to Girl Power 2 Cure, Inc., an organization dedicated to finding a cure for Rett Syndrome, a neurodevelopmental disorder that affects girls almost exclusively. The author knows a special young lady living with Rett Syndrome and wants to help her find a cure soon. To learn more about the inspiring work of Girl Power 2 Cure, visit the author's website at:

www.eleventhcommandmentbook.com